PROLOGUE

It's a well-known fact that brides don't look good in black. But newly-weds look even worse, and Claudie Gale was no exception. Her skin was porcelain-white against the ebony of her dress as she sat shivering in the tiny church. The very church she'd got married in just six weeks before. She could almost smell the flowers; almost feel the warmth of the June sun filtering through the stained glass windows. Almost, but not quite. It wasn't quite there because she wasn't quite there either. She felt suspended from her body as if a puppeteer had attached strings to her and was hovering somewhere up in the church rafters.

She knew she'd promised till death us do part, but she hadn't reckoned on the death part coming round so quickly. It all felt so incomplete, like an unfinished conversation, or the curtain falling five minutes into a play.

She could remember their last conversation at the train station so clearly. She'd insisted on seeing him off. It was what newly-weds did, wasn't it? Like lovingly smiling when you're picking up socks off the bedroom floor, or putting down the toilet seat for the fourth time that day. It soon wore off, she'd been warned, but she'd insisted on basking in it whilst it lasted.

'Do you *have* to go?' she'd complained, her finger making tiny circles in his great, thick palm.

'Claudie, it was arranged months ago. You knew that when we booked the wedding. I can't let the lads down now, can I?'

'I know,' she'd lied, desperately wanting to be selfish and keep him all to herself for a little while longer. 'But it's so dangerous.'

Luke had smiled down at her, his intense blue eyes twinkling mischievously. 'It's no more dangerous than crossing the road,' he'd told her before giving her a kiss which had set her toes on fire.

'You will take care?' she said.

'You know I will. And you will too? There are a lot of roads round here.'

She'd smiled and thumped him in the belly, an d then he'd given

1

her one of his crushing bear-hugs which flattened her nose and squashed her chin. She remembered how she'd protested the first time he'd hugged her like that.

'I'm suffocating! Let me go!'

'No, never!' he'd yelled back.

But he had let her go. He'd left her, hadn't he?

She'd watched him hop onto the train, wielding his mammoth rucksack as if it were a mere wisp of material. They'd blown kisses and waved as the train pulled out, and Claudie had stood on the platform, like a character from a 1940's movie, watching as her husband turned into a funny little dot on the horizon.

It wasn't simply the fact that she'd never see him again which upset her, but that *he'd* never see *her* or anything else ever again. For Luke, the world had stopped on the twenty-first of July. No more songs would be sung; no more books would be written. On the twenty-first of July, the world had become complete for him: no additions, no evolutions. And Claudie couldn't bear that.

Life with Luke had been like living in the land of Oz: a perfect Technicolor dream-sequence. But now she was back in Kansas: drab, colourless, and threatened with tornadoes.

What was she going to do without her daily intake of jokes? He'd turned her into a joke junkie. She laughed now as she remembered one of them, blissfully forgetting where she was for a moment.

'Claudie?' her mother, who'd flown over from Marseille for both wedding and funeral after not having seen her daughter for four years, sounded sharp and stressed-out.

'Claudie? What's the matter?'

What's the matter? *What's the matter?* The sheer idiocy of the question caused Claudie an unprecedented fit of giggles.

'*Claudie!*' her mother's manicured hand clasped her arm but it didn't do any good. She'd slipped out of the world around her, and was miles from anywhere and everybody.

And that's when the voices had started. All suspended. Were there puppeteer's strings attached to them too? Claudie looked up into the rafters but it was too dark; she couldn't see.

'It's only to be expected.'

'She shouldn't have come.'

'She needs to be on her own.'

'Just give her time.'

Everything was echoey and dreamlike, and she felt her vision blurring as hot tears spilled from her eyes. It was the joke that was making her cry, wasn't it? She just couldn't stop laughing.

And then, all of a sudden, she couldn't remember what it was that she'd found so funny. What was the punch line? What had he said to her?

Where was he?

'Luke?'

She was no longer laughing.

CHAPTER 1

'How long has it been now?' Angela asked after swallowing a mouthful of machine-processed coffee.

'Nine months,' Kristen replied, opting for the hot chocolate after seeing Angela's weak specimen.

'Is that long enough, do you think? You know - to get over it?'

Kristen puffed out her cheeks and sighed. 'Well, it once took me nine months to get over an ex-boyfriend.'

'Blimey! How long had you been going out with him?'

'Six weeks.'

Angela nodded in sympathy and drained her cup, filling it up again. This time, the coffee came out looking like molasses.

'It's not natural, is it?' she said, not noticing the contents of her cup. 'I mean, he was so young. It just seems so unfair.'

Kristen nodded, looking across at Claudie who was staring vacantly at her PC, her pen hanging out of her mouth as if it were a particularly potent joint. 'I hardly recognise her these days. She's just shut herself away.'

'So what did all those books say? You must have read every one written on the subject by now.'

Kristen sipped her chocolate, licking the undissolved particles from her lips. 'They're perfectly useless. One will say one thing, the next: another. I don't think anybody really knows.'

'But wasn't there that emotional equation thing?'

'That the stronger the love, the longer you grieve?' Kristen looked at Angela. 'So, the only way to avoid grief is by not loving.'

Angela shook her head. 'It's not natural. How can a person get through life without loving?'

'I don't think you can.'

'No. It can't be done, can it?'

They stood in silence for a moment, drinking and thinking.

'We've got to do something, though, haven't we?' Angela began.

'She's still seeing that bloke in York. That must be helping,' Kristen reasoned.

'How do you know? Are you sure she doesn't just get on the train and go shopping?'

'No! She wouldn't do a thing like that.'

'Or just go and sit in the cinema? You know what she's like with films.'

Kristen knew only too well. There'd been many a Saturday evening when she'd tried to drag an unwilling Claudie away from her collection of MGM musicals and actually leave the house.

'What *is* she doing with that pen pot?' Kristen whispered, watching Claudie's glossy brown bob swinging from side to side as she examined the stationery on her desk. 'That's the third time she's emptied it this morning.'

'And she's sorted through her in-tray a dozen times too. She must have lost something.'

Kristen nodded. She'd been afraid of as much for the last nine months.

Claudie looked at the growing pile of work leaning precariously over the edge of her table like a paper version of the Tower of Pisa. She had enough to keep her busy for a week but she just couldn't muster any enthusiasm.

It was odd but, since that morning, she'd had the strangest sensation that she was being watched. Yes, she knew Kristen and Angela had been talking about her again: they were about as subtle as a sledgehammer, but there was something else. It was almost as if her computer had turned into an enormous eye; a great spying Cyclops on her desk, watching her, recording her, assessing her. It gave her the shivers. She kept having to get up and leave her desk. A bit of filing here, a quick trip to the ladies, a lengthy session at the photocopier. But, as soon as she sat down, the feeling would come back.

She'd soon become paranoid and had started looking round the room, half-expecting to see a hidden camera, as if she were the unwilling guinea pig on a new television programme. But everything seemed normal; depressingly so.

Then there was the other problem. She kept losing things. Yesterday, it had been her calculator, today her silver Parker pen. She was sure she'd left it by her keyboard, but it wasn't there any more. Was she going mad? It was very probable. She really couldn't trust herself with anything at the moment.

And then it had happened. From the corner of her eye, she saw something move: quick and fluid as a fish. She turned round and blinked, but whatever it was had gone. She shook her head and smiled. She knew what her problem was. She needed a dose of caffeine.

Still, as she wondered whether to have weak-as-rainwater tea or thick-as-quicksand chocolate, she couldn't get it out of her head. For a moment, she'd sincerely believed she'd seen a tiny person diving into her pen pot.

CHAPTER 2

Claudie wondered if Dr Lynton would believe her. She always enjoyed the sessions she had with him. There was an unexpected cosiness about being somebody's focus of attention for a whole hour, but was it doing her any good? She'd been going for several weeks now, and still wasn't sure that she was making enough progress. Still, it kept her best friend, Kristen, off her back. Honestly, she could be worse than a mother at times and, with Claudie's mother, that was saying something.

Claudie had never been close to her mother. At the age of eight, she'd put her on a plane from Marseille under the pretence of wanting her daughter to have an English education, but it really had been to enable her to divorce Claudie's father and set up home with the toy boy milliner Claudie detested. It had been his idea in the first place, Claudie had later found out. He'd had a cousin who lived near the boarding school, and gave it a glowing report, but he was a middle-aged man and would never have to go there.

Claudie had staunchly stood her ground during school holidays back in France, and would have nothing to do with the hat man. No man could buy her with a hat. Not even a feather-festooned, *Gigi*, affair.

It had been an ugly, grey time, and Claudie had never seen her real father again, but at least her mother had had a hat for every occasion. But she never really forgave her for what she did. Eight years was far too young to end up in a gothic grange in the middle of the North Yorkshire Moors, and Claudie had screamed the rafters down every night until her mother had been forced to withdraw her from the school.

'What *are* we to do with you?' she'd complained, as if having a child had been nothing to do with her, and bitterly resenting the fact that her daughter was now compromising her life.

So they'd settled in Whitby; a strange and unlikely place to end up when you were used to the Southern France climate, but compensated by being relatively cheap, and punctuated by regular flights back to France where her mother could top up her tan and her hat collection.

Claudie didn't care too much about having such a disjointed life because it was at that time that she'd met Kristen. Big-haired, big-mouthed and loveable, she'd instantly taken over the role of mother and, when they both left school and secured bedsits and jobs at a local solicitors, Claudie's mother had sold-up and left England forever. But Claudie had no wish to return to her birthplace. She loved Yorkshire: weather-warts and all.

Crossing the road from York station, Claudie followed the city walls. There was something about the place that always sent a pleasant shiver down her spine. Perhaps it was the thought of Romans, Vikings, Highwaymen and modern-day tourists all drawn to the same city.

And now her. She'd found her own little corner of York at number fifteen Elizabeth Street, a three-storey town house, in pale blonde stone with a bright yellow door and a brass plaque on the wall. Claudie had laughed the first time she'd seen it because, following Dr Lynton's name, there was a list of letters long enough to form a short story. She had no idea what any of them stood for but trusted Kristen's friend of a friend's recommendation.

What he was a doctor in she had no idea. She was well aware that you could get a doctorate in Disney nowadays, and that titles before your name and letters after it could count for very little, but Dr Lynton had proved wonderful. Warm and welcoming, he'd quickly put her at ease and was the perfect blend of silence and advice that she had so desperately been looking for in order to help her through the quagmire of her mind.

At first, she'd had to remind herself that he was a professional, and not a friend. It was so easy to forget that she was paying him for his time rather than him offering it as a friend, and so they had maintained the kind of distance shared between teachers and pupils.

She didn't even know what the 'P' in Dr P Lynton stood for, but had often speculated on what it might be. For weeks she'd had a strong suspicion that it was Peregrine: aristocratic and well-educated, but she'd since gone off that idea. No, it had to be Percival. Percy Lynton. Dignified yet approachable. Yes, she liked that.

She hadn't been at all sure what to expect from her sessions in York, and whether Dr Lynton was orthodox or not, and she'd always been a little sceptical about therapy; she just couldn't quite see the point of being able to say: 'Hi, my name's Claudie, and I'm a widow.' Would that sort of personal acknowledgement make her feel any better, and what would Luke think of her seeing a counsellor? He'd always been so self-reliant, so very independent, and would probably be horrified that she was seeking outside help. But she wasn't as strong as he had been.

At their first meeting, he'd explained how every person was an individual, and that it was almost impossible to timetable progress, so that didn't exactly help. So how could she tell if she was making any progress? Did she get up one morning and feel better? Was surviving grief like coming round from anaesthetic, or shaking off a bad dose of flu? Could she ever expect to be the person she once was?

One thing was for sure, her visits to York were certainly better than a long afternoon's typing at Bartholomew and Simpson. Claudie loved these old houses with their lofty ceilings and picture rails, and it was almost worth coming just to spend an hour in the sumptuous surroundings.

She pressed the doorbell, which always reminded her of a great Liquorice Allsort, and didn't have to wait long for Dr Lynton to appear. Big as the door frame but with a smile as soft as butter, he ushered Claudie in. His study occupied a room at the back of the house which overlooked a tiny courtyard stuffed with overflowing troughs and chimney pots. Claudie often felt her eyes drifting towards it when she was meant to be soul-searching. She didn't know much about plants but she liked to have a go at identifying them. She recognised the rosemary with its green spikes, and the lavender, but she didn't know what the others were. Perhaps they were all medicinal? Perhaps he'd administer her some if she asked? But maybe it wasn't possible to grow opium in York.

The room itself was painted a warm yolky-yellow, and had two alcoves stuffed with the sort of books you can only buy second-hand. Selected watercolours of local scenes hung on the walls in old gilt frames, and a large Swiss Cheese plant grew happily by the patio door. There was an air of faded grandeur about the place which perhaps contributed to the sense of calm Claudie felt whilst there.

'How are you, Claudie?' Dr Lynton began with his usual opening question.

'I'm fine,' she said, as she always did, acknowledging the fact that if she *was* fine, she would be at work on a Friday afternoon and not sat opening her mind to a bereavement counsellor. She couldn't help remembering her very first visit, and how the simple act of allowing herself to be helped had crippled her with tears for the first half-hour.

'Did you find time to read the book I gave you?' Dr Lynton asked, walking over to the little table in the corner of the room where a kettle and tea tray were laid out.

'Yes.' Claudie's hand dived into her handbag. 'It's here somewhere.'

'And what did you think of it?'

Claudie passed it back to him and he immediately returned it to its home on one of the shelves.

'I thought,' she began, scanning her brain for her opinion. 'I thought it was interesting that there are actually different stages of grief.' She took off her jacket and sat down in the smaller of the chairs in the room.

'You don't take sugar, do you, Claudie?'

'Well, I like just a little,' she said, not daring to say that she actually liked one very large sugar. But it was the same every week. He could never get it right.

'Black?'

'Just a little milk, please.'

'And did you agree with the stages of grief suggested?' he asked, handing her a cup of tea which looked far too strong and not milky enough by half.

'Yes,' she said, taking the cup and sipping nevertheless.

'And do you think you can identify any which you've experienced?' He sat down heavily in the large chair next to the Swiss Cheese plant.

Claudie took another sip of tea. It tasted worse than the stuff at work. She didn't want to talk about stages of grief, but how could she get away with it and move on to what she really wanted his opinion on?

'Dr Lynton?' she began. 'I've been thinking about what the book said about hallucinations.'

'You've been hallucinating?'

'No!' she said quickly. 'Not about Luke. Although, sometimes, when I'm shopping, or walking to work, I'll see somebody who looks like him. I know it's not him, of course, but it's terrible.' She paused. 'I sometimes find myself staring at strangers, almost as if they were to blame for not actually being him. Sometimes, they don't even look like him at all, but there'll have a similar way of walking, or a similar tilt of the chin. Do you know what I mean?'

Dr Lynton nodded.

'Hallucinations can take any form, can't they?'

He nodded again, obviously not wanting to interrupt her train of thought.

'Well, I've not only been seeing people who remind me of Luke. I've also been seeing *other* people.'

'What? Other people who have died?'

'No.' She put her tea cup down and bit her lower lip, anxiously twisting the little band of gold on her left hand. 'Little people. *I think.*'

Dr Lynton removed his tiny glasses and squinted across the room at her. 'What exactly do you mean?'

Claudie puffed out her cheeks and shrugged. 'I think I saw a little person hiding in my pen pot at work.'

Dr Lynton's head jerked forward like an inquisitive bird's. She gave him a moment to comprehend exactly what she'd said.

'You *think* you saw?'

'Yes. I can't be sure. I mean - it was so quick - like a little bolt of lightning - only in the shape of a human.' She watched as he turned his pen over and over in his hand. He didn't say anything, but that was quite usual. He was probably thinking, which always gave Claudie the opportunity to stare at him. She looked at his mass of white hair. It was extraordinarily thick, and his eyebrows alone could have stuffed a cushion quite comfortably. And then she stared at his nostrils: great, dark, flaring affairs, like twin caves. He really was quite striking.

'And you've been sleeping all right?'

'Oh yes.'

'Eating properly? Not drinking too much?'

'No, nothing like that.'

'Because there are all sorts of explanations for hallucinations. You might have just got something in your eye.'

'Dr Lynton, I assure you, it was nothing like that. This was real - physically, it was very real.'

'Did you have physical contact with it?'

Claudie shook her head. 'I didn't dare. I thought about it, briefly, but I was too scared that it might break the spell.'

'How do you mean?'

Claudie sucked in her cheeks. She probably sounded completely mad. 'I don't know,' she said at last, 'I guess I thought that if I'd tried to reach out and touch it, it would be like pressing the stop button on the video in the middle of a wonderful film.'

His forehead wrinkled, as if he was perplexed by her terminology. She had a habit of comparing everything to films, and Dr Lynton obviously wasn't on the same wavelength.

'And it wasn't Luke you saw?' he asked.

'Oh, no. I'm almost sure this was a girl.'

'Because it's not unusual to look for your loved one - in any form. People find comfort in the most unlikely things.'

'You must think I'm mad.'

'You're not mad, Claudie, and you must stop thinking that you are.'

'But is any of this normal?'

He gave the tiniest of smiles. 'Who can truly define what normal is?'

There was a few moments' silence. Finally, Dr Lynton got up from his chair. Immediately, Claudie knew what was coming.

'I can highly recommend this-' he stretched up to reach the third shelf in one of the alcoves, his red jumper riding up his broad back.

'Oh, no - please! No more books, Dr Lynton.'

He turned round, looking slightly disappointed.

'But may I ask for a cutting of your lavender?'

For a moment, he looked puzzled. 'You're into aromatherapy, are you?'

'No. Not really. But it's worth a try.'

Cabin Cottage stood at the far end of Lantern Yard, its sky-blue stable door and tiny windows crammed with herbs always a welcoming sight after a hard day at the office.

Kristen adored it, but would often curse the precipitous steps that led to her and Jimmy's home as they didn't do her high heels any good. That was the problem with living in Whitby. It was all very pretty to the visitor, but they didn't have to negotiate the neck-break steps and tiny alleyways that became impossible during the tourist season.

'We live here!' Kristen often wanted to shout as she'd try to sneak home in her lunch break, elbowing her way through coachloads of jet jewellery-seeking, ice cream-licking holidaymakers.

But oh! When they went home at the end of summer - what bliss! It was true that the weather would close in for almost six months, but there was nothing cosier than to snuggle down in Cabin Cottage; the sound of the wind whipping up the harbour, and the seagulls reeling in the lead grey sky.

'I'm home!' Kristen shouted, closing the door behind her with her foot, and walking straight into the kitchen. She didn't need to shout as the place was so small, but she could never guess what Jimmy was up to. He might have his saw on the go, or be lost in a world of six-inch masts and never actually hear her.

'Jimmy?'

'Through here,' he shouted back.

'I hope you're not making sawdust in the living room again,' Kristen warned, immediately tripping over a cardboard box. She picked it up. She didn't recognise what it had once housed but it was certainly some kind of woodwork tool.

She sighed, her mouth forming a firm, narrow line. 'What are you up to in there?' She threw the box behind her and walked into the living room. And there he was. He'd pushed all the furniture back against the wall and was sat in the middle of the carpet. Newspaper was spread out everywhere and he was hovering over a pile of timber.

'You're home early, love,' he said, his eyes remaining fixed on his new project.

'No, I'm not.'

Jimmy looked up, his pale eyes looking bloodshot from intense concentration, and his sleeves rolled up to real his thick, tattooed arms which Kristen loved. 'Blimey. Is it teatime already?'

'I don't suppose there's anything to eat, is there?'

'Probably not.'

'Jimmy! Didn't you go out at all today?'

'Yes, but-'

'You only made it as far as the DIY store?'

He looked up and grinned at her. She knew him too well.

'I'll go and get some chips,' she sighed. 'You tidy up in here. Simon's coming round later.' Kristen took a fiver out of her purse and dumped her handbag on the old flower-festooned sofa. 'I won't be long, so make sure the table's set.'

'Aye-aye, Captain!' he laughed. It was his little nickname for her when she became too authoritative.

Kristen walked back through to the kitchen, tripping over the cardboard box again. She picked it up and took it out into the yard. God, the place was tiny, she sighed. She often wished she could add a square metre of space for every time she thought how small the cottage was. If they could, they'd own half of Whitby by now.

She leant across to the windowsill and deadheaded a plant that had seen better days, its flowers dry and brittle, crumbling into nothing between her fingers. The windowsill could do with tidying up too. In fact, the whole place would benefit from a lick of paint.

The cottage had belonged to Jimmy's mother and, when she'd died, she'd left it to him. Newly divorced, Jimmy had been only to pleased to move in and, when he'd met Kristen, he'd staunchly refused to give it up.

Kristen had done her best to make the place their own, insisting, point blank, that he got rid of the collection of lace doilies which made it look as if it had been snowing indoors, and the musty-smelling antimacassars which haunted the sofa and chairs.

Several trips to the local charity shops, and a few tins of Country Cream later, and Cabin Cottage had looked like a completely new place. But it was still too small to start a family in, Kristen mused as she walked back up the steps into town. Not that Jimmy had any plans of that sort. He'd never once mentioned marriage, no matter how many hints Kristen dropped. He'd been bitten very badly the first time round and had no intention of inflicting further injuries on himself, despite their two years of domestic bliss together. Still, there was always tomorrow, Kristen thought, ever the optimist.

When she got back, Jimmy had managed to set the table, but they were forced to step over his project in the middle of the floor.

'What are you making?' she asked.

'The shop wants more of those yachts I made last year.'

Kristen nodded. She supposed she should be glad that he had something to keep him occupied during the low season. Come high season, she hardly ever saw him as he owned one of the pleasure trip boats down in the harbour. The money wasn't brilliant, but Jimmy never wanted more out of life than an occasional pint and a packet of cigars.

'You're quiet,' he said, his mouth crammed with fat chips.

Kristen nodded, aware that she was usually full of office gossip.

'Anything wrong?' he asked.

'It's Claudie.'

'Oh.'

Kristen knew it was a phrase that had been bandied around so often during the last few months that it was as familiar as what's for tea? or move that bloody saw from the front room, will you?

'She's been acting very strangely lately.'

'Isn't she meant to?' Jimmy asked.

'Yes. But this is a different strange. She's become - well,' Kristen hesitated, 'odd.'

Jimmy picked up his fish and bit into it. Kristen watched him for a moment, awaiting his response, expecting some words of wisdom at any moment. But they didn't come.

'Well?' she prompted. 'What do you think we should do?'

Jimmy looked up from his wrapper. 'Eat our chips before they get cold.'

Kristen tried not to mind Jimmy's response, but she did wish he'd listen to her more.

What many people didn't realise was that friends suffered too when someone died. Claudie just wasn't the girl she used to be, and Kristen missed her so much that it sometimes hurt. She missed the warm-hearted, honest advice Claudie would give her when she needed to share her problems. Right now, though, it wouldn't be fair to burden Claudie with her niggling worries about Jimmy. It wasn't the done thing, was it? Look, I know your husband died, but can't you give me some advice about where my own relationship is going? No, Kristen had to be the shoulder for Claudie, and where did that leave her to turn?

She couldn't help but miss the old Claudie. The girl who'd made her laugh by dancing round the harbour imitating Ginger Rogers when she'd had one too many. The girl who hid cream cakes in the stationery cupboard until the bosses were safely ensconced in a meeting. What had become of her? Where had she gone? And would she ever come back again?

Kristen sighed as she squirted tomato ketchup over her chips because she knew it wasn't just Luke who'd been lost. It was Claudie too.

Claudie lay back in a lavender-scented froth of warm bubbles. She'd gone a bit over the top with the lavender in York, buying candles, bubble bath, soap, and a tiny bottle of essential oil. She'd potted her cutting from Dr Lynton, but determined to buy her own complete plant for her kitchen windowsill as soon as she could.

She was tired. York always left her feeling drained, but lavender was meant to be good for fatigue, as well as a whole host of other complaints. She closed her eyes for a moment, remembering the way that Luke used to shout through the bathroom door at her if she was more than half an hour.

'I don't want my wife drowning!' he'd call, poking his head round the door with a cheeky wink. She'd thought about it too. It would be so easy to slip under the foamy world into oblivion.

Suddenly, her eyes snapped open, her skin covered in tiny goosebumps. It was that strange sensation again: the feeling of being watched which she'd experienced at work. She sat upright and looked round the tiny bathroom as if she half-expected to see somebody there.

'Who is it?' she whispered. But there was nobody there. Of course there wasn't.

She sighed, and sank back down until her shoulders were dressed in bubbles again. She must try and relax. Perhaps she hadn't added enough essential oil to her bath.

She was just about to reach for the little glass bottle when she saw her. And there was no mistaking this time.

For there, dancing between the shampoo and the loofah, was a perfect tiny, diamond-bright girl.

CHAPTER 3

Simon Hart was not in a good mood. After an hour and a half of two-finger typing, he sat back in his threadbare office chair to proof-read his work. Then, just as he thought he'd got things sorted out, his computer had crashed. He hadn't saved his work, of course.

It wouldn't have been so bad if it had just been one of those days. Trouble was, it was turning out to be one of those years. It was all very convenient to blame everything that went wrong in his life on Felicity Maddox, but it wouldn't be a complete overstatement.

October was when the trouble had begun. He'd known something had been wrong with Felicity for some time because she'd been acting strangely. Not that that was terribly unusual for Felicity, but this was different. She seemed restless and hostile.

For almost two years, they'd shared a house on the edge of town, far removed from the picturesque cottages surrounding the harbour. But it was cheap and convenient. Trouble was, Felicity, belying her name, wasn't happy with it.

'When are we going to move?' she'd moan every couple of days. 'I hate this dump!' Simon hated it too, but he was doing his best to make it as a self-employed website designer, so couldn't possibly think about upgrading something as frivolous as living quarters. There was no cash. Except for the emergency rations in their joint account.

'Just be patient. We'll get there,' he always promised with a smile and a kiss. But his words would always fall on deaf ears.

And so, the circle of discontent continued until, one day in July, he'd come home to an empty house. And an empty bank account. Felicity Maddox had done a runner with the rations.

There was nothing Simon could do about it except get over it and start again.

Six months later, he was still getting over it, and it didn't help that he couldn't type or couldn't spell.

He switched the computer off, not bothering to reboot it. Stretching his arms out in front of him, he sighed heavily. He'd have to start it all again. Later. First, he'd have a cup of tea.

He walked through to the kitchen, grimacing at the intestinal debris from his take-away the night before. He had to get himself sorted out. He opened the cupboard and took out a white mug with a lip-shaped chip before shuffling towards the tea canister. Opening it up, he delved inside, his fingers scraping the metal bottom. He'd run out of teabags.

He rolled his eyes up to the ceiling and, in doing so, caught sight of the clock. It was ten past eight and he should have been at Kristen's over an hour ago.

'God - Simon! You look terrible!' Kristen gasped half an hour later, ruffling his hair affectionately as he stepped into her kitchen.

'Thanks,' he said, letting her kiss him.

'Are you all right?'

He ran his fingers through his curly fair hair and sighed by way of an answer.

'Oh dear,' Kristen said. 'Have you eaten?'

He shook his head.

'How about shepherd's pie?'

'Hey! How come I didn't get shepherd's pie?' Jimmy called from the living room.

''Cause you got fish and chips!' Kristen yelled back.

'I don't want to put you out,' Simon said, his belly rumbling loudly at the mere mention of food.

'Don't be silly. Here,' she said, pulling a can of Jimmy's lager out of the fridge. 'Go through and sit down. If you can find room.'

Simon took a swig from his can and wandered through to the living room. He liked Cabin Cottage but could never quite work out how two people lived in such a tiny place and still got on so well with each other. He and Felicity had shared a large, three- bedroomed semi and still managed to get on each other's nerves. Kristen and Jimmy were lucky.

'Hi, Jim,' he said, stepping carefully into the living room which looked like Whitby Harbour in miniature. 'How's the ship-building going?'

Jimmy looked up from his home on the carpet and grinned. 'Marvellous.' He beckoned to Simon who got down on all fours to examine the latest masterpiece.

'I don't know how you do it. I just wouldn't have the patience to work on something so small,' Simon confessed, turning the miniature boat around in his hand, admiring each tiny detail.

'Well, I couldn't do your job,' Jimmy said, resting on his thick denimed haunches. 'It would drive me mad being sat in front of a computer all day.'

'It's great,' Simon defended. 'When it goes right.'

Jimmy nodded as if he understood. 'Like everything else in life.'

Simon gave the briefest of smiles and handed the boat back to Jimmy.

'God - look at you two on the carpet!' Kristen said as she entered the room, looking at the two men in her life. 'Just like a pair of kids!'

'Well, that was a complete waste of a lager and shepherd's pie,' Jimmy said after Simon had left, putting his arms round Kristen's waist and pulling her towards him.

'What do you mean?' Kristen frowned.

'We didn't get a word out of him. I've known budgies that talk more than him. I don't know why you bother.'

'Oh, it's just his way.'

'You know what your problem is?'

'What?'

'You care too much.'

'Is that so bad?' she asked, eyes widening.

'It is when it makes you unhappy,' he said, ruffling her hair with his thick fingers.

'I'm not unhappy.'

'No?' Jimmy didn't sound convinced. 'Then what?'

'Thoughtful?'

'Is that what you call it?' he pursed his lips. 'You take on too many problems which don't belong to you. If it isn't Claudie, it's Simon.'

'They're going through a rough time at the moment-'

'That doesn't mean you have to as well.'

'Doesn't it? I thought that's what friends were for.'

Jimmy raised a gentle hand and pushed back a strand of red hair which had fallen across her face. 'You know, I could put my foot down. I mean, what man in his right mind lets his partner see an ex-boyfriend on a regular basis?'

'There's nothing going on between Simon and me. Nothing ever did. He's a friend! Anyway, we only went out a couple of times.'

'A couple?'

'Well, a couple of months, and it was years ago.'

'Not that many,' Jimmy said sounding unnaturally sulky.

'Do I detect a hint of jealousy?' Kristen teased.

'No. But you shouldn't get so involved in his problems. He's a grown man. Let him sort them out for himself.'

Kristen sighed. In her heart of hearts she knew he was right. She couldn't fight Simon's battles for him. Or Claudie's for that matter.

'I need you too, you know,' Jimmy added.

Kristen tutted good-naturedly. 'You've never needed anyone in your entire life.'

'No?' he pulled her towards him again. 'What's this then?'

She giggled. 'You know what I mean.'

His eyes twinkled softly and suggestively in the lamplight before blurring into darkness as she closed her eyes to kiss him.

When Simon got back home, he paused for a moment in the hallway, resting his head on the cool wood of the stair banister. It was so quiet. He hadn't quite got used to being greeted by silence when he came home. He didn't like it. Despite his rather isolating job, Simon was a gregarious person by nature, and just didn't feel right living on his own, and he always felt it acutely after a visit to Kristen and Jimmy's.

As much as he knew Kristen hadn't been the girl for him, he still couldn't help feeling a little bit envious of Jimmy. Did he realise how lucky he was to have her there? To have someone to holler to when you got home. Someone to share a meal with, a bath with, a bed with. God, he sometimes even missed the things that had really grated on him, like the lipstick-rimmed cups left by the sink, and the rows of wet tights which would hang like strangled snakes over the bath.

He switched the front room light on and winced as the sixty-watt bulb blinded him. When Felicity had left, she'd remembered that the chintzy light shade was hers. She'd also remembered to empty the cupboards of her collection of pots and pans, fleeced the under-the-stairs cupboard of items worth more than ten pounds, and had even managed to get up into the loft in spite her fear of ladders. In fact, the only thing that she'd left of hers had been Pumpkin.

Simon walked over to the little glass bowl and sprinkled some food on top of the water and watched as Pumpkin rose eagerly to the surface. Poor little mite, he thought. Won at a local fair, Felicity had been thrilled with Simon's skill with the hoop for all of ten minutes. Then, as soon as her make-up had demanded a retouch, she'd flung her fish in a bag towards Simon and disappeared into the ladies' loos. She hadn't bothered with the goldfish after that.

She hadn't even bothered to give him a name but, peering into his bowl one day, had announced that he looked like a mini pumpkin floating around. The name had stuck.

Simon wiggled a finger above the water. It was a useless pet really. You couldn't pick it up, couldn't stroke it, couldn't take it for a walk, and he always felt self-conscious when he spoke to it, as if somebody was secretly filming him.

'All right, mate?' he said, stooping to look into the beady, non-communicative eyes. 'Had a shit day too?'

Simon's eyes glanced round the glass bowl. With its one small ornamental bridge, it was even barer than his front room. He once again determined to buy a deluxe tank with all the trimmings. He might not be able to live in the lap of luxury, but he'd make damn sure Pumpkin would. Perhaps he'd even buy him a companion to while away the watery hours.

Oh that life were as simple for him.

CHAPTER 4

After the strange bathroom sighting, Claudie had gone straight to bed. Lavender essential oil was, she'd read, meant to induce a sense of well-being, not a sense of madness.

But she hadn't been able to sleep. It had all been so vivid: like watching a little film. She really had seen a beautiful woman in a pale lemon dress dancing without a care in the world, as if the white enamel tiles were a ballroom rather than a bathroom.

Claudie had even got up in the middle of the night and tiptoed back into the bathroom as if she'd still expected to see her dancing, or at least find some little wet footprints to confirm that what she'd seen had been real. But no. The shampoo bottle and the loofah remained alone. Nothing had been disturbed.

She couldn't help but feel a little disappointed. It was almost as if she'd discovered an amazing new drug and just had to have another hit. She really wanted to believe in what she'd seen.

'What would Dr Lynton say?' she said aloud to herself in the broad band of morning. '*Why* do you want to believe what you saw?' she mimicked his soft, low voice and giggled at her accuracy.

'Because?' Claudie paused. What possible reason could she have for wanting to hallucinate?

'Look deep into yourself and question what you find.' That's what one of the self-help books had told her, but what did they know? Who wrote those books anyway? What could they possibly know about her? Anyway, she didn't want to look deep into herself. She was still too afraid of what she might find there, and even more afraid that there might be nothing to find at all. Just a great abyss.

That probably explained why she was watching more MGM musicals than ever before. Her usual diet of one a week had multiplied by seven. One a day - after work with a large cup of hot chocolate. What better combination to combat the world than Gene Kelly and Cadbury's? As soon as she heard that lion roar at the start of a movie, she could feel herself slipping gently into another world. A world of colour and music, of love and laughter. A world populated by a cast of characters she knew so well that they were like friends to her. And she didn't care what Dr Lynton said about barriers and blockages. Her diet of musicals certainly beat the hell out of all the self-help books which had been thrust at her by friends and therapists.

Ever since Claudie could remember, she'd relied on musicals to get her through the tough times. She had a vivid image of herself sitting on her bedroom floor at weekends, snuggled in a nest of cushions, her curtains drawn tightly against the wet Whitby weather as she immersed herself in early Deanna Durbin, Judy Garland, Gene Kelly and Doris Day on her portable TV. It was the perfect way to escape her mother, the drudgery of homework and, during her late teens, the trauma of boyfriends. The world was a better place when it was filled with song and dance. June Allyson never yelled at her for not tidying the kitchen, Marilyn Monroe never gave her detentions for not doing homework, and Gene Kelly never *ever* stood her up.

It had started innocently enough but soon become an obsession, with Claudie scanning the weekend television guide and circling her favourite films with a bold red pen and becoming inconsolable if something was cancelled owing to extended sports coverage. Over the years, she came to know many of the films by heart and that was where the greatest pleasure lay. There was enormous comfort to be had in knowing what was coming next; of the absolute knowledge that a happy ending was just around the corner and that, although there may be tears and heartache along the way, there was nothing but bright eyes, smiles and a grand finale before the end credits.

Despite constant teasing from friends and family, this obsession hadn't abated through adulthood so, after a weekend immersed in *High Society*, *Singin' in the Rain* and *Brigadoon*, Claudie entered the office on Monday morning with her head chock full of uplifting lyrics and neat little dance steps. She even attempted a little routine as she walked up the stairs, but it proved rather unwise in her kitten heels.

'Ouch!' she winced, rubbing her twisted ankle. She would never cut it as a Cyd Charisse, that was for sure. But then, she thought, Cyd Charisse would never be able to cope with Mr Bartholomew and his mounds of paperwork, his hieroglyphic handwriting and unpredictable mood swings.

Like Dr Lynton, Mr Bartholomew had never given Claudie leave to call him by his Christian name, but she knew what it was. George.

Not terribly inspiring but thoroughly suitable.

'Morning!' Claudie chirped as she entered the office, pulling her seat out with a flourish and igniting her computer with a wand-like finger.

'You're in a good mood,' Kristen said. 'Good weekend?'

'Lovely.'

'Don't tell me - Warner Brothers?'

Claudie shook her head. 'Too serious.'

'RKO?'

'Not enough colour.'

'Then it's got to be -' Kristen hesitated, 'MGM?'

'You bet!' Claudie laughed. 'MGM - the three most magical letters in the English language.'

'Oh, Claudie! You haven't spent a whole weekend watching musicals again?'

'No. Not a *whole* weekend. I reread that Doris Day biography too.'

'Claudie! You really should get out more.'

Claudie laughed again. She'd heard it all before, and she chose to ignore it again.

'Coffee?' Kristen sighed.

'Please.'

Kristen disappeared down the hall for their early dose of caffeine. Claudie logged onto her computer and sifted through the papers that had miraculously collected in her in-tray since Friday.

'Claudie?'

'Yes?' She turned round, but there was nobody there. Strange. She felt sure she'd heard someone. Perhaps she'd imagined it. She still had half-a-dozen film scores whizzing through her brain.

'Claudie!'

She turned round again. Somebody *had* called her name, hadn't they? She hadn't imagined it.

'Clawww - deeee!'

It wasn't coming from behind her. In fact, there wasn't anyone in the office to call her name. She looked around the desk, moving her pencil pot, picking up files, peering behind her computer screen as if she might come across some kind of voice throwing machine.

'I'm over here! Look up *here!*'

Claudie looked up, and there, perching on the giant fig tree behind her desk was the little woman who'd been waltzing in her bathroom the night before.

'Well, don't look so surprised to see me! You *can* see me, can't you?'

Claudie nodded at the dark-haired girl in the yellow dress who was sitting, quite comfortably, on one of the thicker branches of the fig tree, legs dangling happily.

'Thank goodness for that! I was beginning to think you were ignoring me. Or that maybe you couldn't see me after all. People are always trying to pull one over on us.'

'What do you mean?' Claudie whispered, looking round her in case somebody saw her talking to a plant.

'You know - they like to be in charge - like to think they've got things sussed and that they don't need our help.'

'Are you real?' Claudie frowned, her eyes narrowing.

'Of course I'm real!' she said somewhat indignantly. 'Don't you believe your own eyes?'

'Frankly, no. Not lately.'

The dark-haired girl stared at her with sudden tenderness. 'People always think they're so tough, but they aren't tough. They're tender. Tender as baby birds.' She spoke the words as if they were lines from a poem. 'And that's where we come in.'

'You?'

'Us.'

'What? You mean there's more than one of you?' Claudie suddenly looked round her desk, half-expecting to see a whole troupe of little people.

'Gracious, yes! I couldn't do this job on my own.'

'Claudie?' another voice called her name. Claudie felt her body freeze.

It was Mr Bartholomew. How long had he been standing there? Had he been watching her? Listening to her talking to a fig tree?

'Is there anything wrong?' he peered at her closely: something he didn't normally do so it was rather unnerving to have his beaky nose pushed into her face.

'I'm fine,' she replied hesitantly. She felt herself turning round quickly again to look at the tree. The dark-haired girl was still there, swinging her legs merrily, humming a little tune.

'Are you sure?' he repeated his words very slow, his beaky nose only inches away from her face.

Claudie nodded. Could he not see the little girl, then? She looked at her boss, her eyes wide and questioning.

'Look!' he said, remembering why he'd come into the office in the first place. 'I've made some amendments to this letter. Can you get it typed and run three copies off before lunch?'

Claudie took it from him and nodded, trying not to grimace at the amount of red pen and scribble on it. It looked like one of her old school assignments.

'No problem,' she added hastily, lest he thought her away with the fairies. Claudie started at the thought, turning back round to the dark-haired girl when her boss had walked back to his own office. Was that what the little figure was - a fairy? And why hadn't her boss seen her?

'Look,' Claudie began, 'I don't mean to be rude, but what on earth are you?'

The girl smiled back at her. 'Before you say it, no, I'm not a fairy!' She held her tiny hands up in mock defence. '*Everybody* asks that.'

Claudie found herself smiling unexpectedly. 'I mean, who are you?' She scratched her head. 'Am I finally losing it?'

The dark-haired girl shook her head. 'You're not losing it, Claudie. You're finding it!'

'Can't anyone else see you, then?' God, she thought, this was madness. Talking to apparitions! You could still be locked up for that, couldn't you?

'Of course nobody else can see me! I'm *yours*!'

'Mine? What do you mean?'

'I'm here for you - nobody else. Don't you realise that?'

Claudie shook her head very slowly. 'And you're not-'

'A figment of your imagination?'

'Yes! How did you know I was going to say that?' Claudie was becoming more perplexed by the second.

The girl shrugged. 'Because I've done this before. I know all the questions.'

'God! I think I'm going mad!'

'Claudie?' It was Kristen's voice.

Claudie jumped for the third time in ten minutes. This was getting ridiculous, she thought. Perhaps she should just admit defeat and go home and get some sleep. Maybe she was just over-tired.

'Coffee.' Kristen placed it on her Peter Rabbit coaster and perched on the edge of her desk as she sipped hers. Claudie knew that meant trouble.

'Are you all right, Claudes? You look a bit pale.'

'I always look pale,' she joked, giving what she hoped was a cheerful smile but it was hard to tell under the circumstances. 'I've just been handed this.' She pulled the letter her boss had given her out of her in tray in the hope that Kristen might believe she'd been talking to herself about that.

'Blimey! No wonder you're pale. Why does he do that? You've typed that letter at least five times before.'

'Six. This will be number seven.' Claudie peeped surreptitiously over to the fig tree. The dark-haired girl was still there but she was sitting perfectly still now, watching the pair of them with intense eyes. Claudie smiled to herself. She was losing it, wasn't she?

'Claudes,' Kristen began again. Claudie recognised that tone of hers. It always preceded a probing question.

'Yes?' she said airily, bringing up the saved letter on her computer screen, with just a quick flick of the eyes to the dark-haired girl who had now descended and was dancing behind her computer.

'How are your sessions going in York?'

'Fine. Why?'

'Just wondered,' Kristen said, injecting far too much nonchalance into her voice. 'What's he given you to read this week, then?'

'Nothing. I told him I didn't want any more books.'

Kristen scowled, pushing her red hair away from her eyes in disbelief. 'Are you sure that's sensible?'

Claudie looked up at her friend, trying to ignore the girl who was dancing in the corner of her eye. 'I'm tired of reading,' she said.

Kristen's grey eyes narrowed. 'Your accent's come back.'

'What do you mean?'

'I mean, you always return to your French roots when you're under stress.'

'Rubbish!'

'See! Perfect!' Kristen nodded, pointing a finger at her friend.

Claudie shook her head, not daring to admit defeat, or to speak again.

Kristen sipped her coffee slowly, not showing any signs of leaving until she had a full confession out of her.

'I'm half-French. What do you expect?'

'Aye, lass, but yer can't 'alf speak Yorkshire when yer want to.'

Claudie smiled. 'Look - I'm perfectly all right. There is absolutely no stress here.'

Kristen chewed her lip. 'Well, if you're sure?' She made to go back to her own desk.

'I'm sure,' Claudie reiterated, eager to get rid of her.

'Okay. But you know where I am if you need me.'

'Thanks.' Claudie watched as Kristen sauntered over to her desk, shaking her head at her own growing heap of paperwork. Then, turning round, Claudie spotted the little woman again. She was sure she would have disappeared by now; that she really was only a figment of her overactive imagination. But no, she was still there - smaller than life - but there all the same.

'Well!' the little lady began, her tiny hands resting on her exquisitely slender hips. 'You've got to be the worst liar I've ever come across.'

'What?' Claudie whispered, shocked by the candid remark.

'*There is absolutely no stress here.*' She repeated Claudie's remark with more than a hint of irony. 'Well, what do you think I'm here for?'

CHAPTER 5

'I think, perhaps, I'd better explain exactly who I am,' the little woman began. 'I always forget my manners when I meet clients for the first time. I just get so excited.'

'Well, you already seem to know who I am,' Claudie said, forgetting about Mr Bartholomew's letter, and sitting back in her chair to listen to the little apparition.

'Of course! We're all briefed, you know.'

'Oh?' Claudie was becoming very intrigued.

'Yes. It's all in the job description. We must read through the client's file before contact is made.'

'I have a file?'

The little lady suddenly clasped her hand to her mouth. 'Oh, dear! I'm not supposed to talk about it.'

Claudie's eyes narrowed. 'Talk about what exactly?'

'Our job.'

'Which is?'

'You know - angels!'

'You're an *angel*?' Claudie heard a little laugh escape from her but quickly bit her lip in case she appeared rude. 'What? Like a guardian angel?'

'If you like. But who coined that term, I don't know.'

'But,' Claudie paused, observing the figure as if for the first time, 'you haven't got any wings?'

'I know!' she said, rolling her eyes in a practised manner. 'And we don't wear white feathers or haloes. And we don't play harps either. We're just normal.'

'Then why are you so small?' Claudie asked, peering down at the pen-high figure.

'It's simple if you think about it. Just imagine all the people who've died, and then all of those who are alive now. We wouldn't all be able to move around if we were all the same size, would we?'

'But I thought you were invisible?'

'Doesn't make any difference - we still take up space.'

Claudie pondered this for a moment. With everything else she'd heard, she might as well believe it. 'Do you have a name then? Or do I just call you *angel*?

She laughed. 'My name's Jalisa,' she said with a little curtsy.

Claudie smiled. 'What a pretty name.' She looked round the office to check if she was being watched. Luckily, although it was open-planned, the desks were far enough apart to allow a little privacy.

'So what happens now? I mean,' Claudie struggled, not quite knowing how to talk to an angel, 'what are you going to do now that you're here?'

'There are a few boring preliminaries we have to go through, I'm afraid,' Jalisa said, her pretty mouth twisting as if in apology.

'Such as?'

'Like where you want us? Here at work, or at home?'

'You mean you're going to follow me around?'

'No! But we need to know where you need us most. We can't be all over the place. We need to be contactable, you see.'

Claudie didn't see at all, but she didn't say anything.

'We have to run reports and all sorts of dull things,' Jalisa confessed. 'When I was first given this job, I had no idea that being an angel would be anything other than fun, but it's actually very hard work, and not at all glamorous.' She let out a little sigh and turned a little pirouette.

Claudie watched in delight at the spectacle on her desk. It was rather like an MGM musical in miniature.

'Were you a dancer, then? In life?' Claudie asked.

'No,' Jalisa said. 'I would like to have been, though. I was a teacher of dance. For kids.'

'Isn't that the same thing?'

'Not exactly. I was getting paid to teach rather than to dance.'

'But you're so good.' Claudie watched as Jalisa executed a few effortless turns on top of her computer.

'Thank you.' And then she stopped. 'So - where do you want us? At home or at work?'

Claudie sucked in her cheeks. 'What would you advise?'

'Well, where do you feel more stress? That's usually a sign of where we're needed.'

Claudie thought of her little home overlooking the harbour and of how she tucked herself away in it with her films. In the early days, she had hated it - everything had reminded her of Luke. In the kitchen, she remembered the careless way he'd wash up; in the bathroom, she remembered the way he'd stand in the door, watching her as she brushed her hair; and in the bedroom, well-

'Where's Luke?' The question came out before she had time to check herself.

'Now, Claudie. We're not allowed to talk about things like that.'

'Why not?'

'Because I'm here to help you.'

'But *that* would help me, and I want to know.'

There was a pause. Jalisa sighed and leant forward slightly. 'I'll probably get fired if I'm found out, but,' she looked around anxiously, as if somebody might be eavesdropping, 'he's safe.'

'Can I see him?'

Jalisa shook her head. 'No, I'm afraid not.'

This was getting more and more illogical by the second. Surely, Claudie reasoned, if she did have her own angel, it would make sense if that angel was Luke.

'Why-' she began but Jalisa interrupted her.

'Claudie - it's not my decision, but I'm your angel, so you have to make do with me. If it's any consolation, Luke's probably looking after someone else. That's the way it works.'

The sudden thought of Luke on a stranger's desk made Claudie smile, but she couldn't help feeling just a little bit upset, and a little bit jealous too.

'Surely it would make more sense to have him protecting me?' she said.

Jalisa looked up at her, her eyes soft and tender. 'But you've got to move on, Claudie. It wouldn't be right to give him back to you.'

'Not right?' Claudie's voice almost vanished with emotion.

Jalisa shook her head. 'It's a tough rule, I know. I have no idea who came up with it, but it's set in stone all the same. I'm sorry, Claudie.'

They were both silent for a moment. Claudie spoke first.

'So when do I meet the others? You mentioned something about "us"?'

'Oh - don't be in a rush to meet them! I'm enjoying my time with you alone first.'

'But there will be more than just you?'

Jalisa nodded. 'We operate in flights of five.'

'Flights? You mean like in *flights of angels*? That's from *Hamlet*, isn't it?'

'What?'

'Is that where your collective noun comes from? Shakespeare?'

'Oh, *Shakespeare*! Yes. You're right. He was quite honoured when the term was employed.'

Claudie smiled. 'You've met him, then?'

'Of course! Everybody knows everybody on the other side. Anyway, a flight is a group - a company, if you like - of carefully selected angels who've been trained for the job.' She nodded her head as if pleased with her summary. 'So this idea of people only getting one angel is outrageous. Whoever thought that only one angel could do the job?'

'It all sounds so fascinating.'

'What sounds so fascinating?' The voice wasn't Jalisa's but Mr Bartholomew's. Claudie's heart danced the quick-step. She did wish he wouldn't creep up on her like that.

'Er -' she struggled. 'Nothing. I was just thinking aloud.'

'I found this on my desk. It should have gone out on Friday.' He handed her a memo.

'Oh,' Claudie said, knowing full well that he hadn't given it to her on Friday morning, and knowing that he knew perfectly well that she was out of the office on Friday afternoons. 'I'll deal with it straight away.'

Mr Bartholomew nodded absent-mindedly and left the office.

'What a horrible man!' Jalisa cried.

'Shusshh!'

'Don't worry - he can't hear me! Only you can, Claudie. How many times do I have to keep telling you that?'

'I'm sorry. It's just this is all rather a lot to take in at once.'

'I know. That's why I was sent ahead of the others. It would be disastrous if the whole flight appeared on your desk at once. That's how it used to happen in the old days, of course. Terrible system, apparently. Drove people insane. But there's this new charter now,' Jalisa said, stretching her arms out either side and spinning on one foot like a mini Leslie Caron. 'But-'

'I know!' Claudie grinned. 'You're not meant to talk about it.'

'So - back to where you want us. Here? Or at home?'

Claudie pursed her lips and watched Jalisa dancing round her desk. She'd never be able to see her desk in the same light again.

'I think here would be fine. If that's all right with you.'

'Perfectly!' she replied, swinging round Claudie's Rolodex.

'Can I ask you something?'

'Of course! I may not be allowed to answer it, but I'll do my best to be helpful.'

'How were you chosen for me?'

Jalisa stopped spinning. 'I don't know. That's not my department. But I suppose it's rather like real life. Sometimes a job chooses you.'

Claudie nodded knowingly. 'And why now? Why not before?'

'It's called a testing period,' Jalisa explained. 'Everybody has them, after something bad has happened, and everybody's is different, and we're not always needed.'

Claudie wanted to ask more. Like how did they know she needed help? Who made that decision? Had they all been watching her, and assessing her? And were there flights of angels everywhere, and you could only see your own flight? But Jalisa looked as if she'd said all she was prepared to say on the subject.

'So,' Claudie said, trying to inject a little colour in her voice, 'what about the others? When do I get to meet them?'

'Whenever you're ready! Though I must warn you - they're rather a motley bunch.'

CHAPTER 6

There must surely be something in amongst all his junk that was worth money, Simon thought, head bowed as he looked at a lifetime's accumulation in his attic. Okay, so he knew he wasn't very likely to come across a Rembrandt or a Chippendale amongst his stuff, especially since Felicity had already ransacked the place first, but he at least hoped to find a few items that were taking up unnecessary space and, if sold, might tide him over until his next commission.

It was a poor do when you had to resort to selling possessions to make money in order to compensate the lack of ability to earn it, he thought remorsefully. Was this what three years at university had prepared him for?

He flicked the switch on and stood and surveyed his secret kingdom. He couldn't believe that Felicity had even thought to rifle through this place because there really wasn't much worth rifling through. A couple of old chairs: one with a dodgy leg, the other with a dodgy seat; an old-fashioned record player and a stack of records which would never see the light of day again if Simon wanted to keep his street-cred; an empty bird cage from a former pet canary, and a tower of old comics.

But that wasn't all. Most of the space was taken up with something far more precious. Books. Piles of them from the literature component of his degree. IT and literature had been an odd but satisfying combination, even though he'd constantly had the mickey taken out of him by his mates.

He walked into the heart of the attic and crouched down, picking up the first book on top of a large pile. He should have stored them in boxes. He was lucky they hadn't been rained on, or pooed on by bats.

What was he to do with them all? Though much loved, they weren't any use to him now. It wasn't very likely that he'd pick up George Eliot's *Middlemarch* again, and as for *Sense and Sensibility*, well, he'd had trouble stomaching it the first time, and *Far From the*

Madding Crowd wasn't likely to help him as a website designer.

He scratched his head. There wasn't much money in books, he knew that. Cracked spines, faded covers, and scribbles in the margins. He'd be lucky if he'd get anything at all for them at all. He'd probably be told to take them down to Oxfam, or the recycling bin, but it was worth a try, and it would definitely clear some space.

And then he spied his old favourite. *Great Expectations*. He could still remember the night he'd stayed up to finish it. He'd never experienced anything like it before. The characters were like old friends: Pip, Magwitch, Joe and Jaggers. Could he part with them now?

'When needs must!' he said, and placed it on to his growing sale pile. The books weren't going to do him any good by collecting cobwebs up in his attic, festering away like Miss Havisham. He might as well put them to use.

'What else?' His eyes scoured the towers of paperbacks he'd collected over the years, grimacing at his teenage taste in science-fiction. They could go for a start. One, two, three. He blew a fine layer of dust off each one and placed them on top of Dickens.

'Sorry, old chap!' he said with a grin.

'And Tolstoy. Never could see the magic there. Must be a woman thing,' he said, stretching forward and removing the great tome from storage pile to selling pile.

After half an hour, and much deliberating, he had two carrier bags of books to sell. That was the easy part, he thought. The hard part would be drumming up the nerve to try and sell them to the old witch who ran the bookshop.

He trundled downstairs, nodding to Pumpkin as he collected his keys on the way out. 'Got to keep us in food, mate,' he explained, before walking out into the harsh midday light to catch the bus for the short ride into town.

God, it was so embarrassing. Even though there was only one young woman in the shop, Simon thought twice about emptying his life out onto the counter. But it had to be done.

'They're mostly classics,' he announced unnecessarily.

'You know, you can get most of the classics for a pound now,' the witch-woman told him.

'You couldn't when I was a student.'

She pushed her thick lips out as she turned each of the books over in turn, her eyes squinting.

'I can't give you more than six pounds.'

'Six pounds! But there's fifteen books here!'

'Take it or leave it,' the woman said smugly. 'I have to make my profit.'

'Jeepers!' Simon intoned. But what choice did he have? Six pounds! He must have paid over eighty pounds for the books in the first place. Blimey. He'd heard of depreciation but this was ridiculous.

'I'll take it,' he said woefully and the woman opened the till and produced a manky-looking fiver and a black pound coin. It would just about buy one new paperback novel. Or, if he was careful, half a basket of shopping.

Whilst he was in the shop, he thought he might as well have a look around. Second-hand books always fascinated him. There was no telling what might turn up: first editions, signed copies, out of print gems. He inhaled the distinct aroma of old books and briefly wondered if he could patent an aftershave in it.

He had the shop to himself now and he wandered into the anteroom, away from the counter. He ignored the novels. There was absolutely no point in selling a load only to accumulate more. He went straight into the film and TV section. There weren't many there, so one yellow-spined hardback positively leapt out at him.

He'd always been a sucker for Judy Garland. She'd been one of his mother's favourite film stars, and he'd been force-fed Andy Hardy films since he could remember. The great old hardback begged to be picked up and he flicked through it eagerly, nodding at the familiar photographs. It was beautiful. He checked the pencilled in price at the front and winced. Typical of the old witch, he thought. When he was selling, he got peanuts, but when he wanted to buy-

'Excuse me?' a female voice caught his attention. It was shy, and distinctly French.

'Yes?' He looked up and saw a pair of chocolate eyes in a pale, heart-shaped face.

'Are you going to buy that book?'

Simon stared at her. She was beautiful. Skin like moonshine, glossy brown hair and an expression as delicate as cobweb.

'What?'

'Are you planning on buying that book?' Her voice was anxious.

'Er - I don't know.'

'Oh.' She sounded disappointed.

'Why?' he asked.

'Because I was going to buy it.'

Suddenly, the witch was upon them. 'Is there a problem?' she all but shouted, poking her nose in between them. Simon grimaced. It really should have been a green nose with a big hairy wart on the end of it.

'No!' Simon said, snapping the book shut. 'There isn't any problem.'

The old witch stared up and down at him, and then at the young woman before retreating behind her counter. Simon looked back at the young woman.

'Here,' he said, 'you take it. I really can't afford it.'

'Are you sure?'

He nodded and smiled, and she smiled back.

'Thank you,' she said, gently taking the book from him before approaching the till.

Simon looked on in fascination as the old witch, a staunch recycler, placed Judy Garland in one of his old carrier bags.

And then the moonshine woman was gone. Simon watched from the shop window as she disappeared up the street, swinging his carrier bag by her side.

CHAPTER 7

Claudie almost skipped into the office the next morning. Today was the day. Today, Jalisa had promise to introduce her to the rest of her flight.

Where would they be? Would Jalisa have taken up her position in the fig tree or would she have adopted something more formal in order to introduce everyone? And who would they be? It was hard for Claudie to imagine. Jalisa had said that they were a motley bunch but what exactly did that mean? Claudie didn't even know if they'd be men, women or both, and if they were all modern-day angels or angels from another period in time. Jalisa had said she'd met Shakespeare so there was really no telling who these other angels might be. She smiled wistfully. Just imagine. She might end up with a tiny Gene Kelly on her desk. She'd never get any work done.

It was all very exciting but, as she walked towards her desk, she felt her mouth drooping as she realised there was nobody around. A wave of insecurity hit her. What if she'd imagined the whole thing? What if this Jalisa had just been an externalisation of her inner desire for help? Oh, God! She was beginning to think like Dr Lynton. *Inner desire for help* indeed!

'Morning, Claudes!' Kristen sang.

'Morning,' Claudie replied, suddenly remembering that she was actually here to do a job, not be entertained by little angels other people couldn't see.

And then she spotted it. A tiny little scribble on her top post-it note. It was barely discernible, but Claudie could just make out the message.

'Claudie. Sorry but we'll be a bit late today. Love, Jalisa x.'

So she hadn't imagined it then.

She pulled her chair out and switched her monitor on, flexing her fingers in preparation for a heavy morning's typing. Kristen was already in full flow, and Claudie guessed she'd got in early to catch up on some of the work before the bosses arrived.

'Has anyone got a post-it note?' Kristen suddenly asked, looking round the office hopelessly and catching Claudie's eye. 'I swear those things have legs!' she said, walking towards her as soon as she spotted some.

'Can I pinch some of yours? I promise I'll replace them as soon as the stationery order comes in.' Her hand was already over them. Claudie placed her hand on top of Kristen's. She couldn't let her have the post-its. Not with that message on. What on earth would she make of it?

'I only want a few, Claudes!' Kristen laughed. 'Before I forget what I'm meant to be doing today.' She picked them up.

Claudie closed her eyes, waiting for the questions to start. Could she possibly deny all knowledge? Could she get away with saying she'd never heard of anyone called Jalisa? Probably not. She knew Kristen too well, and she always had a way of wheedling things out of her.

'Kristen? I think I've may have scribbled something on one of the post-its.'

'What? Where?' Kristen held them up for inspection. 'There's nothing here, Claudes. They're blank. See?' She held them out and Claudie's eyes widened as she saw Jalisa's tiny message in blue ink.

'*I'm yours!*' she remembered Jalisa telling her. It was true then. Nobody else could see or hear them at all.

'Have you lost something?' Kristen asked.

'Oh, no!' Claudie shook her head vehemently, a smile stretching its way across her face.

By eleven o'clock, Claudie had almost forgotten about the imminent arrival of her flight. Mr Bartholomew had placed a great wodge of notes on her desk and had even given some to Kristen, who was really Mr Simpson's PA. She'd lost herself in a maze of black ink, and almost leapt out of her seat when Jalisa's legs dangled over her monitor without warning.

'Morning, Claudie! Bet you'd forgotten about me!' she said, cocking her head to one side, her dark ringlets spilling over her left shoulder.

'Jalisa!'

'Did you get my note?'

'Yes! But I-'

'Good,' she interrupted. 'Sorry about the mix up - terrible delay in

Angel Resources, and then the Despatches team were running late. They really should get themselves organised. They've no idea how much chaos they cause. But we're here now. All together at last.'

Claudie's eyes flicked round her desk in wonder but couldn't see anything that resembled another Jalisa.

'No!' Jalisa smiled. 'We're here, but not quite *here*, if you know what I mean.'

'No,' Claudie said honestly.

'You have to be quite sure that this is the right thing for you.'

'Oh, but I am!'

'You realise that, once we're here, you can't just decide to send us back on a whim. We have to do our job and we're not allowed to leave until it's completed.'

'Yes! Yes!' Claudie whispered eagerly. 'I know.'

'Okay!' Jalisa laughed, throwing her hands up as if to deflect Claudie's enthusiasm a little. 'Then you're ready to meet us all?'

'YES!'

'Claudes?' Kristen looked round from her desk. 'You're talking to yourself again.'

'Sorry,' Claudie quickly apologised, feeling herself blushing.

Turning back round to face Jalisa, she whispered, 'Yes, 'I'm ready.'

'Okay. As I said before, each member has been specially chosen for the job: possessing some quality or ability to help you. I'll introduce them to you one at a time.'

Claudie bit her lip as she watched Jalisa, wondering where the other members of the flight would appear.

'Albert?' Jalisa called quietly, looking down the side of Claudie's computer. Claudie's eyes followed and there, miraculously, appeared a little old man, figure stooped like a wind-blown tree, wearing grey hair and the biggest, reddest nose Claudie had ever seen. She tried to stop herself from laughing. It wasn't exactly what she'd expected, not after the beautiful, elegant Jalisa.

'How do you do,' Albert said as he removed his hat, his large amber eyes beaming up at her.

'How do you do,' Claudie replied, smiling down at him.

'Albert died in 1955, which explains the clothes.'

'Hey! Cheeky young miss!' Albert shouted, brushing down his tweed coat with pride.

'But he's got a great sense of humour, haven't you, Bert?'

'I wasn't chosen to entertain the troupes because I was a miserable git, was I?'

Claudie giggled.

'See!' Jalisa said, 'he's working already.' There was a pause. 'Now there's something I need to explain about Elizabeth,' Jalisa said.

'Who's Elizabeth?'

'You're about to find out. She can be a bit stroppy and, to be perfectly honest with you, I'm not at all sure why she was chosen for this flight. I have a feeling that she's your token person from history.'

'What do you mean?' Claudie asked, becoming intrigued.

'Wait and see.'

'Elizabeth. We're ready,' Jalisa announced and Claudie watched as, by her pot of pens, there appeared a beautiful young woman in a cream and burgundy gown. As soon as she came into focus properly, Claudie could see that she had a deep scowl etched across her forehead and was standing with her hands placed very firmly on her hips.

'It's Lily! How many times do I have to say it?' Elizabeth remonstrated.

'Now don't start the minute you arrive,' Jalisa sighed.

'Who is she? Is she a princess?' Claudie asked, seeing Elizabeth smile at the comment. 'Oh, my God!'

'What?' Jalisa sounded worried.

'I haven't got the young Queen Elizabeth I in miniature on my desk, have I?'

Jalisa laughed which made Elizabeth scowl beautifully again. 'Good gracious, no! Although she did come from a very good family, didn't you?'

'The best.'

'Where are you from, then?' Claudie asked.

'1540.'

'No, I meant what place?'

'I see! Suffolk.'

'There's something else I should tell you,' Jalisa said from her vantage point at the top of the computer.

'What's that?' Claudie asked, strangely reminded of the grand ballet sequence at the end of *An American in Paris* which she always thought couldn't possibly get any better, only to be proved wrong over and over again.

Jalisa cleared her throat, 'Eliz, - I mean *Lily*, has a twin,' she explained, somewhat apologetically.

As soon as the word *twin* was out, an identical image appeared next to Elizabeth.

'Wow!' Claudie gasped. 'She's beautiful.'

'Thanks a lot!' Lily intoned.

'I mean - *they're* beautiful.'

'This is Mary. The other half of the Tudor twins,' Jalisa said.

'Hello, Claudie,' Mary said, a pretty smile lighting her face.

'Hello,' Claudie replied, feeling her eyes saucering in wonder. She'd never met identical twins before, and the experience was astonishing enough without them being sixteenth century, six-inch tall angels to boot. She peered closely at their dresses: the square, bejewelled necklines, the tight bodices and double-skirts, and large trumpet sleeves. At last it clicked.

'They look like Anne Boleyn!' Claudie told Jalisa.

'Anne Boleyn!' Lily declared, outraged. 'That witch! *Jane Seymour*, if you please.'

'Jane Seymour? The actress?' Claudie asked, rather puzzled.

'The *queen!* The one Henry chopped Anne's head off for. Anyway, if you think I'm wearing all this stuff any more, you've got another thing coming.'

'Now listen, Lily. I just *knew* you were going to be trouble,' Jalisa said, waving a warning finger.

'All I'm saying is that we should be able to dress in up-to-date clothing.'

'What's wrong with what you're wearing?' Claudie asked. 'I think it's beautiful.'

'It might very well be, but it belongs in the Victoria and Albert.'

Albert's ears pricked up at the mention of his name. 'Did someone call?'

'Go back to sleep, Albert, dear,' Lily whispered and turned back to Claudie. 'I love what you're wearing though,' Lily continued. 'Is that this Gooky I've been hearing about?'

'Gucci?'

'That's the one.'

'Goodness, no!' Claudie exclaimed, her hands flying up to her navy jacket. 'This is from Debenhams.'

'Debenhams. Who's he? I've not heard of that designer.'

'God! All she ever goes on about are clothes,' Mary complained.

'Well why shouldn't I want some modern things to wear?'

'What's wrong with what you've got?' Mary asked.

'I've been wearing it for nearly five hundred years. I'm getting a bit bored with it,' Lily snapped back.

'Girls! Enough already! Mr Woo's still got to make an appearance.'

'Heaven preserve us!' Bert snorted, making himself comfortable on Claudie's strawberry lipbalm.

'Er, Bert,' Jalisa began, 'we all know you two have your differences, but this isn't the time to air them. We're here to work, okay?'

He nodded dolefully.

'Mr Woo?' Jalisa called, and suddenly there was a fifth figure on the desk. A perfect little Chinese man, with jet hair, a wide face, and the kindest, softest eyes Claudie had ever seen. They were just the kind of eyes Claudie had needed ten months ago but which, apart from Kristen, had been sadly lacking.

'Mr Woo died only last year, so he's rather new to all this. You'll have to bear with him as he's still rather shell-shocked,' Jalisa explained. 'Keeps thinking he's going to wake up and be back at his herbal remedies shop in North London.'

Claudie took a moment to compute this. What was she meant to say to him? *I'm sorry you've just died?* What was the etiquette on meeting a newly dead person? She had no idea, so decided to play it cool. 'Pleased to meet you,' she said, nodding to the little man who was wearing the most exquisite olive coat with large embroidered buttons and long, loose sleeves. He gave a half-smile and lightly nodded his head, but didn't say anything.

'He's brilliant with alternative medicine, so feel free to ask him for anything you need.' Jalisa clapped her hands together. 'So that's the flight! Hope you like us!'

'Yes, I do! You're - they're -' Claudie struggled to find the right words

'- amazing.'

'We'll just take up residence round the desk. We can make ourselves scarce when you need us to and we don't make any mess,' she laughed. 'We can entertain ourselves when you're busy but, if you need us, just call us.'

*

Kristen left the office on the stroke of five thirty. Nobody got overtime out of her unless it was arranged in advance and paid for. She went home via the supermarket, guessing Jimmy wouldn't have managed to find his way there during the course of the day, not unless they'd started stocking parts for model boats.

Three bags of groceries and high heels made the steps down into Lantern Yard rather difficult to contend with. Kristen huffed, puffed, cursed, almost snapped a heel, and then swore she'd start taking a pair of trainers into work. Of course, she'd promised that before but couldn't face the reality of teaming an old pair of Reeboks with her gorgeously girly outfits. It just wouldn't do.

'You're going to wreck those pretty little feet of yours,' Jimmy had once warned her, and she knew he was right. It just seemed a long way off to start worrying about right now. She had far too many other things on her mind.

'I'm home!' she shouted as she pushed the door open into the kitchen, trying not to notice the pile of dirty dishes in the sink.

'Jimmy? You in?'

'Yep!' he called back from the living room.

Kristen quickly unpacked the frozen food and then wandered through to the back of the house.

'Still fixing that boat?'

'Not fixing - making,' he asked, eyes fixed on something Kristen couldn't see. 'How was work?'

'Oh, you know - Mr Simpson in his usual panic mode. Angela had a big row with her boyfriend, Mikey. And Claudie-' she paused.

'What?'

'I'm sure she was talking to herself. All day! I've never heard that before. I couldn't quite hear what she was saying but it seemed to be full-blown conversations rather than thoughtful mumblings, 'cause we all do that from time to time. But she was definitely talking to herself.'

Jimmy didn't respond.

'Like me,' she added, turning on her heels and heading into the kitchen to make tea.

CHAPTER 8

'I'm not doing any more shopping this week,' Kristen told herself as she spooned an extra sugar into her coffee. 'And I'm not doing any more washing up either. No siree. This girl is on domestic strike.'

The sigh that left her body could have sent half the boats in the harbour out to sea. She was fed up: fed up of being a skivy; of being taken advantage of; and fed up of being unappreciated. And, if she was perfectly honest with herself, of being unmarried too.

She knew it was pathetic and outdated, and that she should be counting her blessings. She had a good man, after all, and there was more to life than marriage vows, she knew that - but, in her heart of hearts, it was what she wanted. It was the little girl inside her craving the romance and security promised by a wedding. It wasn't even as if she wanted the full works. No, she was one girl who could do without tiaras and taffeta; a quiet register office would do nicely. As long as there were plenty of flowers and confetti.

Jimmy, of course, was dead set against marriage after his one and only disaster. He just couldn't see past his ex-wife and, although he knew she and Kristen were not only cut from different moulds but had also been manufactured in completely different factories, he didn't seem convinced by the idea of a second marriage. That was for foolish Hollywood actors, not a part-time skipper from Whitby.

Kristen lit a cigarette, cursing silently to herself after her first delicious puff. She'd been doing all right too. Down to just five a week. Not bad after years of at least eight a day but, with friends like Claudie and Simon, and a man like Jimmy, what chance did she stand?

Jimmy was still in bed. It was his favourite place until about eleven o'clock, after which time he'd get up, and walk around for half an hour in his bath robe. She rarely saw him before she went out to work, not until the end of May, when the tourist season began to kick in and he'd be up early to get the boat ready. Come to think of it, she hardly saw him then either.

For the first time in their two years' together, Kristen was not a happy woman. Nothing had changed, of course, only her perception of things. She was restless and unsatisfied, finding fault in everything.

It was, she thought, time for a girly talk.

'Claudie - what are you doing tonight?' Kristen asked, pouncing on her almost as soon as she walked into the office.

'Er - ' Claudie knew this was dangerous ground. 'If she said she wasn't doing anything, Kristen would slap her wrists for cocooning herself away from the world, and would, no doubt, try to persuade her to go out.

'How's about a girls' night out? Just you and me?' Kristen said, giving Claudie her biggest and brightest smile. 'It'll be like the old times.'

'I don't know,' she said, hating the feeble tone of her voice.

'Why not?'

Claudie started. It wasn't Kristen's voice but Jalisa's. Claudie hadn't seen her when she'd sat down at her desk, but there she was, tap dancing on top of her printer. 'Why not go out with her?' she said in between steps. 'It will do you both good.'

'You think so?' Claudie mouthed. Jalisa stopped dancing and nodded.

'If you ask me,' Lily observed, walking out from behind the pencil pot, 'it's Kristen who needs a friend at the moment. Just look at her.'

Claudie turned round and, sure enough, Kristen looked as if a steam train had flattened her face. Claudie instantly felt terrible. She'd been so wrapped up in her own world, and couldn't remember the last time she'd asked after Kristen and bothered to find out what was going on with her.

'Go on! *Say yes!*' Mary urged, appearing next to her sister. Claudie suppressed a chuckle at the scene, all of which was, of course, invisible to Kristen.

'Why not?' Claudie said out loud, and felt instantly happier when she saw Kristen smile with relief.

When five-thirty came round, two computers were switched off simultaneously, and two girls grabbed their coats and bags and ran out of the office before anyone had the chance to ask them to type out another letter or photocopy another wodge of minutes.

'God, it's just like school, remember?' Kristen laughed as they legged it down the street.

'Mr Samson's science lessons!' Claudie laughed.

'Blimey! I used to think I'd die of boredom. Watching that bloody clock crawling round, waiting for the bell.'

'And Mrs Jones's English lessons!'

Kristen erupted into laughter at the memory. 'I've since discovered that *Macbeth* is actually quite an interesting play.'

'I thought we'd never get to the end of it. How long did we spend reading it round the class? Why do teachers make kids do that?'

'I don't know. I'm sure Shakespeare would be rolling in his grave if he knew.' Kristen halted. 'God! Claudie - I'm sorry.' She grabbed her friend's arm. 'I shouldn't have said that.'

'Don't worry,' Claudie said.

'What a stupid thing to say.'

'It's all right.'

Kristen bit her lip. 'Sorry.'

Claudie placed a hand on her shoulder. 'Fancy a drink?'

'You bet,' Kristen smiled, glad to change the topic of conversation. 'And I'm dying for a cigarette.'

'Oh, Kris, I thought you'd given up.'

'No,' she said, reaching into the depths of her handbag, 'not yet.'

'But I haven't seen you smoke for ages.'

'That's because I sneak them in the ladies when there's nobody around. It's like being a teenager all over again.'

'Oh, Kristen!' Claudie chided, remembering the numerous detentions Kristen had had for being caught smoking in the upper school toilets.

'I know! I know! I'll pack in one day.'

Kristen was half way down her Lambert and Butler when they reached the pub.

'Listen, I've just got to grab some cash,' she said.

'Don't worry. I'll pay.'

'No, you won't. This was my idea and it's going to be my treat,' she said, disappearing to the cash point before Claudie could stop her.

If there was one thing in the world Claudie hated, other than a film on TV being cancelled due to extended sports coverage, it was walking into a pub on her own. She always felt so conspicuous, which was silly because people probably weren't the least bit interested in her. She hovered around for a moment, waiting for Kristen, but she seemed to be having trouble with the machine, and a bitterly cold wind was trying to disrobe Claudie of her many layers, so she decided to go in.

She hesitated at the door, peering in through a thick cloud of smoke. The sound of after-work laughter hit her, as did the sharp clack of a cue on a ball. She turned her head and saw a group of men hovering over the snooker table. She smiled briefly. Luke had always loved snooker. Or was it pool? Or maybe billiards? She could never remember.

She looked across at the table. There were five men standing under the harsh light. Claudie watched for a few seconds without actually walking into the pub. One of the men had his back to her, but there was something very familiar about him. It was his hair. A mop of pale golden curls.

It was the man from the bookshop. The one who'd nearly stolen Judy Garland from her!

As he turned round, Claudie's suspicions were confirmed. For a moment, their eyes met. Definite recognition.

How strange, Claudie thought. One day, you don't even realise that someone is alive and then you start seeing them everywhere at once.

'God almighty!' Kristen's voice suddenly called from the door. 'Bloody machines. Nearly swallowed my card, and then it wouldn't print me a statement out! Come on, Claudes. It's too cold for a drink.' Kristen pulled her arm from behind. 'Let's go and eat.'

'So Jimmy, the bastard, just fell asleep!' Kristen almost yelled, causing a couple on the neighbouring table to look round. 'I mean! I'd gone to all that effort!'

'I know! I was with you when you bought that negligee. Forty-nine pounds.'

'Forty-nine *ninety-nine*!' Kristen corrected. 'In the sale! Bloody waste of money.'

'What a shame, Kris.'

Kristen shook her head and plunged her spoon into the quagmire of cream on her knickerbocker glory.

'Perhaps he was just tired. You could try again.'

'Tired? He does nothing but build model boats all day.'

'But that must be awfully tiring on the eyes.'

'Claudie, you're such an angel!'

Claudie felt herself flinch at the word *angel*. 'No, I'm not!'

'You'd defend Satan.'

'Jimmy's not that bad. Is he?' Claudie had always got on with Jimmy, and knew he was a decent chap. Kristen could do a lot worse and, deep down, she was sure Kristen knew it.

Kristen's spoon paused halfway to her mouth. 'I just feel so-' she waved it around in the air as if trying to catch the right word with it, 'so - unwanted.'

'But he *adores* you! You know that.' Claudie was beginning to panic. She felt sure she could see tears in Kristen's eyes. Great fat tears ready to spill any second. 'He'd hate to see you unhappy. Come on! Try it again tonight. Or tomorrow. And if he doesn't respond, I'll come round and give him a punch on the nose.'

Kristen gave a strangled laugh and managed to blink the tears back. 'I'm just being silly, aren't I?'

Claudie knew it was a rhetorical question but she couldn't resist answering, 'Yes.'

Kristen half-smiled. 'I don't know what's got into me lately.'

'Not Jimmy from the sounds of things.'

Kristen spluttered, and her mouth widened with laughter, her face burning red. 'That's for sure! I've forgotten what it's like to have a good seeing-to.'

They both laughed, this time causing half the restaurant to turn and stare at them.

'Excuse me, ladies.' One of the waiters, who was ridiculously over-dressed, had approached the table. 'Would you mind keeping the noise down?'

'Don't worry, mate, we're leaving in a minute,' Kristen snarled back at him. 'And don't bother looking for a tip,' she said to his retreating back. 'Pompous penguin!'

'God, Claudes. I feel terrible!' Kristen confessed after they'd left the restaurant.

'I'm not surprised after all that wine you drank.'

'No! I mean, I've done nothing but talk about myself all evening.'

'So?'

'Well, I didn't mean to. I mean-'

'I know what you mean.'

Kristen smiled. 'I wanted to ask how you were. You know?'

Claudie nodded. She knew, and she was glad Kristen hadn't given her the third degree. But she had also wondered, just once or twice throughout the meal, whether or not to tell Kristen about the angels. However, each time, she'd bitten her lip and taken another mouthful of food before she'd divulged anything.

'We'd better get home,' Claudie said, changing the subject. 'Will you be all right from here?'

''Course I will. Will you?'

Claudie nodded. It was always the same after they'd had a night out. Always arguing over who got to walk who home.

'Your place is further.'

'Yours is spookier.'

'Yours is down those steps.'

'Yours is under the church.'

And so on, until they were so tired they just said goodnight and went their separate ways.

But Claudie had insisted on seeing Kristen home. Or to the top of the steps at least. Kristen wouldn't admit it, but she'd definitely overdone it on the wine, and she was tottering somewhat unsteadily in her heels.

'I wish you'd wear sensible shoes.'

'Don't you start,' Kristen slurred, linking Claudie tightly.

'Are you sure you can manage the steps?'

'Yes! Now get on home before Dracula starts roaming the streets.'

'Okay!' Claudie giggled, wishing Kristen hadn't mentioned Dracula. She knew it was only fiction, but there were nights when she seriously believed that Bram Stoker had had good reason to dock his vampiric hero in Whitby.

'Night, Claudes,' Kristen said as she began disappearing down the steps.

'Night, Kris.'

Claudie stood at the top of the steps watching as Kristen descended, waiting until she heard her key in the lock. Then she turned and began the ten-minute walk home. Alone. In the dark.

She tried not to look down the myriad alleyways, and avoided eye contact with the shadows. And she didn't think of Dracula. Too much. But it was at times like this, when she was walking alone at night, or those quiet moments just before she tried to find sanctuary in sleep, when she felt most alone. It was strange, but she hadn't been aware of it before she met Luke. It wasn't that she'd handed over her independence when they'd met; she'd never been the sort of woman to be reliant on a man but, when you'd been in a relationship for a while and then it suddenly ended, there was an undeniable void which took the place of somebody looking out for you. Somebody waiting at home for you, to ask you how your day went, to give you a goodnight kiss: these were everyday pleasures that had been ripped away from her.

Walking in the dark now, Claudie felt that the weight of being alone was almost too much too bear. There'd be nobody waiting for her at home. Kristen, at least, had Jimmy. No matter how much she complained about him, he'd still be waiting up, making sure she got home safely, but what did Claudie have to go home to? A few Gene Kelly posters and a bed that was half-empty. She sometimes wondered if it was really worth going home.

Pulling her coat collar snugly against her bare neck, she cast her eyes down the street. A few windows shone yellow and, peeping into one as she walked by, she saw a young couple pulling at a table-sized pizza as they watched TV together. It was just an ordinary domestic scene. There were probably hundreds of couples all over the country sharing pizza at this very moment, and Claudie found it hard not to hate every single one of them. Did they know how lucky they were? Probably not. For a start, this couple were watching the TV when they should have been watching each other. See how his fingers are red with tomato, and how the crust has flaked down the front of her jumper? It was little things like this that you remembered when somebody was no longer there.

Turning away from the window, Claudie headed down the street, bending her head low against the icy wind. Where were her angels when she needed them? Could she call them now for a bit of company? She knew she'd said she wanted to have them at work, but did that preclude them from everywhere else?

She wondered what would happen if she called them.

'Jalisa?' she half-whispered into the night. 'Are you there?'

There was no response, so Claudie quickened her pace and headed home.

CHAPTER 9

As Claudie gazed out of the train window, she thought that the last week had probably been the strangest in her life. Bar one.

Friday had come round so quickly, and it was time for her weekly session in York. But did she have the nerve to tell Dr Lynton about the weird and wonderful things which had been going on on her desk at work? Could she tell him about Jalisa, Lily and Mary, Bert and Mr Woo? Did she have the nerve to say that there were five mad angels occupying her workstation? Would he believe her, or would he call for the men in white coats straight away?

Perhaps, she thought optimistically, his other clients had experienced something similar? For all she knew, it could be a very common phenomenon. There might even be group meetings: Angels Anonymous. Hmm, she thought, perhaps not.

But surely she wasn't the only one to be visited? Jalisa had said that there was a whole army of angels, ready and waiting to be despatched into flights as soon as they were needed, and Claudie was beginning to wonder how on earth she'd coped before their arrival.

On Wednesday morning, despite just one glass of wine at the restaurant, Claudie had awoken feeling as if King Kong had been jumping up and down on her head. She'd wandered into the office like a zombie and had been greeted by much laughter from the flight.

'I thought you were meant to look after me,' she'd complained bitterly.

'But you must still look after yourself!' Bert chided. 'I don't know. If you drink like a fish-'

'But I didn't!' Claudie complained. 'I wouldn't care if I had, but I was very restrained.'

'You should have taken the day off,' Mary said.

'My head feels like a cannonball.'

'Goodness me!' Jalisa giggled again. ''Fraid that's not my department. But Mr Woo's probably got a solution for you. Mr Woo?' Jalisa called, and he walked out from behind the pile of files Mr Bartholomew had left on her desk.

'Here, Claudie,' Mr Woo said shyly, head bent so that he hardly looked at her. 'Take with little water.'

'What are they?'

'Will taste bitter but very good for headache.'

Claudie took the little brown packet from him and peeped inside. The contents looked like fragments of burnt paper. 'What on earth is it?'

'You're probably best not knowing,' Jalisa pointed out.

'No! Don't ever ask when Mr Woo gives out medicine. It's probably worse than the stuff we used to use in the sixteenth century,' Mary said.

Claudie had taken it and, as promised, almost spat it out at the first taste. But it had worked miraculously quickly. She'd thought of asking for some for Kristen, who'd looked decidedly ropy that morning but, she supposed, Jalisa wouldn't allow that.

Then there'd been Bert's show. Ever since the angels had arrived, Bert had gone on about putting on a show.

'We not entertaining troops now, stinky bird egg!' Mr Woo had said.

'No, we're entertaining *Claudie*,' Bert had said graciously, 'a far more important audience.'

So, somewhere between Claudie's Rolodex and in tray, Bert had organised a rehearsal. Claudie had been told not to watch but it was rather hard to ignore five little angels singing, dancing and ordering each other around, and it was far more entertaining than Mr Bartholomew's amendments to the staff regulation handbook.

Claudie couldn't help but smile as she remembered the scene: Bert taking centre stage in front of her computer whilst Jalisa, Mary and Lily did their chorus-girl bit behind. Poor Mr Woo had looked completely confused by it all and had hovered in the background, a scowl scarring his face.

Claudie felt so lucky to have the angels. They were a brilliant beacon in her dark landscape; they were MGM brought to life and, above all, they were her guardians, in spite Jalisa's hate of that particular word.

Yes, she thought as the train pulled into York station, there was a lot she could tell Dr Lynton about. But should she? Should she tell him about the fierce argument Bert and Mr Woo had had on Thursday afternoon? Claudie shook her head as she got off the train.

What a thing to witness: two grown men, no bigger than a couple of Biros, arguing on her desk. Mary and Lily had tried to break them apart and Jalisa had finally intervened when Mr Woo had called Bert a *stinky bird egg*. Jalisa had sent them back, to a kind of angel detention room, she'd said, but didn't explain any more than that. It was quite common, she'd assured her.

Claudie grinned at the thought, trying to imagine Bert and Mr Woo sat in a classroom writing lines. *I must not argue on my client's desk.* But what would Dr Lynton make of it all?

Sitting in his room, seeing his serious face and pen at the ready, she decided against telling him about any of it. Although it did make her wonder what stories he must have heard from his other clients. Was anything beyond the bounds of possibility? And what right did he have to question what he was told?

'So, Claudie,' he began in his usual manner, 'had a good week?' He always waited for her to speak, never prompting her on anything.

Claudie nodded, looking down and noticing that he had bright green socks on. Most unusual. 'It's been an extraordinary week,' she confessed, without really meaning to. The words just spilled out.

'Oh?' Dr Lynton's white eyebrows shot into his forehead and, for the first time in a long while, he smiled.

Claudie looked on in amazement. This was turning out to be a very odd week indeed.

'Do go on, Claudie. Tell me about your week.'

'Okay!' she said, wondering how she was going to get round this now. If she wasn't going to tell him about the angels, what else could she possibly tell him about? He wouldn't be interested in her night out with Kristen and, other than a group of little people taking up residence on her desk, nothing else extraordinary had happened at work. She sifted through her brain as quickly as possible, aware that time was money and she was paying.

'I was pottering around during lunch early this week and thought I'd pop into the bookshop,' she began somewhat hopelessly, but thinking it would have to do. 'It's old and smelly and the owner's a complete witch, but I just love browsing round. You never know what you might find. Anyway, I happened to come across this wonderful book.'

'About?'

Claudie paused. If he was hoping she'd name a title on the reading list he'd presented her with recently, he was going to be disappointed.

'Judy Garland.'

'The actress?'

Claudie nodded. Didn't everyone know who Judy Garland was?

'I've always adored her,' she went on enthusiastically. 'Ever since the first time I walked down that yellow brick road with her. So imagine my delight when I found out Luke's surname was Gale! I couldn't believe that I was going to be Claudie *Gale!*'

Dr Lynton looked nonplussed.

'*Dorothy Gale!*' she stressed, musing on the fact that the 'P' in Dr P Lynton might very well stand for 'philistine'. She made a mental note that she should lend him some of her videos. It would make a pleasant change from him lending her his books.

'Anyway, I wanted that book but I didn't have enough money. The old witch always overcharges,' she said, getting into her stride for recounting her week, 'and she'd never accept an offer. So I went out to my bank, which is about a five-minute walk there and back and, when I got back to the bookshop, this man was standing there holding my book - reading it as if it was his!' Claudie's eyes widened at the memory. 'I couldn't believe it.' She paused, as if replaying the scene.

'What did you do?'

'I asked him if he was going to buy it. And he looked at me for what seemed like ages. He had amazing grey eyes - they were so clear and pale - like a Whitby sky in winter.'

'And what did he say?'

'He said that, no, he wasn't going to buy the book - it was too expensive and handed it to me.' Claudie smiled at her triumph.

'Well, this is quite a breakthrough,' Dr Lynton said at length. 'And, of course, it's all perfectly normal.'

'Is it?'

'Let me remind you what you said.' He looked down at his notes. "He had amazing grey eyes - like a Whitby sky in winter"?'

'Oh?'

'Don't you see?' He sat forward in his chair as if he'd made quite an important discovery. 'You're beginning to notice other-'

'No!' Claudie interrupted, her voice a little terse. 'Don't go pinning that one on me. I just made an observation. I do that all the time.'

Dr Lynton flicked through the reporter's notepad that was

Claudie. 'Not as far as I've noticed.'

'Oh,' she said quietly.

'It's nothing to get upset about.'

'I'm not upset,' she said, her voice a perfect monotone.

'It's perfectly natural.'

Claudie stared at him. What was he getting at? Sex? Was he accusing her of fancying another man? After so short a time. This was outrageous, and she felt extremely angry with him for even daring to suggest such a thing. That wasn't what she was paying him for.

'It's too soon,' she said in a very quiet voice. 'Perhaps it's natural for some people to fall in love again so quickly, but that won't happen to me.'

Dr Lynton narrowed his eyes. 'Claudie, I didn't say anything about falling in love again. I know how you feel about that. I only mentioned that you noticed someone. Please,' he said, his voice a little less excitable and a little more gentle now, 'don't take it as such a criticism of you.'

But how else was she meant to take it? She felt as if he'd accused her of forgetting Luke, of daring to move on, grow another heart, and learn to live and love again.

She fidgeted in her chair and looked at her watch, squirming when she realised that they weren't even at the halfway mark. What could she say to fill the time in? She didn't want to continue with the present line of questioning, that was for sure.

Perhaps she should tell him about the angels as well? Surely the angels would take Dr Lynton's mind off the subject he'd latched upon with such enthusiasm. But no, she really didn't want to talk about them. They were, for the moment, her little secret. Her private world. Anyway, perhaps there were rules about telling anyone about them. She'd be best talking it over with Jalisa first.

Dr Lynton cleared his throat. 'I'm sorry, Claudie, if I upset you.'

She looked across the room at him. He genuinely looked concerned, and she felt bad. He was only trying to help her. Deep down, she knew that. But she also knew that she didn't feel ready to have that kind of pressure put on her. Not now. Not just yet.

'I'm sorry I flared up,' she said.

'It's all right,' he said, giving his second smile of the day. 'Shall we move on to something else, then? What else have you been doing this week?'

'Kristen and I went out to dinner and got chucked out of the restaurant,' Claudie started.

'You haven't been out for some time, have you?'

'That's what the ang -' she paused, the cat half out of the bag. 'That's what Kristen said.'

'And you had a good time?'

'Yes!' Claudie smiled. 'I did. Even though I had a terrible hangover from one tiny glass of wine. It was good to get out.'

Dr Lynton stroked his chin, as if thinking of how to phrase what he was about to say. 'That's good,' he said. 'It's a step in the right direction, isn't it?'

Claudie nodded, her heartbeat accelerating lest he dared to mention anything that might set her off again.

'These things take time,' he continued. 'You know that, don't you? But you will get your life back. It won't be the life you had before, but things will get better. You believe that, don't you?'

Claudie nodded again, but her action and her belief weren't one hundred percent connected.

Later that evening, when she closed her door behind her, she suddenly understood what Dr Lynton had been getting at. She'd been half-aware of what he was implying during their session, of course she had, but, as if protecting herself, she had chosen to ignore it, staring at his outrageously green socks instead, and waiting for the clock to chime four so that she could escape and go and buy one of her favourite musicals which had just been released on DVD. But now, in the isolation of her home, her hands started to shake, gently at first, almost as though tapping along to a friendly tune. But the tapping soon travelled up her arms until her shoulders were jerking as if they meant to hit her earlobes.

And then the inevitable. Her face fell into spasms, and, for the first time in weeks, she was crying. Hot tears blurred her vision, and the living room disappeared as she buried her head in her hands and just let go. There was nothing she could do to stop herself. She'd tried that once before - stopping her tears by sheer will power then leaving her house, forcing herself to walk into town. It had been a huge mistake. She'd broken down in the local newsagents and someone had had to call Kristen to come and take her home again.

She didn't dare try to block her emotions any more but it was equally terrifying to give them free reign. Sometimes, if she'd had a particularly rough day, whole hours would be swallowed up, and she'd be spat out the other end feeling exhausted and isolated.

Sitting up from the sofa now, she tried to find a tissue in her pocket but there wasn't one. Neither were there any on her bedside table so she had to make do with toilet paper. Not for the first time did Claudie think that widows should be entitled to free boxes of tissues for at least the first year.

Drying her eyes and blowing her nose, she dared to look at her reflection in the mirror and immediately wished she hadn't. An ashen-faced woman with a tangle of brown hair and dull red eyes stared back at her. And then something rather strange happened. Looking at the reflection of her Gene Kelly poster on the bathroom wall behind her, she could have sworn she saw him smile and wink at her.

CHAPTER 10

'You're not telling us everything, are you?' Jalisa said, swinging her legs across Claudie's computer screen in a most irritating manner.

'I'm trying to type, Jalisa.'

'Not before a full confession.'

'What confession? I don't know what you're talking about,' Claudie said impatiently, her fingers fast and furious across her keyboard.

'Claudie - Mr Woo can spot tear stains with his eyes closed. You've been crying, haven't you?'

Claudie stopped typing. '*Merde!*'

'Pardon?' Jalisa said.

'*Merde!*' Claudie repeated.

'Language, please!' Bert complained, waking up from a quick forty winks up against Claudie's pen pot. 'Most unlady-like.'

'Yes! I didn't expect you to come out with such things,' Mary said, somewhat abashed.

'What? Didn't they have "shit" where you come from?' Claudie asked, not in the mood to be lady-like.

'Oh, yes!'

'Streets full of it!' Lily added with a giggle. 'And, for your information, all the best swear words are old. Like arse and f-'

'Er - that's QUITE enough!' Jalisa warned.

'I'm just making a point,' Lily said with a shrug of her shoulders which, today, she'd shoved into a cashmere cardigan in pale pink.

'Goodness me!' Bert exclaimed. 'I've never known such language from women.'

'Welcome to the twenty-first century, Albert,' Lily said smugly, as if she were a modern girl herself.

'You all so noisy,' Mr Woo complained wearily.

'Shut up, you old fart.'

'Old fart yourself!'

'EXCUSE ME!' Jalisa bellowed from her favourite position at the top of the monitor. 'Did you two learn *nothing* from the other day?

Do you want me to send you back there?'

'No,' Bert said penitently, removing his hat and stroking his thinning hair flat.

Mr Woo didn't say anything, probably anxious to avoid eye contact with the infuriated Jalisa. Claudie wondered what it must be like for him to suddenly find himself in this predicament: being bossed around by a young lady, called names by an ex-army troupe entertainer, and having to put up with the antics of the Tudor twins. All that, and cure her of her heartache too. Claudie couldn't help but giggle as she saw him shake his head in despair before sitting down on her make-up bag to read his paper.

'What are you reading, Mr Woo?' Claudie asked, peering closely at the tiny print.

'Express,' he muttered.

'The *Angel* Express,' Jalisa corrected. 'News still happens, even after life,' she explained, seeing Claudie's look of bemusement. 'But we've managed to get right off the subject again, haven't we?'

'Have we?' Claudie narrowed her brown eyes, and did her best to turn her attention back to the letter she was meant to be typing.

'Yes! We were trying to find out what was wrong with you.'

'Oh.'

'Yes, *oh!*' Jalisa said, starting to sound very matronly. Any minute now, Claudie thought, she'd stop dancing and develop an enormous bosom across which she'd fold her arms in disapproval.

'I don't want to talk about it.'

'Talk about what?' Mary asked, looking up at Claudie with her pale, bright eyes.

'You can't wheedle it out of me that way either.'

'Have you forgotten that we're here to help you? We're not just here to keep you amused whilst you're at work, you know,' Jalisa pointed out.

'I know,' Claudie said, giving a little smile. 'But do I have to tell you everything?'

'It might help,' Jalisa suggested, and Claudie watched as the five figures on her table fixed their eyes on her. They looked so sweet and caring that Claudie wanted to cry all over again.

'I, er-' she hesitated, looking from one tiny face to the next. Could she tell them? Could she explain to them how she felt? She looked at the Tudor twins whose eyes were both filled with the same concern.

She looked at Bert, who'd removed his hat in preparation for a bout of head scratching. She saw Mr Woo, who looked as if he might be about to dig in his voluminous pockets to find some more herbs for her. And then Jalisa, whose eyes were wide and concerned. Yes, Claudie thought, she felt she could tell them, couldn't she?

She took a deep breath. 'I-'

'Claudes?' Kristen called from the other side of the room, oblivious to the confession about to occur at Claudie's desk. 'It's your turn to get the drinks.'

Bloody hell, Simon thought, pushing the rotating door into the building society and picking up his badge from reception. What the hell am I doing here?

The receptionist beamed him a smile and pointed to where he was to use his swipe card, but Simon knew the routine all too well. He could do it all with his eyes closed. Through the door, turn right up the stairs, right at the top into the open-planned room he'd lived in for six years. It had seemed a lifetime then but, even though he'd only been away from it for a few months, it also seemed a lifetime ago.

As he trudged up the stairs, his feet feeling heavy for the first time in months, he looked around him, trying to spot a familiar face, but they were all new. It was the nature of the job. People came and people went. Few stayed longer than three years. A mixture of boredom and bad pay ensured a high turnover of staff.

Simon sighed. Yes, few stayed. And even fewer came back of their own free will. Trust him to be an exception.

'Simon!' Mark, his old boss, called in greeting as Simon entered the room. 'Good to see you, mate.' A quick handshake was all he managed. 'You're over there, next to Mandy.' As ever, Mark was about to rush off somewhere. Too busy to string more than a couple of sentences together.

Next to Mandy. Bloody hell. Mandy the Man-eater. That was all he needed.

Mandy looked up as Simon crossed the room.

'Hi, Si!' she said, batting great, blue coated lashes at him from beneath her ebony-dyed fringe.

'Morning, Mandy,' he said, trying to keep things as formal as possible.

'Nice to see you again,' she said sweetly, swinging her chair round in order to give him a flash of her legs in an embarrassingly short skirt. 'Didn't think you'd be back here.'

'No. Neither did I,' Simon confessed, sitting down in the chair and adjusting the height. No. After his break for freedom last year, Simon had never thought in a million years that he'd be crawling back to his old job. It was the stuff of nightmares. But times were hard and he had more red bills than a flock of kittiwakes.

'But it's nice to have you back,' Mandy added, her ruby smile positively glowing at him.

Simon had always tried to avoid Mandy, and bemoaned the fact that Mark hadn't managed to get him his old desk back. He turned round to look at it ruefully. There was a new bloke occupying it. Straight out of college, Simon guessed. He had that youthful glow about him; enthusiasm as yet untainted by experience. Let him enjoy his moment, Simon thought cynically.

He looked around the desk he'd been parked at. It was appalling. Papers spewed all over it, two old cups of coffee even the cleaners hadn't dared to touch, and a medley of photos peeping from between the pot plants. Simon looked at the faces staring up at him from out of the multi-coloured frames. Two mucky-faced children, a mother with a sleeping baby, a father with a child almost falling off his back, and a toddler being pulled across a patch of grass by a puppy. Well, Simon thought, it beat having a photo of a goldfish on your desk. He puffed his cheeks out at the thought. Was that all he had to show for thirty years on the planet? A photo of an animal that didn't even respond when you came into the room?

'So what have you been up to?' Mandy began again, innocently enough, but Simon was immediately on his guard. She had a habit of this - talking about the weather, or holidays or some such rubbish and then *wallop!* She'd be pestering you for a date.

Whatever he did, he mustn't let on to her that he was no longer with Felicity. He'd once made the mistake of buying Mandy a drink after work, and she'd hooked onto him as it they meant to bond for life. He'd dropped enough hints but she was one of those women who didn't understand the word no.

'Not much,' he said, raking over the last ten months of his life with half a sentence.

'Well, how's business?' She stretched her left hand out in front of her to examine her perfectly polished cherry-red nails. Simon felt himself squirming. He'd always got the impression that she meant to slide them down his back when she did that. Only ten minutes in the office and he was already beginning to feel the strain. How on earth would he make it to lunchtime, let alone home time? He ran a finger along the inside of his shirt collar. 'Er - business?' he hesitated, wishing she'd shut up and leave him alone. 'It's a bit slow at the moment,' he said quietly, not wanting anyone to hear.

'I'm sure it will take off soon,' Mandy said. 'You've always been brilliant, Si. I'm sure things will work out for you.'

He felt himself stretch his mouth into a smile quite independently of his better judgement, and immediately wanted to kick himself for doing so because she inched forward across the table.

'Between you and me,' she whispered conspiratorially, pouting her mouth prettily, 'everyone else here is a waste of time. But you, Simon,' she breathed his name out as though it were an incantation, '*you're* different.'

'I, er - ' he stuttered, wishing she had a delete button he could hit.

Luckily, his phone went. The office workers had woken their computers up and were breaking them already.

'I'll be right with you,' Simon promised the distraught sounding lady from Human Resources. 'No - don't touch anything just yet. I'm on my way.' He got up from his chair and hurried out of the office, his heart beating like a jungle drum in his ears. Human Resources was on the third floor. If he took his time and visited his old mate, Brent, in Accounts on the way back, he could, he thought, be away from Mandy for at least twenty minutes.

'Spot of lunch in the pub?' Mandy asked hopefully as the clock approached one, giving her lips another slick coat of the letterbox-red she was so fond of.

'No, thanks. Going to meet Fe-Felicity,' Simon stumbled over the name.

'But I thought she'd left you?'

Simon felt a rush of fear chill his body. Who'd told her that? Felicity, probably - in a moment of spite.

'Where on earth did you hear that?' Simon said, standing up hastily and scratching his head in an anxious manner.

'Oh, you know, word gets around.'

'Yes,' he said knowingly, cursing living in a place the size of Whitby where everyone knows more about you than you do yourself.

'So, if you'd like to join me for lunch,' she said, tossing her hair back coquettishly.

Simon could feel sweat breaking out on his forehead. 'I've got a few errands to run actually. You know-'

'I can come with you if you like.' She was on her feet in a millisecond.

'No!' What could he say? How could he make this woman go away? 'I'm meeting someone.'

'Are you?' Mandy didn't look convinced. 'Well,' she said slyly, 'I know it's not Felicity.'

'No,' he said, defeated. 'You're right. It's not.' He paused for thought. 'It's a little bit delicate actually. So I'd be grateful if you didn't say anything. You know - keep things quiet for a while. I know I can trust you,' he said, putting his best smile on in an attempt to win her over.

It worked. Mandy beamed back. 'You can rely on me,' she winked at him. 'But does she know how lucky she is?'

Simon's smile faltered as Mandy brushed passed him and wiggled her way out of the office.

Blimey, he thought, he was only half-way through Monday morning and he already felt like he'd never left the place. Thank God he was only doing holiday cover for a fortnight.

CHAPTER 11

By the time Claudie came back with drinks for their department, the angels seemed to have forgotten about her big confession. Lily and Mary were arguing over who should wear the cashmere cardigan, and Bert was trying to look at Mr Woo's paper, much to Mr Woo's annoyance. They'd all forgotten about her. Except Jalisa.

She was sitting on an A4 file, waiting for Claudie to return. Her face was attentive, and she hadn't broken into a dance routine for at least half an hour. This was serious.

'You okay?' she asked as Claudie sat down.

Claudie nodded. 'You?'

Jalisa looked mildly shocked that somebody should ask how she was. 'Yes. Thank you.'

'Good.'

'Look, Claudie - you've got this incredible habit of getting everyone off the subject. Don't get me wrong, it's an amazing trait to have, but it's the flight who'll have the explaining to do if we're found not to be doing our job properly, so are you going to tell me what's wrong or not?'

Claudie flinched at the direct approach Jalisa was taking. She didn't know what they taught them in Angel School, but she was quite sure abruptness wasn't a good policy to adopt with clients.

'I don't think that's very fair, Jalisa. I was interrupted before. It had nothing to do with me going off the subject.'

'Yes, I know,' Jalisa conceded, 'but you're going off the subject again now.'

So she was.

'So what's the matter?' Jalisa pressed.

'It's nothing,' she lied. 'It's just something Dr Lynton said to me.' She sighed, wishing she didn't have to think about the whole horrible incident again; wishing she could pop it in the filing cabinet of her mind. 'I made an observation about a stranger I saw in a bookshop, and Dr Lynton blew it out of all proportion.'

'A male stranger?' Jalisa asked.

'Yes.'

'I see.'

Claudie looked straight into Jalisa's eyes. What did she see, exactly? Could Jalisa see the hurt and distress which she felt? The sense of betrayal - hers in Dr Lynton, and, if it was possible, Luke's in hers? Could she possibly sense the guilt she felt by merely looking at another man? It was all too horrible, and it was all way too early.

'Yes. I see,' Jalisa said again, as if reading Claudie's thoughts. And they left it at that.

At about two o'clock, a stern voice called Claudie away from Jalisa's latest tap-dance routine. It was Mr Bartholomew. Claudie turned round and saw that the beaky nose was only inches away from her again. His usually sallow face was burning red and his eyes looked ready to pop out of his head at any moment.

'I'd like a word,' he said in a subdued tone. 'In my office.'

Oh, dear, Claudie thought, watching him disappear before she had a chance to keep up with him. She turned to Jalisa who had stopped dancing. She looked up at Claudie and then blew a massive raspberry.

'Don't you go taking any nonsense from him, Claudie!' she said.

Claudie giggled, took a deep breath, and followed Mr Bartholomew.

She'd always liked her boss's office. It was all cream and chestnut, and there wasn't a grotty grey filing cabinet in sight. And there was, of course, the painting. Claudie had spent many a furtive moment wishing she could leap right into. Her eyes would peep over her memo pad as she was taking down shorthand, or gaze right into it if the telephone interrupted Mr Bartholomew's flow. It was an ordinary landscape: a country field with a river meandering through it like a piece of ribbon flung from heaven. A light breeze tickled the trees and, Claudie thought, you would almost be able hear it sometimes, if Mr Bartholomew wasn't in full dictation mode.

She wished she could leap into it right now. Wished she could walk along the river bank, her feet slicing through the long grass like a lady in a Monet painting. She wanted to disappear through the trees and walk on, on towards the horizon until she was nothing more than a little dot in the distance.

But she was going nowhere, and there wasn't even a memo pad to hide behind today. She peered up from under her dark fringe. Mr

Bartholomew was still red in the face, as if he were about to explode. She had a feeling she knew what was coming.

He sank back into the big leather armchair which squeaked like a rude schoolboy. Claudie tried hard to suppress another giggle. She always had the urge to fall about in giggles when she was nervous.

'Claudie,' he began, his voice barely above a whisper, his fingertips steepling in front of him. 'I've been concerned about you lately.'

Concerned. Yeah, right, Claudie thought. 'Oh?' she said instead, faking bewilderment rather badly.

'Yes,' he said ponderously, the redness of his face draining slightly. It was embarrassment. Of course. He wasn't angry with her at all. She'd never seen him angry before. He just got uptight and walked around the building slamming doors behind him, but this was definitely a case of acute embarrassment. He wasn't a person to person sort of man; couldn't stand having to talk to anyone for more than was absolutely necessary to conduct business. He never socialised, and never sent out Christmas cards.

'I've noticed a distinct lack of,' he paused, his heavy eyelids half-closing as he searched for the right word.

Claudie began to get nervous. Distinct lack of what? What was she lacking? She hadn't noticed anything was missing recently.

'Concentration,' he finished.

Claudie breathed a sigh of relief. Was that all? 'Oh,' she said again, in a suitably subdued tone of voice, as if it genuinely concerned her.

'Now, I know it's not been-' he paused, squirming in his seat, making it fart again. Claudie watched. She felt terrible for him, she really did. She'd had this effect on people lately: the ability to make them squirm; to make them highly uncomfortable; to render them both speechless and senseless.

'It's not been an easy time for you, but I had thought you'd settled back into work rather well.'

Claudie nodded. She thought she'd settled back in rather well too. Especially since the arrival of the angels, but she couldn't very well say that.

'But lately, I've noticed you've been rather abstracted.'

Claudie leant forward very slightly. Abstracted. He hadn't hesitated when he'd used *that* word. Claudie blinked hard and swallowed, as if trying to digest what he'd said. She'd been called some things before in her time, but never abstracted. Dreamy - yes, wistful - yes, but abstracted was a new one. She'd have to write it down in case she forgot it.

'Is anything the matter, Claudie?' he asked.

'No, Mr Bartholomew.'

'Because you've got that look about you again. As if you're going to float right out of your chair and vanish.'

Claudie felt herself frowning. 'Do I?'

He nodded vehemently. 'Yes!' he said, his beaky nose bobbing up and down as if it meant to slice the air. 'Yes!' he repeated. 'You do.'

She didn't suppose it was a good thing, otherwise he wouldn't have mentioned it. He never gave praise, didn't Mr Bartholomew, only advice on what you could do better. But floating out of her chair! That didn't sound too bad. Claudie could almost imagine it. It was like something out of one of her MGM musicals. Of course she wasn't quite dressed for it. She'd have to get something a little more appropriate, something with lace and sequins in cloudy blue would be more suitable for floating. A dress like the one in that number, *Smoke Gets In Your Eyes*, from *Till The Clouds Roll By*, she thought. Yes! Perfect.

'Claudie?'

'Yes?' she looked him square in the face. She *must* try harder to concentrate. This was important.

'Do you need more time? Would you prefer not to be at work at the moment?'

'No!' she said anxiously. 'No. I love my work. I'm happy here.'

'But is it good for you? I mean,' he combed his hair with his long fingers, 'would you be better off at home?'

'No!' Claudie all but screeched. She didn't want him to send her home.

'I think, perhaps, for the rest of the week. Things are pretty slow here at the moment,' he lied. 'And I can easily pass things over to Kristen and Angela.'

'But I -'

'I think it would do you good.'

Claudie opened her mouth to protest again but Mr Bartholomew was out of his chair.

'You're still seeing this Dr Lindell, are you?'

'Dr Lynton. Yes.'

'Good. That's good,' he said, ushering her awkwardly out of the office. 'Now, Claudie, if there's anything you need, just let - er - us know.'

'Mr Bartholomew?'

'Yes?'

'You haven't just fired me, have you?'

'No. No! I just think a little time off would be good for you. But I want you back here on Monday morning.'

'I see,' Claudie said, watching his face as it reddened again. Then the nodding began as he desperately tried to think of a suitable way to wind up the conversation.

'I'll see you on Monday,' Claudie said, deciding to help him out of the awkward situation.

'Yes,' he said, and she turned to walk back to her desk.

'Is everything all right, Claudes?' Kristen asked as she walked back in.

'I'm not sure,' Claudie said.

Angela stood back up to full height after having had her head in the filing cabinet for the last ten minutes. 'What's happened?'

'He's given me the rest of the week off,' Claudie explained, feeling as if a ginormous question mark was hovering somewhere above her head.

'You lucky thing!' Angela piped. 'And it's only Monday.'

'I don't know what to do.'

'You enjoy it!' Angela said.

Kristen got up and gave Claudie a big hug. 'It will do you good.'

'That's what he said. But there's nothing wrong with me!' Claudie protested.

'Of course there isn't,' Kristen laughed, giving her friend's shoulder a reassuring squeeze. 'But you go home and make the most of your time.'

'I don't want to go home!' Claudie said. She was beginning to sound like an angry child but that was exactly how she felt: the desperation of having nobody listen to her - not *really* listen to her. They had no idea what she wanted and needed at the moment, did they?

'I wish I could go home in your place,' Angela said, motioning to a mountain of filing which had spread across the top of the filing cabinets like a snowstorm.

'Be my guest,' Claudie sighed, wandering back to her desk and sitting down heavily. Jalisa immediately appeared.

'Oh, dear,' she said in a tiny voice. 'Have we got you into trouble?'

'Yes,' Claudie whispered back, chewing her lip as Lily, Mary, Bert and Mr Woo appeared, all looking very apologetic.

'What are you going to do?' Bert asked.

'I have special herb for -'

'She doesn't want any more bloody herbs!' Lily told Mr Woo, slapping his hand.

'That hurt!' he said, his head shrinking into his mandarin collar.

'Lily! What did you go and do that for?' Mary asked, poking her sister in the arm.

'Because he's getting on my nerves, always going on about bloody herbs. Well they can't cure a broken heart, can they?'

'Shut up!' Jalisa shouted. 'We were trying to find out what Claudie wants to do.'

Silence was restored to the desk as five pairs of eyes looked up at Claudie, waiting for her response.

She looked down at them and sighed heavily. 'I just want to get on with my life. But nobody's letting me.'

CHAPTER 12

It was Monday afternoon and Claudie didn't know what to do with herself. She didn't need to go food shopping and she'd never been a great one for clothes shopping, despite being half-French. And she didn't want to go home yet. The magic of MGM just wasn't the same in the middle of the afternoon.

She felt strangely out of place as she left the office and headed into town, as if she'd stepped outside her own life. That had been a familiar feeling over the last few months. She felt like she was living in a twilight world and didn't seem to fit in any more. She had become a stranger to herself and, it would seem, to her job too. And just as she'd thought she was doing so well.

Claudie sighed. Her job was her touchstone, and she knew she'd be lost without it. Didn't Mr Bartholomew know that he was doing her more harm than good by sending her home? After all, what did she have to go home for? There was nothing there any more but an empty bed and a collection of over-watched videos.

She decided to go for a walk. There was an icy bite to the breeze but it would be invigorating, and would, perhaps, help her think what to do with her unexpected week off.

She took the well-trodden route up the one hundred and ninety-nine steps to St Mary's Church. It was a popular pilgrimage for tourists but was quiet today.

The sea looked a uniform slate grey from the top of the hill. Same as the sky. Claudie looked down onto the clusters of town houses, their red roofs dull and uninspiring. She couldn't imagine any artist wanting to paint the scene today.

Whitby really could be the most isolating of places, especially in the winter when both sun and tourists forgot about its existence. Claudie missed the tourists. As much as she hated the tat that was sold in the shops, apart from Jimmy's boats, of course, she really did like the jolliness of the visitors. There was something about crowds of people all wearing the same bright anoraks and ear to ear grins as they licked sky-scraping ice creams which made her smile. But there was nothing to smile about today.

She walked around the churchyard, pulling the collar of her coat up against the relentless wind. She knew where she was going. It was kind of a personal pilgrimage. Something that the tourists didn't know about but which caused great interest if they were lucky enough to stumble across it: a simple inscription above a tomb which told of Francis and Mary Huntroods who were born on the same day and, after marrying on their joint birthday, went on to have twelve children together. They died, aged eighty, on the same day of the year they were born. 'The one not above five hours before ye other.'

Claudie felt a shiver down her spine as she read the words for the hundredth time. Why hadn't *she* died with Luke? She remembered how bitter she'd felt when she'd realised that she wasn't going to die along with him. All sorts of thoughts had assailed her. Wasn't that what true love meant? Why was she still alive? What possible purpose could she have left?

Luke had been the perfect partner; her one chance at happiness. How could she expect to find that again? It didn't happen more than once to a person, did it? She'd been given her crack at happiness. Yes, it had only been a mere wink in the stretch of a lifetime, but she'd had it nevertheless, and that made her feel so hollow inside, so terrifyingly alone, that she wished she could climb inside one of the graves, close her eyes, and fall into oblivion.

Instead, she looked down at the Huntroods' tomb and envied the couple their happy silence together. Did they know how blessed they had been? They had shared the whole of their lives, and now they shared eternity.

Claudie closed her eyes. How could someone so full of life be dead? It just seemed so absurd. It was no wonder people turned to religion at times like this, and began believing in an afterlife. It was the only way to remain sane - to imagine that someone hadn't stopped living at all but merely changed form and been absorbed into another dimension.

Opening her eyes, Claudie peered up at the abbey which loomed darkly over the church against the silver sky. Finding a bench, she decided to sit down. She watched the boats coming in and out of the harbour, listened to the shrieking gulls, and followed the path of the white horses out at sea.

It was true what they said about life going on, but there was no comfort in the phrase or the reality. The seasons, with their cruel predictability, seemed to taunt her as they rolled into one another. She'd hated autumn for replacing the summer when Luke had died, and had detested the winter which had brought the first Christmas without him. Now, spring was threatening to break, mocking her with its beauty: a palette of pale colours that Luke would never see.

She closed her eyes against the world for a moment, and lost herself in blissful blackness. It was a familiar pattern. So often, when the world became too much for her, when her eyes were too sore from crying to stay open any longer, she would try to lose herself in sleep. She felt as if she could fall asleep right there on the bench too, despite the bitter cold, but something was stopping her. She could see a little figure dancing and spinning round in her mind until she felt quite dizzy, and it wasn't Jalisa. It was a man, dancing a beautiful, effortless dance. His face was bright and smiling, and he looked as if he'd swallowed sunshine or had starlight streaming through his veins because he danced with his whole being and then a little bit more.

Claudie watched with mesmeric intensity. One moment, his movements were elegant and easy, the next raw and raunchy. It could only be one man.

'Gene?' Claudie started, her eyes opening to see a man in a sailor suit sitting beside her on the bench.

'Hello, Claudie,' Gene Kelly said, his bright eyes crinkling at the edges.

'Is it really you?'

'It's really me,' he smiled, briefly lighting the leaden Whitby day. But his smile soon vanished. 'Gee, Claudie. I hate to see you looking so sad,' he said, his voice quiet and sombre.

'But what are you doing here?' Claudie asked in astonishment.

'I came to see you. Thought I might be able to cheer you up,' he said, shrugging his shoulders. 'You looked as if you could do with some company.'

'First, I find angels on my table, and then I get Gene Kelly sitting next to me in a graveyard!' She tried not to laugh in case she appeared ungrateful. 'You're not another angel, are you? I mean, I wouldn't mind if you were.'

'No!' he smiled. 'I'm not an angel.'

'I didn't think so. You're a little bit bigger than Jalisa and the gang.'

They were silent for a moment. Claudie just gazed at him, her mind a perfect blank. What exactly did you say when you found yourself sitting next to your idol? Was now the time to list her favourite films to him? Could she ask him who his favourite leading lady was? And did she dare to ask him to dance with her?

'You're not having an easy time, are you?' he said.

Her mouth parted slowly and she could feel tears threatening to spill. All she could do was shake her head. 'I'm trying - I really am, but it's not easy.'

'Aren't the movies helping?'

Claudie met his eyes. 'They are,' she said, 'but the grief floods in again once the screen goes black.'

'Movies don't last forever, do they?'

'No,' Claudie said, shaking her head. 'And then you're left wondering where all the music and colour vanishes to. Where does it all go?'

Gene looked out across the sea for a moment. 'Into your heart? So you can carry it with you.'

Claudie looked at him. He sounded so sincere that she desperately wanted to believe him. 'I sometimes find myself rewinding and replaying, over and over again, just to prevent that awful black screen. But there's no rewind button on life.'

'No, there isn't,' he said slowly.

'I thought I'd found my happy ending, Gene. Just as sure as Gaby found Miss Turnstiles in *On the Town*, and Joe found Aunt Susie in *Anchors Aweigh*.'

'That's the movies, Claudie. It's all part of the magical of the musical. Life, I'm afraid, is a bit more complicated.'

'That sounds like something Kristen would say to me.'

They were quiet again for a moment, watching as a little boat chugged out of the harbour.

'I don't like being a widow, Gene,' Claudie said suddenly. 'Especially a widow in Whitby.'

'Sounds like the title of a musical. *A Widow in Whitby!*' he said, making her smile. 'I can see the line up now,' Gene grinned, a hand stretched out in front of him as if he really could see a cast of stars instead of the dull grey sea. 'Judy Garland. Me, of course,' he winked and turned to Claudie. 'Anyone else you'd like?'

'Luke?'

Gene shook his head. 'I'm sorry, Claudie.'

'No,' she said, 'you're right. He'd be terrible. He had a voice like a blocked drain.' Claudie's lip trembled and the tears she'd hidden from her idol for as long as she could started to fall now. 'I'm sorry,' she said as the view over Whitby wavered in watery bands.

'Don't apologise,' Gene said.

'I shouldn't be here today. I should be at work, but my boss thinks I need some time out. It's ridiculous!' Claudie cried, pulling a tissue from her pocket and blowing her nose. 'I'm *fine!*'

'You're a great kid, Claudie, but I think your boss is right.'

'You do?' Claudie dabbed her eyes and looked up at Gene.

He nodded.

'I suppose you would say that. *If you can't be glad and merry, lock yourself in solitary.* Isn't that what you sang to Jerry the mouse in *Anchors Aweigh?*'

'You know all my movies, don't you?'

Claudie blew her nose again. 'But I don't want to be on my own. It makes me feel so -' she wrung her hands together in desperation.

'Lonely?'

She gave a little smile. 'Yes.'

'Sometimes, we have to take a little time to be by ourselves. It's the only way to seeing ourselves as being part of the bigger picture again.' He paused. 'You're a swell kid, Claudie, and you'll be fine, believe me. It just takes a little time.'

Claudie closed her eyes again and, when she opened them, he was gone. She felt as if a cloak of loneliness had been wrapped around her, and a cold chill shook her body as she stood up. There was no point wandering round in the cold so she returned down the steps and walked along a little alleyway that would lead to home. When she looked at her watch, she was surprised to find that it was after five. She must have been gazing out to sea for longer than she thought. Soon be time for a movie. It would definitely have to be a Gene Kelly tonight. Preferably with him as a sailor. *On the Town* or *Anchors Aweigh?*

But the decision was taken away from her as she rounded the corner to her cottage.

There was a man sitting on her doorstep and, after Gene Kelly, it was the last man she'd expected to see in Whitby.

'Hello, Claudie,' he said. She'd know that grin anywhere. It was Luke's younger brother, Daniel.

Once the initial shock had worn off, Claudie had managed to fumble for her key and let him in. She'd put the kettle on and he'd wandered through into the living room to dump his enormous rucksack.

He'd then come back through, given her a kiss on the cheek and opened the cupboard above the sink in search of food. Typical Daniel, she thought, as she opened a can of soup and threw a baguette into the oven. He was always very good at making himself at home.

After eating, she followed him through to the living room. He hadn't said much throughout tea and, after finishing his soup and bread, he'd fried two eggs he'd found in Claudie's fridge and finished her pizza from the night before.

'So, how did you get to Whitby?' Claudie said, knowing the trains were a fierce price from London and that Daniel never had any money.

'I hitched.'

'Daniel! Don't you know how dangerous that is?'

'I think drivers are more scared of me than me of them.'

Claudie smiled. With his American footballer shoulders and long black hair, he was rather something to behold. 'It's a wonder you got a lift at all.'

'So what were your plans for this evening then?' he asked, sinking heavily into Claudie's favourite chair.

She didn't want to confess to an evening at the musicals, so just smiled as she sat opposite him in the chair with no springs.

'You got home early,' he pointed out.

'Well, earlier than usual,' she said. 'My boss has given me the week off.'

'Has he? Well that's perfect!' Daniel said enthusiastically. 'We can spend it together.'

'You've got some time off too?' Claudie asked hesitantly.

'You could say that.'

'You've not-'

'Yep,' he said, shrugging his shoulders in the same way Luke used to.

'Again? How many's that now?'

Daniel pretended to count on both hands. 'A lot,' he conceded.

'It is, isn't it! How on earth do you make ends meet?'

'I get by,' he said. And Claudie guessed that he spent most of his time dossing on friends' sofas and looking for handouts. Would he ever change? She adored Daniel, but he'd never learnt to take the world seriously.

So what was she going to do with him for a whole week? They'd never really spent that much time together and she felt at a loss as to how to occupy a whole week with him. But, before she could say anything, his eyes alighted on the shelves in the corner of the room.

'Shit! Are they all films?'

Claudie nodded. 'Welcome to my secret world.'

'You must have hundreds.'

'You can watch one if you like,' Claudie said, knowing full well that he'd decline.

'Great. Have you got *Blade Runner*?'

'Er - no.'

'Police Academy?'

'No. I don't think so.'

Daniel got up and scoured the shelves. 'I've never heard of any of these. Hey! You haven't got *Reservoir Dogs*, have you?'

Claudie shook her head again.

'Look! *The Wizard of Oz*. Now I *have* seen that one.'

Claudie watched as he read the spines, his head on one side, hair dangling over his shoulder in a dark curtain.

'What do you recommend then?'

'All of them,' she said, hoping that he wouldn't suggest they watch *The Merry Widow*. She wasn't quite ready for that one.

'But I mean to watch - tonight.'

'Are you serious?'

He turned round to look at her. 'Sure. Why not?'

'You're having me on, aren't you?'

'No, come on, Claudie, I really want to watch one.'

Claudie bit her lip. Luke had known about her great obsession when he'd first gone out with her, and used to have fun teasing her, but he'd never actually sat down and watched any of her beloved films with her. But Daniel sounded quite serious.

She walked over to the shelves and her hand extended up to pull out a familiar tape.

'They're mostly musicals, you know.'

'So I gather,' he said, nodding his head. 'Well, I'm into new experiences.'

Claudie grinned. He had no idea what he was letting himself in for, did he? she thought, as she ejected *High Society* from her video and pushed in.

'Are you sure?' she asked again, watching as he got himself comfy on the sofa, his long legs stretched out across the living room floor.

''course I'm sure.'

'Okay!' Claudie sat down and hit play on the remote control.

It was the strangest experience Claudie had ever had. As far as she was concerned, she was the only person to have watched Summer Stock. Never mind big stars, big budgets etc, when Claudie watched a film, it always seemed as if it had been made for her and her alone. So it was a strange feeling to share it with someone.

But Daniel was brilliant. He laughed at all the right moments, sat in silence during the dance sequences, he even tapped his foot along to Judy Garland's *Get Happy* number. It was quite a revelation, and not at all what Claudie had expected. She'd once got Kristen to watch *Cover Girl* with her, but the whole experience had been a disaster. She'd laughed at all the romantic moments and talked through all the songs. But Daniel was the perfect audience.

'Shit! I've never seen anything like that in my life!'

'You liked it?' Claudie couldn't help but be mildly shocked at the fact that she'd persuaded a man who normally watched B-type horrors or X-rated adult movies to watch something staring Gene Kelly.

'I liked the lady in it. Who was she?'

'Judy Garland,' Claudie said, trying not to ram the name down his throat. Had *nobody* heard of her? Perhaps she should run an evening class in musicals.

Daniel got up and stretched his arms above his head. They almost scraped the low ceiling. She watched as he went to look at her colourful collection of videos again, and couldn't help but smile. Was he for real or was he buttering her up? It had already become obvious that he had no intentions of booking himself into a hotel for the night. The rucksack had been placed at the side of the sofa, but there was no need for him to pretend he wanted to watch another film.

'What's *Seven Brides for Seven Brothers* like?' he asked, head cocked on one side.

Claudie looked at him, his profile sharp and handsome. Just like Luke.

'Perfect,' she said.

CHAPTER 13

'What the hell is Daniel doing in Whitby?' Kristen bellowed down the phone.

'Kristen! Shush! He'll hear you.'

'I wouldn't care - the good for nothing...'

Claudie held the phone away from her face as Kristen's tirade ensued, and counted silently to ten, putting it back to her ear just as Kristen was winding up.

'He's the devil, Claudes. The devil!'

'Isn't that going over the top just an intsy bit?'

'Do I have to remind you where he placed his hand at your wedding reception?'

'Come on, Kris - it's traditional for the best man and chief bridesmaid to get on.'

'Yes but that doesn't follow that *I* wanted to get off.'

Claudie rolled her eyes. She was in no mood to hear all that again.

'Where is he now?' Kristen asked.

'He's asleep on the sofa.'

Kristen sighed. 'Just watch out, Claudes, you know what he's like. He'll be lodging with you - rent-free - for as long as he can. I bet he's already eaten all the food in the house?'

Claudie tried not to think of the supper he'd prepared at eleven o'clock. But she would definitely have to go shopping today.

'Claudes? Am I right?'

'Kristen - you're always right. But let me handle this my own way, okay?'

'So what were you doing last night?'

'We watched a couple of films.'

'You're joking?'

'No - Summer Stock and Seven Brides for Seven Brothers.'

There was a pause on the other end of the line whilst Kristen digested this piece of information. 'Just so long as he doesn't think that you're one bride for two brothers.'

'Kristen! What a thing to say.'

'I just wouldn't put anything past him. He's no good, Claudes. He's a freeloader. He's probably on the run from someone too. He's-'

'He's Luke's brother,' Claudie interrupted.

There was another pause. 'Just don't let him take you for granted. That's all I'm saying.'

Claudie listened and said *yes* and *no* in all the right places, knowing that otherwise there'd be no getting rid of her. Finally, Claudie thought of a way to finish the conversation. Kristen was sounding rather breathless, which could mean only one thing.

'Kristen?' Claudie interrupted her flow. 'Are you smoking?'

When she put the phone down, she felt like blowing a huge raspberry, Jalisa fashion. She loved Kristen, but she sometimes treated her as if she were a child.

She walked through to the living room and dared to draw the curtains an inch, letting in a sliver of spring sunshine.

'Morning!' Daniel said from underneath the covers on the sofa.

'Sleep well?'

'Like a baby,' he said, pushing the covers down to waist level. Claudie averted her eyes quickly but not before getting an eyeful of a red and green snake heading south from the base of his throat.

'I'll get some breakfast going,' she said, speeding out into the kitchen.

Kristen wasn't at all surprised that Daniel Gale had landed in Whitby. She only wondered what had taken him so long.

She sighed. Had she been forthright enough with Claudie on the phone? Had her message really got through? Claudie could be stubborn sometimes, believing that she could look after herself, but she couldn't.

'Jimmy!' Kristen's mouth dropped open at the sight of him out of bed before eleven in the morning. And it wasn't even May yet.

'Don't look so surprised!' he said, shaking his head in disapproval.

Kristen snapped her mouth shut. 'Cup of tea?'

'If you've time,' he said, looking at the clock, knowing she'd have to leave for work soon. 'Who was that on the phone?'

'Claudie.'

'Bit early, isn't it?'

Kristen nodded. 'She's got a guest staying with her.'

'Oh?'

'Daniel.'

'Bloody hell! In her tiny cottage? Where's he sleeping?' Jimmy blurted, and then suddenly coloured. 'I mean - if he's in the living room, his feet will end up in the kitchen.'

'I know. I've told her to get rid of him.'

'I thought you usually needed a couple of bouncers to get rid of him.'

'You're not joking,' Kristen shook her head in annoyance and watched as Jimmy grimaced. She could see that he was remembering something unpleasant.

'If I ever catch him touching you up again -'

'Jimmy!' she warned, not relishing the idea of an argument first thing in the morning. 'It's sorted. Now leave it,' she said, secretly pleased that her man would defend her honour.

'I'm going to be out most of today,' he announced, shuffling across the kitchen in a pair of red tartan slippers which made him look about eighty. 'And most of tomorrow too. But I'm all yours come Friday night.'

'What do you mean?'

Jimmy turned and grinned at her. 'What do you mean what do you mean? For crying out loud, Kris, it's our anniversary!'

Kristen's mouth dropped open again. She'd remembered it a few days ago and then, with the recent office goings-on, she'd plain forgotten about it.

Jimmy walked over to her, extended a hand under her chin and pushed her jaw up until her mouth closed. 'And I've got a surprise for you,' he whispered, tickling her ear with his mouth, his unshaven face gently grazing her cheek.

'What is it?'

He frowned. 'Do you think I'm going to go spoiling it, now?'

'Come on - just a hint!'

'No! You'll find out soon enough. Now get to work, before the boss lays you off for a week too.'

'So what are we doing today?' Daniel said, leaning up against the sink.

'I hadn't made any plans,' Claudie said honestly, hoping the sink wouldn't buckle under the weight of him.

'Want to watch another film?'

'Daniel, we can't stay in and watch films all day.'

'Why not?' He stared at her with his intense blue eyes. Claudie instantly felt embarrassed. It was as if they saw right through her. As if he knew what she got up to when there was nobody around.

'Don't you think we should go out somewhere?' she said, knowing that she didn't want to spend the entire day trapped in her tiny place with Daniel. It would be too much. He was so like Luke that she couldn't bear to think of the comparisons that she'd be likely to make. No, they had to get out.

'Okay,' he said casually, taking such a large bite out of his slice of toast that he almost ate his fingers in the process. 'Where shall we go?' he asked, his mouth crammed to choking point.

Claudie frowned, not quite knowing where to suggest. She didn't have a car and Daniel had never owned any form of transport other than a motorbike. He'd had a whole series of them, all of them sold in moments of extreme poverty, of which there'd been quite a few.

She watched as he buttered another round of toast and polished it off in seconds.

'We can visit Staithes, if you like,' she suggested. 'But we'll have to go shopping first.'

'Okay,' he said, 'I'm always up for a bit of shopping.'

To say Claudie took advantage of having Daniel in a supermarket with her would be a slight understatement. Where she usually bought one carton of orange juice, she bought a family pack of four. Where she usually selected four single potatoes, she chose a big economy bag. What would have had Claudie keeling over into the harbour with the weight, didn't make an ounce of difference to Daniel. And he certainly had an air about him. He strode up and down the aisles as if it were his natural territory. The only man in Whitby stupid enough to wear a T-shirt in April. But he didn't seem to feel the cold.

And he knew how to turn heads. With his great lolling walk, and arms the size of legs, the women of Whitby didn't stand a chance. Claudie could see the way they looked at him: peeping at him from behind the Persil, batting their eyelids from behind the beans. Claudie briefly wondered if she should link arms with him in an attempt to fend them off, but she was finding the whole thing far too amusing to put a stop to it, and Daniel was obviously enjoying the attention. Claudie suspected it was because he was probably nothing out of the ordinary in London. It was hard to be special in a capital but, at eleven o'clock on a Tuesday morning in a Whitby supermarket, a six foot two guy with long jet hair and blinding blue eyes was like finding a Tiffany diamond inside a Christmas cracker.

However, the amusement stopped when they got to the checkout. During the last few months, Claudie had slowly got used to shopping for one again. That had also meant budgeting for one. But today's trolley load was three times the cost of her usual weekly shop, and Daniel obviously didn't have any money on him. He was conveniently placing their goods into carrier bags when the till assistant said the amount, and Claudie was forced to use her credit card.

All the way home, she wondered what had cost so much. It definitely wasn't the budget box of tissues which would probably disintegrate as soon as you threatened to sneeze on them, nor was it likely to be the dented tins she'd chosen in an attempt to save a few pennies. And she hadn't even dared to look at the magazine rack.

It wasn't until they were unpacking at home and Daniel surreptitiously placed the cans of lager and bottle of wine in the fridge that she realised. How had he managed to sneak those passed her?

'Just a quick bite to eat before we go, eh?' Daniel said, making free with one of the two loaves of bread before she even had time to think about putting them in the cupboard.

Claudie blushed as he winked at her, and watched as he proceeded to cover four slices of bread with a thick coat of butter. Who would ever have thought that this was Luke's *little* brother?

CHAPTER 14

Claudie couldn't think of a single thing to say to Daniel. They'd virtually covered all the normal topics of conversation on their short journey to Staithes and, now they were walking down to the little harbour, she couldn't think of anything else to talk about.

Just what do you say to someone whose brother's just died? There were no words adequate for the job. And what could he be expected to say to her? The only thing they'd had in common had been Luke. Yet the silence between them wasn't awkward at all. They seemed perfectly at ease with each other, as if the grief they shared cemented them together in silent friendship.

They walked down the deserted street in between the rows of fishermen's cottages. It reminded Claudie of a Western before a shoot out, it was so quiet. Did anyone live here at all?

'The tourists haven't arrived yet, then?' Daniel laughed, as if reading her thoughts.

'No,' Claudie said, but, peering up at the sky, which had slated over, it wasn't surprising. People didn't visit Yorkshire before June if they knew what was good for them.

When they reached the beach, they stopped for a moment. The tide was out and they decided to walk over the damp sand. Claudie usually loved visiting Staithes. Although she saw the sea every day, there was something rather magical about this particular stretch of coastline. But today, it looked intensely sad, as if all its vibrancy had drained away. The sea was the same hopeless colour as the sky, and the sand looked washed out and unwell. The whole scene looked as if it should be tucked up in bed and fed hot soup and affection until it was restored to health. Perhaps they should have just stayed at home and watched old films, Claudie thought. At least there was plenty of colour in an MGM musical.

'Claudie,' Daniel suddenly said in a tone which made her panic; a tone which sounded pensive and forced. She could feel what was coming, and it was what she'd been dreading.

'I'm sorry I haven't seen you. You know,' he paused, 'since the funeral.'

Claudie stopped walking and gazed down into the sand as if she meant to bore a hole into it. Daniel stopped beside her and, for a moment, she stared down at his cracked leather boots speckled by sand. 'It's all right,' she said calmly.

'I meant to. It's just - I didn't know what to say.'

She looked up at him and nodded. 'I should have called *you*.'

'I don't know where the time's gone,' Daniel said. It was the kind of statement that would have sounded lame coming from most people, but Claudie didn't hear it that way. She knew what he meant. Time was doing funny things with her too.

She'd become obsessed with time since Luke had died. The first couple of months had been the worst. Time had tortured her with sleepless nights and endless days, and she'd kept on turning the clock back in her mind to when he'd been alive, desperately trying to work out what they'd been doing, and if they'd made the most of things. Had they loved enough? Lived enough? Could there have been more if they'd known how little time was left?

Two years ago, she'd remembered that they'd been house-hunting together. A year ago, they'd got engaged and were in the throes of planning their wedding. Just a year ago. How many hours was that? She'd worked it out once. The world had been complete then; a safe, comfy haven where unhappiness happened to other people, and death was a word you didn't associate with those closest to you.

'Your mother stayed with you, didn't she?' Daniel asked, breaking into Claudie's thoughts.

Claudie nodded, noticing how Daniel had so aptly used the word *mother* instead of mum. It was something that Claudie had long acknowledged; that her mother had never ever been a *mum*.

'She stayed for ten days, then she handed me over to Kristen,' Claudie said, staring up at the cliffs which looked almost black today. 'She wanted to get back to France. She's useless anywhere else. And it was better that way, really. We've never exactly been close.'

Daniel shoved his hands in his pockets and kicked the heel of his right boot into the wet sand. 'And you're all right?'

Claudie turned to look at him. 'Not many people dare to ask me that.'

'I know what you mean,' he confessed in a low voice.

'In case the flood barriers break.'

He nodded, and, from the look of him, Claudie could see that it was something he'd had first-hand experience in too.

'But,' she continued, 'what people can't handle is the fact that I'm so quiet. I think they actually *want* me to explode or physically crumble in front of them. But I'm not like that. I don't do public performances.'

Daniel's eyebrows rose an inch.

'Except at the funeral,' she added, before he had a chance to mention it. 'I'm told I rather let rip there.'

'You don't remember?'

Claudie shook her head. 'Do you?'

Daniel nodded but didn't say anything.

'Oh, dear.' Claudie had so desperately wanted to forget that day. As it was, it played in her memory like a movie projected onto a river; the individual scenes were all there but the pictures seemed to swim around as though she'd taken drugs. Perhaps she had. She remembered her mother had given her something before they'd left the house, but she'd thought they'd been paracetamol. There was no telling though. Her mother's handbag usually rattled like an autumn poppy.

Claudie and Daniel walked over to the sleeping boulders under the cliff. It was a strange sight. Piles of black boulders, shiny as Whitby jet, and icy cold to the touch. Claudie trailed her fingers over one and felt herself shiver. Thousands of cold days must be locked away in these stone, she thought.

A lone gull pierced the silence with an agonising cry. Claudie looked up and followed its path across the sky, her eyes settling on the cliffs shielding the beach.

'How high do you think it was?' she said, her neck white and exposed as she craned her head back.

Daniel looked up at the cliff. 'Much higher than that,' he said, following her train of thought without the need for elaboration.

Claudie dragged her eyes back to the ground and, for a moment, she seemed to be counting the individual grains of sand on the beach.

'It's absurd,' she said at last. 'I mean, how can you be angry at a mountain?' Her voice was cold, distant, as if it had been carried away by the gull.

She sat down on one of the boulders and Daniel sat next to her.

'You never went with him, did you?' She said it as a statement rather than a question.

'Only once. But it looked too bloody dangerous to me.'

Claudie managed a little smile.

'You're coping really well,' Daniel said.

Claudie shrugged. She didn't want to tell him it was all an act really, and that she could behave really badly when she put her mind to it. Like the time Kristen had taken her shopping. That had been a close call. She could still see that packet of pine nuts trapped inside her prison-cell grip.

She'd been on the verge of something terrible that moment. If Kristen hadn't come back and woken her, there was no telling what she might have done. Her mind had been on the verge of tripping over itself, and all because of a packet of pine nuts.

Luke had never liked pesto sauce.

'It's like snail's bile,' he said. 'I'm not eating that stuff.'

'That's only the stuff you buy in jars,' Claudie told him. 'Come on, now. Get hold of that pan and heat it up.'

Claudie watched as he tipped the pale kernels into the volcanic orange pan, moving them around with a wooden spoon. She loved watching him cook: the way he rolled his sleeves up, enabling her to worship his forearms. She loved the silly way he tied her pinny around his waist, and she loved the way he always managed to burn something. Last time he'd cooked, he'd burnt their plastic spatula so that it now looked like petrified spaghetti.

'What do I do now?' Luke asked.

'Keep turning them until they're golden.'

'They're golden now, aren't they?'

'They're anaemic!'

'You know I'm no good at this cooking lark.'

'You're brilliant,' she said, leaning forward from her pan of boiling tagliatelle and giving him a kiss.

Pasta boiled, pine nuts golden, Luke stripped the basil plant whilst Claudie dressed the pasta in heaps of pungent cheese, mixing the whole lot together with lashings of garlic infused olive oil.

Five minutes of silent eating ensued.

'This is once seriously sexy meal,' Luke said, blue eyes haunted with lunchtime lust.

'See! I told you you'd like it,' Claudie smiled back at him. 'What?'

He held her gaze. Her brown eyes locked with his blue ones.

'Luke?'

'Claudie!' He was out of his chair and had grabbed her before she had time to work out what was happening. His kisses were hotter than chilli pepper, his fingers melting her faster than butter in a microwave.

Looking back, it hadn't been a good idea. Tagliatelle had got everywhere, and Claudie swore her hair smelt of garlic infused olive oil days later.

'You okay?'

Claudie shivered. She wasn't in the kitchen at home with Luke, she was in Staithes on the beach with Daniel, and he was speaking to her.

Claudie nodded. She didn't want to talk any more. Things were getting a little too close.

She rubbed her hands together. 'Should have bought gloves,' she said.

Without a moment's hesitation, Daniel picked her hands up and cupped them between his.

'You're cold,' he said.

'You're warm.'

He smiled and, for a moment, she thought she saw tears in his eyes, but perhaps it was only the bitter bite of the wind.

Sitting in silence, they stared out to sea.

CHAPTER 15

Simon knew that he was being followed. He quickened his pace, dodging the lunchtime workers, and diving into as many shops as he could.

She wasn't very subtle. She'd make a terrible detective, he thought, wondering where he could go to next, and how he could shake her off his tail. But maybe he shouldn't even bother. God, he was so nice sometimes. Maybe he should just be bloody nasty and give her a piece of his mind. He contemplated this for a moment, idly picking up a packet of throat pastilles then placing them back amongst the toothpastes.

'Excuse me!' a stern voice arrested him. It was the shop assistant. 'Can I help you,' she said with the sort of voice that doesn't sound helpful in the least.

'Er - no, thank you,' Simon said apologetically, stumbling out of the door.

He felt like an actor in a low budget thriller as he weaved in and out of the crowds, hoping Mandy wouldn't be able to keep up with him. What annoyed him more than anything was her attitude. What did she expect from him? After years of turning her down, of going out with other girls, of living with another woman for two years, did she really expect him to suddenly fall in love with her? Unfortunately, Simon believed that the answer was yes. She had no scruples, no shame and, from what Simon had seen of her this morning, no bra on either.

There were some men in the office who would go for her obvious attractions, but Simon wasn't one of them. He'd never been into the long talons, red lipstick, skirt so short and top so low that they almost met in the middle look.

As he took a sneaky glance over his shoulder, he could see that he was losing her now. Either that or she'd lost interest in trying to follow him. Perhaps it was because he'd mentioned he was meeting someone again, he mused.

'The same girl, is it?' Mandy had asked in between mouthfuls of chocolate digestive. She always had a packet of crisps or biscuits on the go, and her desk drawer would have been a haven for mice if there'd been room left in it for them to operate.

Simon had nodded.

'What's her name?' Mandy had immediately asked.

Simon had sighed. 'Now, it's all to be kept very quiet.'

She'd nodded, but her nosiness had obviously got the better of her and she'd decided to do a bit of amateur spying. Very amateur, Simon thought bitterly.

But what would it be like, he wondered, if he *were* meeting a girl during his lunch hour? It seemed like an age since Felicity had walked out on him. He hadn't even so much as chatted anyone else up. The only women he'd talked to for more than five minutes had been his mother and Kristen, and they didn't count.

As he walked with no real direction in mind, a sudden image of the moonshine woman in the bookshop assaulted him: her creamy complexion and glossy brown hair, her eyes like great gleaming chestnuts. He tried to remember what she'd been wearing, but he couldn't. But it hadn't been a thigh hugging skirt or a cleavage pushing top, that was for certain. And she'd looked so incredibly fragile. Simon had never seen anyone who looked so fragile: not anorexically fragile but the kind that's passed down through the genes. Then there'd been that French accent. Why was that always so sexy?

Above all, there had been a gentleness about her. She'd had a grace, which seemed sadly lacking in most of the women he met.

Just imagine, he thought, his pace slowing down to normal now that Mandy had retreated, just imagine if he was going to meet the moonshine woman. He wondered what her name was, and where he would meet her. Not in a pub, that wouldn't be her style. But hey! Hadn't he seen her walk into the pub a few nights ago? Well, she nearly had. He wondered what had stopped her. Perhaps she hadn't liked the look of the pub, or maybe she hadn't liked the look of him. Could he have possibly scared her off? He wondered if she lived in Whitby, and, if she did, why he hadn't seen her before. But maybe she was a tourist? A French tourist shopping for second-hand books and seeing what English pubs were like.

But he wasn't meeting up with her, was he? He was meant to be shopping for Pumpkin. Hadn't he promised him a companion?

Simon turned and headed towards the pet shop, wondering if goldfish came in a moonshiny-silver colour, because he was going to buy Pumpkin one hot-babe of a fish.

After getting back from Staithes and virtually eating all the food they'd bought that morning, Claudie and Daniel had settled down in front of the television again. He'd only been there two days but they'd already developed a rather cosy routine together.

It was, Claudie consoled, all about being a family. That's what they were, wasn't it? Brother and sister-in-law enjoying some time together. As an only child, she felt exceptionally lucky in having Daniel now; after all, it wasn't every man who would want to travel so far north to a windy old fishing port to see his sister-in-law.

She looked across at him as he stretched his huge legs out into the middle of the living room. His toes were practically tickling the video player from where he was sitting. The cottage just wasn't big enough for a man of his size. It had been fine for her when she'd been on her own, and Luke had never complained about the lack of space. He'd been a lighter build than his brother and a few inches shorter, and he had never dwarfed the place in quite the way that Daniel was now.

'Are you comfy?' Claudie asked.

'I'm fine,' he said.

'Can I get you anything?' Claudie asked, feeling stuffed after the amount of food they'd eaten.

'A can of lager would be great,' he said. 'And have you got any crisps?'

Later that evening, when Claudie believed that no more food could possibly be consumed, she said goodnight to Daniel. She let him use the shower before her and got undressed, waiting in her bedroom until the coast was clear.

She wondered what Daniel would make of her Gene Kelly poster, and remembered how Luke had objected to her putting it up.

'I don't want to be ogled at coming out of the shower!' he'd grimaced.

Claudie had merely laughed. 'Don't be so vain. He won't be ogling you!'

'Well I don't want him ogling my wife either.'

It was nice that he got a little bit jealous, even if it was over a dead movie star, and he'd let her get away with it on the condition that he could put up his relief map of Britain on the back of the kitchen door.

It was still hanging there.

Turning on the lamp on her dressing table, Claudie sat down to comb her hair. The coastal wind had played havoc with it today. It was only chin length, but it had managed to tie itself into fierce knots, causing her to wince as she attacked them.

She remembered the delicate way Luke had had of brushing her hair, starting with his fingers, massaging her head, then working down towards her neck.

'You have the most beautiful hair in the world,' he'd say, breathing it in like perfume. Claudie had never believed him. It was just what husbands said, wasn't it?

She placed her brush down and almost screamed out loud as she nearly squashed an angel.

'Lily? What on earth are you doing here?' Claudie was so surprised that she forgot that Daniel was in the house and might hear her.

'Ssshussh! Look, I'm not meant to be here at all. I sneaked out and, if I get caught, they'll probably fire me and I'll end up in that bloody office filing death warrants again.'

'You gave me such a shock! I nearly flattened you with my hairbrush!'

'Occupational hazard, being so small.'

Claudie sighed, her heartbeat returning to something approaching normality. 'So what are you doing here?'

'I wanted to see how you were. I feel just awful about you being sent home by your boss like that. We all feel terrible about it. And I think it was my fault.'

'Don't be silly.'

'No! I'm always arguing. It's a terrible fault in me. I'm a dreadful angel.'

'No you're not,' Claudie said, resting her head in her hands and looking at Lily standing in the lamp light like an actress on a stage. 'You can't be all that bad for you to risk being fired just to see me.'

Lily looked up at her. 'You think?'

'I *know*. And I really appreciate it. I was just beginning to miss you guys.'

'You were?'

'Yes. It's odd but I've really got used to having you around.'

'But we do nothing but cause you trouble.'

'That's not true. You've all been so kind. I can't quite imagine a time when I didn't have you all to look after me. I don't know how I coped without you all. You make me feel so-'

'What?'

'Looked after!' Claudie said. 'And it's not just that. I find myself thinking of all these things that I must tell you. Like, I'll be flicking through a magazine and see a picture of a beautiful dress and think, I must show Lily this. Or, I'll hear a joke on TV and be dying to tell Bert the next day. You're all like a family, but not like any family I've ever belonged to. I feel so very proud to be a part of this one,' Claudie said, smiling down at Lily.

'Really?'

'Yes! *Really!* You don't realise how much joy you bring me. I only wish I could have you all at home with me as well as at work.'

'Wow!' Lily said. 'Would you put that in writing for me? For my file? This is the best feedback I've ever had. They've only let me out two times before this, and they were both complete disasters,' Lily confessed, giving a little snigger. 'I thought they'd never give me another chance, but this is brilliant.'

Claudie smiled. 'So what did you get up to the other two times?'

Lily looked sheepish. 'You know we're not meant to talk about our assignments but,' she looked around her in case someone might be listening in, 'I mucked up big time. There was one client - a little boy who'd just lost his pet dog.'

'Poor boy.'

'That's what I thought. Until I met him. He was horrible! Just so mean to everyone. I think his dog had a lucky escape.'

Claudie stifled an urge to giggle.

'Anyway, one day, when he was in a particularly gross mood, I hid in his school bag. I wasn't meant to leave his bedroom, but I just couldn't stand him any more. He had to be taught a lesson.' Lily paused.

'And then what?'

'I kept well hidden all day and, believe me, that was hard with what I found in the bottom of his school bag - but that's another story. So I kept hidden, but I kept on biting him and pinching him so that he'd yell out in lessons. It was so funny, the teachers got really annoyed and he ended up with two hundred lines and three lunchtime detentions.'

'Lily!'

'It wasn't the half of what he deserved, but I got found out all the same and put in the Death Warrant department, where some evil woman gave me all the filing. Still, you got to find out who was about to expire.'

'It all sounds so fascinating,' Claudie said.

'Don't you believe it! You enjoy life while you're here.'

Claudie nodded, waiting for her next divulgence.

'Can I have a look in your wardrobe?' Lily asked, breaking the spell.

Claudie nodded. 'Yes, of course, but I don't think you'll find anything in your size.'

'Elizabeth Chandler! What *do* you think you're doing?' a little voice suddenly bellowed, and Mary appeared on Claudie's dressing table, hands on hips, and nostrils flaring like a mad horse.

'Mary! What are you doing here?'

'What do you mean - *what are you doing here?*' Mary shouted back.

'This was my idea, and you know it!'

'Ah! What a liar. You promised me that you wouldn't follow when I said I was coming here.'

'I did not!' Lily protested, looking deeply offended.

'You know you did! You're *always* breaking promises. Remember that time we went to market and you promised you'd introduce me to Robert Samuels?'

Lily sighed. 'I can't believe you're still holding that grudge after nearly five hundred years!'

Mary shook her head. 'Goodness, how I hate being a twin sometimes.'

'Look!' Claudie said, not wanting Daniel to become suspicious with the level of noise in the room. But it was too late. A light rap on her bedroom door told her that he'd already heard too much.

'Claudie?' he said, pushing the door a little and peeping in.

She turned round and, even though she knew it was Daniel, in the half-light she could have sworn it was Luke. Her heart banged against her chest and her eyes widened in shock.

'Claudie? Who were you talking to? Are you okay?'

Claudie could only nod as she looked at Daniel. God, he looked so like Luke at times that it quite took her breath away. 'I'm fine,' she whispered, her voice barely there. '*Really*,' she insisted when his eyebrows rose in disbelief.

She watched him nod and turn away, walking down the hall to the living room.

'Who was that?' Lily sighed, her eyes agog. 'They didn't make them like that where we come from.'

'Elizabeth!' Mary admonished.

'Doesn't he wear clothes?' Lily asked.

'What do you mean?' Claudie said.

'Well he was all bare - he was only wearing shorts.'

'Was he?' Claudie sounded surprised.

'Don't tell me you didn't notice?'

'I didn't!' Claudie said. 'I was looking at his face.'

'A likely story!' Lily sniggered.

'Elizabeth,' Mary began, 'I don't think this is at all appropriate.'

Lily suddenly looked bashful. 'Sorry. I didn't mean to offend you, Claudie. It's just that - well - he's gorgeous!'

Claudie looked down at Lily who was ankle deep in her jewellery box. 'It's all right,' she assured her. 'It's actually a compliment, because he looks exactly like Luke.'

CHAPTER 16

Claudie had no idea what it was that woke her up but, once awake, she was sure of one thing: there was something in her room. It wasn't quite the same experience she'd felt just before the angels had descended: that of being watched, but it was a definite presence.

'Lily?' she whispered, wondering if she'd dared to come back. But there was no answer. Anyway, after the Daniel incident, they'd left pretty sharpish for fear of being missed. Something about an angel refresher course they were meant to be attending.

Claudie swung her legs out of bed and fumbled around for the lamp switch; flicking it on and letting her eyes adjust.

It was through the mirror that she saw it. There on the wall, just above her bed, was a spider the size of a saucer. There weren't many things that could awaken Claudie with such surety, but spiders were one of them.

How on earth did these things get into the house? She never saw them sneaking in through the windows, and they certainly never came through the front door. Maybe it was that little one that had given her such a shock when it had descended over her Gene Kelly poster in the bathroom. Poor Gene. He'd smiled through the whole horrible incident, but she bet he was fuming inside.

Claudie bit her lip as she looked at the monstrous-legged one. She should have got when it had been small enough to cope with instead of letting it grow into a Goliath.

She watched the cheeky way it clung on to the wall, as if it were a permanent fixture, but Claudie knew that, if she hadn't woken when she had, it would more than likely have dropped right in the middle of her face or crawled into her ear.

She shook her head, trying to expel the images. It was like a horror movie right in the middle of her bedroom, which wasn't at all fair because everybody knew she loved musicals.

She had to take action, and that meant one thing.

'Daniel?'

What else could she do? It was a potentially embarrassing

situation, but there was no way that she could go back to sleep until the offending creature was got rid of.

'Daniel?' she called softly, grabbing her dressing gown and tying the cord as she ventured into the living room.

'Are you asleep?' she said, rolling her eyes at her own stupid question. It was three o'clock in the morning, what else would he be doing?

'Daniel?'

He murmured something as he floated up from subconsciousness. 'Hayley?'

'No. It's Claudie.'

'Claudie?'

'Yes. I've got a problem.'

He sat up immediately, and scratched his head. 'What is it?' he asked, coming round and focusing on her.

'There's a spider in my bedroom.'

He chuckled.

'It's not funny. It's enormous, and I can't go back to sleep until it's got rid of.'

'You want me to deal with it?'

'Yes please.'

'Okay.' Daniel yawned and pushed his blanket down, swinging his enormous legs off the sofa bed and revealing a pair of navy boxer shorts.

Claudie tried not to gasp. So that's what Lily had been looking at with the most unangelic expression. Daniel caught her eye and she turned her gaze away quickly. He seemed to sense her discomfort because he reached for his jumper and pulled it on before standing up.

'Come on then. Where is it?'

Claudie led the way back down the hall but stopped outside her bedroom door, pointing at the offending creature like a frightened child.

'Jesus! It's enormous. What do you expect me to do with that?'

'Well I don't know! Just get rid of it!' Claudie screamed back at him.

'Okay. Okay,' he said, restoring a little calm to his voice.

Claudie dared to venture a little way into the room, her face crumpled in a mixture of horror and disgust. She didn't dare watch, but felt compelled to all the same.

Before Claudie had time to wonder what Daniel was going to do, his fist had flattened it in one quick movement.

She screamed.

'It's dead!' Daniel said. 'What are you screaming for?'

'That was horrible!'

'Well what did you expect me to do?'

'I don't know. Not *that! Merde!*

'It wouldn't have felt a thing, Claudie. It was so quick.' He grabbed a tissue from the box by her bed and dealt with the mess quickly. But Claudie wasn't watching. His words had triggered something inside her.

He moved through to the bathroom, placed the spider's Kleenex shroud into the toilet and flushed. Then he watched his hands. All the time, Claudie was stood on the threshold of her room, as if she couldn't quite bring herself to go back inside.

'Claudie? What is it?' he said, his voice low.

'I -' but the words were stuck in her throat. She felt utterly helpless. Her words wouldn't start and her tears wouldn't stop.

'Hey!' Daniel stepped closer and she was immediately wrapped in his great thick arms. 'I know,' he said, 'I know.' Over and over, stroking her hair, just like Luke had used to, but that just made matters worse. She couldn't stop crying. She was spilling out all over the place.

And Daniel just let her. His hands stroking, his voice soothing. They seemed to stand there for ages, the semi-darkness and Daniel's calmness having a hypnotic effect of her. But, somewhere amongst the brotherly hugging, a kiss occurred. Claudie wasn't quite aware of it at first. A kiss on the crown of the head seemed harmless enough in the scheme of things. It was one of those cosy, comforting things that you did to children or pets. The trouble was, Daniel's was beginning to travel. She could feel him kissing her ear, her neck, and then her mouth. And it had felt wonderfully strange at first because it felt so like Luke.

But it wasn't Luke. It was Daniel.

She tried to push Daniel away but it was like attempting to move a wall with a knitting needle, so she tried to shout but her throat was still thick with tears.

There was only one option left. Her knee. His groin.

'SHIT!'

Without a moment's hesitation, Claudie ran into the living room and began picking up all his things. His shirts, his shoes, his bag. It didn't take long.

Opening the front door, she threw the lot out into the damp night. How could he? How could he have crossed the line and taken advantage of her like that? He'd spoilt everything.

'JEEE-SUS!' she could hear him cursing in the hallway.

'GET OUT DANIEL!' she yelled, aware that she had probably woken her neighbours up.

'Claw - deeee,' he whined, hobbling through to the living room, his body bent double with pain. 'I'm sorrr - eeee.'

'Too bad,' she said, her voice quiet but infused with a steely quality she didn't quite recognise as her own.

'I want to ex -'

'Well *I* don't want you to,' she interrupted, watching as he staggered slowly towards the door, her eyes still stinging with tears.

'I've got nowhere -'

'Too bad,' she cut in, slamming the door behind him and double bolting it. If he had any sense at all, he'd hitch the first available ride home and not bother to call again.

She walked back through to the living room and, to vent some of her anger, flung the covers from the sofa bed and folded it back up into itself. She wanted no reminders of him in the morning.

She couldn't believe it. She'd truly thought she had a friend in Daniel when all the time he was using her. Her head pounded with the indignation of it all. But not only that. In a way, she felt as if she'd failed. Somehow, within a year, she'd succeeded in loosing both brothers, and she couldn't help feeling responsible for it all somehow.

Slumping into the armchair, she stared into space, completely numbed by what had just happened. If she'd had any idea, she would have preferred to have slept with the Goliath spider in her bedroom. This wasn't how she wanted things to turn out.

She sat until her body started to feel the cold. Heaving herself out of the chair, as if she had just aged fifty years, she went back to bed. Although she felt exhausted, she knew she'd never be able to get back to sleep now.

She twisted her body into knots as she tried to get comfortable.

What was it Mr Woo had told her to do in times of stress? "Imagine beautiful place where you feel safe". Claudie closed her eyes and tried to visualise one.

A place with no mountains. No spiders. And definitely no Daniel.

CHAPTER 17

'Kris! Am I glad to see you!' Claudie said, ushering her friend into the kitchen and closing her door before old Mrs Kettering, who was pottering around in the yard, could question her about the noise the night before.

'Right, what the hell happened?' Kristen's scowl was a terrifying sight to behold first thing in the morning.

'Can we have a cup of tea first?' Claudie suggested somewhat timidly.

'Claudes, I know *something* happened, otherwise you wouldn't have phoned. And I can't see any evidence of Daniel, so you might as well just come out with it.'

Claudie tried to ignore her, making a show of filling the kettle and opening cupboards for mugs and teabags in an attempt to put off the moment when she'd have to confess to Kristen what had really happened. She'd telephoned her instinctively, for a little bit of support, but, now she was here, she just felt confused and embarrassed.

'Claudeee!' Kristen had her arms folded across her ample chest, and was looking every inch a school marm.

She put a big spoonful of sugar into her mug and half a one in Kristen's before she began.

'Daniel tried to kiss me.'

'I just knew it!' Kristen cried. 'He couldn't keep his hands to himself could he? It's a good thing he had the sense to leave or he'd have *me* to deal with.'

'Now be fair! He's been under a lot of strain too,' Claudie said.

'I don't believe you, Claudes! How can you even think about defending him? He had *no right*!'

'I know he didn't.' Claudie handed her a mug of tea and urged her to go through to the living room.

'He took complete advantage of you.'

'Yes he did,' Claudie nodded in assent. 'I still can't believe it.'

'How did this all begin anyway?' Kristen demanded, pacing up and down the living room in her anxiety.

'I don't know,' Claudie said, not wanting to relive the experience. 'I was crying.'

'What about?'

'For goodness sake, Kris, sit down? You're making my head spin.'

Kristen sat as told. 'Is this where he was sleeping?'

Claudie nodded.

'You'll have to sell it,' Kristen said with a snarl.

'Don't be ridiculous.'

There was a moment's pause as they sipped their tea and dwelt on Daniel's bad behaviour.

'So why were you crying?' Kristen asked again.

Claudie drew a deep breath. 'It was silly really,' she said. 'But there was a spider in my room, and Daniel squashed it.'

'You mean you let him into your bedroom?'

'What else could I do? You know I hate spiders! I couldn't deal with it myself.'

'And then what happened?'

'I don't know. I just got upset. I think it was the way he just flattened it. The way - one minute it was alive, minding its own business, and the next it was dead.'

'But it wouldn't have felt a thing, Claudes.'

'That's what Daniel said.'

'You just got to thinking again?'

Claudie nodded. She'd done a lot of thinking over the past few months and she sometimes thought her head would explode.

'And that's when the bastard took advantage of you? God! If I ever lay my hands on him, I'll murder him!'

'Don't worry, I did a good enough job on my own with my knee.'

'He might have raped you!'

'I don't think so.'

'How do you know? If you hadn't kneed him, who knows what would have happened?'

Claudie felt a smirk tickling her mouth.

'You *did* knee him, didn't you?' Kristen's lips were also beginning to twitch.

'Oh yes,' she said with great satisfaction. 'I reduced him to a pulp all right!'

'Ouch!'

'He won't be trying that again in a hurry.' They both laughed. 'Thanks for coming round, Kris,' she smiled across at her friend, wondering what on earth she'd do without her.

'That's all right.'

'What did you tell Mr Simpson?' Claudie asked, aware that it was nearly half past nine, and that Kristen should have been in the office by a quarter to.

'Nothing. Angela's covering for me.'

Claudie chewed her lip as she thought of life at the office continuing without her.

'I might come in later this afternoon,' she said.

'What? Are you mad? Mr Bartholomew will just send you home again.'

'I don't care. I'm fed up of being at home. And besides, I miss-' she paused. What was she going to say? 'I miss you all.' There, that was true enough. She couldn't really say that she missed her flight of angels. But it was true. She missed Jalisa's dance routines, and Mr Woo's kind face. She even missed Bert's hurrumphing and continual scratching of his head.

'Well we miss you too.'

For a moment, Claudie could have sworn it was Jalisa's voice she'd heard. She cast her eyes quickly round the room, half-expecting to see her tap dancing on the television, but there was nobody there.

'I suppose you'd better be off. I don't want to get you into trouble,' Claudie said.

Kristen nodded but she didn't look as if she wanted to make a move just yet. 'God I feel miserable,' she said suddenly.

'Sorry if I've ruined your morning.'

'It's not you. I don't know, I'm just fed up lately. Got anything to cheer us up? Just a quick fix.'

'Well I haven't got any cigarettes, if that's what you mean, but we could just watch the opening of *On the Town*.'

The young girl in the pet shop hadn't been able to tell whether the fish Simon had chosen was a male or a female. And they hadn't had any goldfish in silver either.

Poor Pumpkin, Simon had thought, as he'd lowered the plastic bag into the water and watched as the new arrival swam out into its new home. What if it was another male, and what if the two of them didn't get along? Was that possible? Did goldfish argue? Pumpkin wouldn't thank him at all. At least, at work, *he* could get up and walk away from Mandy the man-eater. Poor Pumpkin would have no choice but to keep on swimming around his little bowl.

Now, sat at his office desk again, he was beginning to feel very much like Pumpkin. Mandy hadn't dared to mention her amateur sleuth role of the day before, and Simon was too much of a gentleman to mention it either. But he felt trapped by her. All morning, he could feel the intensity of her gaze upon him. He felt like he was under a microscope never mind in a goldfish bowl, and she hadn't stopped talking all morning.

Simon did his best not to respond.

'So,' she began again, 'are you meeting her this lunchtime?' Did Simon detect a slight derisive note in the way she said her?

He cleared his throat. God, he wished she'd shut up and leave him alone. As if he was likely to divulge personal details to her of all people. But was he meeting her? As far as Mandy was concerned, Simon was really seeing somebody. It was a ridiculous scenario but, if he wanted to keep her off his back, he had to keep it going.

The image of the moonshine woman filled his mind again. Now, she would be a great girl to meet at lunchtime. She would be able to get a man through a nightmare morning at work. He wondered briefly what it would be like to meet up with her, and then a naughty thought occurred.

'No,' he said, 'she's got to go shopping.' He immediately pictured her browsing in the little bookshop, her large chocolate eyes mesmerised by the magical world of the books. She might very well go there regularly during her lunch hour for all he knew. 'But I'll be seeing her tonight.'

'Right. Doing anything special?'

'No,' Simon said, 'just hanging out.' A smile was playing about his mouth as he tried to imagine what it would be like hanging out with Miss Moonshine. What would his living room look like with her in it? Far more exciting an option than two goldfish, that was for sure.

'And you won't tell me her name?'

Simon shook his head, not taking his eyes away from his monitor in case they gave him away.

'Still your little secret, is she?'

'Yes,' he replied, replaying the scene in the bookshop when he'd handed her the book she'd coveted. That beautiful rainbow smile. 'She's my secret,' he added. So secret, he mused, that she doesn't even know herself.

CHAPTER 18

Kristen was determined not to get excited about Friday. She knew Jimmy pretty well, and it wasn't very likely that he'd be booking a romantic meal for two. During their whole two-year relationship, the closest they'd got to a romantic meal had been lunch in a pub in Wensleydale. He was a simple man with simple tastes, and would much rather spend his money on a few pints than a plate full of unpronounceable food. Still, it was fun to try and guess what it was he had planned for them. Probably a bag of chips by the harbour, looking out at the boats and dreaming of summer.

Looking out of the window whilst her bosses set up the meeting room, she realised that she couldn't imagine a time pre-Jimmy. All past boyfriends seemed as remote as the stars. Apart from Simon that was. He was far too precious to forget. Their relationship had probably been the shortest of Kristen's, and yet there'd definitely been something about him. Something wonderful, but very platonic.

And Jimmy? What was she going to do about Jimmy-the-completely-unweddable? To be fair, he'd been quite plain with her from the start of their relationship on the issue of marriage, and, being a woman, Kristen had nodded and agreed very politely whilst secretly thinking that she'd be able to change him; that she'd be the one to make him see the light.

Two years on, and several near rows on the subject, they were still rolling along together in unwedded bliss, and she'd been doing very well over the past few months. She had hardly made any references to marriage at all, except at Claudie and Luke's wedding. Well, who wouldn't make the most of an opportunity like that to drop a few hints?

But it was only a matter of time, Kristen knew that. She couldn't help herself. She wanted more than he seemed prepared to give her and, although she loved him, she really couldn't see a future with him if he didn't want the same things as her.

Claudie sneaked up the stairs to the office, checking that the bosses weren't around before she dived through the double doors.

'Claudie!' Angela shouted in surprise.

'Shush!' Claudie waved her hand up and down.

'What are you doing back?'

'I got bored.'

'Really? Away from this dump? You're mad!'

'I know,' she said, looking apologetic. 'It's just, I spend enough time on my own as it is.'

'You don't have to explain,' Angela said. 'I know what you mean. But won't old Bart kill you?'

'I don't think so. Listen, I'm just going to sit here quietly for a couple of hours and then sneak home before five.'

Angela nodded. 'Well they're in a meeting anyway, so they probably won't even know.'

'Is that where Kristen is?'

'Yes. She's got the ghastly job of taking the minutes.'

Claudie nodded, thinking that at least Mr Bartholomew would keep out of her hair.

Pulling out her chair, Claudie began inspecting her desk for angels. It seemed very quiet. Unnaturally so. Perhaps there was something in their contract to say that if a client went missing, then they would withdraw their services. But surely they knew that the circumstances had been beyond her control, and surely they would have given some notice, or left a message or something?

Claudie began to look around for a possible note from Jalisa and panicked. They weren't coming back, were they? They'd abandoned her. Left her to it. The flight had fled. It served her right, she supposed. She hadn't been the best of clients. Still, wouldn't Lily and Mary have said something to her if they had been planning on leaving?

Claudie sighed. It was ridiculous even thinking about it. After all, how could she possibly be expected to explain the behaviour of angels?

'For she's a jolly good fel-low!' suddenly, from out of nowhere, an unmistakable voice assaulted her ears. It was Jalisa.

'For she's a jolly good fel-low!' she sang. But where was she? Claudie's eyes danced around the desk.

'For she's a jolly good fe - el - low! And so say all of us!'

In a blink of an eye, the five of them were standing by her

keyboard. 'And so say all of us. And so say all of us!' they chorused. 'For she's a jolly good fe - el - low. And so say all of us!'

Claudie's smile almost shot off her face, taking her ears with it. 'Gosh! I've missed you guys!' she all but screamed.

'Have you?' Bert was the first to speak, his eyes almost watering in delight.

'Of course I have! It's only been two days but it feels like a lifetime,' Claudie said, looking over her shoulder and making sure Angela's head was still in the store cupboard.

'And we've missed you,' Jalisa confessed. 'They put us all in storage for a while, which was awful, and we were just praying that you'd come back.'

'Storage? What's that?' Claudie's forehead buckled with wonder, as she imagined the five of them placed neatly on a shelf and told not to move.

'Well, it's called The Waiting Room really, but it's secretly known as storage. It's where angels go when clients are having a break - for whatever reason,' Jalisa explained diplomatically. 'Instead of training us up for another mission, we have to wait, just in case.'

'I'm glad you did,' Claudie said. 'It wouldn't have been much fun having to break in a new flight.'

'To tell you the truth,' Jalisa said in a hushed voice, 'I thought they were going to have to do just that.'

'Really? Why?'

Jalisa turned round and glared at Lily and Mary who were both looking decidedly guilty. 'They were under the impression that *some of us* had been visiting out of bound areas.'

Claudie could feel herself blushing. 'Really?' she said, trying to inject some innocence into her response.

'Yes!' Jalisa said. 'And if they were ever found out, it would mean a filing job in Death Warrants for a very long time!'

Claudie glanced quickly at the Tudor twins who had suddenly become engrossed by a pile of paper clips and were avoiding eye contact with Jalisa.

'Well, everything seems to be all right now,' Claudie said, clearing her throat and anxiously thinking of how she could change the subject. 'And how are you, Mr Woo?'

Mr Woo looked up from where he'd positioned himself on Claudie's pocket dictionary, his expression a little merrier for being addressed. 'I good. You good also?'

Claudie smiled. Some people asked as routine, but when Mr Woo asked how you were, you knew that he genuinely wanted to know. 'I'm well, thank you. But I've been missing having your advice to hand.'

'Have you?'

Claudie nodded, thinking of how she'd wished he could have been there the night before when she kicked Daniel out.

'But I bet you've missed my jokes more, eh, Claudie?' Bert interrupted, his face breaking into two with a cheeky grin.

Claudie nodded, the word *jokes* hitting her for the first time. Bert - the joking angel. *Each member has been specially chosen for the job: possessing some quality or ability to help you*, that's what Jalisa had told her, and jokes were one of the many things she'd loved about Luke. She hadn't made the connection before, but it made perfect sense to her now.

She gazed down at Bert. 'You must tell me all your latest jokes. I need cheering up.'

He beamed back up at her. 'You bet!' he said, giving her a cheeky wink.

Mr Woo turned around and glared at him, his gentle demeanour disappearing in an instant. 'Stinky bird egg - she talking to *me!*'

'Shut up, you big woman's blouse.'

Claudie smiled. It was good to be back.

CHAPTER 19

There weren't many friends Simon kept in touch with from his university days, but he was glad that he still gave Paul a ring every now and again because he'd recently put in a good word for Simon with his employers who were looking for a website designer. It was only a small job, but the company had a number of contacts which could lead to much bigger things.

They'd even asked him to come into their office to discuss what they wanted. So what better way to escape Mandy than an expenses paid, Friday afternoon in York?

Forgetting how bored he usually got on trains, Simon hadn't taken anything with him to read, so had to make do with staring out of the window and sharing a personal stereo. It wouldn't have been so bad if the young girl, who looked as if she should have been in school, wasn't kicking the leg of their shared table with irritating regularity. He thought about getting up to move, but he hated making a fuss about anything. And where would he move to? The train was pretty packed and, short of moving carriages, he had the choice of sitting next to a man who kept clearing his throat every eleven seconds - Simon knew because he'd become incensed enough to time it - and a woman eating a smelly egg sandwich.

He opened his briefcase and flicked through his portfolio. Everything was in order. It was the only thing about him that was.

Claudie stared out of the window as a rush of fields passed. Another week, another session with Dr Lynton. She'd thought about cancelling it this week, but she thought about cancelling it every week, so no change there.

Again, there was the dilemma of what she was going to tell him. The Daniel incident, for example. What would he make of that? What would he accuse her of this week?

She shut her eyes, trying to visualise Mr Woo's suggested tranquil landscape, but nothing came to mind. She thought of the painting in Mr Bartholomew's office, but she couldn't be bothered to walk into it. Not today.

She glanced at her watch. They were nearly there. Thank goodness too. She was almost losing her patience, what with the teenage girl's constant foot tapping from somewhere behind her and the appalling smell of egg that was filling the carriage from an unknown source.

When the train arrived, Claudie almost ran through the station, the luxury of fresh air invading her nostrils in a heady rush as she darted across the road.

Dr P Lynton was going to get the full Daniel story, she'd decided. Make of it what he would. But one thing was for certain: the angels were going to remain a secret. For another week at least.

Was it her? Simon stood dead in his tracks as he watched her crossing the road, a little dance in her step. Was it really Miss Moonshine? How strange. How wonderful. He wondered if he had time to follow her, but caught himself in time as he realised that he was turning into a Mandy. He looked at his watch and scratched his head as if that might help. He was having a life-deciding moment outside York Station. Choose now. Job or woman? Paycheque or romance? Which is more important? Choose now and, either way, you'll live to regret it.

He tapped his right shoe against his left. On one side he saw a beautiful, delicate face; on the other, a corkboard full of bills at home. He knew what to do. He knew which was the right decision. But he chose the other option.

He turned round and started walking towards the Swanlea Insurance head office.

CHAPTER 20

Rosehip, Coral Kiss or Pink Shimmer? Kristen unscrewed each of the lipsticks in turn and held them up to the light. They looked like a girly version of a Star Wars light saber.

She'd got it down to three from a possible choice of twelve, but she was stuck now. She supposed she could count Coral Kiss out on account that Jimmy probably had bad memories of it after she'd got it all down his one good white shirt whilst getting romantic with a loose grape. And Pink Shimmer? It was far too cold to think about wearing anything remotely frosty on her lips. So Rosehip it was.

She'd opted for a Whitby weather-defying tight dress, which just skimmed her knees, and had left her auburn hair loose. Just let the wind try to ruffle it tonight, she thought with a little smile.

Dress smoothed, make-up on, and hair in place, Kristen stood in front of the mirror gazing at her reflection. She thought about giving herself a few words of advice or comfort, but what would they be? Hang in there, girl. Don't press him. Let him work his way round to it in his own time. Things that are worth having are worth waiting for, and other clichés. She shook her head. In his own time, she tutted. If women didn't give the occasional prod, the human race would come to a complete stand still. She'd read a dozen novels and a hundred articles that said the same thing: women had to make their presence felt. It was no longer enough to look pretty and hope for the best. A woman had to be forthright if she wanted to succeed.

'Are you ready?' Jimmy shouted from downstairs, breaking into her thoughts.

'Yes!' Kristen shouted back. 'As ready as I'll ever be,' she added, giving her reflection a wink, and taking a deep breath before heading downstairs.

Claudie sank back into her sofa and breathed a sigh of relief. It had been another fraught session with Dr Lynton. She really must think about giving them up altogether. After all, she felt that she was getting on well by herself since the arrival of her little flight. Surely five personal angels were enough to see a girl through the rough times? Having a bereavement counsellor on top of that was just plain greedy, wasn't it?

She'd told Dr Lynton about the unfortunate incident with Daniel.

'How did you feel about his advances?' he'd asked.

'How did I *feel?*' Claudie had asked, aghast. 'I suppose you could say I had a knee-jerk response to the whole thing.' She'd watched as Dr Lynton's face had turned a veritable shade of puce. Well, ask a silly question.

She wished Jalisa and the gang could be called upon for a quick house visit, but guessed that just wasn't permissible. For a rash moment, she thought about breaking into the office at work. She still had a key from ages ago, which Mr Bartholomew had long forgotten about, but just imagine if she got caught. What would she say? I'm just visiting the angels on my table? She'd be locked away for sure.

So it was going to be another lonely evening in. She'd call Kristen round if she hadn't been going out on her mystery date with Jimmy. Claudie smiled. If she hadn't needed her fingers for the remote control, she would keep them crossed for Kristen all evening. She hoped Jimmy came up with the goods tonight. If there was one person who deserved to be happy, it was Kristen.

Claudie sighed. She was fed up of evenings in on her own and, as much as she adored her collection of musicals, there came a time when all you wanted was a bit of company. She'd never really understood the notion of being lonely until she'd lost Luke. She'd thought it was just another way of saying you were bored, but there was more to it than that. Loneliness was like a disease you couldn't find a cure for. Movies were only a temporary relief and, as soon as the words, The End, appeared, that feeling of hollowness would return once more, and it couldn't be cured by picking up a book or flicking through a magazine.

The End. Claudie had often felt cheated by those words. Although they gave closure and a necessary structure to the films, they always seemed so smug and taunting. There you are, they seemed to say, you've had your ninety minutes of perfection. Now, get back to your real life. The music faded, the dancing stopped, and real life seeped in once again.

Walking through to the kitchen, Claudie reached into the drawer under the sink and found the key she needed. She knew exactly what she had to do. In fact, she didn't know why it hadn't occurred to her before. Hadn't Jalisa told her that the flight were there for her whenever she needed them? Well, she knew that her home was out of bounds so that meant *she* had to go to *them*.

'We're here to work for you, Claudie!' Jalisa constantly reminded her. 'You only have to give us a call.'

Claudie still felt a little uncomfortable admitting that she needed help, even to her own angels. But, now, she was more than ready to admit she needed them and, with a smile of anticipation dressing her face, she grabbed her coat. It was a familiar movement, she thought, the grab-the-coat-workout you had to get used to if you lived on the North Yorkshire coast. She opened the door, and was surprised that it wasn't as cold as she'd expected. Perhaps excitement was heating her up as she half-walked, half-ran towards the office.

It was after eight thirty, which meant that the cleaners would have left long ago. There was nobody around in fact, and it was easy to approach the building from the back entrance and slip the key into the lock.

As she turned it, she wondered, for a moment, what she'd do if they'd changed the lock. But no, the key turned effortlessly, and she was inside, sighing with relief at the realisation that she hadn't set any alarms off.

She felt like a thief as she walked through the corridors and up the stairs in the dark. But she didn't want to turn any of the lights on. She was rather enjoying the secrecy of it all.

Everything had a rather sinister look about it at night. The great hulk of the photocopier was like a strange, sleeping beast, and the empty desks looked quite lost without their cheerful occupants.

But would the angels appear? Would they be prepared for a night-time call, or did they work nine to five like normal people? Perhaps there were angel pubs and night-clubs which they could go to. Hadn't the girls said that they partied at weekends? Claudie hadn't thought of that as the mad rush of adrenalin had propelled her to break into the office.

She walked in trepidation towards her desk, lit softly by a street lamp outside. Her eyes were beginning to adjust to the low light of the building, and she peered around the familiar objects which had taken on a surreal quality in the dimness.

And then her heart filled with fear. What if she'd made it all up?

What if the angels were mere figments of her imagination and didn't exist at all? It was easy to believe that she was going mad, creeping round her place of work at night in the expectation of having a chat to a six-inch angel.

She stopped for a moment, her heart thudding like an angry fist in her chest, her breath short and irregular. They didn't exist, did they? Her mind had been performing visual somersaults; something she could only blame on herself for her over-rich diet of MGM musicals.

And yet they'd seemed so very real. Claudie bit her lip so hard that she almost drew blood. There was an explanation for that, wasn't there: she'd needed help. She'd needed help so badly that she'd had to create five different personalities. Not one but five! Wasn't that just a little excessive? Who did she think she was?

Suddenly, it was all so clear. Each angel seemed to represent a strand of her personality: Jalisa was her secret dancer locked deep inside her office persona; Mr Woo was the sensible, level-headed part of her; Bert, well Bert was the joker - the little part of her which loved to laugh but which hadn't been around for a while. And the twins? Perhaps they just went to prove that Claudie really had lost it.

No, she needed Dr Lynton far more than she was willing to let on. She closed her eyes and leant up against a filing cabinet, the dark grey metal cold against her back. What was she doing? She had Kristen to talk to, and Dr Lynton to open up to. Why did she feel the need to create five mini angels? And why angels? Had Clarence in *It's a Wonderful Life* finally got to her?

But she knew what the heart of the problem was. No matter how many people she had around her, and no matter how many others she created, it didn't make up for the one she'd lost. No amount of friends, counselling or angelling could replace the pair of arms around her which she'd loved so well.

She took a moment to think about what she should do next. As much as she'd convinced herself that she was finally slipping into madness, she still couldn't resist finding out for sure. Leaving the solid safety of the filing cabinet, Claudie walked towards her desk.

'Hello?' she called softly into the darkness. 'Is anyone there?' She moved closer, pulling her chair out and sitting down. 'Jalisa? Lily? Anyone?' She bit her lip again, and waited silently for a moment.

'Claudie?' a little voice greeted her.

'Mr Woo?' Claudie's voice had risen an octave higher than normal, and she felt like crying as she spied him on her desk.

'Why you here so late?' he asked, walking out from the shadows behind her computer.

'I got lonely. I just wanted a bit of company,' she explained shyly, blinking hard to make sure that he was real.

'But you in trouble if catch you?'

'Well what are you doing here?' she asked, very glad that he was actually there.

He looked up at her, his big brown eyes soft and gentle. 'Policy to be on call - just in case.'

'Then, you *are* here if I need you?'

He nodded. 'Jalisa not explain to you?

'Well, I wasn't sure,' Claudie said, not wanting to get Jalisa into trouble. 'I mean, I took a bit of a chance coming here.'

Mr Woo looked slightly apprehensive, as if he wasn't quite sure what he was meant to do. 'So you need herb to sleep?'

Claudie shook her head. Mr Woo and his herbs reminded her of Dr Lynton and his books. But books and herbs weren't the answer to everything.

'I just wanted someone to talk to,' she explained.

Mr Woo nodded. 'I understand.'

'You do?' They looked at each other for what seemed like the longest moment.

'I miss my wife,' he said, giving a sad little smile. 'But I make you feel sad if I talk.'

'No! No! Honestly,' she tried to assure him. 'You can talk to me. I'm a good listener.'

Mr Woo sat down on a sleeping file and gazed at nothing in particular. 'It seem long time since I see her.'

Immediately, Claudie could feel tears prickling the back of her eyes as she felt the connection of a fellow sufferer. And she knew that there wasn't a single herb that could vanquish what he was feeling.

'Oh, Mr Woo.'

'So many thing I remember. So many thing I wish can come back.' He paused for a moment, and then quickly shook his head as if coming out of a trance, and held his hands up.

'I'm so sorry,' Claudie whispered.

'I also sorry for you,' he said, looking up with gentle eyes.

'We're two sorry people,' she said with a nervous giggle, blinking back her tears.

Mr Woo nodded in agreement. 'Now I make you sad.'

'No,' Claudie said. 'Don't think that.'

There was a moment's silence as they wondered what to say next. 'It's just that I've never thought that the person who died might actually miss the people they left behind,' Claudie said.

Mr Woo nodded again. 'Angel school teach us to comfort bereaved. But person dead also hurt.'

'You mean Luke will be mourning for me too?' Claudie's eyes widened in the dark room.

'Yes.'

Claudie felt a lump in her throat, and her eyes welled up with the thought of Luke confessing as much on somebody else's desk somewhere. 'Oh, Mr Woo, can't I please see him?'

Mr Woo shook his head. 'You know cannot do, Claudie.'

'But that's such a silly rule. I'm sure I'd be fine if only I could see him again. And don't you want to visit your wife, and comfort her?'

'Very much,' he whispered, as if anxious not to be overheard. 'But not working tha way.'

'Why isn't it?'

'Have to continue life, go to new thing - what you say? "Move on".'

'Move on!' Claudie gave a laugh like a splinter of glass. 'That's the most ridiculous thing about all this. People keep telling me that, but they obviously have no idea about what you're feeling. *No idea.*'

'I have same feelings also.'

She looked down at him. 'I know. I'm sorry. It's just, I get so angry sometimes. It's like I've swallowed a volcano and I'm about to erupt.'

'I feel same also. Except from other side.'

Claudie blinked. 'Do you suppose Luke was angry too?'

'I thinking leaving you make him have fury of dragon.'

'Then, you've met him?'

Mr Woo shook his head. 'I look for him now.'

'You will?'

'Yes.'

'And you'll tell him how much I miss him? How much I love him?' Claudie's voice was breathless now.

'But no say anything to other. You in much trouble if find out.' Mr Woo gazed up at her, his expression serious.

Claudie felt her shoulders slump in defeat. 'Okay,' she said, 'I promise.'

'You understand,' Mr Woo began again, 'anger is most difficult feeling.'

'Do they teach you that at angel school?' Claudie asked.

'No. I learn in life.'

Claudie gave a half-smile. 'I saw this little boy in the street the other day screaming his head off,' she said. 'He was just standing there howling. His mother didn't know what to do with him, and everyone was staring. And do you know what I thought? I thought that what he was doing was the most natural thing in the world, and I really envied him his ability to stand in the middle of the street and just let it all out - all those pent up emotions - for everyone to see.'

'Adult not show feeling with freedom?' Mr Woo said.

'But why? When does that happen? When do adults tell children that they have to pull themselves together and bottle it all in? It's so unnatural. And imagine if adults took a leaf from the children's books. The whole world would be filled with a cacophony of crying!'

'Best medicine in world.'

Claudie looked at Mr Woo. 'Bert told me it was laughter.'

'That one reason why we not okay together,' Mr Woo said, but Claudie could see a little twinkle in his eyes.

'But you not cry in street?'

Claudie rested her head on her hands. 'I wanted to at first,' she said. 'And I think people expected me to. It was awful. Everyone was treating me like a pressure cooker about to go off. But I was just too aware that it wasn't the done thing.' She paused for a moment, her eyes a very soft brown as she gazed into her past. 'I wanted to shout more than anything.' She gave a little laugh. 'You know, Luke once gave me shouting lessons!'

Mr Woo's eyes narrowed and he cocked his head on one side.

'We'd climbed up this mountain in the Lake District, and he insisted that we couldn't leave before we'd shouted something from the top.' She felt herself smiling at the memory, as if she had travelled back to the very scene she was describing. 'He was always a little bit mad.'

'You shout for him?'

Claudie giggled and covered her mouth. 'Yes! I did.' Claudie looked at Mr Woo, but the happiness had melted from her eyes. 'I shouted, *I love you.*'

For a few moments, they were silent, lost in their own private web of thoughts. It was as if both were trying to get back to their own past lives because the present was a hard, hurtful place.

At last, Claudie spoke.

'I know I'm probably not meant to ask this, but what do you miss the most?'

Mr Woo looked up, startled by the question. 'Miss?'

'If you had to name one thing. Other than your wife, of course.'

Mr Woo pursed his narrow lips together and rubbed his knees. And then he gave a little chuckle.

'What?' Claudie asked.

'I miss sweet almond jelly. And also cake'

'Cake? Really?'

'Yes!' He laughed again, a great vibrating sound that seemed to roll around in his stomach until it built into such a size that it had to be released. 'You're not allowed cake in heaven.'

'Really?'

'I know what you thinking. You thinking you allow favourite thing in heaven: but not true. You eat salad and rice and brown bread. It not fair if you spent earth life with good diet. But they say indigestion and cholesterol not good for angel.'

'I suppose not,' Claudie laughed, trying to imagine an angel with indigestion. 'So you'd advise us to enjoy our food whilst we're here?'

'In moderation, yes!'

They laughed together, and then silence fell again, broken only by the chime of a distant church clock.

'I suppose I'd better go,' Claudie said at last. 'It's getting late.' She pushed her chair out and stood up.

'Claudie?' Mr Woo's voice sounded cautious.

'Yes?'

'You want me come with you?'

She looked down at him. Was he serious? 'Can you do that? I thought you weren't meant to.'

He looked a little bit embarrassed. 'That not question asked. You want me come with you?' he asked again.

Claudie thought of walking home alone, of the evening stretching darkly ahead. She thought of what it might be like to take Mr Woo with her. Would he sit comfortably on her shoulder and watch films all evening? She couldn't quite imagine it somehow, and yet his kind offer made her positively glow with warmth.

'No, thank you,' she said. 'It's very kind of you, but I'll be fine. I'll see you in the morning.'

Mr Woo didn't look convinced. 'Here,' he said, digging deep one of his pockets which appeared to have no end. 'Take. Put under pillow for sweet and easy dreams.'

'Thank you.' Claudie took the familiar little package and placed it in her own pocket and, when she looked up, he had gone.

'How much further is it?' Kristen asked, stumbling on the uneven pavement for the fifth time in as many minutes.

'Patience. We're almost there.'

'You said that ten minutes ago.'

'Are you sure you've got your eyes closed?'

'Yes!' Kristen wailed.

'You're not peeping?'

'Through your massive hands? I don't think so! Come on, Jimmy - let me see!'

'Okay. After three,' he said, milking his opportunity for every ounce of suspense. 'One ...'

Kristen pictured a restaurant with a table decorated with red roses.

'Two ...'

She imagined Jimmy on his knees in the street outside the restaurant, a red rose between his teeth.'

'Two and a half ...'

She imagined them outside a jewellers, and Jimmy holding out a little black velvet box.

'Three!' he whipped his hands away. Kristen was smiling from ear to ear until she saw where they were. They were in front of a shop all right, but it wasn't a jewellers. It was the shop where Jimmy sold most of his model boats.

'Well?' he said, a child-like glee edging his voice. 'What do you think?'

If Kristen had told him precisely what she was thinking at that moment, they would probably have had a parting of the ways. Instead she stared at the shop window, trying to spot what it was that was so important to him. Maybe, she thought optimistically, he'd attached a diamond ring to the mast of one of his boats? She scoured the models for evidence, but couldn't see anything out of the ordinary. There were definitely no eye-socking solitaires in this window.

But something did catch her eye. In the centre of the window, for all to see, was a large sign. Models and display by Jimmy Stanton.

'What do you think?'

Kristen bit her lip as she tried to hide her disappointment. 'It's - er-'

'It's my biggest display yet! The owner let me have the whole window this time,' he said excitedly, grabbing her shoulders from behind and giving them a firm squeeze.

'It's - wonderful.'

'I knew you'd like it! I've been keeping it a surprise all week.' He kissed her hair. 'Took me three days to put together.'

Kristen nodded, trying not to let her smile drop.

'And you really like it?'

'I do,' she said, thinking it would be the only time she'd be likely to say those words to Jimmy.

'I thought you could take a photo of me here some time,' he said excitedly. 'For the scrapbook.

'Yes. Good idea,' Kristin replied, forcing a tiny smile onto her face.

'Great! Now, how 'bout a Chinese? I'm starving,' he said. Kristen looked up and smiled. It was, at least, a step up from a bag of chips.

Poor Mr Woo, Claudie thought as she walked passed the pub where she had spotted the man who had almost stolen her Judy Garland book. Tonight, music was blaring and the pub walls were vibrating with laughter as she walked by. It was just the very place where she and Mr Woo should spend a couple of hours. Just imagine that: sitting in a pub with an invisible, six-inch high herbal practitioner. Who was dead.

She slowed her pace and peeped through the window. There wasn't a chance of her going in on her own, but she couldn't resist a quick look. She couldn't see the snooker table from this angle, but she could see that the place was packed. Heads nodded in animated conversation as cigarette smoke turned the air grey. These were people who knew nothing about lonely nights in with MGM musicals.

Claudie watched the strangers for a moment, her eyes skipping over their faces until they fell on one in particular. There, sat in a quiet little corner was a raven-haired woman in a tiny skirt and low, revealing top. Claudie squinted, taking in the flirtatious bat of her eyelashes and the letterbox-red mouth. But it wasn't the woman who was the focus of her attention. It was the six-foot giant with long, dark hair next to her.

So, Claudie thought, Daniel hadn't left Whitby after all.

CHAPTER 21

'Poor old Kris,' Simon said, ruffling her newly-hennaed red hair.

'I mean, I'm not being unreasonable, am I?' she looked up at him with eyes the colour of wet slate.

'Of course you're not,' he said. He'd lost count of the number of times they'd had this conversation.

'It's been two years after all, hasn't it?'

'It certainly has,' Simon agreed.

'You're a man.'

'Yes,' Simon nodded, trying to keep the smile from out of his voice.

'Wouldn't you have done something by now - proposed or something?'

Simon swallowed hard. This was dangerous ground. If she took a close look at his own life, then she'd see what a great mess he'd made of it. She'd see how having not proposed to the feckless Felicity had been the best thing he'd ever done. But Kristen didn't want to hear that.

He took a deep breath. 'Perhaps he just needs a bit more time to get comfortable with the idea of marriage again.'

'Comfortable!' Kristen all but shouted.

'Shush!' Simon waved her. Even with the television on full blast, there was still a chance that Jimmy might overhear them, and Simon did not want to get in a row with Jimmy.

'Comfortable! If we get much more comfortable,' Kristen whispered angrily, 'we'll stagnate.'

'But some men need more time than others.'

'Do they?' Kristen's voice dripped sarcasm.

'Yes they do. Don't forget he's only just got out of one marriage.'

'Two years, Simon. It's been two years!'

'But that's not long. He probably just wants to make absolutely sure. Look at it this way - it's probably for your own good. You get a chance to back out too. He's doing you a huge favour really,' Simon smiled, trying his best to cheer her up.

'And how do you work that one out?'

'Because you're getting to see him in all his glory. You're getting the best of both worlds here: living together, but with none of the forced commitment of marriage. You can up and leave any time.'

'But I don't want to up and leave.'

'And you don't have to.'

Kristen screwed her face up, not understanding any of Simon's logic.

'Look,' Simon began, 'I'm not the best person to ask for advice on relationships, am I?'

'Oh, Simon! I'm sorry,' Kristen said, her face falling into a frown. 'How selfish of me to keep going on and on.'

'You're not selfish. Just a bit worked up, that's all.' He took a swig from one of Jimmy's cans of lager. 'So tell me,' he said, a slight smile curving his mouth, 'was this window display any good, then?'

Kristen pursed her lips together and made as if she was going to hit him.

'Only asking!'

'God, Si,' she said in frustration, 'I feel as if I'm going to go out of my mind sometimes. Is it so wrong to want just a little bit more?'

'No. 'Course not. And it will happen. Trust me,' he said, reaching out and giving her arm a squeeze. 'You're one of the lucky ones, Kris. You're going to be fine.'

Kristen's face broke into a little smile. 'Sorry I keep boring you with all this.'

'You're not boring me. I'm getting a free meal, aren't I.'

'Yes, you are,' she said, turning her attention back to the industrial size pan of pasta. 'So tell me what you've been up to. Any new women on the horizon?'

Simon flinched slightly at the question, a vision of Miss Moonshine flickering through his mind.

'Only if you can count a goldfish. And I don't even know if it *is* a female.'

'God, Si! You've not been buying more fish? You've really got to get a life!'

'I know. I know,' he complained. 'I must be having one of the worst years on record.' He picked up the jar of tomato sauce, reading the Italian-sounding name. Turning it round he read, *made in England.*

'No, not quite,' Kristen chipped in.

Simon raised his eyebrows. How could anyone have had a worse year than him?

'You've heard me talk about Claudie, haven't you?' Kristen said, a huge wooden spoon in her hand.

Simon nodded. 'The lady whose husband died?'

'Yes. She's been acting very strangely lately - talking to herself.'

'Well I do that.'

'At work? All day?'

'Er - no.'

'Well *she* does. But the strangest thing about it is that she seems happier than she has for a long time. I keep trying to talk to her about it, and she swears she's fine.'

'So what's the problem? Why not leave her to get on with things in her own way?'

'Because it's not normal, is it?'

'Who are we to say what's normal, and what isn't?'

'Stop getting all profound on me. I invited you round for some advice and I'm getting all your university notes regurgitated at me.'

Simon grinned. 'Sorry.'

Kristen picked up the jar of sauce. 'My speciality,' she said. 'You know I spend hours making this sauce and then pouring it into ready-bought containers.'

'So that's the secret, is it?'

'I don't think I'd make a very good housewife, actually,' she said in a more serious tone of voice. 'I'm a terrible cook.'

'Who said that?' Jimmy asked, poking his head round the door. 'You're not a terrible cook. I love your cooking.'

'It's hardly cooking,' Kristen said, draining the pasta and emptying the pot of sauce over it.

Jimmy walked over to her and squeezed her round the waist, planting an embarrassingly loud kiss on her cheek.

Feeling a little uncomfortable in the middle of a scene of domestic bliss, Simon walked through to the living room and left them to it.

The post hadn't arrived before Simon had left for Kristen's, and he wasn't surprised to find three window envelopes on his mat when he got home. He opened them, grimacing at the amounts he owed to various people, and wondering how long he could delay payment.

But one envelope caught his eye. It wasn't brown, and there was no window in sight. He tore the envelope open and lifted the letter out, immediately seeing the words *congratulations, you have won*. He didn't bother reading any further. Or he wouldn't have, if two Eurostar tickets hadn't fallen out from behind the letter.

Simon picked them up and read them. They looked official enough. There was no red rectangle asking him to telephone anywhere to claim his free prize.

He picked the letter up and read it again. *Yours was the winning caption in our "Paris Passion" competition*, it stated. Winning caption? Was it referring to that daft thing he had filled in and posted months before without thinking? He couldn't even remember what his caption had been. Something slushy, in the hope of winning a romantic weekend for two, and thereby keeping Felicity sweet. But that was two weeks before she'd upped and left.

'Blimey!' he laughed. He'd won a trip to Paris for two. But who on earth was he going to take?

CHAPTER 22

'Why is it that every woman thinks she's the perfect matchmaker?' Jimmy asked between mouthfuls of bacon butty.

'Because they probably are!' Kristen said. 'Anyway, it was your idea.'

'I don't think so,' he mumbled, shaking an extra large dollop of brown sauce onto his plate. 'I only mentioned Simon and Claudie in the same breath and you slapped the two of them together as if they were destined to be with each other.'

'I really think they might be. I don't know why I didn't think of it sooner,' Kristen said, her eyes gleaming with excitement.

'Well you can count me out of it. It will only end in disaster. You'll probably make a fool of yourself, and lose both Claudie and Simon in the process.'

'Don't be so melodramatic. This could really work.'

'And how many times have I heard that one?' Jimmy asked, shaking his head in despair. 'Look what happened to Linda and Patrick.'

'That was different,' Kristen said sharply.

'How?'

'They just didn't get into the spirit of the thing.'

'They nearly murdered each other, Kris.'

Kristen pouted. She didn't like being proved wrong. 'That had nothing to do with me.'

'Really!' Jimmy dunked his butty into the brown pool of sauce that was turning his plate into an Irish bog.

'They obviously weren't meant to be together.'

'Obviously. And what makes you think Simon and Claudie are?'

'Well, it's-' she lifted her eyes to the ceiling, 'it's indefinable. I've known them both for so long now. I know how they tick. I know that they'll just slot together.'

'Kris, they're people, not pieces from a jigsaw puzzle. You can't just piece them together and expect things to work out.'

'Why not? Isn't that how we were introduced? At a mutual

friend's party.'

'Yes but-'

'But nothing! We were sat next to each other, when Penny knew perfectly well that we were both single.'

Jimmy declined to answer.

Kristen shook her head. What if Jimmy was right? What if she messed things up good and proper? She'd even almost failed to get to first base by deciding to make fresh pasta with a pesto sauce. Thankfully, she'd remembered just in time.

Pine nuts. Something as simple as pine nuts could spell absolute disaster. Kristen remembered the day she'd gone shopping with Claudie. It was only a few days after the funeral, and Claudie had been as limp and lifeless as a ragdoll. Kristen had put her in charge of the trolley, thinking it best that she had something physical to hold on to, whilst she had hunted down the items on the list.

She'd just returned with a bumper box of tissues for Jimmy's hayfever when she saw her. Standing stock still, Claudie was staring down at something as if she meant to melt it with her gaze. Kristen had approached slowly and looked down to see what it was she was holding. It was a little packet of pine nuts. She didn't know what they meant; what significance they held, and she wasn't sure that it would have been wise to ask.

'*Do you want to buy those, Claudes?*' she'd asked in a very calm, quiet voice.

Claudie had shaken her head and, with a hand that trembled like a catkin in spring, replaced the packet on the shelves.

No. Kristen didn't suppose she knew what she was getting herself into, but she was determined not to let Jimmy change her mind. She'd just have to keep her fingers crossed and hope that fate was on her side.

'Anyway,' she started again, pulling herself firmly out of her anxieties, 'what's the big deal if I want to invite my two best friends round at the same time? It's a wonder it hasn't happened before. In fact, I'm quite surprised with myself that it's taken me so long. They're the two nicest people in the world - just waiting for me to get them together.'

'Don't forget that Claudie's only been-'

'I know,' Kristen interrupted again. 'You don't need to tell me that. But I really do think it will do her good.'

Jimmy shifted uncomfortably in his seat. 'Well, you know how I feel about it.'

'Shut up, and leave me to it,' Kristen said, throwing him another bacon butty.

On Monday morning, Simon was still smiling. It was as if he'd won the lottery rather than a holiday break. He knew that it wasn't exactly life changing, but it was the symbolism of the thing. He'd been feeling so miserable, so self-absorbed and put-upon lately; nothing had been going right, and then, within the space of two days, he'd secured the website design for the company in York, and had won the competition. Was his luck finally taking a turn for the better?

Walking into the office, he wondered whether he should tell anyone. Mandy, for example. Or would she think that, by telling her, he would want her to go with him to Paris? Could be dangerous, he thought. Best not to mention it.

Strangely enough, Mandy didn't seem to be in a very talkative mood. She'd nodded and said morning as he'd sat down, but hadn't broken into her usual non-stop gossip routine. It was rather disturbing. He'd kind of got used to her drone as he worked. Perhaps something was wrong. Perhaps he should do the decent thing and ask if everything was all right.

He looked across at her as she sat smiling away to herself. There didn't appear to be anything the matter. In fact, now he was actually paying attention to her, she seemed to be even happier and perkier than normal. Her lips were cherry-red and turned up into the most dazzling smile, and her face was glowing like a Halloween pumpkin.

She turned round to face him, as if she knew he was looking at her. And that was when he saw the love bite at the base of her throat. He tried not to stare at it, which was rather difficult because it looked like an old teabag glued to her neck.

Mandy the man-eater had obviously found a guy who knew how to bite back.

CHAPTER 23

Simon's hair was still wet from his shower as he left for Kristen's. It was a mild evening, and he decided to walk into town. It gave him a chance to think about the night ahead.

He'd rang the competition organisers to explain how his circumstances had changed since he'd entered back in the autumn, and a very nice lady had said that there wouldn't be any problem in exchanging his double room for two singles. He'd been so grateful to her that he'd almost invited her along as his guest.

Which posed the question, who was he going to take with him? Paris was definitely not a place to take a mate to. It just wouldn't work, walking down the boulevards with a guy. Unless you really were into "gay Paree".

There was only one choice: Kristen. But that posed a whole set of other problems. They were best friends, and it went without saying that a weekend away with her would be great fun, but what would Jimmy have to say about it? Would it be worth invoking the wrath of Jimmy Stanton?

Kristen was in the kitchen when he arrived. For someone who claimed to be a lousy housewife, she spent an awful amount of time hovering over the oven with a pinny wrapped round her waist.

'Your hair's wet,' Kristen observed as Simon peered over the hob to see what was cooking.

'Here.' He passed her a bottle of wine.

'Thank you. Do you want to do the honours? The glasses are over there.'

Simon uncorked the bottle and poured the wine out into the glasses on the worktop.

'Four?' he queried.

'Yes. Didn't I mention?' Kristen turned round and smiled coquettishly. 'Claudie's here.'

'No. You didn't mention it.'

'I thought I had. Silly me.'

'Yes,' he agreed, knowing instantly that Kristen was likely to have her own agenda for the evening.

'I've a funny feeling you're going to get on really well together.'

'And I had a funny feeling you were going to say that.'

'What? Don't you believe me?'

'It's not that I don't believe you, it's that I don't like the idea of anyone making my mind up for me.'

'Don't be such an old windbag.' Kristen play-punched him in the stomach. 'Come on,' she said, untying her pinny. 'I'll introduce you.'

Simon grimaced but followed her through to the living room. It was impossible to get angry with Kristen. She had a heart the size of Hull, and truly believed she knew what was best for people. He'd just have to humour her for the length of the evening. Anyway, he'd always wondered what this friend, Claudie, was like.

'Claudie,' Kristen began as she entered the room, 'this is Simon. Simon, this is Claudie.'

Simon stepped out from behind Kristen and immediately felt his mouth spring open. It was Miss Moonshine.

'Hello,' Simon said, a smile warming his face as he leant over to shake her hand.

'H-Hi,' she said, eyes widening.

Kristen looked from one to the other. 'You know each other?'

'No,' Simon said.

'Yes,' Claudie said.

'Not really,' Simon agreed. 'But we have kind of met before.'

'In the bookshop,' Claudie said, her French accent tickling his ear musically.

'Over Judy Garland,' Simon added, almost laughing.

'Judy Garland?' Kristen looked puzzled. 'I didn't know you were an old film buff like Claudie.'

'Ah!' Simon began. 'You see, there's a lot about me you don't know.'

'Obviously,' Kristen said.

'He tried to steal the book I was going to buy,' Claudie said with a little laugh in her voice.

'Only because I had no idea you wanted it.'

Kristen looked from one to the other, quite baffled by the situation. 'So that's how you two met?'

'Well, we didn't exactly *meet*,' Claudie said, 'I mean - we didn't know each other's names or anything.'

'But we did see each other again, you know,' Simon added, sitting down opposite her. 'At the pub. Do you remember? You were hovering at the door.'

'Yes! It was that night we went out,' Claudie explained to a bemused Kristen. 'When we didn't quite make it into the pub.'

'You saw Simon?' Kristen asked. Claudie nodded. 'Why didn't you say something? I could have introduced you.'

'But I didn't know you knew him then, did I?' Claudie giggled at her friend's mistake.

'Oh, yes!' Kristen said, looking from Claudie to Simon, and back again. 'This is all very strange, you know.' Kristen turned to Jimmy, but he merely gave his head a little shake as if reminding her that he wanted nothing to do with it.

Kristen did most of the talking throughout the meal, leaving Claudie and Simon to eat, nod, and stare at each other. It was unavoidable really. Claudie had often wondered what the mysterious Simon was like. He was the man to whom every other man in Kristen's life was held up against and measured. Even Jimmy.

'He's smart,' Kristen might say, 'but he isn't as smart as Simon.' Or, 'He's got a good sense of humour, but it isn't a patch on Simon's.'

Claudie had got a little fed up with it over the years. Why hadn't she just married this paragon of manhood instead of harping on about him all the time? Claudie couldn't work it out. Looking at him now, it was hard to imagine why he hadn't been marched up the aisle already. He was smart, kind, attentive and attractive. And he had a head of pale curls like an angel. Not like one of her little angels, of course, but like one expects an angel to look like - as if they've just flown down from a Renaissance ceiling - all fat cheeks and golden hair. Yes, he had the kind of curls you wanted to twist around your fingers in little rings.

Claudie blushed at the thought, and found herself staring deep into her soup in order to prevent staring, but then told herself that she'd make exactly the same observation about a beautiful animal. A dog, say, or a horse. Why shouldn't she make observations about a man? It didn't have to mean anything, no matter what Dr Lynton might say, and men did it all the time, didn't they? Simon was an attractive man, and that was all there was to it.

She thought about his hair again. It glistened in the low light of the room as if it had been sprayed with diamonds. She shifted uncomfortably in her seat and tried to pay attention to what Kristen was talking about. Her mouth was going ten to the dozen this evening, obviously keen to engage them all in conversation. Then, at the end of the evening, Kristen uttered the predictable words, 'Simon? You wouldn't mind walking Claudie home, would you?' And, even though Claudie had protested, saying she didn't want Simon going out of his way, he did the gentlemanly thing and obliged.

'So,' he began, as they wended their way through the dark alleys, 'how's Judy?'

'Judy?' For a split second, Claudie wondered whom he was referring to. 'Oh! She's fine, thank you.'

'Good.'

'She's keeping my other two books company.'

'You have *three* Judy Garland books?'

Claudie nodded. 'It was silly of me to buy a third, I know. I just have this fascination that has to be fed. With Jimmy, it's boats; with me it's musicals.' She shrugged her shoulders as if what she'd said was the most natural thing in the world.

'So what is it with you?'

Simon's mouth opened but nothing came out. 'I suppose it's computers. It's my job,' he said after a moment's thought.

'But outside your job, what then?'

Again he paused. 'I don't know.'

'Really?'

'Yes. Sad, isn't it? My whole life is centred around my work.'

'That's not sad,' Claudie said. 'Not if you like your work.'

'I do. I just wish there was a bit more of it around.'

They were silent for a few moments.

'Well, this is it.'

Simon looked up.

'I'm just at the end there,' she pointed towards a dimly lit cottage in the middle of a yard. 'Thank you for walking me home. I hope I've not made you late.'

'No. No.'

Was it Claudie's imagination or did he seem out of breath? 'Night then.'

'Night,' he said and, for a moment, Claudie thought he was about to add something, but he didn't.

By the time Simon reached home, he was completely shattered. It was hard work looking at a beautiful face all evening. He'd been annoyed that Kristen had tried to set him up with her friend, but that had evaporated the moment he realised who the friend was. He could hardly believe that his Miss Moonshine was Kristen's best friend. God, he thought, he must stop referring to her by that name. He'd be sure to come right out with it by accident one day and seriously embarrass himself.

This was the woman he'd heard so much about over the last few months. The dear friend who had lost her husband so shortly after getting married. How did you survive something like that? No wonder she had such an air of vulnerability about her. She looked like a snowflake: so perfect and delicate but with the constant threat of melting hovering over her. He hadn't known what to say to her, especially on the way home. He hoped she didn't think he was an idiot.

And then he remembered something. In his excitement at realising that Claudie and Miss Moonshine were one and the same person, he'd completely forgotten to tell Kristen about Paris.

CHAPTER 24

Kristen put the phone down and sat back in her chair, a huge smile filling her face. A weekend in Paris. She was honoured that Simon had asked her to go with him and, without a moment's hesitation, she'd said yes. It was only after Simon had hung up that she'd remembered Jimmy.

With the thought of a free holiday, she'd completely forgotten that she was a woman who was cohabiting. Jimmy might not have actually married her as yet but, as far as he was concerned, she was his woman, and weekends away with an ex-boyfriend, even though there'd never been anything between them, just weren't acceptable. Still, it had been a nice idea for about half a minute.

Poor Simon. She was going to have to let him down, but she'd rather do that than risk Jimmy losing his temper. And risk losing Jimmy, of course. She sighed, and swung round neatly in her chair as she wondered how she'd tell Simon.

As she turned a perfect half-circle, she caught sight of Claudie. She was smiling to herself, and chatting away quite happily as if she had a group of friends round her. Now there, Kristen thought, the beginnings of an idea floating into her mind, was a girl who needed a holiday. Paris was, after all, the romance capital of the world. What better place for two people to get acquainted? She could just imagine Simon and Claudie there, strolling by the Seine, and walking arm in arm down the Champs Elysee.

Kristen slowly nodded to herself, feeling a Cheshire cat grin splitting her face in two as her idea began to take shape.

Claudie was quite unaware that Kristen was watching her, and plotting her fate. She was busy having a nice chat to the flight.

'I'm not sure I'd advise that,' Jalisa was saying as she spun across the top of the printer in a wild dance.

'Why not?' Claudie was puzzled.

'I think it still might be wise to keep going to Dr Lynton. I mean,' she stopped in mid-spin, 'it's not as though we're professional.'

'I thought you were?' Claudie said. 'I thought angelling was a profession.'

Jalisa chewed her lip. 'But Dr Lynton is trained.'

'But so are you.'

'Yes,' Jalisa said, 'but-'

'I think what Jalisa is trying to say,' Bert interrupted, 'is that it would be wise to have a number of different people to help you. You shouldn't be reliant on just us.'

Claudie leant forward and looked at him. 'Really?' Claudie didn't sound convinced. 'What do you think, Mr Woo?'

Mr Woo walked forward silently in his pillow-soft shoes. 'You more happy now but Dr Lynton still important.'

Claudie suddenly felt like a laboratory rat being examined, and she didn't like it.

'I think I've made quite enough progress already.'

'Yes, you have!' Jalisa encouraged. 'But you mustn't turn your back on people who want to help you in your own world.'

Claudie bit her lip. 'I see,' she said slowly, reading between the lines at last. 'Does this mean you'll be leaving me soon?'

'Of course not,' Jalisa said. 'We're here for as long as you need us.'

'Really?'

'Yes!' Jalisa smiled.

Claudie breathed a sigh of relief. If she lost the angels, she felt sure it would be like losing Luke all over again. It was strange. Even though she hadn't seen Luke, she felt as though she was living in his world a little by having the angels with her, and she couldn't bear for them to go. Not just yet anyway.

Mr Woo interrupted, 'Not good to have one help. Many help always best.'

'You mean I need all the help I can get?' Claudie looked round the table at her angels. She looked at Lily, who had been suspiciously quiet throughout the whole discussion.

'What do you think, Lily?'

Lily looked up and smiled prettily, delighted to be asked for her opinion. 'I think they're right. I don't think you should stop seeing Dr Lynton. You shouldn't become too reliant on us.'

'And that's what you all truly believe?'

There was a moment's pause as Claudie analysed each angel in turn. She heard the whirr of the coffee machine from the end of the office, the flash of the photocopier, and the slam of a distant office door before she answered. 'Okay. I won't stop seeing Dr Lynton just yet. If you all truly believe I shouldn't.'

'It's definitely what we all believe,' Jalisa nodded heartily.

'You make good decision,' Mr Woo agreed.

'Absolutely,' Lily said. 'Besides you haven't even found out what his first name is yet,' Lily added, and they all laughed.

After some serious pen chewing, Kristen came to the realisation that she wasn't going to be able to let Simon down over Paris after all. Not if she was going to persuade Claudie to go. No, she mused. If Claudie and Simon were to go to Paris together, then she was going to have to pretend to be going to Paris with both of them. She'd have to tell Claudie that she had won the weekend in Paris for two, and that Jimmy really hated travelling.

Would she be able to pull it off? She was a terrible liar, she knew that. Ever since Jimmy had found that packet of cigarettes stashed inside the cushion cover on the little armchair, he'd been able to tell when she was pulling a fast one. She shook her head at the memory. What on earth had Jimmy been doing sitting in the little armchair anyway? He was far too bulky for its tiny frame. And how on earth had he felt a packet of cigarettes? Was his mother the lead from 'The Princess and the Pea'?

And Claudie was a far better detective than Jimmy. Hadn't she been the unraveller of many an untruth in the past? Kristen exhaled a long and slow sigh. It was going to take a little bit of practising if she was going to pull this particular lie off.

When Kristen got home, she kissed Jimmy on the cheek and then hid herself away in the bathroom. It was practically the only private room in the tiny house, and Jimmy was perfectly at home with her monopolising it.

She brushed her tangle of red hair and filled her lips in with her favourite gloss lipstick. These things took planning. She had to get it absolutely right or the whole plan would fall apart.

Rolling her shoulders back, and taking a deep breath, she began.

'Claudes! You'll never guess! I've won a weekend for two in Paris!' She shook her head. Her voice sounded as phoney as a daytime soap actress.

'Claudie! What would you say if I told you we're going to have a holiday?' No! Too much of the wide-eyed wonder look.

'CLAUDES! I just had to tell you!' Again, Kristen shook her head. This wasn't going well.

She turned away from the mirror for a moment, phrases tumbling round her head.

'Hey!' she began, spinning round to face her reflection again.

'Hey, what?' Jimmy suddenly appeared in the doorway.

'Bloody hell - you scared the life out of me!' Kristen's heart thudded in her chest as she saw two heads in the mirror instead of one.

'What are you up to?' Jimmy's eyes narrowed.

'What do you mean?'

'I mean, why are you talking to yourself?'

'I wasn't.'

'You bloody were, you liar,' he said, grabbing her by the waist and nuzzling into her neck. 'And you worry about Claudie being mad!'

'Jimmy!' She pushed him away.

'What? Come on, Kris, what are you up to in here?'

'Nothing,' she said, but she could see that she wasn't going to get away with that for long. 'Okay,' she sighed, 'if you must know, I'm thinking of joining the amateur dramatic society.'

Jimmy laughed loudly. 'You are joking!'

Kristen could feel her face flushing. 'Why should that be so funny?'

'You - act? I've never heard anything so ridiculous.'

It was Kristen's turn to frown. 'I don't see what's so ridiculous about it.'

'You want to spend your free time with a bunch of retired people, spouting Shakespeare in a draughty old hall?'

'Well,' she said defensively, 'I haven't quite made up my mind yet.' She swallowed hard, wishing he'd just leave the room before her lie escalated out of control.

'And you'd expect me to come and watch you prancing round in a pair of old curtains?'

'Yes!' She was slowly beginning to get annoyed that he wasn't there to support her, even though she had no intention of joining the local group of thespians.

'God almighty, Kris!' He laughed. 'You do amaze me.' And with that, he left the bathroom, chuckling to himself.

As soon as he was out of earshot, she closed the door and turned back round to the mirror, but the words had evaporated. Still, she thought, with a certain amount of satisfaction, if she could make Jimmy believe that she wanted to join the local amateur dramatic society, surely she could convince Claudie that she'd won a holiday?

CHAPTER 25

It was Friday morning, and Kristen still hadn't told Claudie about the trip to Paris. It was proving much harder than she'd anticipated. She'd been on the verge of telling her on Thursday morning; even getting into the office early to prepare herself. Then, as soon as Claudie had arrived, Mr Bartholomew had charged in and promptly whisked Claudie away. She'd quite lost her momentum on her return.

There had been odd moments throughout the day when she'd thought she might be able to break the news, but she'd failed. Claudie had kind of sussed that there was something Kristen wanted to say too, which didn't bode well at all. It would all look so set-up and unnatural if Claudie got wind of it beforehand.

They'd been a particularly dodgy moment in the ladies. She'd been about to blurt it all out when Angela had come prancing in.

'Were you going to say something?' Claudie had asked.

'No. What makes you think that?'

'You've got that look about you. As if a hundred words are going to tumble out of your mouth at once. Like when we were at school - after you'd been on a date and couldn't wait to tell me.'

'Do I?' Kristen had shrugged.

'Yes, you do,' Claudie had said. 'Are you sure there's nothing you want to tell me?'

Kristen had nodded, and had tried to move away from talking altogether by applying a thick layer of lipgloss.

Still, she had great motivation for imparting her news soon because, if she didn't, she'd end up going to Paris with Simon herself and getting into terrible trouble with Jimmy.

Claudie had had the feeling that there was something on Kristen's mind. Perhaps it was that whole business with Jimmy and the boat display that was still bothering her. It certainly hadn't helped when Angela had come swanning into the office on Monday morning sporting a diamond solitaire.

'Look! Look!' she'd cried, flashing the obscene rock around the office like a lighthouse beam. 'He proposed! Can you believe it? My little Mikey finally proposed!' And she'd hopped between departments the whole morning, flexing her fingers and smiling like a Marx Brother.

Kristen had been in a foul mood ever since. Claudie was sure that she was happy for Angela really, after all, Angela had been waiting much longer for her boyfriend to pop the question than Kristen had. But happiness in one often highlights misery in another, Claudie mused.

Poor Kristen. Ever since her own parents had separated when she was thirteen, she'd craved the security of marriage herself. It was funny. It had worked the opposite way with Claudie: her parents' split had put her off the idea of marriage altogether. Until she'd met Luke, of course.

But she'd let Kristen talk about things in her own time. At the moment, she had her own problems to think about.

'I do wish you could all come with me,' she said again to Jalisa a little after eleven o'clock.

'To York?' Jalisa asked. Claudie nodded. 'We'd have to get special dispensation for that. It's out of bounds, you see.'

'But it could be done? If you asked in advance?'

Jalisa looked thoughtful. 'I think it could, but I don't see why you want us there. Wouldn't we just be a distraction?'

'I don't think so.'

'I mean, you're meant to be in therapy, and that means concentrating.' Jalisa nodded towards the back of the desk where Bert and Mr Woo were arm-wrestling and Lily and Mary were cheering them on. 'I rather think that we'd just be a big distraction.'

Claudie nodded slowly. 'I see what you mean.'

'Then why do you want us there?'

Claudie paused for thought. She was nervous even talking about it, but had really grown to trust Jalisa. She sometimes felt as if she'd known her all her life. 'Recently,' she began, 'I feel that Dr Lynton's pushing me towards something I'm not ready for.'

'What's that?' Jalisa's voice was gently probing, but Claudie still felt distinctly uncomfortable. 'ANGELS!' Jalisa suddenly bellowed. 'Will you *please* keep the noise down? I can't hear Claudie think.'

Claudie bit her lip anxiously.

'Claudie?' Jalisa said hesitantly. 'What is it you don't feel ready for?'

Claudie looked down at her, suddenly feeling quite exhausted by it all. 'Love,' she said quietly. 'I don't feel ready for love.'

Kristen walked as quickly as was polite towards the ladies toilet. It had been a terrible morning. Not only had she been unable to impart her news to Claudie, but Angela had started talking about wedding dresses, even though her dearest, darling Mikey hadn't discussed a date as yet. But still she went on and on about scooped necklines, flaring waists and trains to rival Virgin.

It had all become too much for Kristen. She'd wanted to share in Angela's joy, she really had, but it was hard to smile when your heart was wearing a great fat scowl.

In the relative privacy of the ladies, Kristen stood over the sink and stared at her reflection. She looked as mean as a dog. God, Kristen chided herself, what was the matter with her? Could she really not be happy in someone else's happiness? Was she that selfish? No, she thought, just miserable: miserable that she was seeing Angela's whole future unfurl in a way she'd longed for for herself.

CHAPTER 26

Even though Simon now had enough work to fill his days two-fold, he still found that he was wandering round the house like a lost thing. It hadn't taken him long to realise that it was one of the occupational hazards of working at home. There was nobody to tick you off when you were slacking, or to keep you in check when you were rooting in the biscuit tin. You were your own boss, and that sometimes became too great a responsibility because it was so much harder to discipline yourself than anyone else.

Still, it had been a relief to leave his office days behind him - again. And an even greater relief to find that Mandy the man-eater hadn't seemed particularly perturbed about it. Perhaps the perpetrator of the love bite necklace had something to do with that, Simon mused, as his fingers reached into the tin for the final broken custard cream.

It was eleven o'clock, and he still hadn't got further than booting his computer up and making three cups of tea. Friday, he thought. Just one week since he was in York. One week since he'd seen Claudie at the station. Would she be going there today, he wondered, screwing his face up as his teeth sunk, rather than crunched, into the biscuit?

He could do with going into Swanlea Insurance, couldn't he? And wouldn't it be brilliant if he could make the same train from Scarborough to York as last week - the train that Claudie had caught. It would be a complete coincidence, of course. It wasn't as if Claudie had actually seen him in York before, and he did have legitimate business there, didn't he?

He shook his head. He really must stop all this with Claudie. He didn't really know her at all. She might just be another Felicity but with a prettier face.

It had been a strange experience to finally meet her, and she'd been nothing like the half-crazed, half-French woman Kristen had been fretting about for the last half-year. She looked like a little angel who had peeped out from the clouds one day and quite liked the look of Whitby.

A bit of goldfish consulting was what was in order. He walked across the room towards the small tank he'd bought them. Nothing fancy, but it was a mansion compared to the one-up, one-down bowl they'd previously occupied.

Pumpkin and his still unnamed companion were swimming about, which didn't really surprise Simon. He watched for a moment, wondering if they'd go under the lurid green bridge he'd spent ten minutes choosing in the pet shop. They didn't.

Calm and collected, they regarded him with their glassy black eyes.

'What would you do, guys?' he asked. 'Would you follow the woman of your dreams?'

They barely moved in response.

'Or would you knuckle down to some graft?'

Neither batted an eyelid. But maybe that was because they didn't have any.

'Come on, it's an easy enough question,' he said, starting to get ridiculously irritated. 'Stalk or work?' He watched closely for any response or movement that might help him make a decision.

'You're right.' Simon stood back up to full height and went through to the kitchen to make his fourth cup of tea before settling down to work.

Dr Lynton leaned over the corner table and measured an imperceptible amount of milk into Claudie's cup.

'You don't take sugar, do you?' he asked.

'Just one, please,' Claudie all but laughed at his shocking memory. Surely he should write her tea-needs into that little notebook of his, instead of all the incidental stuff like her dreams and feelings.

He handed her the appalling cup of tea and then sat down heavily in his chair.

'Is there anything you want to talk about today, Claudie?'

'I don't think so,' she said.

'Shall we continue to examine where you think you are in your life, then?'

Claudie felt a volcanic-sized sigh building up. It was like being back at school again, an experience surely no sane person would want to repeat. If only the angels had got their special dispensation to accompany her, she might have enjoyed her visit to Dr Lynton's.

She could just see it now: his little room peopled by her flight.

Jalisa would just love dancing across the corner table and sliding down the great Swiss Cheese plant, and she felt sure that Mr Woo would find something of interest in Dr Lynton's ever-expanding library. Bert would probably be kept adequately entertained by observing and mimicking Dr Lynton, whilst Lily and Mary, well, since Claudie had given them some travel-size make-up, they'd barely said a word to anyone.

'We've been examining the four tasks of mourning, haven't we? Claudie?'

'Yes.'

'And do you remember what they are?'

She nodded. 'To be able to accept the reality of the loss.'

'Good.'

'To experience the pain of grief.'

'That's right.'

'To adjust to an environment in which the deceased is missing,' she rolled off, as if she'd been jamming for an exam.

'Splendid. And the last?'

Claudie bit her lip, wishing that her flight was to hand.

'Do you remember the last one, Claudie?' he asked again.

'No,' she said.

'It was to withdraw emotional energy from the deceased, and to reinvest it in another relationship.'

She remembered.

'And where do you feel yourself to be?' His eyes looked up from his notebook, his great flat hands neatly crossed over his scribblings. 'How far do you think you've come?'

Claudie shifted her weight again, and turned her teacup round in its saucer.

'Do you think you've adjusted to your environment?' Dr Lynton probed.

Claudie stared into the brown depths of the tea, but there were no answers there. And, even if the flight had been with her, nobody could really answer the question but herself.

'Yes,' she finally said, in a little voice that didn't seem to belong to her.

'I think you have,' he said. 'From the things you've told me.'

'Didn't you say something about it taking three months?' Claudie asked without looking up.

'That's right. But that's only an average. Everybody is different.'

She nodded again.

'So,' he said, breathing the word out slowly, 'what about stage four? Have you had any thoughts about that?'

Claudie looked down into her lap. She'd had thoughts about it, of course she had, but she didn't want to voice them.

'I sometimes feel I'm changing. But I'm still not the person I was, and I don't think I ever will be.'

Dr Lynton nodded. 'It's true that fewer than half of widows are themselves again at the end of the first year. And you mustn't think I'm pushing you into anything.'

She looked up at him. Was he a mind reader? It was scary sometimes how he was able to reach inside her head and pull her thoughts out for dissection.

'But it can almost be a comfort to move on. Would you agree?'

Please, she thought, don't ask me to do that. How can I be expected to withdraw from my own husband? I'm still wearing the ring he gave me. She gave it a little twist round her finger. Surely, she thought, I'm not married any more? Does that mean I should take it off? Is that what this is all about? Can I really be moving forward when I'm still wearing his ring?

Dr Lynton got up from his chair. 'I want you to take this home,' he said, stretching up to his shelves. 'Now, I know you didn't want any more books, but I do believe you'll find this one of help.'

He handed it to Claudie. 'Page sixty-three,' he said. 'Have a look at Freud's quotation.'

She nodded politely and no more was said on the subject.

When Claudie got home, she slumped into a chair and stared at her boots for about half an hour. She hated Friday evenings. Her trips to York always left her feeling depleted even if she'd had a good session with Dr Lynton. The fact remained that she needed to see him. She wouldn't even have known of his existence if Luke had still been alive, and that thought depressed her beyond words. She didn't want to be in counselling; she wanted to be a newly-wed, doing what newly-weds did best.

She closed her eyes for a moment. The cottage was so quiet; too quiet to be that of a twenty-six year old. She should be laughing, kissing, making love, arguing, shouting - the usual things a young adult would be doing - not slumped in her front room, alone and unloved with the weekend stretching ahead of her like a vast desert.

Emptying her handbag, she took out the latest book Dr Lynton had given her and placed it on the coffee table. She wasn't going to look at it. In fact, shaking herself out of her slump, she did everything she could to distract herself from the book. She prepared tea, did her washing, had a bath, vacuumed the front room, and then watched the final half of *Invitation to the Dance*. She didn't want to read Freud. What possible use could she have for a dead sex maniac? And how could he possibly say anything as eloquent as a Gene Kelly dance?

Nevertheless, the book sat there on the coffee table, making its presence felt. *Page sixty-three, page sixty-three*, it seemed to chant, and, by a quarter past ten, Claudie could ignore it no longer.

She picked it up and bent it open somewhere in the middle. Page one hundred and four. *No! This isn't the right page*, the book almost shouted. *Turn back! Turn back!*

Claudie turned back. Ninety-eight. The pages flicked. Her eyes caught strange charts and tables. Seventy-one.

Page sixty-three.

Her eyes scanned the page quickly, looking for Freud, and, when she found it, she read.

"We find a place for what we lose. Although we know that after such a loss the acute state of mourning will subside, we also know that we shall remain inconsolable and will never find a substitute. No matter what may fill the gap, even if it be filled completely, it nevertheless remains something else."

CHAPTER 27

Kristen battled against the April wind which seemed to whip up all the cold from the sea before hurtling it through the town. She battled her way up and down the supermarket aisles cursing the other shoppers, cursing her drunken trolley, and then cursing the fact that she lived somewhere which made owning a car impossible.

She then struggled up and down the steep steps on her way home, swearing at her shoes for being pretty but completely impractical.

Jimmy barely noticed Kristen as she crashed into the kitchen with the three bags of shopping. In fact, he didn't even bother to look up from his latest model boat, even when Kristen slammed cupboard doors and banged tins down on the worktops.

'God damn tins,' she swore under her breath, rubbing her thigh where they'd knocked into her. She'd no doubt have a Lake Windermere bruise by the morning.

The only time Jimmy responded to the terrible noise she was making was when she yelled out after catching her finger in a netted bag of satsumas.

'Are you all right?' he bellowed through, so as to avoid getting up off his home on the carpet.

'I'm fine!' she said, with all the conviction of somebody who is on the brink of insanity.

'What's for tea, then?'

By teatime, Kristen's mood had deepened as only an ignored woman's can. They sat together at the tiny table in the living room, foreheads almost touching as they ate the jacket potatoes which, along with the tinned food, had also contributed to Kristen's bruised thighs. Jimmy, however, still hadn't noticed that anything was the matter or, if he had, he was steering well clear of the subject.

'The window display has caught the eye of a chap from that posh magazine,' he was saying. 'You know the one with all them glossy photos?'

Kristen nodded.

'He left his card with Bill at the shop, and wants me to give him a call about a feature or something.'

Kristen grunted in response as she pushed the skin of her jacket potato around her plate.

'Well?' Jimmy said. 'That's good news, isn't it? It could be quite big.'

There was a moment's silence, apart from the strange sound of a potato in transit.

'Kristen?'

'What!' she snapped.

'What's the matter? You haven't said a word all evening.'

'Neither have you.'

'What do you mean? I've been telling you about my boats. Haven't you been listening?'

'I don't want to hear about your bloody boats. It's all you talk to me about,' she said sulkily, her voice sounding like a particularly obnoxious teenager's.

Jimmy dropped his knife and fork onto his plate. 'Kris-'

'Don't start. I'm not in the mood.' She scraped her chair back from behind her and walked through to the kitchen, throwing her plate, potato skin and all, into the sink.

'Kris?' Jimmy followed close behind her. 'Will you tell me what's wrong?'

'What's wrong!' she said, turning round to face him, her grey eyes wide and wild. 'US! That's what's wrong!'

Jimmy's forehead immediately furrowed as if he knew what was coming. They'd been here before, many many times.

'You never talk about us. It's always you. You never stop to think what I want from this relationship. It's just the same old stuff week after week, month after month, and I don't know if I can take any more.'

'Kris, listen-'

'We're stagnating, Jimmy. Just look at us. We're not going anywhere.' Jimmy's mouth opened to say something, but Kristen interrupted him again. 'You know how I feel about having a family of our own, but you never want to talk about it.'

'I was going to-' Jimmy began, but Kristen pushed passed him.

'I've just about had enough, Jimmy.' She ran into the bedroom and locked the door, standing perfectly still in the middle of the room. Her heart was thudding and her eyes were swimming with tears. She waited for a moment, half expecting Jimmy to come banging on the door. She knew he could break into the room if he had half a mind to. Trouble was, he would never have half a mind to, and that's what was bothering Kristen. She'd constantly laid herself bare in their relationship, urging him to move forward with her but no, he never listened.

She sat down heavily on the edge of the bed. The bed they'd shared for two years. She could hardly remember what life had been like in a single bed. And would she have the courage to face it again?

She blinked away her tears, her eyes resting on the chest of drawers in the corner of the room. She took a few hesitant steps towards it, knowing exactly what she had to do.

Somebody was banging on the front door. Claudie reached out and switched her light on, grimacing at the clock that read half past ten. Who on earth would be banging on her door at half past ten at night?

And then a cold shiver passed through her body. What if it was Daniel? There was a good chance that he'd had one too many to drink and had remembered her.

She tiptoed across her room and grabbed her robe, tying it tightly round her body. The banging had become more insistent. Trust whoever it was to have picked a night when she'd decided to have an early one.

Claudie padded down the hallway, thinking that she really must go to the local RSPCA shelter and buy something with fangs and a terrifying growl. That was something she'd never had to worry about when Luke was around. He only had to pop his head round the door to deter hapless salespeople or local political types. Claudie, by comparison, was a soft touch, and would always end up buying mops and brushes she didn't need, and promising to read the political manifestos thrust at her.

She wasn't sure whether to put the kitchen light on or not, and paused for a moment, looking at the silhouette at the back door. But the figure was far too short to be Daniel. She breathed a sigh of relief, putting the light on before opening the door cautiously, making sure the chain was on.

'Who is it?'

'Claudes!' a voice wept out from the dark courtyard.

'Kris?' Claudie whispered in disbelief. 'What's the matter?' She quickly removed the chain and ushered her friend inside. After she locked the door again and looked round, she saw that Kristen had a rather large bag with her, and her face looked like blotting paper on which a red ink pen had been cleaned several times.

'Kris!' Claudie gave her a big hug. 'Whatever's happened?'

There were a few loud sobs before she answered.

'I think I've left Jimmy.'

CHAPTER 28

It was two in the morning and there was still a light on in the front room of Claudie's cottage. There were also two wineglasses and an empty bottle of white on the coffee table.

'I've screwed up! Really screwed up this time,' Kristen said, her voice shaking. 'I should never have pushed him. It was so silly of me.'

Claudie, who was sat beside Kristen on the tiny sofa, placed an arm around her. 'You only did what you thought was right.'

'I should tell him that it was all just a big misunderstanding - that I don't care about getting married.' She blew her nose loudly.

'But it would all just blow up again later,' Claudie pointed out. 'At least you've been honest about how you feel, and now he knows it's up to him to decide what he's going to do.'

Kristen closed her reddened eyes for a minute. She knew what Jimmy would do: nothing - absolutely nothing. He wasn't the type of man to be goaded into giving a response. He just shut down, and the thought made Kristen cry all the more.

Claudie sat quietly for a while, letting Kristen get it all out of her system. There was no point talking over the noise she was making, so she just rested her head against her shoulder and cuddled her.

'You know,' Kristen said at last, giving her nose another loud trumpet, 'I feel like a spoilt child, I really do.' She leant forward from the sofa and picked up her handbag. Claudie watched as she removed a familiar looking packet.

'Kris? Those aren't what I think they are?'

'They're *lights* - look!' She held out the cigarette packet towards Claudie for inspection.

'But you've been doing so well.'

Kristen took one out and lit it. 'Yeah, well, it's not exactly been the best of weeks, has it?' She inhaled deeply and closed her eyes. A second later they sprang open. 'Oh, Claudes, you don't mind me smoking in here?'

'I do as a matter of fact. So please remove yourself to the yard,' she said in a voice too stern to be serious. 'Anyone but you would be given their marching orders.'

Kristen managed a weak smile. 'Thanks, hon.'

Claudie watched as the tiny front room began to fill with fumes. She'd only once had a puff herself, and had responded like a novice dragon, much to the embarrassment of Kristen.

'Do you want to watch a film?' Claudie said hesitantly.

Kristen shook her head. 'It's very sweet of you, Claudes, but Judy Garland isn't very likely to shift this particular mood.'

'Can I get you something to eat?'

'No thanks. But how about another bottle?'

One hour later, and one more bottle of wine, and Kristen had almost forgotten about her argument with Jimmy. Almost.

'I should have just left, but I didn't. I had to go and open my big mouth.'

'There's no point beating yourself up over it. It's done now,' Claudie soothed, pouring the last few drops of wine into Kristen's glass. She was starting to feel its effects now.

'God! What did I say? I was horrible! A real bitch.'

'Kris - don't.'

Kristen shook her head as she remembered what she'd said. 'I said he didn't care - never had - and that he didn't love me.' Her eyes were beginning to fill up again. Any minute, Claudie would have a full breakdown on her hands.

'I know he loves me! Why couldn't I be satisfied with that? Why do I have to go and push him for more?'

'Because it's what you want, in your heart of hearts. Anyway, every woman's the same. It wouldn't be natural if we didn't keep pushing for more. I was the same with Luke. I don't think he would have proposed if I hadn't kept dropping hints all the time.' Claudie felt surprised by what she'd just said. She hardly ever spoke about Luke to anyone other than Dr Lynton, and she certainly never mentioned him in as light-hearted a way as she just had with Kristen.

Kristen shook her head. 'Claudie! Just listen to me now. I'm so bloody selfish. Just look what you've been through.'

'Please, Kris-'

'No - listen. You've had such a terrible time, but you've been amazing. Just look at how you've coped. You're incredible, Claudie.'

'No, I'm not.'

'What do you mean *no you're not? Of course* you are! If I'd been you, I would have gone under - completely.'

Claudie stared down at the swirling pattern of the carpet. Did it usually swirl this much, she wondered?

'I don't know how you do it,' Kristen was saying.

'Do you want to know?'

'You mean you've got a formula?'

'No, not quite, but something just as good.'

'What is it? Those musicals?' Kristen nodded towards the shelves of films in the corner of the room.

'This has absolutely nothing to do with MGM or Gene Kelly.'

'What is it then?'

Claudie bit her lip. The wine was getting the better of her, and she knew she'd probably regret this in the morning, but what the heck?

'You know I've been talking to myself at lot at work?' She looked across at Kristen, anxious to see her response.

'*A lot?* It's bloody constant!' Kristen giggled, causing Claudie to smile.

'Yes. But I'm not.'

'Not what?'

'Talking to myself.'

'What do you mean?'

Claudie took a deep breath. 'I've got angels.'

Kristen's red nose scrunched up in her face. '*Angels?*'

'A whole flight of them in fact. They live on my desk.'

'Claudie? I think we've been drinking too much.'

'No! Listen - it's absolutely true!'

'And your accent's come back.'

'It's the wine!' Claudie insisted. 'But I'm telling the truth.' She breathed deeply, giving herself an opportunity to work out what she was going to say next. 'It's hard to explain. But there are five little angels living on my desk at work.'

Kristen didn't speak, but her mouth was a perfect O.

'It's incredible. At first, I didn't believe my own eyes. I thought I was making it all up because - well, you know - but they're absolutely real. They're like you imagine guardian angels to be - only much, much smaller, and they've come to take care of me - to make me smile whilst I'm getting over Luke.'

'You're having me on?'

'I swear, I'm not,' Claudie said, grabbing Kristen's hands and squeezing them tightly.

'You're telling me there's a bunch of guardian angels on your desk at Bartholomew and Simpson's?'

'Not a bunch - they're called a *flight*.'

'How do they all fit on your desk?'

'They're tiny! No bigger than my pencil pot.'

'What you mean like Munchkins?'

'No!'

'Oompah Loompahs?'

'No! They're just like normal people. Only smaller.'

'Claudie,' Kristen said, her serious voice firmly in place despite the amount of wine she'd consumed, 'you know we've been friends for years, and I've supported you in everything you've ever done, haven't I?'

Claudie nodded. 'Even when I didn't want to take Chemistry in my options.'

'Yes,' Kristen said, remembering. 'And even the time you went out with Craig Evans.'

Claudie rolled her eyes. 'What on earth did you bring his name up for?'

'Because I want to make a point. I'm always here for you. You know that, don't you?'

'Of course I do.'

'So you've got to listen to me now. I've been so worried about you, Claudes. I really thought that doctor what's-his-name in York was doing you some good, but I can see that he's just been ripping you off.'

'He's not, Kris.'

'But all this talk of angels?'

Claudie bit her lip. There wasn't going to be any convincing Kristen, was there? She'd always been a far more down-to-earth, logical person than she was, which was probably why they were such good friends: they balanced each other out. But Claudie should have known that she wouldn't be able to convince her. If Kristen couldn't suspend disbelief and watch an MGM musical, then there was little hope for her as far as angels were concerned.

'Okay!' Claudie suddenly said, leaping up from the sofa. 'Get your coat on.'

'What?'

'We're going out.'

'Don't be daft - it's half past three in the morning.'

'Never mind,' Claudie said, her mind made up.

'And it's freezing.'

'Doesn't matter. Come on.'

Had Kristen not drunk more than her fair share of wine, there's no way Claudie would have got her out of the house at that time on an April morning. It was pitch black and the wind whipped round their bodies as if it meant to skin them.

As for the task of breaking into their office, well, their wine-fuelled spirits suddenly seemed to find the whole thing rather amusing.

'What if we get caught?' Kristen whispered before breaking out into giggles.

'We won't. I've done it before.'

'You have?'

'Yes. They've got absolutely no security. It's dead simple.'

Kristen gave her a look of admiration, as if she hadn't expected Claudie was capable of such daring feats.

Ten minutes later, they were walking up the stairs, pushing and hushing each other en route to their office.

'God, it's a bit spooky,' Kristen said.

Claudie grabbed her arm for support. 'Wait until you see the office.' She pushed open the fire doors.

'Blimey. It's like a film set or something.'

'It is, isn't it?'

'Remind me why we're here again.'

'I'm going to introduce you to the angels.'

'Oh, God. I'd forgotten.'

'Here.' Claudie pushed Kristen towards her desk. 'Sit down.' She pulled Angela's chair over from the other side of the room and sat next to Kristen before reaching over to put her desk light on.

'Ouch!' Kristen and Claudie shut their eyes simultaneously, and opened them slowly to adjust to the room.

'Mr Woo?' Claudie whispered.

'What?'

'Mr Woo,' Claudie repeated, 'he's one of the angels.'

'Oh!' Kristen said, scrutinising Claudie's face with worry.

'Are you there?' she asked.

'*Is anybody there?*' Kristen giggled.

'Kris!'

'Sorry.'

'He might not be there, you see,' Claudie said. 'But it was his turn for night-duty the last time I came here.'

'Claudie?' It was Bert.

'Bert! Hi!'

'What's going on?' he asked, removing his hat to give his head a scratch.

'I've bought Kristen with me, Bert.'

'I can see that, but what for? What are you doing?'

'I wanted to prove to her that you're real.'

'You're drunk,' Bert said, his voice rather serious for such a small man, Claudie thought.

'So?'

'So, think about what you're doing.'

'What's going on?' Kristen asked, focusing on the spot of the desk Claudie was looking at.

'Bert's telling me off for being drunk.'

'Claudie,' Bert began, 'this isn't right. You're not supposed to tell anyone about us. It's one of the rules.'

'Not even Kristen?'

'Not *even* Kristen. There's no point. She can't see us, anyway.'

'But maybe if you picked something up? Moved something?'

'Claudie, you'll get the whole flight into trouble if you carry on like this, and you'll know where that will lead to.'

'I know,' Claudie sighed, 'filing for eternity.'

'Claudes? What are you talking about?' Kristen asked, sounding puzzled and tired.

'Wait a sec, Kris,' Claudie pleaded. 'Please, Bert. Can't you just grab that pen or something?'

'I've already said-'

'*Please!*' Claudie gave him a heart-felt look. 'You'd be my favourite angel in the whole world. I'd love you even more than Clarence in *It's a Wonderful Life.*'

Bert blushed at the compliment, knowing that was high praise indeed coming from Claudie.

'As long as you promise not to tell anyone?' Bert said.

'I promise!'

'And that you'll go home straight away?'

'Yes, yes!'

'All right. What do you want me to do?'

Claudie pointed to her favourite Parker pen. 'Just pick that pen up and bring it to me.'

'What's he doing, Claudes?' Kristen asked.

'He's going to pick that pen up over there. So don't miss it.'

Claudie watched at Bert braced himself. In proportion to his size, it was rather a large item to move, but it was light and he managed it without too much trouble.

'Did you see that?' Claudie all but shouted as Bert held the pen out to Claudie.

'Yes, I did,' Kristen admitted.

'It was Bert!'

'It was the wine.'

'No, Kris - Bert moved it. He's one of the angels.'

'I'm going home, Claudes. Come on.'

'But, Kris?'

Kristen got up from the chair and stumbled across the room. Claudie turned to Bert for some words of advice.

'Go home, Claudie. We'll pretend this never happened. Okay?'

'Okay. Night, Albert.'

How the two of them staggered home, they'd never know, but as soon as they got in the door, Kristen grabbed Claudie.

'Listen, Claudes. There's something I've been meaning to tell you.'

'Really? God, this is turning out to be a night and a half.'

Kristen smiled at her. 'I've won a trip to Paris, and I want you to go with me.'

Claudie stood dumbfounded for a moment. 'You're joking?'

'No.' Kristen shook her head.

'And you want *me* to go with you?'

'Who else?'

Claudie couldn't very well say Jimmy in the circumstances, could she? 'I can't believe it!'

'You'll come with me, then?'

'Of course I will.' She gave her a big hug. 'And don't worry, Kris.

We'll have a fantastic time - just you and me. And when we get back, Jimmy will be begging to have you home.'

'I don't know about that.'

'Of course he will. Now, come on. It's time for bed.'

Claudie made sure Kristen had all she needed before tucking her up into her bed. She felt hot and tired and decided to throw herself under the shower before going to sleep.

By the time she climbed into bed, Kristen was sound asleep. It was going to be funny sharing a bed again, and Claudie only prayed that neither of them would reach over and become amorous.

Kristen had stayed overnight before. When Claudie's mother had left Whitby shortly after the funeral, Kristen had camped out on the sofa bed. She'd been a real sweetheart. Claudie hadn't wanted to be on her own but hadn't wanted to share her bedroom, knowing that she'd be lying awake half the night.

Now, she smiled down at the sleeping Kristen, noticing that her hand was clasping a magazine. Prizing it from her fingers, she saw that it was one of Angela's bridal magazines. How had Kristen come to have it?

She looked down at what Kristen had been reading, but the pages were so wet with tears that they looked like multi-coloured waves. She placed it on the floor next to the bed, switched the light out and kissed Kristen goodnight.

Lying in the soft darkness of the bedroom, Claudie felt her body fill with the weight of grief. It was like a heavy-metal drink which dispersed around your body, and there was no telling when it would hit you. Night-time was the worst, though. There were no distractions in the dark. Even Kristen's soft breathing was of little comfort. What she needed was a pair of arms around her. Luke's arms. His big bare bear-hug: that's what she needed. A real nose-squasher.

For a moment, she thought about their wedding day. It had been one of those sultry summer days that don't often visit North Yorkshire, giving all the women a rare opportunity to wear light summer dresses. Claudie could still see the scene in the church. It had been like viewing a great herbaceous border with all the pinks, purples, yellows and blues on display.

And then there'd been Luke. He'd looked so handsome in his dark tuxedo, just like a movie star. Claudie had gasped at her first sight of him as she'd walked down the aisle on Jimmy's arm. This was the man who lived in fleece all year round and whose idea of getting dressed up was to make sure there was no mud on his boots.

'You look like Cary Grant,' she'd whispered to him at the reception.

He'd grinned and shaken his head. Either he hadn't believed her or he'd had no idea who Cary Grant was. But then he'd whispered back, 'And you look like Audrey Hepburn in that dress.'

Claudie had beamed. He might not have known Audrey Hepburn from Katherine Hepburn, but he knew how to pay a compliment when it counted.

A hot tear slide down Claudie's face as she remembered. They'd had so little time to love each other, so little time to collect memories together. She thought of the wedding album and how she'd have loved to have pored over it with Luke in the years to come but how that joy had been denied her.

'Remember your Uncle Hugh dancing with Kristen and the way he kept trying to look down her dress!' she might have said.

'And when Daniel belched in the middle of his best man's speech!' Luke would have joked.

Who would Claudie remember these things with now? Lying in the dark, she felt like the only person in the world left to remember Luke. Nobody else had remembered, had they? There'd not been a single phone call or word of support today, and Claudie hadn't mentioned it to anyone. It was Luke's birthday. But what did a birthday become when you were no longer alive? And how could those left behind possibly pass by that day again without remembering?

Claudie turned over onto her side, her tear dying on the pillow underneath, and, in a voice barely above a whisper, she said, 'Happy birthday, Luke.'

CHAPTER 29

Simon had decided that Saturday mornings were kind of an odd time when you were on your own. You didn't have anyone to plan the weekend with, nobody to go shopping with, and no partner to get excited about visiting. It was a strange, hang-around- the-washing-machine kind of time. A well-I'd-better-pick-my-socks-up-off-the-bathroom-floor-because-nobody-else-is-going-to-do-it time. At least when Felicity had been there, there'd been somebody to talk to. Her constant griping was, at least, company.

Simon walked from room to room, too restless to stay in one for longer than a few minutes. The whole weekend stretched out before him like an enormous blank canvas, with no promise of shape or colour, and certainly no opportunity for him to get his brush out.

He shook his head at his crudely extended metaphor. He was going mad cooped up in the house by himself all day, every day. He had to get out. It was about time he took control of his life once more.

And that's when he'd decided to call round on Claudie. It would just be a casual thing: a just-happened-to-be-in-the-neighbourhood-and-wondered-if-I-could-spend-the-day-gazing-at-your-beautiful-face kind of call.

He was out of the door in less than five minutes, and down by the harbour in fifteen. He paused outside the supermarket for a few moments, wondering if he should nip in and grab a bunch of flowers. Was that terribly old-fashioned? Was he out of date? Or did women still go for that sort of thing?

He tried to imagine it from Claudie's point of view. She'd be pottering around the house, Judy Garland book open on a coffee table, and some old film playing on TV. Suddenly there'd be a knocking at her door. She'd go to open it and there, broad as daylight, sporting a crescent moon grin, would be Kristen's friend, what's-his-name? The one who'd tried to steal her book and hadn't had a single interesting thing to say when she'd been forced to walk home with him. And he'd got a ridiculous bunch of flowers with him.

What exactly did he want?

Simon shook his head. The whole thing was a terrible idea. He should just hang around the harbour for a while. The early May sunshine had brought the crowds out. He might even spot Jimmy out in the boat with the first of the year's tourists.

'Good heavens!'

Kristen's voice startled Claudie out of a very deep sleep, and it took a few minutes to work out why her best friend was in bed with her.

'Kris?'

'Don't you have curtains in this bedroom?'

'Of course I do, and they're lined too.'

'Then why is it so bright in here?' Kristen groaned.

Claudie struggled up onto one elbow and blinked hard. 'Try two bottles of wine and hardly any sleep.'

Kristen groaned. 'God, I feel terrible. My head feels like a granite boulder.'

'We've hardly slept. It must have been after five when we got back from the office.'

'And what's the time now?'

Claudie peered round at her alarm clock. 'Eleven.'

'Blimey.'

Claudie rubbed her eyes. They felt heavy and sore and in need of at least another four hours' sleep. 'At least we don't have to get up for anything,' she said, her head sinking back into her pillow.

No sooner were the words out of Claudie's mouth than there was a knock at the front door.

'I don't believe it,' she sighed.

'Who's that?' Kristen sat up, dramatically clinging to the duvet to her chest as if she was having an illicit affair and was about to be caught.

'Don't worry, it's probably just the postman with something that won't go through the letterbox. Like an envelope.'

'It's Jimmy. I just know it.'

'It won't be Jimmy. Just relax.'

'What should I do?'

'Go back to sleep. I am.'

'What? You're not going to answer the door?'

'Like this? You've got to be joking.' Claudie ruffled her hair which felt like a hedge which had been slept in by several restless hedgehogs.

There was another series of knocks at the door.

'Please, Claudes! You've got to answer it.'

'Why don't you?'

'*Me?* I don't want Jimmy seeing me like this. Anyway - it's your door.'

'All right.' Claudie grabbed her robe in resignation, and walked down the hall. She stopped short of the kitchen, peering round the door and looking at the silhouetted form behind the frosted glass. It wasn't the postman. And it wasn't Jimmy either. It was Simon.

What was he doing here? What could he possibly want? He had never been in her home before so he couldn't have left anything behind. She stood, her feet fixed to the floor as if they'd been stapled. What could she do?

'Claudes? Who is it?' Kristen's voice called through.

Claudie ran back through to the bedroom.

'It's Simon!'

'Simon? What's he doing here?'

'I don't know!'

'Why didn't you answer the door?'

Claudie bit her lip. 'Because I look a mess.'

'You're blushing!' Kristen said, grey eyes watchful as she sat upright in bed, suddenly very awake.

'I am not.'

'Yes you are! And very prettily too.'

'Shut up.' Claudie flopped down on the chair by her dressing table and picked up her hairbrush.

'You should have answered the door, Claudes.'

Claudie stared at her reflection. She *was* blushing. How ridiculous. 'I have no idea why he was here,' she said, more to herself than to Kristen.

'And you won't know now, will you?'

Claudie shook her head slowly. 'I don't suppose I will.'

'He likes you,' Kristen smiled. 'He probably just wanted to say hello.'

Claudie suddenly felt very guilty, but she was still rather annoyed at Kristen for having taken it upon herself to set her up with her ex. Although Kristen had maintained that the dinner had been perfectly innocent, Claudie knew how her friend worked.

It had always seemed rather strange that she'd never met Simon before. In a town as small as Whitby, where gossip spread quicker than warm butter, it was rare not to get the chance to vet your best friend's beau. Whilst Kristen had been dating Simon, she'd tried to get Claudie and Luke to make up a foursome on several occasions, but Luke had never been into that idea at all. 'I'm not sharing you with anyone,' he used to say, which had always made Claudie swell with pride.

So she'd never got to meet Simon the saint: the man who'd sounded so perfect but had failed to make Kristen swoon. They'd had a few dates where they'd talked endlessly but rarely kissed. Kristen had always said that he was more like a brother than a potential lover. No, Kristen had only ever had one love, and that was Jimmy.

Claudie watched as Kristen threw the bedcovers back. Despite the profusion of red hair and the determined face, Kristen looked so vulnerable as she sat with her bare legs sticking out from beneath her oversized T-shirt. If Jimmy could see her like that, he wouldn't be able to refuse her anything, Claudie thought.

'Mind if I have a shower?' Kristen asked.

''Course not. Towels are in the airing cupboard.'

Claudie dragged the hairbrush through her hair. Through the mirror, she could see the unmade bed. A bed so obviously slept in by two. She listened as the shower hissed into action and, for a moment, she could almost believe that it was Luke in there.

Somewhere between the supermarket and the harbour, Simon had decided to visit Claudie after all, minus the bunch of flowers. He had absolutely nothing to lose. Except his pride. And he'd felt sure she'd been in. In fact, he had almost been able to make out an indistinct figure at the kitchen door in a long red robe. Or had it been his over-active imagination?

Perhaps she'd been there and had recognised him? How awful if she hadn't wanted to answer the door to him. Or what if she'd had a man in there? That could explain her wearing a robe at eleven o'clock in the morning.

He'd walked all the way home, wishing he hadn't tried to add any colour to his blank canvas of a weekend.

CHAPTER 30

'You've got to stop worrying, Kris,' Claudie said as she made a light lunch. 'We're going to have a fantastic time in Paris, when we get back, Jimmy will be begging to have you home.'

Kristen gave a weak smile.

'You should really be going with Jimmy, you know.'

'I know,' Kristen admitted, 'but it wouldn't be right to be somewhere so beautiful with a man who doesn't love you.'

'Kris! Stop it!' Claudie said in a hands-on-hips manner. 'Jimmy loves you. How many times do you need to be told that?'

'If he loves me, why doesn't he want to marry me?'

'Marriage doesn't guarantee a happy ever after,' Claudie said, passing Kristen a cheese and Marmite bap.

'I know,' Kristen said, sighing the words out hopelessly, 'but it would make me feel so much better.'

Claudie knew what she meant. When Luke had proposed to her, Claudie had felt her whole body fill with warmth even though they'd been on a particularly windy shoulder of a mountain in the Lake District. It was the symbolism of the thing. The fact that somebody wanted to spend the rest of their lives with you, and that they wanted to show the rest of the world that too.

'Do you believe in fate?' Claudie suddenly asked.

Kristen's forehead wrinkled. 'I'm not sure.'

'Because it's something I've been thinking a lot about lately. I mean, I often wonder how it all happened, you know? How I started off in a small French town and ended up as a widow in Whitby? It sounds like the plot of a ridiculous play, don't you think? A farce, even, with banging doors, and too many characters and a plot that isn't really funny.'

'Oh, Claudes.'

'No, don't feel sorry for me, Kris. It's just that I often wonder what would have happened if I'd never left France. If mother hadn't sent me over here.' She stared out of the tiny kitchen window as if looking into an alternative future. 'I wouldn't have met Luke for a start. But do you think I might have met somebody else? And what then? I mean, am I fated as a person? Would it matter where I lived or who I met?'

'I don't follow.'

Claudie shook her head as she tried to make herself understood. 'I mean, do you think we're destined to live the same lives, no matter where we live in the world?'

'I really don't know.' Kristen looked up and suddenly her eyes widened.

'What is it?' Claudie asked.

'Is that Gene Kelly?' Kristen asked, nodding towards a small corkboard crammed with black and white postcards. 'Blimey. He's gorgeous.'

'You've only just noticed?'

'I couldn't help noticing really. You've got him in every room of the house. He's even in the bathroom!' Kristen laughed. 'It was a bit embarrassing standing completely naked in front of a life-sized poster of him.'

Claudie giggled. 'He keeps me company.'

Kristen looked at the postcard again, momentarily forgetting her cheese and Marmite bap. 'God! Just look at those arms.'

'I know.'

'And that cute smile. He's a real sweetheart.' Kristen beamed at Claudie. 'But not as cute as Simon.'

'Kris!'

'Just making an observation.'

'Yeah, right.'

'Come on though, you've got to admit that Simon's cute.'

'I'm not getting into that discussion,' Claudie said very firmly.

'I wonder why he was calling. He must think *you're* cute if he's calling round already. You'll have to ring him and find out.'

'I'm doing no such thing.'

'Why not?'

'Because I just don't do that sort of thing.'

'No, Claudes: heroines in fifties musicals might not do that sort of thing, but twenty-first century women have to.'

Claudie grimaced. 'I don't see-'

'Aren't you just a little bit curious?' Kristen asked. 'Gosh, if I had someone as cute as Simon chasing after me, I wouldn't run away.'

Kristen suddenly laughed. 'But I did run away, didn't I? Ah well,' she said, flapping her hands, 'we weren't meant to be. But you-'

'I just don't think it's right,' Claudie pleaded.

'Right or not, you're going to do it. In the next hour too.' Kristen got up and grabbed her coat from the back of the sofa.

'Where are you going?'

'To Simon's.'

'Why?'

'Because I need to talk to him.'

'Kris! Don't you dare go stirring things,' Claudie said, panic rising in her voice.

'I'm not! Don't worry. I just need a word. It's got nothing to do with you, believe me. But,' she said, peering across at Claudie with a very serious expression on her face, 'by the time I get to Simon's, I want to hear that you've called him. All right?'

'I don't think-'

'Claudes!'

'I'll think about it.'

'Good. Here's his number,' Kristen said, writing it down with a great grin on her face. 'Give him a call.'

Kristen hovered at the front door for a moment, something else obviously on her mind. 'Claudes?'

'What?'

'What was all that about angels last night?'

Claudie almost dropped the carton of milk she was holding.

'Were you just a little bit tipsy or do I have to start worrying about you again?'

Claudie put the milk carton on the draining board out of harm's way. 'You don't have to start worrying about me again.'

'Are you sure?'

Claudie nodded. 'Now get on out. I'm not going to ring Simon in front of you. And don't forget your bap.'

Kristen blew her a kiss from the door before disappearing out into the yard, bap in hand.

As soon as she was out of sight, Claudie looked down at the phone number, the paper trembling in her hand like a leaf about to take flight. Was she really going to do this or had she just been humouring Kristen? She looked down at the six numbers. Just six numbers divided them. All she had to do was pick up the phone and dial them. It was easy, wasn't it?

She walked through to the living room and sat down by the telephone. No, she thought, it wasn't easy at all. The telephone sat there, white and fat like a sleeping cat. But would it bite her if she dared to pick it up?

Taking a deep breath, she picked up the receiver and dialled before she had a chance to change her mind. He could be on the internet, of course. No. It was ringing. Or out? He might not have gone straight home after calling by hers.

'Hello?'

Claudie felt her heart skip a beat. He *had* gone straight home.

'Simon? It's Claudie.'

'Clawwdeee!'

'Hello,' she said, feeling nervous and excited all at once.

'How are you?'

'Fine. I'm fine,' she stumbled, twisting the telephone cord around her index finger until she almost cut off her circulation.

'Good.'

God. What was she going to say now? 'Simon? Did you call round before?' She rolled her eyes up to the ceiling of her living room.

'You were in?'

She stumbled over her own thoughts. 'Ye-es. Sorry. I didn't quite make it to the door.'

There was a pause. Claudie guessed it to be an awkward one.

'Don't worry,' he said at last.

'I had a late night,' she said, and almost clamped her hand to her mouth. That sounded just awful. 'Me and Kristen. *We* had a late night.'

There was another awkward pause, and then Claudie thought of a way out of her dilemma. 'Was it Kristen you called for?'

'No. Why?'

'Because she's here. You know, because of Jimmy.' Claudie suddenly bit her tongue. Perhaps he didn't know.

'What's happened?'

'They had a row. I think it's just the usual thing, but she's pretty upset.'

'Of course.'

There was another pause.

'So, Simon?'

'Yes?'

'Why did you call round?' Claudie cringed at her question. Did it sound too confrontational?

'I was,' he began and then cleared his throat, causing Claudie to pull away from the phone for a second. 'I was going to ask if you were doing anything this weekend.'

Claudie blinked. She didn't know what to say. 'You mean other than sleep and get over drinking too much wine last night?'

'Yes. Did you want to go out?' There was no hesitation or throat clearing this time.

'Yes,' Claudie replied, shocking herself for being so direct.

'Good.'

Please, Claudie thought, don't let there be another pause or I might change my mind.

'How about tonight? We could go somewhere for dinner,' Simon suggested.

'Okay,' Claudie said, before remembering that she was meant to be Kristen-sitting.

'Great!'

Claudie felt like laughing. He sounded so happy.

'I'll call round at about half past seven?'

'Fine,' Claudie said. 'See you later.'

'Bye.'

Claudie put the phone down and began to panic. She had only six hours to get ready.

CHAPTER 31

She'd said yes! And the word had practically flown from her mouth. Simon sat down. First the Paris trip and now this. Life was simply too stunning for words.

Paris and Claudie. Now there was a thought. What a shame he couldn't link the two of those together. He shook his head. She'd only agreed to go out to dinner with him. She'd probably only said yes because she didn't like cooking. Or maybe she'd grown tired of watching old movies. The possibilities were endless, and they probably had little to do with romance. But he could hope, couldn't he?

He stretched back on the sofa, kicking his shoes off and not bothering to pick them up and place them neatly in the hallway. He could do that now Felicity wasn't around, and he liked it. For a moment, he wondered if Claudie had any feminine quirks such as neatness, but he dismissed the thought as soon as it entered his head. No, she was perfect, or that's what he'd let himself believe for a while. She wouldn't yell if he left a trail of lights on round the house like Blackpool illuminations, or if there were still breakfast dishes on the table at dinnertime.

He was just losing himself in a world of domestic bliss where dishes washed themselves, and shirts ironed themselves when his doorbell went. His heart skipped a beat until reality kicked in and told him that Claudie couldn't possibly have made it to his front door, even if she'd had a private plane.

He stuffed his feet into his shoes, just in case his mother had decided to make an impromptu visit and noticed that his socks were more hole than wool. But it wasn't his mother. It was Kristen.

'Hey!' He ushered her inside, noticing the red-rimmed eyes that had one of two sources: heavy drinking or heavy crying and, since Claudie's phone call, he happened to know that Kristen had succumbed to both.

'Hope you don't mind me calling round unannounced?' Kristen said.

'When have I ever minded?'

Kristen gave him a smile but he could tell it was forced, and then he remembered what Claudie had said.

'Come on through. It's time we had a talk.'

Kristen nodded as if she'd worked that out for herself.

Simon knew he made a mean cup of tea and, once two steaming mugs had been placed side by side on the table in the living room, he thought he'd better start making his apologies.

'Look, Kris. If your row with Jimmy has got anything to do with this trip to Paris, I'll be happy to call the whole thing off.'

'Paris?' she said in surprise. 'It's got nothing to do with Paris.'

'But I thought he'd found out about the weekend?'

'No! *God, no!* He has no idea about it. And you mustn't say anything either.'

'I won't,' Simon assured her. 'So what's happened?'

Kristen sipped her tea by way of delaying her answer. Simon didn't want to ask her if it was the usual old argument but he had a feeling that it was and, the longer Kristen took to answer, the more he suspected it.

'I've left him,' she said at last in a very small but very calm voice.

Simon almost spilt his tea down the front of his shirt. 'What - really?'

'Really.'

He weighed her up for a moment. After all, there were degrees of leaving. There was Kristen-leaving and Felicity-leaving, and Kristen-leaving didn't usually amount to more than a night's separation from Jimmy whilst Felicity-leaving involved fleecing the house of everything of value, and a little bit else besides.

'What happened?'

Kristen gave Simon the Technicolor version of Friday evening, and he made all the appropriate noises at the appropriate times until Kristen had purged herself, and they were left shaking their heads at each other.

'Anyway,' Kristen said at length, pushing her hair away from her face and smiling brightly at him, 'did Claudie call you?'

Simon smiled, partly because he was relieved that they'd changed the subject, and partly at the memory of the phone call with Claudie.

'*Simon?*' Kristen goaded. 'She did, didn't she?'

Simon's smile grew into an obscenely large grin. 'Yes.'

'And?' Kristen leant forward like an inquisitive chat show host.

'And we're going out tonight.'

'NO!'

'YES!'

'That's great!'

'It is, isn't it?'

Kristen nodded. 'So what did you say to her? Or did she ask you out?'

'Kris!'

'Okay! It's none of my business,' she agreed, probably making a mental note to quiz Claudie about it later on, Simon thought mischievously.

'But you like her, right?'

'Of course I like her! I wouldn't be exchanging an evening alone watching family quiz shows if I didn't like her.'

'So I might have got something right for a change?'

'I'm not going to answer that - yet.'

'Okay,' Kristen said. 'Mind if I use the bathroom?'

Kristen nipped upstairs feeling rather pleased with herself for having introduced Simon to Claudie. Her suspicions had been correct. They were just so right for each other.

As she caught sight of her reflection in the bathroom cabinet, Kristen suddenly thought of how much fun she'd have telling Jimmy about it all. She loved proving him wrong, but she wasn't able to tell him, was she? She'd be spending another night at Claudie's. Alone too, if Claudie was out late with Simon.

As she looked around the bathroom, she noticed that there was a distinct lack of female. There were no fancy bath salts or feminine bottles of lotion; there were no fluffy make-up bags or soaps on ropes. And then a thought occurred to her. What would the bathroom in Cabin Cottage look like if she removed all of her things? She tried to imagine Jimmy' toothbrush standing alone in the blue enamel mug, but it was too sad to contemplate.

She was just coming out of the bathroom when she heard the front doorbell ring. Watching from the top of the landing as Simon opened the front door, she couldn't quite see who it was. It wasn't until she heard a familiar voice that her stomach flipped in horror.

'Is that what you call a greeting?' a loud, lordly voiced asked.

'Felicity?'

An arm pushed past Simon, and Kristen watched as Felicity charged into the house, suitcase in hand.

'Well?' Felicity asked, expectancy fuelling her voice. 'Aren't you going to welcome me home?'

Simon watched in stunned silence as Felicity brought her suitcase into the front room. She sat down on the sofa but not before brushing a few biscuit crumbs onto the floor and plumping the cushions. She looked pale, and had maybe even lost a few pounds since he'd last seen her.

For a split second, Simon almost felt sorry for her, but he could still see that cold edge to her. She practically exuded coldness as if wearing it as a perfume.

He sat on the only other chair in the room and stared hard at Felicity. He had about a hundred things he wanted to say to her, and none of them were very pleasant, but he waited for her to speak first. He couldn't wait to hear this particular explanation, and could only hope that she was here to return the money she'd stolen from him. He was in dire need of it at the moment.

'What have you been doing with yourself?' she started clumsily.

Simon gave her a blank look. 'It's Saturday. I've not been doing anything.'

'That's not what I meant.'

Simon had a feeling that he knew exactly what she meant. How much money was he earning now? That's what she wanted to know, and he wasn't about to tell her. She'd taken enough of what was his already.

'Has your business taken off?' she said, her tone sounding exasperated.

'It's doing okay.'

She eyed him for a moment, lining up the next question in her head. 'So you're doing all right now?'

'I'm getting by,' he said, being as polite and evasive as possible.

There was a moment's pause as they looked at each other, and Simon thought that he had said all that he wanted to this woman. Their business was done. It was over. History.

'Well if you're not going to make me a cup of tea, *I am*,' Felicity said, suddenly getting up and walking through to the kitchen. Simon didn't bother to follow; instead he remained sat down and counted to three.

One. Two. Thr-

'Bloody hell, Simon. You could have done the washing up!'

Simon closed his eyes. This wasn't happening. This was a nightmare from which he'd awake at any second.

'Pssst!'

There, he thought. That was his alarm clock.

'Psssssssst!'

Although he'd never heard it make a noise like that before.

'Simon!'

He opened his eyes. It was Kristen. He'd forgotten all about her. He got up and walked quickly to the door whilst Felicity was cursing in the kitchen at the state of the place.

'What's she doing back here?' Kristen whispered angrily.

'I don't know yet. She hasn't told me.'

'Why didn't you just tell her to f-off?'

'She didn't give me a chance.'

'God, Simon! Are you a man or a mouse? Give you a chance! Don't you remember what she did to you?'

'Of course I bloody remember! Just give me some time to work it out.'

'What do you need to work out? She's a bitch.'

'Shush!' Simon waved his hand in the air, terrified Felicity might hear them.

'What perfect timing, as usual. What are you going to do?'

Simon scratched his head and frowned. 'Try and find out what she's done with my bloody money, and then get rid of her.'

'I mean about Claudie?'

'Claudie? Bloody hell! What's the time?'

'Time you should be getting ready for your date with Claudie.'

Simon rolled his eyes. 'Kris, you've got to help me.'

'Didn't I just know it? And I came here thinking you could help me!'

They smiled hopelessly at one another. 'I really don't want to let Claudie down.'

'And I don't want you to let her down. I feel responsible for all this.'

'So what are we going to do?'

Kristen sighed, peeking through the gap in the door to make sure Felicity was still ensconced in the kitchen. 'You sort Felicity out, and I'll explain to Claudie. Just make sure you get rid of her this time - don't let her wangle her way back in with you.'

'I won't,' Simon said, pushing Kristen towards the door.

'Because I know what you're like. You're a soft touch.'

'Just what I needed to hear.' He opened the door and they stood looking at each other for a moment. 'Kris - Claudie-'

'I'll tell her, don't worry.'

'Thanks.' Simon closed the door as quietly as he could and returned to the living room just as Felicity was walking back through with the tea. He quickly picked up his previous cup and that of Kristen's before Felicity could spot the great red lipstick mark on it, and took them through to the kitchen.

When he returned, Felicity had curled up on the sofa as if she'd never been away, her face like a Siamese cat: beautiful and cruel. Should he shout at her? Should he rant and rave about how much she'd hurt him? Should he mention the mammoth withdrawal from their joint account? Or should he listen to what she had to say? If he was perfectly honest, he couldn't wait to hear her pathetic excuses. After the months he'd spent trying to work out what had gone wrong between them, and coming to the conclusion, via dozens of conversations with Kristen, that it had nothing to do with him, he couldn't wait to hear the lies Felicity had had time to concoct.

Yes, he thought, he'd listen. And *then* he'd throw her out.

But nothing could have prepared him for what she said in a voice as cold and still as a frozen canal.

'I'm pregnant.'

CHAPTER 32

It was just after seven when Kristen arrived back at Claudie's cottage. She knocked on the door and was surprised by the speed at which it was opened.

Claudie stood in the doorway, her little black skirt and black velvet jumper on. Her face was glowing with make-up and her hair was up in curlers.

'Kris!'

'Hi, Claudes.'

'I can't stop, I'm afraid,' Claudie said as she walked through to the living room, fixing a pair of silver hoops in her ears. 'Did Simon tell you? We're going out.' Claudie suddenly stopped. 'Is he with you?'

'No,' Kristen said, her face pale and grim. 'He's with Felicity.'

Simon looked across the expanse of living room at the cold eyes that stared expectantly at him. Had he heard her right? He *had*, hadn't he? It was only two words but they were enough to change the course of a lifetime.

He looked across at her. She looked very beautiful in her own, icy way: her vanilla blonde hair cropped short around her heart-shaped face, and her pale eyes wide with expectation. Yes, Simon thought, she expects something from me.

He realised that it wasn't so long ago that he'd wanted to marry this woman. He'd thought they'd had a future together. But all those thoughts and dreams had evaporated when she'd walked out nearly seven months before.

Seven months. The thought struck him singularly and powerfully. He was no mathematician, but a baby only took nine months to cook, didn't it? He looked across at Felicity's stomach. It looked more like an ironing board than a space hopper.

Felicity seemed to be following his train of thought.

'I'm eight weeks pregnant,' she explained.

'Eight weeks?'

She nodded.

Simon rubbed a hand over his chin. For a few dreadful moments, his mind had spiralled away from logical thought and he'd sincerely believed that she was carrying his child. But this revelation put a whole new slant on things.

He began tentatively. 'So, who is-'

'Does it matter?'

Simon frowned. 'Does it matter who the father is? Well, call me old-fashioned, but I rather think it does.'

Felicity responded by grinding her teeth. 'We broke up. It didn't work out, okay? Happy?'

'I'm happy,' he said, unable to resist the opportunity. 'But you aren't it, would seem.'

'Look,' her voice suddenly took on a more gentle timbre, and Simon knew at once that she was in seduction mode. 'I've made a mistake. I thought the grass was greener. I don't know what I was thinking.'

Simon wanted to laugh at the clichés that were pouring out of her mouth, but he wasn't that cruel. Or was he? After all, *she'd* been that cruel. She hadn't spared a thought for how he might feel so why should he now?

Something clicked and whirred in his brain. Something which reeked of revenge. 'And what is it you want from me?' he asked, deciding to be absolutely honest with her from the start.

'I want to come back, Si.'

Simon winced. He'd forgotten how sharp she could make his name sound. It wasn't the friendly way Kristen said it, or the slightly exotic way he imagined Claudie would shorten his name to. It was short and spiky and rather sinister, because he knew she only used it when she wanted something from him.

'I want to come back,' she repeated. And it wasn't a question uttered in a moment of humble contrition; it was a simple statement.

Claudie didn't say a word. Instead, she raised her hands to her head and began to untwist her curlers one by one. It was the singlest, saddest movement Kristen had ever seen.

'Claudes-'

'No!' Claudie interrupted quietly but with great force. 'Don't say anything.' And she walked through to the bedroom, her glossy brown curls bouncing happily around her sad face.

Kristen sat down on the edge of the sofa bed and sighed heavily. She looked around the tiny front room which was even smaller than that of Cabin Cottage. Her eyes caught a couple of MGM videos lying on the floor. She shook her head slowly. Life was a mess not a movie. There were no happy endings here, none that she could see at any rate. MGM were the biggest liars ever. They should have been fined years ago for painting the world in colours that just didn't appear into the ordinary person.

Kristen gave the films her best Medusa look knowing that if they'd been her videos, she'd have got a kitchen knife and slashed them. But they weren't, so she cried instead.

Claudie sat down at her dressing table, but she didn't dare look at her reflection in the mirror. She didn't want to see what she'd turned herself into for Simon. She knew she should never have gone along with it. What had she been thinking of? She was furious with herself for imagining that she was ready for all this again, but what hurt the most was that she'd been so excited about it all. She'd been thinking of Simon, and not Luke and, now that it had all fallen through, she couldn't help thinking that she was somehow being punished for attempting to be happy again.

'What are you doing, Claudie?' a little voice asked her, but she didn't answer. She wasn't in the mood to pander to her inner voice.

'Claudie?' the voice came again. And it wasn't her voice. Her eyes attempted to come out of blur mode and focussed on her jewellery box lid where Jalisa was sitting.

'Hello!' Jalisa said, her eyes big and bright like gemstones. 'You okay?'

'What are you doing here?'

'That's not much of a welcome,' Jalisa answered in a quietly scolding tone.

'I mean,' Claudie bit her lip and tried again, 'I thought my home was out of bounds.'

'Well, you see, it isn't - all the time. Just *most* of the time. It's special occasions only.'

Claudie stared at her. 'And I'm having a special occasion now, am I?'

Jalisa blinked hard and nodded. 'Yes.'

'I see.'

'It's all right,' Jalisa said softly. 'Everyone has special occasions, and what's the point of having a flight if it can't accommodate them?'

'Please,' Claudie began, 'I don't think I can cope with any angel philosophy tonight. I don't mean to sound ungrateful-'

'But you're going to anyway?' Jalisa suggested, and they both smiled.

'Sorry,' Claudie said, secretly pleased that Jalisa cared enough about her to know when she needed some company of the non-human variety.

'That's better,' Jalisa said, seeing Claudie's slight change of mood. 'I'd hate to sit here and be ignored.'

'I'd never ignore you,' Claudie said, 'it's just I don't feel much like talking tonight. Do you know what I mean?'

Jalisa nodded. 'I do,' she said, and with such conviction that Claudie felt she wanted to know more.

'Really?' Claudie said, suddenly aware that she hadn't been paying enough attention to the needs of her flight. It would seem that they needed to talk too. Angelling was obviously a two-way friendship.

Jalisa sighed. 'Only this week, back at you know where, I was let down by somebody.'

'What - a boyfriend?' Claudie asked.

Jalisa gave a little smile. 'Not really. But he definitely has potential. If only he had the time.'

'You were meant to go out together?' Claudie looked puzzled as Jalisa nodded.

'You still get to date, you know. It doesn't all stop because of a little thing called death. Anyway, we weren't talking about me. We were talking about you.'

'I don't remember us talking about me.'

'Claudie!' Jalisa reprimanded. 'You can't run away from this.'

'Run away from what, exactly?'

'*This!* This situation that you're in.'

'I don't under-'

'Don't you dare say you don't understand! Don't you *dare!*'

Claudie looked down at her in surprise, and with a certain amount of admiration too. She liked Jalisa. She made a great angel forerunner, and Claudie really couldn't think how she'd ever coped before the arrival of the flight.

'Right,' Jalisa began again, confident that she now had Claudie's full co-operation, 'we're going to talk about this, even if it takes all night.'

'It can't take all night,' Claudie sighed. 'Kristen's in the living room.'

'I know. So we'd better make a start, hadn't we?'

'I suppose so.' Claudie rested her head in her hands, absent-mindedly fingering her fat sausage curls.

'Okay,' Jalisa said, sitting back on Claudie's jewellery box, forsaking the urge to test its lid in a quick tap-dance routine. 'So what's been happening?'

Claudie closed her eyes for a second, half-wishing she could shut it all away and do her best to forget about it, but Jalisa wouldn't allow that, so she began. 'Dr Lynton's been going on about me reinvesting in new relationships: that it's time to move on. And I believed him.' Claudie's eyes were sparkling with tears the size of Christmas baubles.

'Claudie,' Jalisa said quickly 'it was never going to be easy, and you can't blame yourself for taking his advice. It was good advice!'

'Was it?' Claudie didn't sound as if she believed Jalisa. 'Then why has it all ended so disastrously?'

'Has it?'

'Simon asked me out and I said yes,' she said, making it sound as if she'd started World War III single-handedly.

'Well, that's *good!* What's disastrous about that?' Jalisa asked.

'He had to cancel because he's old girlfriend's shown up.'

'That's not so good,' Jalisa admitted.

'I trusted him. And I trusted myself to go out with him.'

Jalisa gazed up at her and nodded slowly. 'Claudie, it just hasn't worked out *this* time. I'm sure there's a good explanation. Simon is a good man, isn't he? He hasn't done this to hurt you. He's probably as upset about it as you are. Just give it time.'

'Time,' Claudie said the word quietly. 'It's all about time, isn't it?'

'Yes it is, so you've got to be patient.'

'I don't think I can do patient,' Claudie said, feeling the horrible hollowness that sometimes filled her heart.

'Of course you can! Just don't give up.'

Don't give up. Claudie wanted to write the words down on poster-sized paper just so she could tear them up. Those three simple words: so easy to say but so damned hard to put into action.

'What is it?' Jalisa asked, seeing Claudie's faraway look.

Claudie shrugged. 'I feel so numbed by everything sometimes, as if I'm not really living at all.'

'That's only natural,' Jalisa said. 'I know that's not what you want to hear, but it does get easier, believe me. Everybody who loses someone they love goes through this.'

'It's hard to believe that other people feel like I'm feeling now. This pain seems so completely exclusive to me,' Claudie said. 'Does that make sense?'

Jalisa nodded. 'Oh, yes.'

A light knocking on the bedroom door broke into their conversation.

'Listen,' Jalisa said, 'I'd better be going. Will you be okay?'

Claudie nodded. She didn't want to let Jalisa go but realised that she couldn't keep her with Kristen in the house. 'Thanks for coming, Jalisa.'

'That's all right.'

'See you on Monday?'

'You bet.' And she was gone.

'Claudes?' a rather husky Kristen called from the hall.

Claudie got up and opened the door.

'Claudes? Are you all right?'

'I'm fine,' she said. 'But you look terrible!'

Kristen suddenly sobbed. 'I feel dreadful.'

'What? Why?'

'As if it wasn't enough to mess my own life up, I had to go and mess yours and Simon's too.'

'You haven't! What are you on about?'

Kristen's lower lip did a great jelly wobble as she tried her best to stop crying. 'I'm sorry, Claudes.'

'There's nothing to be sorry about.' Claudie gave her a hug, because she needed one as much as Kristen did.

Kristen sniffed loudly in Claudie's ear. 'I think I'll have an early night before I cause any more trouble. If that's okay?' she added, as if suddenly remembering that the bed wasn't actually her own.

'Of course it's all right. But,' Claudie said guardedly, 'there's one condition.'

Kristen looked worried for a moment, as if she was about to get a scolding. 'What's the condition?'

'You don't hog all the duvet like last night!'

CHAPTER 33

After Felicity had choreographed an Oscar-worthy breakdown in the front room, Simon was forced to change his mind about throwing her out on the streets. Even as he told her she could stay, he realised he'd probably regret it, but it would also give him time to work out what to do.

He did, however, make sure she understood that, as long as she was staying, or as *short* as she was staying if he had anything to do with it, she was sleeping alone in the bedroom at the back of the house; the room she'd previously monopolised as her walk-in wardrobe.

As he'd taken her suitcase upstairs, Simon couldn't help feeling just a little bit smug as he imagined her unpacking in the tiny room. What was that wondering phrase? What comes around goes around? He wasn't usually a vindictive, but he was quite enjoying the feeling of power he now had and, although Felicity was her usual hard-nosed self, she did seem to be aware that Simon wasn't prepared to take any nonsense.

He spent the rest of the evening carefully avoiding Felicity, aware of her presence yet refusing to acknowledge it fully. And then, after shouting a curt goodnight, he went to bed.

The main bedroom was at the front of the house, and the combination of street lighting and unlined curtains meant that it never got completely dark. But that wasn't the reason he couldn't fall asleep. He lay staring up at the ceiling trying to make out faces in the tatty old paper as if he were cloud gazing.

Even though he had it in mind to hatch some wonderful revenge, he knew in his heart of hearts that he had failed already. He should never have taken pity on Felicity, and he certainly shouldn't have let her stay the night. But what was he meant to do? She was probably bluffing about being pregnant, but he had no way of disproving her, even if she looked as pregnant as a paintbrush.

He turned over and pushed his face deep into his pillow to muffle a pained yelp. As he lay, pleading for sleep to rescue him, he heard the bedroom door creak open. It was one of the odd jobs he was always meaning to do round the house, but now he thanked the good lord that he'd never got round to buying any WD40.

'Simon?'

Simon lay stock still, his eyes shut in a pretence of sleep.

'Are you awake?' Felicity asked. 'I can't sleep.'

Before she even bothered to find out if he was really asleep or not, she'd whipped the bed covers back and had climbed in next to him.

'Woah!' Simon yelled into the semi-darkness. 'What do you think you're doing?'

'I'm cold,' she complained, snuggling further down into the double bed they'd once shared quite amicably. But this was not her bed any more.

'For God's sake!'

'I only want a little cuddle. Come on,' she said, moving up closer so that he could feel her long, silky legs against his. 'You're so cold,' she whispered, her breath hot in his ear.

He didn't feel especially cold; in fact he was burning up but, when he tried to push her away, she coiled her right leg around him like an amorous snake and, before he could protest again, her lips clamped his in a colossal kiss.

Her hands worked their way down his body which, rather annoyingly, was starting to come alive. But he forced his mind away from the physical as he tried to think about how she had treated Pumpkin; how she had walked out on him with his life savings, how she had the nerve to come back and expected him to pick up the shattered pieces of her life.

And, before it was too late, he found his voice.

'Get out, Felicity - *now!*' he bellowed. At first, she was too shocked to move but, after she realised he wasn't likely to be persuaded, he watched as she rose up from the bedclothes, resting her body weight on her elbows and showing that she still didn't wear anything to bed. He tried not to look. 'Out!'

'Don't be such a bore, Si.'

'We'll talk in the morning.'

There was a moment's pause as they stared at each other in the semi-darkness.

'I'm not moving,' Felicity said in a quiet voice.

Simon felt his heartbeat accelerate, but he was determined to stay in control of the situation. He wasn't going to get involved in one of her silly little games. He was the one calling the shots now, he reminded himself.

'Fine,' he said, calmly getting out of bed and walking across the room. 'I'll sleep in the other room, then.' And he left her alone in the bed, smiling to himself as he crossed the landing and locked the door of the smallest bedroom behind him.

If she thought, for a moment, that she could follow him into a single bed, she'd be disappointed.

CHAPTER 34

'I don't know if I can do it,' Kristen said, pushing a heap of pale chocolate krispies round her cereal bowl and examining the brown milk with intense eyes.

'Do what?' Claudie said, biting into a slice of toast.

'Spend another day away from Jimmy.' She sighed. 'And another night.'

'You miss him?'

Kristen put her bowl down and looked up at Claudie. 'Oh, Claudie. I don't know how you coped.'

Claudie looked down at the black and white floor of the kitchen. The black was faded and scuffed and the white was really more like grey.

'I didn't cope,' she said, 'I just existed.' She shrugged her shoulders as she tried to remember if there was some sort of formula she could pass on to Kristen. 'You become the most basic of creatures. You breathe and sleep. Sometimes you get the urge to eat, but not very often. You become somebody else.' She switched her gaze from floor to ceiling. 'It's like there's a little person deep inside you who takes over the controls.'

Kristen nodded as if Claudie's words were the wisest she'd ever heard.

'I feel so miserable without Jimmy,' she confessed. And it's making me more miserable because I know my situation isn't *anything* compared to yours.'

Claudie pulled a stool up next to Kristen at the breakfast bar.

'How do you continue?' Kristen asked.

Claudie gave a tiny half-smile as she sat down. 'You should never underestimate the will to live. It's more powerful than you realise.'

They looked at each other with the kind of peace and understanding born from years of friendship.

'But life can be such a bitch,' Kristen said.

Claudie nodded. 'And sometimes you feel you're not really living at all. Those first few months after Luke died were so bleak, so black, that I felt I'd died as well but, gradually, it did start to get better - not much - but it was no longer so black. It was more like a strange kind of twilight.' Claudie's eyes misted over as if she were experiencing it again. 'You can see life going on around you - just like it always did but, somehow, you're not quite ready to be a part of it again,' she said, remembering Gene Kelly's words to her in the grounds of St Mary's.

'And it doesn't help when you've got bullies for friends - who are always trying to get you to do things you don't want to do. When I think of all the terrible things I must have said to you -'

'You were wonderful, Kris. The best friend anyone could hope to have.'

Kristen swallowed hard. 'Life's a bitch, isn't it?'

'Sometimes,' Claudie agreed, 'but we've got Paris to look forward to, haven't we?'

Kristen nodded, but the ensuing silence gave the impression that neither of them thought it was that big a deal in the scheme of things.

A strange plop from outside grabbed their attention, and Claudie and Kristen turned round to see that a huge dropping had been fired at the kitchen window by what must have been an enormous seagull.

'How on earth do they manage to do that?' Claudie gasped, walking over to the window and staring at it in undisguised horror.

'It's meant to be lucky, isn't it?' Kristen said, joining her at the window.

'Not for the poor sod who has to clean it up.'

They looked at each other and, before they knew it, they were laughing.

What was it that made Sunday the most boring day of the week, Simon wondered? Even having a pregnant ex-girlfriend around the house didn't seem to liven things up.

As he booted his computer up, he thought of the night before and how he'd not been able to sleep after leaving Felicity in his bed, even with the door of the little bedroom locked behind him. He'd turned on the bedside lamp and had stared around the room at Felicity's things.

Her double-decker bus of a suitcase lay open on the floor and she'd already managed to hang most of her clothes away in the single wardrobe in the room. Where were her other clothes, he wondered, and had she made plans to have them sent over? She'd better not have.

He peered into the suitcase. He wasn't normally a nosy person, but his eyes were drawn to the strange collection of things she had in there. There were three pairs of strappy heels that were just perfect for walking round Whitby; a hairdryer the size of a small car; and three huge photo albums. No wonder her case had almost pulled his arm out when he'd hoisted it up the stairs.

It hadn't taken him long to dip into the photo albums. At first, it had been to look for clues as to what Felicity had been up to since she'd left. But there were no new boyfriends to be found, and no signs of any candidates for father of the baby; only photos of him. Had Felicity left it out hoping that he'd find it?

The whole of their life together was in those three large photo albums. There was the day they'd moved into the house. How happy they'd been, and how funny everything had seemed back then, from the damp on the kitchen wall to the boiler that thumped whenever you wanted more than a cupful of hot water.

He turned a few pages and there they were on their nasty package holiday to Spain with Felicity in an amethyst swimming costume at the side of the pool, and Simon with an ice-cream the size of his head.

They'd been happy back then. Life had been one big adventure, one big laugh. So what had gone wrong? Where had all the fun gone? Had all the love simply drained away as if some emotional plug had been pulled?

As he'd closed the final photo album, he'd felt something inside him soften towards Felicity. As absurd as it seemed, he could feel a few maybes floating around his head. Maybe. It was the most dangerous of words.

Now, he looked out of his study window as an elderly couple walked passed on their way to church. He looked at their frail arms, intertwined and delicate as December twigs, and a sadness enclosed his heart. Would he ever walk arm in arm with somebody on a Sunday morning?

And then the word maybe popped into his head again. Maybe Felicity really was the one?

He turned back to look at his desk and his eyes narrowed as he saw Felicity standing in the doorway. She looked pale and tired, her long limbs milky and bare in an insubstantial dressing gown. How long had she been standing there watching him? Had she been able to read his thoughts?

She walked into the room and he could smell her perfume. She hadn't got dressed but she was wearing lipstick and perfume, and the scent reminded him of the very first time he'd seen her.

'Simon,' she whispered, extending a hand out to stroke his face.

It felt good. It felt like the first time. Maybe it was?

He closed his eyes and let her kiss him.

CHAPTER 35

Back at work on Monday, Kristen was waiting for Claudie to go to lunch. She was certainly taking her time: faffing about with Mr Bartholomew's booklets, closing down all her files, straightening her in tray, and fiddling with the contents of her handbag. Any more time-consuming nonsense and Kristen was going to have to march over there and physically propel her out of the office.

It wasn't that she didn't love her friend dearly. She did. Which was exactly why she wanted rid of her: to enable her to make her phone call to Simon to see what was happening with the trip to Paris.

'Sure you won't come with me for a sandwich?' Claudie called over to Kristen, completely oblivious to her friend's train of thoughts.

'No! Er - thanks. I've got to finish this letter before lunch. Mr Simpson's orders.'

'Okay. See you later, then,' Claudie smiled, throwing her bag over her shoulder and leaving the office.

'Thank goodness for that,' Kristen said under her breath, picking up the phone and dialling Simon's number. She'd been longing to hear what had been happening with him and Felicity all weekend, but hadn't been able to ring in private from Claudie's.

Listening to the ringing tone, she bit her lip, trying to anticipate what he would say. With any luck, he'd have sent Felicity on her way the minute she had left his house on Saturday. But, if he'd done that, surely he would have called Claudie to apologise?

'Hello?'

'Simon?'

'Kristen?'

'Yes. Look, I'm at work, so I can't talk for long.'

'Neither can I.'

'Why?' Kristen asked, fear coursing through her body.

'Felicity's upstairs.'

'What do you mean, she's upstairs? What the hell's going on, Simon?' Kristen hissed, turning her back on Angela who was peering round from her computer at the far end of the office.

'It's complicated.'

'Don't give me that old cliché!'

'It's not a cliché. There are things we need to sort out. It's not as simple-'

'Bollocks!'

'Kris!'

'God!' Kristen gave a fiery sigh. 'You haven't slept with her, have you?' There was a moment's pause. A pause which seemed to indicate Simon's guilt. 'Simon?' She could hear him cursing quietly at the other end of the phone.

'I didn't sleep with her,' he all but shouted.

Kristen closed her eyes. Why didn't she believe him? Because she knew Felicity? Because Simon didn't sound at all like Simon at the moment?

'What about Claudie? How do you think she's feeling about this?'

'Oh God.'

'She was really upset on Saturday night.'

'Was she?'

'Of course she was, you bastard. You're the first date she's had since Luke, and you went and stuffed it up.'

'I didn't do it on purpose. And don't call me a bastard!'

Kristen bit her lip. 'I'm sorry. I didn't mean to. But it doesn't change the fact that you've probably set her back a fair few months on the emotional healing scale.'

'This is terrible,' he groaned.

'Yes, it is. I trusted you with this, Si, and only you can sort it out. So get sorting!' She was about to hang up but remembered something. 'What about Paris? What are you going to do about that, then?'

'Don't worry. Paris is still on. I'll sort things out before then.'

'You're damned right you will.' Kristen had noticed that Angela had suddenly found an important job to do just in front of her desk, so she sent her a narrow-eyed glare.

'Well,' Simon sighed, 'you've had your turn at telling me off - what's happening with you and Jimmy?'

'What?'

'Have you two made up yet?'

'No,' Kristen said.

'Well it looks as if *you've* got some things to sort out too.'

'I don't think they can be sorted,' she said.

Simon suddenly whispered into the phone. 'I've got to go, Kris. Felicity's coming downstairs.'

'Okay,' she said, her voice sounding loose and pathetic.

She put the phone down and stared across her desk. Angela had returned to her own and had used her sense in not questioning Kristen about her call.

In truth, Kristen half wished that she hadn't called Simon. It had brought Jimmy to the forefront of her mind again.

How could she sort things out? She was the one who'd done the walking out, so surely it was up to her to make things up? Or had walking out meant that the ball was now in his court? It was all so complicated.

'Right,' Angela said from her retreat at the other side of the office, 'I'm off to lunch.'

Kristen nodded and watched as she walked towards the door, her hideously large diamond engagement ring seeming to leave a wake of light behind her. Kristen drummed her ringless fingers on her mousemat and stared down at the telephone. Should she? Could she? And, if she could, what exactly would she say?

She picked the receiver up and dialled the familiar numbers. Monday lunchtime. He might well be down at the harbour on his boat but there was a good chance that he would be in.

'Hello.'

Kristen gulped. He was in.

'Hello?' Jimmy said again, making Kristen freeze. It seemed an age ago since she'd heard his voice. 'Kris? Is that you?'

Kristen nodded but her voice had gone AWOL.

'Kris? Talk to me.'

I want to. I want to! she cried to herself but her mouth, dry as a desert, refused to co-operate, so she hung up.

'Who was that?' Felicity asked as she walked into the living room.

'Just someone about a website,' Simon said quickly, as if he'd rehearsed the line.

'That's good,' Felicity said, and Simon swore he could see pound signs registering in her eyes. 'Anyway,' she said, moving close enough to inflict a heady dose of perfume upon him, 'what are you doing this afternoon?' She snaked a long arm round his waist.

'Well, I -'

'Only, we could always have a repeat of yesterday.'

Simon wasn't sure which was hammering faster: his heart or his brain. 'I don't think that's a good idea,' he said, aware that her long nails were toying with the waistband of his trousers.

'But it was so good,' she cooed into his ear.

'No.'

'What do you mean, *no?*'

'It wasn't a good idea.'

Felicity leant back and glared at him. 'Not a good idea?'

'No,' Simon replied, trying to keep calm as he watched the dragon rising behind Felicity's pretty face.

'I see,' she said, her good humour slipping away at an alarming rate.

Simon scratched his head. 'I've got to do some work,' he said, making to leave the room.

'In that case,' Felicity said, an injection of venom in her voice, 'I'm going out.'

Simon watched as she stalked out of the room, and couldn't help wishing that she was going - full stop.

CHAPTER 36

Claudie had been idling round the shops during her lunchtime when she'd come to a sudden halt. It was something she hadn't done in months. Not since the angels had arrived anyway.

It had happened quite a lot in the weeks after Luke had died. She'd be walking round the shops and would see something she knew would appeal to Luke: a pair of boots or a rucksack in a window display, and she'd think, I must remember to tell him that. Call it instinct or habit, but whatever it was, it wasn't an easy thing to shut down. And it was surfacing again.

Claudie stared hard at the mannequin wearing the dark red shirt. It was the sort of shirt a man chopped wood in, the sort of shirt whose sleeves were always rolled above the elbows. Luke's sort of shirt.

Her eyes misted over as she stared at it. Who would buy it? Who would buy Luke's shirt? For one moment, unable to bear the idea that a stranger might have the nerve to wear it, Claudie thought about going in and buying it herself. But that was silly, wasn't it? And didn't she already have half a wardrobe of his clothes at home?

Shortly after the funeral, Luke's mother had visited and taken it upon herself to pack her son away into boxes and bin liners, but Claudie had drawn the line at his shirts. And his green wellington boots.

'What can you possibly want with those?' Mrs Gale had asked as she looked down at the pair of scuffed rubber boots flaking mud by the back door. But how could Claudie get rid of those? That was the mud they'd trod through together a week before he'd died.

God, that walk! Luke had bought her her first pair of wellington boots since she was five, and had driven her out into the middle of the countryside.

'You'll love it!' he'd enthused, marching her through a wood whose path had been lost under a chocolate river of mud.

They'd squelched and skidded, unable to look at anything but their feet for fear of falling over, and had arrived back at the car looking as if they'd bathed in the stuff.

Getting rid of his boots would be a kind of amputation, and she hadn't been able to do it. She hadn't even been able to clean them. They just stood there, sentinel-like, by the back door.

Claudie thought of Mrs Gale for a moment. She'd rung almost every day during the first couple of weeks after the funeral, but then the calls had stopped. There'd been nothing to talk about any more, and Claudie's role as a daughter-in-law had ended.

Outside the shop, Claudie closed her eyes for a moment but the red of the shirt burned bright in her mind. She could buy it; just get it over and done with, but it wouldn't make it Luke's, would it? He would never wear it and make it his.

Sometimes, Claudie would just open the wardrobe door and stare at his clothes, as if trying to breathe life back into them. She'd even stuck her nose deep into the soft materials in an attempt to seek out a little piece of him. She'd seen people do that a thousand times in the movies. But it had been hopeless. She'd smelt nothing but Lenor.

She opened her eyes and looked again at the red shirt and, as much as she wanted it, she knew that it didn't make any sense.

When Claudie got back from lunch, Kristen got up from her desk to go.

'You okay?' Claudie asked her.

'I'm fine. I'm just going to pop home and get some things. I'm beginning to run out of undies.'

'Won't Jimmy be in?'

'No. He usually goes out around lunchtime for a quick pint.'

Claudie gave her a smile. 'Will you be all right?'

'Of course I will,' Kristen said, but the expression on her face didn't echo the sentiment of her words.

Claudie looked down at where the angels were playing cards together in the most amicable group scene she'd ever witnessed.

'Don't you think Kristen should have her own flight of angels?'

The angels looked up and, smiling, all shook their heads.

'Why not?' Claudie asked.

'Because if we were sent out to everyone who suffers a break-up, there wouldn't be enough of us to go round,' Jalisa explained. 'Besides, before we're sent out, the client has been given a few months in which to deal with their problems in their own time. It's only if this time elapses, and the problems still aren't sorted that we step in.' Jalisa did a little flourish.

'So Kristen isn't-'

'Kristen hasn't suffered enough by half,' Lily said.

'I see,' Claudie said. 'That's rough, isn't it?'

'I think you have saying: *that's life?*' Mr Woo said.

Claudie nodded. So, she thought, by that reasoning, she *had* suffered. She was deemed angel-worthy. That was pretty bad, wasn't it? She hadn't been able to cope on her own.

'I know what you're thinking,' Jalisa said, breaking away from the group, 'and you mustn't think like that.'

'But it's not normal, is it?'

'What isn't normal?'

'To need help.' Claudie was feeling weighed down with her own self-doubt again. She hated that feeling. It was almost as bad as the actual grief.

'Not normal?' Bert abandoned his cards and stood up. 'Are you trying to do us out of a job?'

'Yes!' Mary added. 'What on earth would we do all day if we didn't have people to help?'

'I hadn't thought about it,' Claudie said honestly.

'Exactly!' Mary said. 'There's no fun sitting around doing nothing for eternity.'

Claudie giggled. 'Then how do you explain what you're doing now?'

'This isn't *nothing*,' Lily said, coming to the defence of her sister. 'We're keeping you company.'

'And making you laugh,' Bert said, pulling a very silly face.

'And entertaining you,' Jalisa said doing a quick Ann Miller tap dance. 'Why? Are you not happy with us?'

'It's not that! No! I love you all.'

'I can feel a *but* coming any minute now,' Mary said.

'It's just I know so little about what you do and why you're here.'

'Ask away, then,' Jalisa said encouragingly. 'Although I must warn you that-'

'I know! There's a lot of classified information.'

Jalisa nodded. 'Sorry.'

Claudie sighed and looked thoughtful for a moment. 'Are there famous angels?' she asked. 'Does anyone get Marilyn Monroe, for instance?' Claudie smiled, wondering, not for the first time, what it would be like to have a mini Gene Kelly or Judy Garland on her desk, and if she could put a request in.

'There are famous angels, yes,' Jalisa said somewhat guardedly, 'but they're not very popular. They still carry complexes over from their lifetime of fame, and it can be very hard for clients to cope with them. Believe me, a pigmy prima donna is the last thing you want on your desk.'

'You're better off with us,' Bert said.

'I'm sure I am,' Claudie agreed with a nod.

'Why?' Jalisa asked. 'You weren't thinking of trading us in, were you?'

'Gracious, no! Why would I do that? I didn't even know I could!'

'Not advisable,' Mr Woo said.

'Better the angel you know?' Claudie joked.

'Absolutely!' Bert laughed.

'So,' Claudie said, another question surfacing, 'does everybody become an angel?'

'Oh, no!' Jalisa said. 'This is the crème de la crème job. Most of us are just admin staff. You wouldn't *believe* the paperwork involved in death. On the other side, I mean.'

Claudie sighed. She could very well imagine, and it would be just her luck to spend her eternity typing letters and filing.

'And you all enjoy it?'

'Of course!' They all chorused.

'Do you get paid?'

They looked perplexed for a moment.

'Not as such,' Bert said.

'There are other rewards,' Mr Woo said.

'Like?' Claudie said.

'That's classified information,' Jalisa said, shaking her head.

'You mean I have to wait until I die to find out?'

Jalisa nodded. 'Yes.'

'Is it worth the wait?' Claudie asked. Lily and Mary giggled, and Mr Woo blushed.

'Like anything worth having,' Jalisa said, 'it's definitely worth the wait!'

Kristen entered Lantern Yard with nervous footsteps. She had her keys in her pocket but her fingers just couldn't get a grip on them because she was shaking so much. She noticed that the bin had been put out, a job that was usually left to her, and that the plants had been watered too. So, she thought, he could manage without her.

Taking a deep breath, she placed the key in the lock and opened the door, but she didn't cry her usual hello. She sneaked inside and quietly pushed the door closed behind her instead of kicking it with her foot.

The first thing she noticed was the big pile of dishes in the sink. She wrinkled her nose in disgust at the unwashed plates coated with the peculiar sauce from microwavable dishes: the stuff that set like cement unless washed immediately, and secretly, she was a little pleased that he might actually have noticed how well she used to look after him.

She walked into the living room and was relieved to spot Jimmy's tartan slippers in the middle of the carpet: a sure sign that he was out. That meant she could pack her things and be out of the cottage without disturbance.

Moving through to the bedroom, she reached under the bed for her sports bag and began to empty the drawers of their contents. Knickers, bras, socks, tights, gloves, hats, scarves. She stopped for a moment as her hand alighted on a pink scarf and its matching hat. Jimmy had bought them for her. They were horrible really; in that girly pearly pink that she hated so much but which men always assumed women liked. The hat had clashed horribly with her red hair, but Jimmy had insisted she wore it whenever it was cold.

'You look like a fifties pin up,' he'd once assured her with a kiss. But Kristen couldn't imagine even Betty Grable making this hat look good. Nevertheless, she put it in the bag.

Next stop was the dressing table. It wasn't a proper dressing table though, just a drawerless table picked up at a car boot sale, but it housed Kristen's two large jewellery boxes and a host of lotions and potions. She chose a few bottles and slung them into the bag.

She was just about to make a start on the wardrobe when she heard the front door open and close.

'Kris?'

She bit her lip. She'd left her key in the door. What a stupid thing to do. If she hadn't have left it there, she might have been able to sneak out again, but she was trapped in the bedroom now.

'Kris?'

She turned to face the door and saw Jimmy standing there, his hair ruffled by the wind. He had oil down the front of his shirt and there was a button missing but Kristen curbed her maternal instincts and turned back to the wardrobe to pack.

'What are you doing?' Jimmy asked, his voice unusually quiet.

'Don't worry, I'm not going to be long.'

'That's not what I meant.'

Kristen grabbed a few skirts from their hangers and stuffed them into her bag. There wasn't time to be neat.

'Kris?' The tone of his voice made her stop for a second. 'This is silly.'

'Yes,' she said, 'it is.' And she began packing again.

'Listen,' he said.

Kristen was listening. She was listening for the words she'd so longed for but had almost given up on hearing. Almost any words Jimmy said to her now would do.

'I don't know what to say.'

Except those words.

'That's the trouble,' Kristen said, 'you never know what to say.' She blinked back the tears as she continued to stuff her bag to bursting point. It was time to go.

'No, Kris - listen-'

'No!' Kristen rolled her shoulder away from his hand. If she let it stay, she would lose her resolve for sure. She walked to the door, willing him to say something: to plead with her a little bit more. To say he'd been an idiot. Or just to tell her to stay.

'Kris?'

She took the key out of the door and paused for a moment. Waiting. But he didn't say another word.

CHAPTER 37

Simon was glad Felicity had gone out. It gave him the chance to think about things, and, as Kristen had so succinctly pointed out, he was in serious need of the time.

He flopped down on the sofa, forgetting any notion of actually getting any work done today. He'd have to make up for it later otherwise he'd been in serious trouble in that department as well.

It was hard to believe that, just a week ago he'd thought himself the luckiest man alive: to finally be making progress in his chosen career, to have won the trip to Paris, and to have met Claudie. So why had fate thrown a Felicity-shaped spanner into the works?

He shook his head in dismay. He'd been sucked into the vortex again; the vortex that was Felicity Maddox, and, if he didn't take charge of things soon, he was in grave danger of being spat out. It had happened before.

Way back at the beginning of their relationship, they'd had a little tiff. Well, it was a little tiff as far as Simon was concerned. He couldn't even remember what it was about now, but Felicity had gone all histrionic on him. He could still see her now, her eyes spurting tears, her voice hard and cold as diamond.

She'd left too. No dramatic scene was complete without a throwing clothes in a suitcase finale. And he'd been happy to leave her to it.

Then what had happened? He wracked his brains. Her mother had called him. Yes, that was it. Marjorie Maddox had rung to say how distraught her daughter was and what was he going to do about it? She'd barked at him down the phone. He could still remember how terrified he'd been and how he'd thanked his lucky stars that he wasn't one of the unfortunate girl guides she regularly marched around the county.

Mrs Maddox had then dropped Felicity off the next day and Felicity had acted as if nothing had happened. Pretty much as she was behaving now in fact. But, this time, they'd had slightly more than a little tiff and, this time, Simon wasn't going to sit back and take it.

It was then that an idea occurred to him. If he was going to do something, he might as well do it in style. Felicity Maddox had screwed him up good and proper. She'd walked away with not only his worldly goods, but his heart too. That, he thought, was what you got for being a nice guy. Well, he wasn't putting up with that again. What was that wonderful line of Lady Macbeth's? "Look like the innocent flower but be the serpent under't." That's what he was going to do. He'd had enough of being a flower. It was time to become a snake.

He got up and went through to the kitchen. Next to the telephone lay a little blue book stuffed with numbers. He picked it up and flicked through the tatty pages and, picking up the telephone, he dialled, giving a casual little whistle as he waited for somebody to pick up.

'Hello? Mrs Maddox? Yes, it's me - Simon. No. Nothing's wrong. Well,' he paused, 'that's not quite true. No, don't be alarmed. She's fine. It's just there's something I think you should know.'

Tears in the toilet were an almost weekly occurrence at Bartholomew and Simpson but, with the workforce consisting mostly of young women playing the dating game, it was hardly a surprising fact. That's why someone had come up with the idea of providing a box of extra strong tissues, and it was into one of these tissues that Kristen was blowing her nose after returning to work with her overloaded sports bag.

'He did try to stop you from leaving though, didn't he?' Claudie asked, stroking Kristen's hair gently.

'Not really!' Kristen sobbed.

'But you know what he's like - he's not the talking type, is he?'

Kristen shook her head. 'Would it be so hard for him to say he loved me? Would it?'

Claudie's eyes widened in sympathy. She didn't dare think of the number of times Luke had told her he loved her. It was almost a part of his everyday vocabulary. But not every man was like that, and Jimmy Stanton was as strong and silent as a pint of Yorkshire bitter. 'Jimmy's just so-'

'Don't give me that strong and silent bullshit!'

Claudie bit her lip. That was exactly what she'd been about to say. 'But he *is!* And isn't that part of why you fell for him in the first place?'

Kristen nodded before trumpeting into her tissue, a sound which ricocheted around the tiled toilet walls.

Claudie sighed. Kristen was looking at her as if she held the answer to all her prayers, but what could she say? She was no agony aunt. She couldn't even sort out her own problems. Weren't her angels testimony to that?

'I'll tell you what we'll do,' she said, suddenly taking charge. 'We'll go home after work and sort your things out. I've been dying to get my hands on your clothes for ages.'

'What do you mean?' Kristen blew her nose again.

'I mean I want you to help me with my wardrobe. There's nothing in it except black and grey. I sometimes feel like a character from a Checkov play.'

'Well,' Kristen dabbed her eyes and looked at Claudie, 'you *could* do with brightening up a bit.'

'Especially with Paris coming up.'

Kristen nodded. 'Yes. You've got to look your best in Paris.'

Claudie grinned. She wasn't sure how long she could keep Kristen's spirits up, but she was going to give it her best shot.

CHAPTER 38

When Felicity arrived back, she found Simon chopping vegetables in the kitchen.

'What are you doing?' she asked, her voice cold and clipped, as if she might suspect him of preparing a dish with which to poison her.

'Dinner,' he said.

'Oh.'

'Wine?'

She nodded.

'There are two glasses chilling in the fridge.'

He watched as she opened the door and took out the glasses and bottle of white. 'Lovely,' she said, her voice softening a little.

'Why don't you put your feet up. Everything's taken care of in here.'

'Okay,' she said, and he watched as she sashayed into the living room, a great smug smile on her face.

Simon smiled too. Not because he was taking pleasure in cooking a meal for the woman he loved, but because he was looking forward to dessert. A dessert that was arriving at about eight o'clock.

Half an hour later, they were sat at the table eating. In typical Felicity mode, she hadn't apologised or explained her dramatic exit earlier that day, but had dived into a conversation about the soft furnishings they simply had to have if the house was to look half-way decent. Well, it wasn't *exactly* a conversation, because Simon's contribution was to nod occasionally. Instead, he ate his food and watched Felicity's pink glossed mouth moving ten to the dozen.

How could anyone become so animated when talking about cushions and curtains, he wondered? Was it a female thing? No, surely not. He'd never heard Kristen go on about pelmets and valances, and he certainly couldn't imagine Claudie getting excited about swags and tails. It must just be a Felicity thing. There had been a time when he'd have argued with her, trying to persuade her that there was very little point in throwing hundreds of pounds worth of chintz around a modern semi, but he didn't have the inclination tonight. Besides, he thought, his sofa would never know the pleasures of an Indian tapestried cushion.

'So which do you prefer?' she asked, waking him out of his reverie.

'What?'

'No, *which?*' she said sarcastically. 'Burgundy or Violet?'

'Er, violet, definitely.'

'You think so?'

Simon nodded. 'Definitely.' He felt the urge to guffaw but managed to suppress it.

'I'm not so sure.'

He smiled to himself. She had a habit of asking for his opinion, *demanding* his opinion, and then disregarding it completely, but he didn't care because it was ten to eight.

'Violet really wouldn't go with the throws I've got in mind,' she said, turning round and indicating to the sofa; the sofa he felt sure Felicity would have taken with her when she'd left him seven months before if only she'd been able to fit it in her suitcase.

'Well,' he said, 'burgundy's a good colour too.'

He could see the mechanics of her mind in action. 'You've got me all confused now.'

'Don't worry about it. It will all work itself out, I'm sure.'

She turned back round and threw him a smile. 'You are sweet,' she said, reaching across the table and squeezing his hand.

'No I'm not.'

'You are,' she insisted, taking a sip of wine. Simon was just about to get up for a refill when he heard a car pulling up outside. He paused for a moment and, sure enough, the doorbell went.

'Are you expecting anyone?' Felicity asked.

Simon looked across the table at her. Her expression was soft and, for a moment, he almost forget that it could be any other way. Almost.

'Yes,' he said. 'I'm expecting someone.'

'Who?'

He walked through to the hallway and opened the door.

'Ah! Simon!' a huge female voice boomed from out of the darkness.

'Come in,' he said. 'How lovely to see you.'

'It is no such thing.' The woman, whose chest seemed to proceed her by several seconds, pushed past him and stood in the middle of the hallway, glaring into the living room. 'Felicity.'

It was only one word, but it had Felicity on her feet in an instant.

Kristen took a pace back from the wardrobe and reviewed its contents. 'There's a lot of grey in here,' she said.

Claudie nodded. 'But I suit grey.'

Kristen face filled with doubt. 'Nobody suits grey,' she said. 'Now, what you need is a serious injection of colour.'

'Colour,' Claudie repeated, knowing full well that her idea of colour and Kristen's idea of colour were completely different. Where Claudie would choose claret, Kristen would choose scarlet. Claudie's colours whispered; Kristen's yelled from the rooftops.

'Yes,' Kristen mused, 'colour. And lots of it. We can't have you walking round Paris looking like a shadow. And you should know that, being French.'

'I suppose,' Claudie said, sitting down on the edge of the bed. 'But I guess I haven't been feeling very colourful lately.'

Kristen sat down next to her, placing her hand on top of Claudie's. 'What you've got to try and do is to take some of the colour from all those musicals you keep watching, and translate them into clothes. Think - yellow brick road blouses, ruby slipper red jumpers-'

'Yuck!'

'Or Glinda-pink trousers.'

'Kris!'

'Yes, maybe a bit much to ask.'

'Definitely,' Claudie agreed, thinking of Glinda floating down from the heavens in her glorious pink bubble in *The Wizard of Oz*.

'But you've got to do something.'

'I will,' Claudie promised. 'I'll go shopping tomorrow.'

'And you *promise* not to come back with a pile of clothes in various shades of grey?'

'I'll do my best. But pewter's really in at the moment.'

Kristen gave her a warning look.

'Okay! I promise.'

Marjorie Maddox was wearing a little blue bobbly hat like one of the

Liquorice Allsorts that everybody leaves at the bottom of the box. But it wasn't the hat that Felicity was staring at in disbelief.

'Well?' her mother boomed.

'Mother? What are you doing here?'

Her mother tutted like a machete. 'What a fine question to choose in the circumstances.'

'I don't understand.' Felicity looked from her mother to Simon and back again in obvious confusion.

'Simon's told me everything,' Mrs Maddox sighed. 'And I must say, I think he's handled the whole thing admirably.'

'What thing?'

'Oh, you are a silly girl,' her mother puffed, her brass buttoned cardigan seeming to burst at the seams. 'I have better things to do with my time than drive across the country to pick you up whenever you're in trouble.'

'But you don't need to pick me up. I'm staying her - with Simon.'

Mrs Maddox's eyebrows rose superciliously. 'That's not what he told me.'

Felicity glared at Simon, but he merely shrugged back at her.

'You've got yourself into a fine mess this time, haven't you? Not even knowing who the father is! That wasn't how we did things in my day,' Mrs Maddox said, her Girl Guide persona firmly in place. 'Now get that suitcase and get it in the car.'

Felicity's eyes caught sight of her suitcase at the foot of the stairs. 'When did you do that?' She looked at Simon, her eyes burning. 'You bastard! How could you do this to me?'

'Oh, it was easy,' he said.

'FELICITY!' her mother barked from the car.

Felicity stood under the harsh glare of the hall light which had been robbed of its shade seven months ago.

'By the way,' Simon said, 'don't worry about all the money you owe me from when you cleared out our joint account. You're going to need it more than I am.'

Felicity opened her mouth to retort but her mother yelled again, and he watched as she struggled down the driveway with her overloaded suitcase.

Simon couldn't stop himself from waving as she glared at him from the front seat of the car. Felicity and her mother deserved one another. If there was one person who was meaner and tougher than

Felicity, then it was her mother. Simon tried to picture them together in the months to come and could hardly keep his smile to himself. There wasn't much he'd managed to do right in this world, but packing Felicity off to her mother's was a stroke of pure genius.

Talking of packing reminded him of his holiday. He rubbed his hands together in excitement, thinking of Paris. It was only three days away now. Thank goodness he'd sorted himself out in time. Kristen was going to be so proud of him.

He wandered through to the living room and said a quick hello to the fish.

'Think yourselves lucky I've got rid of her,' he grinned. 'She would've had you guys swimming round in burgundy water.'

CHAPTER 39

For somebody who generally preferred book shopping to clothes shopping, Claudie wasn't doing too badly. She'd spent all of her lunch hour on Tuesday and Wednesday shopping for clothes, and today was her last opportunity to grab some last minute items before her trip to Paris the next day.

Claudie smiled to herself. Here she was, jetting off to sample spring in one of the most beautiful cities in the world. She and Kristen were going to have such fun.

She tried not to think about the amount of money she'd spent, but it had to be done. She supposed she couldn't go round looking like a nun forever. Instead, she tried to focus on the positive aspects of her shopping trip: the gorgeously feminine jumpers in the softest of wools. And she'd managed to steer away from the pewter and the mushroom she'd favoured of late, choosing amber and lilac instead. She was really quite proud of herself.

For a long time, the world had lost its colour, and Claudie had felt as if she'd lost hers too, wearing a limited palette of navies, browns and greys. She was still a long way off resembling a butterfly but at least the shopping trip was helping her to break free from her colourless chrysalis.

Then she'd bought a brand new pair of long black leather boots that fitted so snugly against her legs, they were like a second skin. And then she'd done something incredibly rash. She'd bought new underwear. It seemed silly to buy something she didn't really need, but the magic of Paris was beginning to weave its spell over her, and the pearly lace creations had just begged to be taken home.

After she'd made her purchase, she had a second look around the lingerie department, thinking about the weekend ahead.

Paris. Wasn't it the most beautiful word? For a moment, she wondered what Luke would have thought about a trip to Paris, and just knew he would have hated the idea. Paris was such an un-Luke sort of place. She'd desperately wanted to go with him, but he'd always teased her about it.

'Claudie, I'm not going to sing and dance with you by the Seine. That's not real life, and it certainly isn't me!'

She hadn't minded the not singing or dancing bit; the thought of Luke breaking into a spontaneous ballet routine was laughable, but she would have liked to have gone to Paris with him. But Luke had always felt trapped in cities. He'd needed to see the mountains or the oceans. That's why they'd gone to Wales on their honeymoon. Land of waterfalls and valleys, forests and mountains. If only he hadn't gone back there.

'Claudie?'

Claudie froze, her hand hovering dangerously close to a pair of strawberry coloured knickers. She turned round. She knew who it was, and she also knew there was nowhere to hide in the underwear department. 'Hello, Daniel.'

'How are you?' Daniel asked, striding forward and filling the aisle with his bulk, his dark hair swinging as he came to a standstill.

'I'm fine,' Claudie said, thinking it absolutely typical that she should be caught in the most embarrassing department of the store.

'Good,' he said, his smile nervous. 'You look well.'

'You too.'

He scratched his head. 'Shopping?'

'Yes,' she said, and then wondered what he was doing in the women's underwear department. Perhaps she shouldn't be so self-conscious. Shouldn't he be just as embarrassed as her? 'Just getting a few new things. You know,' she said.

He nodded, looked around, but quickly returned his eyes to Claudie, a beautiful blush colouring his face. They stood for a moment in awkward silence.

'Look,' he said at last, scouring the floor with his piercing blue eyes, 'I'm really sorry about what happened.'

Claudie looked down at the same patch of floor. 'No, it's okay.'

Daniel shook his head. 'I was way out of order.'

'Me too,' she said, and he looked up at her. 'I'm sorry I reacted so badly. I hope I didn't hurt you?'

'No. No. And I don't blame you. I'm a complete moron sometimes.'

'No you're not.'

'I am,' he said grinning. 'Anyway, I've been meaning to ring you to say I was sorry. I didn't want to leave things like that.'

'But where have you been staying? I've been worried about you.'

Daniel laughed. 'There was no need. I've met somebody.'

'Have you?' Claudie's voice rose as if she'd inhaled helium.

'Yeah,' he nodded enthusiastically. 'She's great. And you won't believe it, but she's coming to London with me.'

'Really? Isn't that rather,' she paused, looking for the right word, 'sudden?'

'It is - yeah! I can't quite believe it myself. But she's got some contacts down there, and even thinks she can get me sorted with a job.'

Claudie's eyebrows leapt up an inch. Daniel in a job? With a girl? 'Gosh, Daniel, that's terrific. I hope things work out for you.'

'Thanks,' he said, and there was another awkward silence.

'So, I guess this is goodbye, is it?' Claudie asked.

'I guess so.' Daniel took a step towards her and gave her a hug. Claudie smiled, although she still felt a little anxious after what had happened last time. Nevertheless, she allowed him to hug her, holding her breath as he squeezed the living daylights out of her with his mammoth arms. The Gale brothers certainly knew how to give a decent hug, she thought. None of that half-hearted air-kissing, shoulder-squeezing for them. If their recipients didn't need resuscitating after they'd finished with them, it wasn't worth giving.

'Anyway,' he said, stepping back a little, 'you wouldn't want me hanging round Whitby, would you? I mean, this is your stamping ground.'

'Don't be silly,' she said, but secretly wondered if it would be such a good idea seeing Luke's double round the town all the time.

'Besides,' he said, 'London's more my style. Bright lights, big city and all that.'

Claudie nodded. Thinking how unlike Luke he was that way.

'We'll keep in touch, though, won't we?'

'Of course,' Claudie said, thinking of the future Christmas cards she'd send which would never be returned.

'And I'll visit sometime soon. And you must come to London.'

Claudie nodded. 'I will.'

'Great! Well then.'

'Take care, won't you?'

'Sure.'

'And good luck with the new job.'

'Thanks. I aim to keep this one.'

Claudie gave a little laugh. 'Good! It's about time you settled down.'

'I know.' He leant forward and kissed her cheek and, for the briefest of moments, she felt Luke in that kiss.

'Bye, Daniel,' she said, aware that tears were threatening to spill at any moment.

'Bye, Claudie,' he sounded her name so softly and so sweetly that her tears spilled down onto her cheeks before she could stop them. 'Hey!' he said. 'Don't cry. I'm not worth it.'

Claudie managed to smile. 'I know! I'm just being silly.'

He hugged her again, giving her a much-needed moment in which to compose herself.

'I'm sorry,' she said at last.

'It's okay,' he said, leaning back and running a hand through his long hair. 'It's rather nice to know I'll be missed.'

'You will,' Claudie said, willing herself not to cry again.

He looked awkward for a moment, looking down at the floor and glancing from side to side, so Claudie decided to help him out.

'I'd better get back to work.'

'Right,' he said. 'Well, don't you forget to come and see me.'

Claudie nodded, and watched as he walked away, his huge shoulders and casual gait causing the usual head-turning reaction amongst the women in the store. She knew that that was the last she'd ever see of Daniel, and she couldn't help feeling that she was losing a little bit of Luke all over again. Her connection with the Gale family had truly ended. Daniel Gale had turned from a brother-in-law to a stranger in a couple of seconds and there was nothing she could do to change that.

Claudie looked at her watch. It really was time she was heading back at work. Time to move forward, and time to sort one last thing out before her trip to Paris.

'Paris!' Jalisa cried. 'What do you mean you're going to Paris? Why didn't we hear about this sooner?'

'I'm sorry, Jalisa, I guess I've just had other things on my mind. And it's come round so quickly.'

'When you go?' Mr Woo asked.

'Tomorrow,' Claudie said, feeling a wave of excitement rippling through her stomach.

'Tomorrow!' Jalisa looked as if somebody had whacked her in the face with a dead fish.

'Yes. I know I should have mentioned it before now.'

'Claudie,' Jalisa said, in head-shaking mode, 'it really isn't usual practice for a client to up and run without telling us.'

'But I thought you'd be pleased.'

Bert cleared his throat to speak. 'We *are* pleased, Claudie. It will be a marvellous weekend.'

'But you should have given us a bit of notice.'

'I know,' Claudie sighed. 'Especially when I was going to ask a favour of you.'

Five little faces craned forward.

'What?' Lily asked.

'I was going to ask you all to come with me,' Claudie said hesitantly.

'Really?' Lily grinned.

'Truly?' Mary giggled excitedly.

'Now hold on a minute!' Jalisa began.

'Oh, *please!*' Lily shouted. 'Paris! I've read so much about it in the fashion magazines.'

'Just think of all those shops,' Mary added dreamily.

'Yes,' Lily nodded, 'just think of the clothes. I can tell you right now, you'll never get me in a corset and bumroll again.'

'Er - girls,' Jalisa interrupted. 'If we did get leave to go to Paris, don't forget it would be a business trip. It's not a holiday for us.'

'So,' Claudie said, 'there is a possibility that you can come with me?'

Jalisa bit her lip and looked thoughtful. It was a look she was very good at. 'It's not the usual thing to do, of course. I mean, we're only meant to position ourselves in one place - in one country!'

'But it could be the chance of a lifetime!' Lily enthused.

'I've always wanted to see the Eiffel Tower,' Bert said.

'Good to see French pharmacy,' Mr Woo said.

Jalisa waved her arms in the air. 'Before we all get over-excited, don't forget that we will have to apply for special dispensation.'

There was a collective groan.

'That usually takes *weeks!*' Bert pointed out.

'Claudie leave tomorrow,' Mr Woo said.

'Exactly,' Jalisa sighed.

'Then I've left it too late?' Claudie felt her face fall into glumness.

'We'll have to see,' Jalisa said, 'but it doesn't look hopeful.'

When Claudie and Kristen got home after work, Claudie showed her latest lunchtime purchases.

'Claudes! They're gorgeous!' Kristen said, picking up the two creamy blouses and daring to finger the lacy underwear. 'And these jumpers! I just love this amber one. Can I borrow it?'

'Not before Paris!'

'It's beautiful. You're going to look so gorgeous.'

'What are you taking?'

Kristen looked pensive for a moment. 'I've still got some things to pick up at Jimmy's.'

'But I thought you had everything here now?'

Kristen shook her head. 'I meant to say, actually, that I'll have to go there en route to the station. So it's probably best if I meet you there. Is that okay?'

"Course,' Claudie said.

'Have you got a camera?'

Claudie reached into the suitcase lying beside the bed. '*Voila!*

'Be sure to take lots of photos.'

Claudie frowned, thinking that was a bit of a strange thing to say, seeing as she was going to be there too but, before she could say anything, the telephone went and Kristen was on her feet in an instant.

'I'll get it.' Kristen ran through to the living room but Claudie couldn't hear who it was she was talking to. When she came back through to the bedroom, Claudie looked up from her suitcase.

'Who was that?'

'Simon,' Kristen said. 'Just to wish us a bon voyage.'

'That's nice of him,' Claudie said. 'We should send him a postcard, shouldn't we? He'd like that. Kris?'

'Oh - yes,' Kristen said quickly. 'That's a nice idea.'

CHAPTER 40

Simon woke up on Friday morning with the vague notion that today wasn't the usual tip-yourself-out-of-bed-and-work-until-nightfall kind of day. He sat upright and examined the syrupy stream of light that fell on the bedcovers, and then he remembered. *Paris*. Today, he and Kristen were going to Paris.

He'd packed the night before, and had given a set of house keys to his neighbour, Mrs Briars, who'd pop in to feed Pumpkin. And he'd checked what time he was meeting Kristen at the station.

Poor Kristen, he thought. She'd sounded a bit stressed when he'd talked to her at Claudie's. She was still probably brooding over Jimmy. Still, he smiled, a weekend away would be just the thing to cheer her up, as long as Jimmy didn't find out at the last minute and turn up at the station and murder the pair of them. Now that wouldn't be the best of starts to the weekend.

Claudie buzzed around her kitchen, humming "Wonderful, Wonderful Day" from *Seven Brides for Seven Brothers*. It was a glorious May morning, and everything was ready for the weekend ahead. Kristen had already left to collect a suitcase and pack some of the clothes she'd left at Jimmy's, and they were to meet each other at the station later on.

Claudie waltzed through to the living room and couldn't help but smile at her own little suitcase ready for take off. She was smiling because it was as if she had x-ray vision and could see its colourful contents. She was even wearing colour now: one of her new creamy pink blouses, and it made her feel as if she'd swallowed a whole MGM musical.

The only thing was, she hadn't heard from the angels. It was a shame that they weren't going to be able to make the trip, and it was sad that she didn't even have an address to send them a postcard.

Still, she thought, she could tell them all about it on Monday morning.

*

Kristen was not having such an enjoyable morning. She'd had to pretend to Claudie that she was going back to Cabin Cottage to collect a suitcase that she didn't really own and to pack clothes that weren't really there. Claudie had been right, Kristen had all her clothes already, but what other excuse could she have for meeting Claudie at the train station? She wanted Claudie and Simon to arrive there separately: to spot each other and, if at all possible, to work out what was going on without any interference from her.

She felt awful about lying to her two best friends but how else was she to get them together? They obviously liked each other, but she also knew that Claudie still needed a shove in the right direction. Simon's Paris holiday had appeared like a falling star from the heavens: so full of promise that you'd have to be a fool not to make a wish on it. The timing was perfect, and she truly believed that lying to her friends was a far better option than not getting them together.

Standing in the station now, she began to panic. She looked at her watch for the tenth time in as many minutes. Where was Claudie? And where was Simon? This wasn't how she'd planned it at all. What if it all fell through? Could either of them possibly have got wind of her idea? What if neither of them turned up? Would she end up going to Paris on her own without any clothes?

She shook her head vigorously from side to side as if trying to dislodge her doubts. They'd be here. She looked at her watch once again. Just give them a few more minutes before she really began to panic.

'Kris!' Claudie's voice carried across the station.

'Claudes!' Kris beamed her a smile as she practically ran across the station, her small suitcase in her hand. 'Where's your luggage?'

Kristen bit her lip. She was hot off the mark this morning, was Claudie.

'I er-'

'Is it on the train?'

'Not exact-'

'Kristen!' Simon's voice interrupted them and they turned round to see him marching towards them, large rucksack slung over his shoulder. '*Claudie?*'

'Simon! What are you doing here? Are you going somewhere too? What a coincidence!' Claudie looked genuinely pleased.

'Going somewhere?' Simon smiled. 'I certainly am. And not just anywhere! I've won a trip to Paris and Kristen's coming with me. I thought you knew?'

'*You've* won a trip?' Claudie's face suddenly clouded over with confusion. 'I don't understand. I thought *you'd* won the trip, Kris?'

'What's going on?' Simon's brows closed together over his nose. 'Is Claudie coming too?'

'Look, I'm confused,' Claudie's forehead wrinkled. 'I thought I was going to Paris with you, Kris?'

'And that's exactly what I thought,' Simon said.

'*Right!* Just wait a minute!' Kristen held her hands up in the air to halt any further questions. She took a deep breath as she looked at her two horrified friends in turn. 'I'm not coming.'

'What?' Claudie whispered.

Simon didn't say anything. He just frowned.

'Simon's telling the truth, Claudie. I didn't win the holiday - *he* did. But I *did* agree to go with him.' She turned to look at Simon. 'I was going to say no, Si, honestly. But then I thought of Claudie, and it just seemed so perfect. I really thought you two would get on well together.'

Claudie's face had drained of all colour. 'You lied to me?'

'*No!* Well, yes, but I knew you wouldn't go otherwise.' For a moment, Kristen wondered if she should just commit herself to the tracks in Anna Karenina style. 'I'm sorry. Really! I shouldn't have lied to you both like that.'

'No, you shouldn't have,' Simon said.

Claudie turned to look at him. 'I'm really sorry, Simon. I had no idea this had anything to do with you.'

'It's all right.'

Kristen watched nervously as they looked at each other, luggage in hand, both hoping to have been heading off to Paris for the weekend. With her. Would they be going now? She had to push just a little harder.

'Come on, guys!' she began, filling her voice with enthusiasm. 'Don't make a big deal about this. You both want to go. You both get on well. So go and enjoy yourselves. It's a holiday!'

Claudie glanced at Simon. He seemed even more uncomfortable with the idea than she did.

'Simon? You *are* going, aren't you?' Kristen asked. 'You've been looking forward to this. It would be silly if you didn't go.'

'I've always been going, it's just a question of who it is I'm going with.'

'Claudie?' Kristen pleaded her friend for a response.

'I don't think it's up to me, is it?' The question was addressed at Simon, but Claudie was looking directly at Kristen.

There was a horrible moment's silence, and then the announcement for their train was heard.

'There isn't much time,' Kristen urged, looking from one to the other.

'What do you think?' Simon asked Claudie, his face softening with a smile. 'Would you like to go with me?'

Kristen almost flung her arms round Simon. But Claudie still had to give her answer. A few anxious seconds passed as Claudie tried to weigh Simon up.

Finally, she spoke. 'Okay,' she said.

Kristen couldn't contain her happiness as she whooped for joy. The plan had worked. She flung her arms round Claudie and gave her a great smack of a kiss on her cheek, leaving a poppy red smear. She then gave Simon one to match.

'Go on, then!' she urged, propelling them towards the train before they were too late. 'Have a great time,' she yelled as they boarded. 'I know you will!'

She stood on the platform, waving her arms around like a human windmill, but neither Claudie nor Simon bothered to wave back.

CHAPTER 41

They'd barely said a word to each other since leaving Whitby behind. Now, as the Eurostar pulled out of Waterloo station, Claudie wondered what on earth had made her agree to come on this trip. After all, a weekend in Paris had connotations written all over it, and Claudie wasn't naïve enough not to realise it.

She sat back in her seat, glancing quickly over to Simon. He'd helped her with her suitcase when they'd got on the train, but he didn't seem in a talkative mood. A feeling of deep guilt suddenly overwhelmed her. She shouldn't be here, she thought. She shouldn't have let Kristen get away with it. *She* didn't want to be here, and she was more than sure Simon didn't want her here either. But there was no going back now, was there? Not unless she got on the next train back to London as soon as they arrived, and that seemed such a waste, didn't it?

She stared out of the window but there weren't any answers to be seen in the endless blank fields. She had to work this one out for herself. Maybe they could go their own ways once they got to Paris? That would be the best solution. Simon could do his thing, and she could do hers. Perfectly simple. Paris was a large enough city so they wouldn't be likely to trip over each other every five minutes. Claudie felt a small smile creeping up on her. Sorted.

No. Not quite. What about breakfast? She didn't want him to feel that she was crowding in on him. This was his holiday after all, and they were bound to have rooms next door to each other? She'd probably spend the entire weekend eavesdropping on him, listening out to hear when he left his room and checking if the coast was clear before she surfaced from hers.

Claudie chewed her lip and looked around the carriage. She'd bet her bank account that nobody else was in the same predicament as she was. How did she manage it? One thing was for certain, free trip to Paris or not, she was going to throttle Kristen when she got back. She'd heard of matchmaking but this was really pushing it to extremes.

She looked around at the other people, trying to guess their own personal circumstances. There might not be any passengers eating smelly egg sandwiches, but there was an awful lot on mobile phones. Everywhere Claudie looked, someone was speaking into his or her little finger. Most were wearing pinstripes and ties, and all looked as dull as ditch water. But then Paris, for some, was a business trip.

Claudie was just about to close her eyes against all her worries when, under the soft glow of the pink lamp on the table, five tiny figures appeared. Claudie blinked, looking up at Simon as if he might have spotted them, but he was staring out of the window.

'Guess what!' Jalisa cried. 'We got our special dispensation!'

Claudie stared down at her in surprise.

'It took some doing, mind,' Bert said. 'We've been up half the night filling the forms in ourselves.'

'And we all had to write an essay on why this trip was so important,' Lily said.

Claudie's eyes widened. Angels having to write essays? Wonders would never cease.

'But don't worry. We won't make a nuisance of ourselves. We just wanted to let you know we can come with you,' Jalisa said.

'Thank you,' Claudie mouthed, and watched as Lily and Mary disappeared only to reappear at the table adjacent to theirs where two middle-aged businessmen had set up office.

Lily and Mary stood hand in hand on a copy of the bald man's Financial Times and pulled faces at him.

Claudie tried not to laugh but failed miserably.

'You all right?' Simon asked, looking at her with a great deal of concern.

'Fine,' she said, feeling herself blush. 'Sorry. I always laugh when I'm nervous.'

Simon gave her a little smile. Claudie glanced quickly over at Lily and Mary again, grinning as they blew raspberries and stuck their tongues out at the pair of ponderous businessmen.

It was very hard to think about picking up a book or a magazine when five angels were doing their best to distract you. Bert and Mr Woo were playing snap and, for once, seemed to be getting along quite nicely, and Jalisa was filing her nails with the tiniest emery board Claudie had ever seen. But Lily and Mary simply refused to behave themselves. Claudie tried to beckon them away from the businessmen's tables, but they were taking absolutely no notice of her. One of the men, in particular, had caught their attention. He was wearing half-moon glasses and was doing a bit of laborious two-fingered typing on his laptop. But that's not what was interesting the Tudor twins.

His tie hovered over the table, just begging to be pulled, and Lily and Mary didn't waste any time with such an obvious opportunity. Mary grabbed hold of it. Lily helped, and together they picked it up until the tip was dangling over the man's cup of coffee. Claudie watched, her mouth parting in anticipation of what they were about to do.

'Oh, for God's sake!' the man yelled as soon as he saw what had happened. Lily and Mary went running for cover as the man retrieved his tie from his cup and did his best to squeeze the excess liquid from it. Claudie watched in amazement. Things like that happened to her all the time: pens disappeared, her sleeve would catch on a doorknob or she'd step on a piece of chewing gum she could have sworn wasn't there a minute ago. Did that mean that she was the unwilling participant in an angel's practical joke?

She glared down at Lily and Mary as they returned to her table, but they merely grinned back at her, knowing she couldn't tell them off in front of Simon. So she decided to close her eyes against them and, with all the excitement of the day so far, she fell into a deep sleep.

By the time they'd pulled into the Gare du Nord, and had snaked their way round the taxi queue, it was after eight o'clock. Claudie, despite her sleep on the train, was exhausted, and would have fallen asleep in the taxi too if the driver hadn't been slaloming his way through the centre of Paris as if competing for Olympic gold. Claudie felt quite carsick by the time they stopped outside the hotel.

'I'd forgotten how bad French drivers were,' she said as Simon picked her suitcase up from where the driver had dumped it on the pavement.

'You're calling your own nation?' he said with some surprise.

'I'm only French by nationality, not by nature.'

He looked at her and smiled, and there was something behind his eyes that Claudie couldn't quite read. What was it? Had he finally resigned himself to the fact they were going to spend a weekend together?

'I think he likes you,' a little voice sang. Claudie looked down and saw Jalisa sitting on her suitcase as Simon carried it towards the hotel. 'Yep,' Jalisa said, gazing up at Simon, 'he definitely likes you!'

Claudie shook her head and followed Simon through a pair of large iron gates.

'This is beautiful,' Claudie gasped. 'I can't believe you won this!'

'Neither can I,' he said, looking up at the rosy red brick of the hotel and the myriad windows winking in the lamp light. 'I thought it would be a dump miles from anywhere.'

Simon opened the door for her and they walked into a large hotel lobby stuffed with antiques.

'It's like heaven,' she said in a quiet voice.

'Oh, no,' Jalisa laughed, 'this is *much* posher than heaven!'

Claudie hovered in the background whilst Simon checked in. When he turned round, he handed her a key. Room twenty. He was in room twenty-one. Both were singles.

Claudie felt herself breathe a sigh of relief as they made their way to the lift, doing their best to squash into the small space with their luggage. She'd read her fair share of romance novels whilst a teenager, and had lost count of the number of stories where the hero and heroine had been thrown together in the last double room left in the hotel. But they weren't in a novel, and Claudie certainly didn't feel very heroine-like as she rubbed sleep out of her eyes and struggled to stifle a yawn.

As the lift began to move, Claudie glanced down at Jalisa who was still smiling up at Simon. She was doing a great job of balancing on her case, but Claudie didn't like the twinkle in her eye. It was as if she was planning something.

'Do you want to go out somewhere and eat?' Simon asked.

Claudie thought of the room and bed that awaited her. If they went out to eat, she couldn't avoid talking to him, and she really didn't know what to say. She still couldn't believe that she was with Simon instead of having a girly weekend away with Kristen, and felt sure that he was just being polite. Anyway, she needed some time out. Alone.

'I'm not really hungry. I think I'll just have an early night.'

'Okay,' Simon said, his voice alarmingly blank.

'Pssst!' Claudie frowned down at Jalisa. 'Go out to eat, you idiot!'

Claudie she shook her head gently. She couldn't believe the cheek of that angel sometimes, and was beginning to wonder why on earth she'd thought it a good idea to ask the angels to come to Paris with her.

When the lift doors opened, Claudie was still staring angrily at Jalisa.

Simon led the way down the narrow hallway decorated in a sumptuous red and gold wallpaper, and placed their bags outside their rooms.

'Well, here we are,' he said.

'Yes.' Claudie stared at the two doors. There was barely room for another door in between them.

'So I'll see you in the morning? Breakfast is seven thirty to eight thirty.'

'Okay,' Claudie said, forgetting her plan to tiptoe around his timetable.

'Say eight o'clock then? Shall I knock for you?'

Claudie nodded.

'Night, then,' Simon said, handing her the key and opening the door into his own room.

Claudie walked into her room, closing the door behind her and leaning against it. Oh, God. Had she sounded ungrateful? Had she been completely antisocial in not going out to dinner with him? Would he send her home on the first train in the morning?

'You should have gone out to eat!' Jalisa sang up at her from her suitcase.

'Jalisa!'

'Just making an observation.'

'Well I'd thank you not to. I feel bad enough about it as it is.'

Claudie walked into the room and smiled as she saw that the rest of the angels had already made themselves comfortable on a small dressing table next to the bed. It was really a home from home for them, wasn't it?

'Jalisa's right,' Mary said hesitantly.

Claudie sighed and crossed her arms. 'If I'd known you lot were going to spend the weekend matchmaking me, I'd never have asked you to come along.'

'Now, fair's fair, Claudie,' Jalisa said. 'We had no idea that you'd be here with Simon, did we?'

'I suppose not.' She looked at each one in turn, trying to read their faces for clues, but they weren't giving anything away. Perhaps she was being a little harsh on them. After all, it was highly unlikely that they would have been able to predict circumstances like the one she now found herself in.

'We're just trying to help you have a good time,' Jalisa reiterated.

'Well, of course I'll have a good time. I'm in Paris!'

'Then why aren't you going out to eat with Simon?' Lily asked.

'He looked so disappointed,' Jalisa told everyone.

'Did he?' Claudie frowned.

Jalisa nodded vehemently. 'Yes, he did.'

'Oh dear. I didn't mean to be so rude. Do you really think I should have gone with him?'

'No harm in that?' Mr Woo said.

'No,' Claudie agreed, 'it's just that I feel a little uncomfortable. I don't think I should be here at all, and I'm sure he's feeling the same way.'

'How can you be so sure?' Bert asked. 'What man in his right man wouldn't want to be in Paris with a beautiful woman?'

Claudie bit her lip. She wasn't at all sure she was ready to be thought of as a beautiful woman.

'I think that's what's bothering her,' Lily stage-whispered.

There was a few moment's silence. Finally, Jalisa spoke.

'Look, you're not going to sort anything out by sitting in this hotel room, are you? I think you should just go out. Stop worrying about everything - just *do it!*

'Just do it, huh?' Claudie tried to listen to her own inner voice but, with the constant chatter of the angels, it was almost impossible to hear. 'You think I should go?'

The angels gave a group nod.

'Bite the bullet!' Bert said.

'Take the bull by the horns!' Mary chipped in.

'And loose yourself in those eyes the colour of a Whitby sky in winter,' Jalisa giggled.

Claudie glared down at her. 'How do you know about that?'

'Never mind! Now get a move on.'

Claudie ran through to the bathroom to tidy up. They were right. There was only one way to face the situation, and that was to face the situation.

She barely had time to notice her plush surroundings as she sent a toothbrush round her mouth like a washing machine on spin cycle. A quick slick of lipgloss and an even quicker brush of the hair, and she was ready.

She stood back from the mirror, watching as her chest heaved in anxiety. She could do this, couldn't she? Everyone was behind her. This was the right thing to do, wasn't it?

She walked back through to the bedroom.

'Good luck!' Bert called, giving Claudie a rather lascivious wink.

She grabbed her handbag and room key and stepped out into the hall. A few deep breaths took her outside room twenty-one where she knocked at the door and waited.

But there was no answer. Simon had already left.

CHAPTER 42

Simon walked out of the hotel and under the cool arches of the Place des Vosges. There were still plenty of people about, dipping in and out of the boutiques, or sitting in the restaurants that spilled onto the pavements. Simon decided that if his wallet was to survive his free weekend, he'd best stick to something a little off the tourist track.

After ten minutes of wandering around the back streets and dodging scooters, he found a nice impersonal bar where he ate by the window, watching the world parade past in pairs. And suddenly he felt more alone than he had done in months. Paris had that effect on people. It was a city made for couples, not a sad single guy who had won a competition and been set-up by his best friend.

He couldn't really blame Claudie, though. It wasn't her fault that she'd been promised a holiday only to have to tag along with him. But they were here now, and they had to face up to the fact that they were stuck with each other.

So what were they going to do? They could go their separate ways of course, but that wouldn't be much fun. Anyway, he didn't want to do that. He liked Claudie.

A little alarm bell went off in his head. He liked Claudie, and he was alone with her in a beautiful hotel in the capital of romance. What was he going to do about it? Something? Nothing? And what was it he wanted? Claudie? The signs were definitely there. He practically felt stoned out of his mind with desire for her. And this was where the crux of the problem lay. How could he be lusting after someone so angelic? She was just so ethereal. It didn't seem proper to want to grab hold of her or do anything else remotely physical. Yet that was what his body was urging him to do.

He was sat there shaking his head and tutting to himself when he became aware that he was being watched. He turned round and saw a beautiful redhead leaning up against the bar, her hair waving down her back like Rita Hayworth's, an obligatory cigarette held in a manicured hand. Simon felt as if he'd been sucked into a film noir scene, and it would have been so easy for him to flirt, to beckon her over with a few smiles, but he couldn't, because his head was filled with somebody else.

He scraped his chair back noisily and paid at the till before heading out into the dark street. It had started to rain, light and feather-soft but enough to send people running back towards homes and hotels. In pairs.

Simon turned the collar up on his jacket and headed back to the hotel.

He still hadn't made up his mind about what to do as he came out of the lift on the first floor. Part of him wanted to knock loudly on Claudie's door and just kiss the living daylights out of her, but the other told him to go back to his room and get a good night's sleep.

For a few seconds he hovered outside room twenty. She was probably fast asleep by now and certainly not dreaming about him.

He was just about to go when he heard the distinct sound of singing from behind Claudie's door. He bent forward, almost pressing his ear to the wood. And then a smile crossed his face and, shaking his head, he walked towards his own room.

Only Claudie could have found *Singin' in the Rain* dubbed into French and chosen to stay in and watch it rather than spending an evening in Paris with him.

Claudie woke up and stared at the ceiling. She'd have to have a quick shower before breakfast because she hadn't made it to the shower the night before, having fallen asleep straight after the finish of *Singin' in the Rain*.

If only it had done her some good, she thought. *Make 'em Laugh* usually had the desired effect, and *Broadway Melody* was a real happy pill, but there was one time when the songs couldn't help her, and that was at night. The dark world of dreams still held the power to shake her to her very core. They were so vivid: as if Luke were really with her; a living, breathing Luke, his smile larger than life and his great rock-climbing hands so warm on her skin.

Sometimes, it was all too much because, when she woke, it was like losing him all over again. The wound was so raw that it really didn't take much salt too make the pain unbearable. And how would Simon react to it all? How could she hide her alabaster face and wild eyes? She couldn't.

She swung her legs out of bed and padded over to the window

and pushed her head through the layers of curtain. They certainly didn't give prize-winners rooms with a view, she thought, as she looked out into a long, thin street filled with traffic. She watched a moment, tutting at the cacophony of pips and toots, and grinning as a little green vehicle drove by, complete with little green man and cleaning materials. Paris, known the world over for its beautiful beige boulevards, its fabulously frivolous boutiques, and its shit-covered streets.

She could have spent the whole morning watching the world pass beneath her bedroom window, but the strangest of sounds halted her attention. It was coming from the bathroom.

Walking through and switching the light on, she stepped into the tiled room and listened. A tiny smile lifted her face as she realised what it was. Simon was singing in the shower next door. And she'd never heard such a funny rendition of *I Want to Break Free* in her life.

She didn't mention it when they walked down to breakfast together. In fact, they were both a little on the quiet side, like two people on a terrible blind date, Claudie thought, thinking that that was exactly what Kristen had set them up on. Except most blind dates didn't involve first-class tickets on Eurostar and a two nights in a luxurious Parisian hotel.

The hotel breakfast room was tucked away under the main part of the hotel and looked like a church crypt with its columns and arches. Tables were laid out in twos and fours, and the food was a grab-what-you-want-affair from a low-lying trestle table.

Simon and Claudie hid themselves away under an obliging arch, sitting down in silence. Claudie was sure she wouldn't be able to eat anything, even though she was starving. She was just too aware of herself, and the fact that Simon was within touching distance. If she reached too far for her knife, her hand would crash into his. She felt herself blushing at the thought. It felt like a long time since she'd shared breakfast. It was such a strange, intimate meal: the first meal after getting out of bed, when your face is still soft and swollen with sleep.

'Claudie? You okay?'

Claudie looked up, startled by his question. 'Yes?'

'You look a bit red.'

She put her hand up to her face. 'It's rather warm in here, isn't it?'

Simon nodded. 'Look,' he said, 'I know how awkward this is.'

Claudie gazed down at her bread roll. As much as they needed to clear the air, she didn't fancy participating in it herself.

Simon sighed. 'I had no idea this was going to happen. But it has, and we're both here now, so we might as well enjoy it. Claudie?'

'Yes. I agree,' she said quietly, looking up from her plate.

'Good,' he said, his eyes smiling and his shoulders relaxing a little.

Claudie felt her own body beginning to relax too. She hadn't realised how uptight she'd been, but now he'd said his piece, she felt a little more comfortable about being there.

'Thank you for letting me come with you.'

Simon's eyebrows rose. 'You're welcome.'

Claudie smiled at him, and no more was said on the subject.

They began breaking open their bread rolls. Claudie had it down to a fine art, her roll neatly sliced in two equal portions, but Simon was making a major hash of his, sending a snow cloud of crumbs over the tablecloth and down onto his un-napkined legs.

'Would you like me to do it for you?'

'No, it's okay,' he said through gritted teeth, 'I've got it covered!'

Claudie smiled at his effort. 'What happened to a good old bowl of Cornflakes?'

Simon looked up in surprise. 'You really sounded English when you said that. Apart from the French accent, of course.'

'I *love* Cornflakes.'

'But you're French! You're meant to like croissants, and all that dry stuff for breakfast.'

'Just because I was born here, doesn't mean I have to like everything about it.'

'You were obviously meant to be British,' Simon said thoughtfully, buttering what was left of his butchered bread roll. 'And what exactly is this butter about? Look! It's an anaemic, unsalted excuse for butter.'

'I agree. Tasteless! And look at this strawberry jam - it's brown. There's no red here at all.'

Simon looked up and narrowed his eyes at her. 'I w*as* hoping for a good argument.'

'Well you're not going to get one here.' She smiled at him, thinking that the weekend wasn't going to be so bad after all.

Once back in her room, Claudie bid good morning to the angels.

Although they'd been granted special dispensation for accompanying Claudie to France, they warned her that they weren't early risers. It had, Jalisa said, something to do with a kind of angel assembly which everyone had to attend. Claudie had tried to picture a giant school hall filled with tiny angels singing hymns, but couldn't quite imagine it, and she hadn't dared ask questions for fear of being told off again.

'How are you getting on?' Jalisa asked as Claudie sat down at her dressing table.

'With what?' Claudie asked, combing her hair and pretending not to understand Jalisa's meaning.

'Not with *what* - with *Simon?*' she said impatiently.

'Fine!' she said, deliberately keeping things nice and vague.

'I don't think he's quite as good-looking as Daniel,' Lily mused.

'Who's Daniel?' Jalisa turned to face Lily.

'Nobody,' Claudie interjected, lest Jalisa should find out about Lily and Mary's impromptu visit to her house.

'I think Simon's very handsome,' Jalisa said, head cocked to one side to gauge Claudie's response, but she obviously wasn't going to give one. 'What do you think?'

Exasperated by the route of the conversation, Claudie turned round. 'Handsome is not an issue here.'

'A handsome man is always an issue, isn't it?' Jalisa said.

'I'm on holiday,' Claudie began, 'albeit by some warped notion of Kristen's - and I intend to enjoy it.'

'Good for you, Claudie,' Bert said. 'Don't let them get all silly and girly on you.' He scratched behind his ear and then examined his hat for rough patches of tweed. 'You enjoy Paris.'

'I thoroughly intend to!'

'Of course,' Mary smiled, 'Paris is the capital of romance.'

'Yes,' Claudie agreed, 'it is. So we'll probably see lots of couples as we go sight seeing.' And, picking up a handbag you could have fitted a small armchair into, Claudie waltzed out of her room, humming *The Last Time I Saw Paris* to herself and slamming the door on five very bemused faces.

CHAPTER 43

As predicted, there were couples everywhere. Handholding, bum slapping, earlobe nibbling couples. There was no getting away from them. They were strolling down the Champs Elysees, kissing on the Arc de Triomphe, snoodling in the Tuileries. Claudie tried not to stare, she really did, but she found her eyes positively dragged towards them, watching as lips gingerly found lips, or tongues gently probed. It was as though a hundred love scenes were being played out before her.

And then there was Simon. Had he noticed the legions of lovers? What did he make of it all? She watched him as he walked a couple of steps ahead of her. But he didn't seem to notice the acts of amore around him. Were all men like that, she wondered? She remembered a weekend in the Peak District with Luke. They'd been walking up some mountain or other, Claudie could never remember the names of them all, and there'd been a family having a picnic. It was a scene straight out of HE Bates but, when Claudie had commented on it, it appeared that Luke hadn't even noticed them. But perhaps that marked the difference the sexes: men noticed things; women noticed feelings.

Simon had his eyes firmly on the tourist sights rather than on the tourists themselves, but it didn't bother her. If she were perfectly honest, it rather amused her. He had all the awe-inspired glee of a child.

'Look!' he'd shout excitedly above the traffic. Or 'Wow!' he'd point, making sure Claudie got an eyeful of whatever it was he had spotted. His enthusiasm was addictive, and it seeped into Claudie quite without her noticing, so that, before long, she was shouting and pointing too.

Of course, Simon *had* noticed the courting couples. It was impossible not to. But he did make a valiant attempt not to stare. And he made an equally valiant attempt not to stare at Claudie, which was hard in the extreme because she looked so beautiful. He distinctly remembered that he had never seen her wearing any colours other than navy or charcoal. Even at Kristen's, she'd chosen a grey sweater and matching skirt. Beautiful, yes, clinging in all the right places, yes, but not exactly a beautiful, young woman's colour.

Perhaps she was still in mourning, he thought. But today, she was in a fantastic dark amber sweater. Simon really didn't mean to stare but it made her eyes the most incredible colour - like autumn conkers, and her face positively glowed against it; lovely and luminous like a Botticelli angel.

She was also wearing the most incredibly sexy boots: long, black and leg hugging, leaving just enough leg to admire between their tops and her short black skirt. Why didn't she wear more clothes like this, he wondered? He almost felt that it was his responsibility as a man to point out how fantastic she looked, and that she really must dress up more often.

But he really mustn't stare. He was also doing his utmost to keep his eyes away from her breasts, but he couldn't help the occasional gaze, bouncing loose and lovely as they were under her amber sweater. He cursed himself for being a man. He really shouldn't be eyeing up the assets of a woman so recently widowed, but how exactly was he meant to respond to her? When he'd first seen her that day in the bookshop, she hadn't seemed real at all. She'd been more like an angel. But she was turning into flesh and blood before his very eyes.

'Are you all right?' Claudie asked suddenly.

Simon started visibly, as if she'd dipped into his mind and found out what wicked things he was thinking.

'Simon?'

Was it his imagination or, when she said his name, was it really as if she was saying 'Sigh - mon' lengthening the first syllable as if she was luxuriating the sound in her mouth?

'Er -' he stumbled for something intelligent to say, something that might explain the strange expression his face was obviously wearing. And then he thought of something. 'I've been meaning to explain about the other night. When Felicity came round.'

'It's all right,' Claudie said lightly.

'But I feel awful about it. I meant to call you, but I didn't know what I could say in the circumstances.'

'You had things you had to sort out. I understand.'

Simon paused. Was this woman too good to be true? When he was expecting anger, he got understanding. She *was* an angel, wasn't she?

He cleared his throat. 'Perhaps we could try again - this evening?'

'What? Dinner?'

Simon nodded. 'My treat.'

Claudie smiled. 'Okay.'

'Good,' he said, thinking that he'd probably rescued her from an evening alone in front of an old movie.

'In the meantime,' Claudie said, as they came to a pedestrian crossing, 'where shall we go?'

'I don't know. Any ideas, French girl?'

Claudie laughed. 'Why does everybody assume that all French people know Paris like the back of their hands?'

'You mean to say you *don't?*'

'Well, I've only been here once when I was eight, but my mother spent all the time shopping for clothes, so we didn't get time to see the city itself. All I can remember are an endless succession of shops and frocks.'

'But your mother lives in France, doesn't she?'

Claudie nodded. 'But she's in the south. Tucked away with a horrible little man who prefers hats to people.'

Simon nodded as if he understood. 'So neither of us has the slightest idea where we're going?'

'It would appear that way, yes.'

'Great!' he smiled, 'that's just the way I like it.'

Simon and Claudie continued to walk with no real direction in mind, which was the easiest thing in the world to do in Paris, especially if one followed the river. And they could only walk the length of the river so long before spotting the darkly Gothic cathedral of Notre Dame.

Simon looked at Claudie and they read each other's minds at once.

'Come on,' he said, and Claudie nodded.

Despite her French roots, Claudie had never been to the top of Notre Dame, but she was glad Simon had suggested it because the views were fantastic. And, what was even more fantastic was that the angels had decided to join them.

Claudie did her best to hide her surprise as they appeared on a stone ledge tucked away from the crowds.

'Did you really think we'd just sit in the hotel room all day when there's so much to see and do?' Jalisa laughed seeing Claudie's expression.

'I don't suppose so,' Claudie whispered back.

'Great Scott!' Bert said. 'Look at the face on that gargoyle. It looks just like Mr Woo.'

Lily and Mary giggled at his comment.

'You stinky bird egg!' Mr Woo retorted.

The city spread below them in tones of beige and grey. The River Seine ran in a straight line, as if it didn't dare argue with the orderliness of the architecture and, in the distance, the Eiffel Tower stood proudly governing the city.

'It's such a romantic place,' Jalisa enthused. 'You're so lucky Claudie - to be here with someone-'

'Don't start!' Claudie quickly whispered.

'I was only going to say with someone as nice as Simon.'

Claudie looked at Jalisa as she tried out a few dance steps on the stone ledge.

'Oh, Jalisa, please don't tap dance up here. You'll give me vertigo.'

Jalisa stopped her little routine, her face glum.

'Are you all right?' Claudie asked, making sure Simon was occupied with the view and wouldn't notice her having a private conversation. Jalisa had that far away, abstracted look that was much better suited to Claudie.

'I suppose,' Jalisa sighed heavily.

'What is it?' Claudie whispered as Simon took photos from the other side of the balcony.

'I guess it's just being here, and seeing all these couples.'

Claudie suddenly felt incredible tenderness towards Jalisa. She knew she could sometimes be a little short with the angels, but she did so want to get close to them, and be there to listen to them when they needed her as much as they were there for her.

'I know what you mean,' Claudie said. 'It's been getting to me too. But I didn't know it was upsetting you. What is it, Jalisa?'

'It's Robbie.'

'Robbie? Is he the one you mentioned before?'

Jalisa nodded. 'I've not been able to see him for ages. As soon as I return from flight duty, he's off on his. When he gets back, I'm away.

It's just awful.'

Claudie frowned, wondering what on earth she could say to a love-struck angel. It wasn't a predicament you read about on problem pages. 'I guess these things take time, don't they?'

'I guess,' Jalisa said despondently.

'And you don't want to rush anything, do you?'

Jalisa looked up at her. 'Who are we talking about here? You or me?'

'You, of course!'

'Right,' Jalisa said, a grin stretching over her face.

They didn't go inside Notre Dame but headed, instead, to the lofty heights of Montmartre, wandering around the streets lined with trees which shone a luminous green with their spring clothing, every pore filled with hope for the coming year.

They watched the myriad artists painting, sketching and caricaturing the tourists. They watched fresh crepes being made, and then stood in line and bought one each, watching as the batter was poured over a hot plate before being covered in chocolate sauce and rolled into a cone. Held in a bouquet of paper napkins, they ate their crepes as they walked down cobbled back streets, cleverly dodging the street artists who seemed determined to paint their portraits.

'Why don't you have yours done?' Simon asked Claudie.

She shook her head, hiding behind her brown bob. 'No, no,' she said, dismissing the idea with a wave of her hand, 'I know what I look like.'

Claudie hated having her picture taken, never mind having a portrait done. In fact, her wedding had been the one and only time that she'd managed to relax in front of the camera. Luke had never understood it.

'Why is someone so beautiful so shy?' he'd once asked, pointing his throwaway camera at her on top of Striding Edge in the Lake District. Him and his camera. He'd always wanted everything on record. Claudie wasn't so bothered about that sort of thing but, after he'd died, every photograph he'd taken had become precious. She remembered looking through the stacks of wallets of photos. These were Luke's view of the world: his special moments - captured forever.

But Claudie had brought her camera to Paris. She felt for it in her pocket and took it out. Simon paused as she took a photo of the street ahead, and then he gave her a smile which brought her firmly back into the present.

Claudie liked this kind of sight-seeing: there was no pressure of a full itinerary, and she liked to see the behind-the-scenes of places. Perhaps that was what came of living in Whitby for so long - she knew that the loveliest of places were often tucked away from the eyes of all but the most discerning tourist.

Walking with Simon, she gazed up at the houses lining the cobbled streets, trying to imagine the people who lived there and the sorts of lives they led. Did they like the tourists as much as she liked the ones who visited Whitby? Or did they object to people cluttering the place and firing cameras at their homes?

They came to the end of the street and wandered back out into the square and gazed up at the great white dome of the Sacre-Coeur. It was rather unusual as domes went. It was a slimmer version of its Italian cousins, almost as if it had been dieting. But that was the French for you, Claudie supposed, always conscious of the way they looked.

'Do you want to go in?' Simon asked.

'I'd love to,' Claudie said, her eyes still fixed on it, 'only-' she paused.

'What?'

'I've not been in a church for a while.'

Simon nodded, as if understanding immediately what she meant without the need for painful explanations.

'Well, this isn't exactly a church, is it? It's the Sacre-Coeur,' Simon said, taking a step closer to her and smiling.

Claudie smiled back. 'You're right. Come on.'

Claudie wasn't sure what she'd been expecting from the Sacre-Coeur, but she certainly wasn't prepared for the dazzling light of the building. It was beautiful, and she had, for a moment, the magical feeling that she'd stepped inside a rather large wedding cake. Yet she also felt an overwhelming feeling of sadness. Why was that, she wondered? Why was extreme beauty always edged with sadness?

She looked across at Simon and watched as he walked forward and took a seat. It was exactly what she'd been about to do. She sat down next to him and, for a few moments, they let time wash over them.

Claudie tried to empty her mind and focus on the things around her: the clack of heels, the squeak of trainers, the whirr of a camera and, almost everywhere, the excited whispers of tourists. She closed her eyes, focussing on these sounds, feeling what it was like to live purely in the present. Somewhere, she couldn't tell if it was to her left or to her right, a man sneezed. There was a faint rustling from somewhere else - a rucksack against a raincoat, perhaps? Then a little creak and the faint tap of a shoe against hers. Simon.

Claudie opened her eyes. He was looking right at her. He probably thought she'd been praying.

'I,' she began hesitantly, as if she had to explain herself, 'I'd like to light a candle before we go.'

Simon nodded. 'Okay.'

'Do you want to wait here?'

Simon's eyes widened a fraction and his lips parted. 'Couldn't I light one with you?'

Claudie felt her eyes vibrate with sudden tears. *I'm not going to cry. I'm not going to cry*, she said to herself.

'I mean, would that be all right?' he asked.

The clack of heels, the squeak of trainers, the whirr of a camera; the place was filled with noise, but Claudie only heard Simon's words.

'Of course it would,' she said, and they stood up, walking silently together towards the candles.

CHAPTER 44

The strange thing about Paris, Claudie thought as they left Montmartre far behind them, was that it didn't seem real. She realised that she'd probably watched one film too many, but she really felt as if she'd walked into a film set, especially whilst walking along the river. She could almost see Gene Kelly and Leslie Caron in *An American in Paris*, and Audrey Hepburn and Cary Grant in *Charade*, and had to pinch herself to believe that she was really here and not sitting in her front room watching one of her films.

She took a deep breath; a breath so happy and contented that she didn't want to let it out. Here she was. Here *they* were. Claudie, Simon and the angels in Paris.

They were on their way back to the hotel now. After a foot-fatiguing day, they were going to have a bath and a change of clothes before going out in search of a restaurant.

Claudie was looking forward to it. All the tension over the mix-up over Paris had ebbed away. She and Simon were having fun together and, for the first time in months, Claudie had worn a smile throughout most of the day.

'Shall I knock for you in an hour?' Simon asked as they reached their rooms.

Claudie nodded, and then opened the door into her bedroom, thinking how glad she was that Kristen had made her go shopping for clothes. She dreaded to think what she'd have taken to wear otherwise.

She was just rifling through her hangers when she heard a little voice from her dressing table.

'Jalisa?'

'Hi, Claudie! I wanted to come and see how things went after Notre Dame.'

'Oh!' Claudie said. 'Well, fine.'

'Come and talk to me for a minute,' Jalisa said, her voice insistent.

'I've got to get ready–'

'It will only take a moment.'

Claudie smiled. She knew when the leader of her flight meant business so she crossed the room and sat down on the stool by the dressing table. 'What do you want to know?'

Jalisa grinned. 'I just thought we should have a little chat. You know I have to write these progress reports every so often. It's all rather dull but necessary, I'm afraid. Anyway, the Executive Flight Controller's been on at me because there's one box on your form I've not filled in yet.'

'Oh? Which is that?' Claudie asked, not really knowing if she wanted to hear the answer.

'It's the RTMO box.'

Claudie frowned. 'What does that stand for?'

'Ready to move on,' Jalisa said, and her cheeks flushed a rosy pink, as if feeling Claudie's embarrassment for her.

'I see,' Claudie said at last, resting her head on her hand as she looked down at Jalisa. 'And do you have a deadline for filling in this box?'

'Not so much a deadline, but there's always pressure within the department to get as many completed in a month as possible. Last month was a record breaker so we've got even more pressure on us than usual.'

'I don't see how I can help you,' Claudie said innocently.

Jalisa glared up at her, placing her hands on her hips like an annoyed headmistress. 'Claudie, you're the only one who can help me! Look! I was with you today. I saw the way you two were looking at each other. Simon's a fine man, Claudie, and he's obviously crazy about you.' She paused. 'Claudie? What do you think?'

'I –' Claudie began, her voice cracking. 'I don't know what to say.'

Jalisa bit her lip. 'It's never easy, this part, but you've got to move forward.'

'I know that.'

'Then how do you feel about Simon?'

Claudie's eyes sparkled like dark jewels with sudden tears. 'I like him.'

'Well, that's a good start,' Jalisa said, her voice warm and encouraging. 'So why do you sound so sad about it?'

'Because I still love Luke,' Claudie whispered.

'But you'll always love Luke. He'll always be a part of you, Claudie, but you've got to think about making some room for somebody else.

I *know* you can do this! You have so much love in your heart and it shouldn't be shut away there. You're young, you're beautiful, and love is out there waiting to be found.'

Claudie's eyes vibrated with tears at Jalisa's words. 'You think so?'

'I *know* so! And so do you in your heart of hearts! Don't you?' Jalisa asked, reaching behind her to pull a tissue out of the box.

Claudie took it and wiped her eyes. 'I'm not sure how to do this. It feels as if I'm betraying Luke just by being here, and yet Simon was so understanding today. Did you know he lit a candle for Luke in the Sacre-Coeur? I was so touched by that. He really cares.'

'Of course he does.'

'I just don't know if I'm ready for this.'

'But you like him, and he likes you. What's the problem?' Jalisa said, slowly and cautiously.

'I'm scared,' Claudie admitted after a moment's silence. 'I'm scared of the hurt that love can bring. I never knew I could hurt like that and I never want to go through that again.'

'But you have to be willing to chance that - if you want to love again.'

Claudie nodded. She knew Jalisa was right.

'It isn't easy, Claudie. There are no promises or guarantees but, when you get it right, it's the most perfect thing in the world.'

Claudie gazed at her reflection in the mirror but it wasn't her reflection she saw, it was a line of people telling her exactly what Jalisa was telling her now.

'It will happen,' Kristen had told her. 'You'll find somebody, someday, and life will be wonderful again.'

Jimmy had said something similar too, as had Angela at work and, of course, Dr Lynton.

'Now,' Jalisa said, bringing Claudie back to the here and now, her eyes twinkling mischievously, 'what are you going to wear for dinner?'

Claudie felt a tiny smile lighting her face and she stood up and walked towards the wardrobe, opening it and surveying the colourful contents. It had been a mild day, but what would it be like out at night? She smiled and shook her head. Who cared if she froze, she thought, reaching for her new red dress? And it really was red too: a Kristen-red rather than a Claudie-red, and it was beautiful.

She turned round, holding the dress out for Jalisa's approval.

'A definite winner!' Jalisa said, clapping her hands and spinning round on the dressing table.

'It's not too much?'

'NO!' Jalisa shouted. 'This is the start of your new life, Claudie, so you've got to make a statement.'

Chez Veronique was not far from the hotel and, even though it was busy, they were shown to a table for two which looked out over a lantern-lit courtyard. It was lovely, and Claudie felt as if she was being spoilt. Other than the recent meal out with Kristen, when they'd been asked to leave the restaurant after disgracing themselves, she hadn't eaten out for ages.

'You're not disappointed, are you?' Simon asked, pulling Claudie's chair out for her.

'What do you mean? It's beautiful.'

'No. I mean about being here with me instead of Kristen.'

'No!' Claudie bit her lip at her response. It sounded way too enthusiastic and, despite Jalisa's mention of RTMO boxes, Claudie was not going to rush anything.

Simon pulled the chair out opposite her. 'Good. Because I want you to enjoy this weekend.'

'I am. *We are!*'

He gave an anxious little smile as he sat down, and then picked up the menu.

The food was too good to necessitate any conversation, but Claudie couldn't help but occasionally glance across the table at Simon. She noticed the way that he nodded his head as he ate, as if passing silent judgement on the food, and how dark his eyes looked in the dim light of the restaurant. She noticed the play of shadows over his face, making it look as if he hadn't shaved, and the way his fingers wrapped firmly around his wineglass. Claudie had declined wine when he'd offered it, knowing it would send her to sleep, so Simon was slowly making his way through the bottle on his own. It made her smile that he was so enthusiastic about everything. Yet she still felt afraid to talk to him. And she desperately wanted to, because something had been worrying her since they'd left London.

She bided her time, waiting for the right moment, and there *was* a moment when she almost managed to get her words together, but the waiter interrupted, trying to sell Simon a second bottle of wine, and Claudie had lost her nerve.

It wasn't until they'd finished that she spoke.

'Simon,' she began, feeling as if the whole restaurant had stopped talking and was tuning in to her broadcast. 'I've done something rather naughty.'

Simon leaned forward a little from out of the shadows, his brow furrowing. 'What?'

'I rang Jimmy.'

'When?'

'Well, I was going to anyway. I don't know. I guess I was going to threaten him or something. He's just so thick-skinned sometimes.' Claudie paused. 'But I was going to tell him to get himself sorted out before we got back from Paris.'

'Oh, God! You didn't mention Paris, did you?'

'No. Why?'

'Because I don't think he knows anything about it. And if he got wind that Kris was coming with me-'

Claudie gasped. 'I hadn't even thought about that. You don't suppose he knows, do you?'

Simon shook his head. 'No. I doubt it. But what exactly have you done?'

Claudie took a deep breath, wondering if she should have accepted a glass of wine. 'Well,' she began, 'I rang him from Waterloo. When I told you I was popping to the ladies.'

'And what did you say?'

'I told him to get a bloody move on! That I was going away for a couple of days and that Kristen would be sat in my cottage, probably watching her way through my collection of musicals, and brooding.'

Simon laughed and then shook his head again. 'Poor Kris.'

'Exactly.' Claudie felt herself relaxing now that the truth was out in the open. She hated to think of herself as a meddler but, sometimes, a meddle was the only way out of a muddle.

'And what did the big man have to say to that?'

Claudie shrugged. 'That's the thing that's been worrying me - he didn't say anything. Although it *was* rather noisy, so he might have said something. I can't be sure.'

'So we won't know until we get back?'

Claudie had a sip of water. 'I guess not. I don't think I should ring again, do you?'

'No!' Simon agreed, leaning back in his chair and pulling an uncomfortable-looking face. 'I don't think Jimmy's the sort of man to be pressurised into making decisions.'

There was a moment's silence as they both contemplated the fate of their best friends.

Simon sighed. 'But they'll sort things out, won't they? I mean, they're not going to end up like me and Felicity, are they?'

Claudie smiled at him, thinking it was sweet that he cared so much. 'I'm sure they're going to be just fine,' she said. 'If Kris and Jimmy aren't meant to be together, I don't know who is.'

CHAPTER 45

Kristen was going to murder Claudie when she got back. She'd just spent an entire evening watching MGM musicals and, rather than being buoyed up by the experience, it had left her in tears.

She trumpeted into a man-sized tissue. Somebody, she thought, should sue that company. Weren't musicals meant to warm the heart and leave you with a sense of well being? Well, Kristen's heart certainly didn't feel warmed. That song in *Cover Girl*, "*Long Ago and Far Away*" was hardly the stuff of rollicking laughter, was it? And the confectionery-sweet ending of In the Good Old Summertime just made her feel worse.

She felt like complaining to someone about the misrepresentation of life in the movies but, instead, she dried her eyes. They felt as if they'd doubled in size like some cartoon character and, to make matters worse, it was only nine o'clock. What on earth was she going to do with the rest of the evening?

For a moment, she wondered what Claudie and Simon were up to in Paris. God, she hoped they were getting along okay. After her abrupt announcement that she wasn't actually going with either of them, she had felt the tension between them. But they'd be all right. If Claudie and Simon didn't get on then she'd throw herself into Whitby harbour.

She gave her nose another blow and then got up, walking into the kitchen with the express purpose of rooting around Claudie's cupboards for chocolate. But she didn't get that far. Standing, silhouetted in the light of the yard beyond the kitchen door was Jimmy. Kristen almost leapt out of her skin at the sight of him. What was he doing here?

She watched as he stepped forward and knocked on the door. He'd obviously seen her in the kitchen so there was no chance of pretending she wasn't in. She took a deep breath and opened the door, looking up into his face but not able to say a single word.

'Kris? he said, stepping into the kitchen. 'What's the matter?' He raised a large hand up to touch her face but she turned away from him.

'Nothing,' she said.

'Have you been crying?'

She turned her face so that she was hiding behind her hair.

'Kristen,' he said gently.

'What?'

'Look at me.' He placed a hand on her shoulder and turned her round. And, as she felt his eyes on her, her resolve crumbled and she found herself crying. Great sobs wracked her body, as if she'd been storing it all up for him. It made the tears in the living room seem like the first drops of the thaw, but this was the real thing now.

And he didn't try to stop her. He wrapped his arms around her as if he never meant to let go, kissing her hair and telling her it was all right, just letting her cry into his ridiculously thin T-shirt.

'Jimmy,' she said at last.

'Yes?'

She didn't dare look at him, but she wanted to so much. 'I missed you.'

He stroked the side of her face, his thumb wiping away a stray tear. 'I missed you too, Captain.'

She gave a little laugh. It felt so long since he'd used her nickname, and it sounded so sweet.

'I'm sorry,' she said quietly.

'That's what I came to say.'

She wiped her nose on her already sodden tissue and looked up at him. 'Is it?'

'Yeah,' he said. 'And that's not all.' He gave her a smile which made her cheeks flush red. 'Is there anywhere in this house to sit down?' he asked.

Kristen led him through to the living room where they sat down on the beaten-up sofa bed.

Jimmy leant forward, his long legs sticking out at peculiar angles on the low sofa. 'I'm probably going to do this badly.'

'Do what?'

He ran a hand through his thick dark hair and cleared his throat. 'I've had time to think since you left, and I've come to realise that life's pretty damn miserable without you.'

Kristen felt her mouth falling open at his words.

'And I've also realised that maybe - just maybe - I took you for granted when you were around.' He picked her hand up and kissed it gently. 'And I want you to come back.' He paused for a moment and Kristen looked into his soft green eyes. 'Will you come home, Kris?'

She felt a basketball-sized lump forming in her throat which almost prevented her from talking. Almost, but not quite. 'Yes,' she squeaked. 'I'll come home.'

'You will?'

She nodded, her eyes filling with tears she didn't think she had left. 'I've been so selfish,' she whispered, 'and childish.'

He squeezed her right hand in his and she placed her left hand on top, making a great hand sandwich. 'And I've been horribly cruel to you. I said some terrible things.' She paused. 'You can interrupt me at any time.'

Jimmy smiled. 'It's all right. I'm enjoying this.'

Kristen smiled back at him. 'You're horrible.'

'You're gorgeous.'

Kristen swallowed hard. 'Am I?'

'Yeah. And I don't tell you often enough, do I?' He squeezed her hand again and then withdrew it, fishing in his pocket for something.

Kristen felt as if she'd stopped breathing completely. She mustn't even begin to think - she shouldn't build her hopes up - he couldn't possibly have. Could he?

'Kristen,' he said, and, from the way he said her name, she knew that he had. 'I know you haven't been too impressed with the amount of time I've been spending on my boats recently-'

'You don't need to apologise,' she said, wishing he'd stop on about boats for half a minute and get on with the serious business of proposing.

'Well, the boats have been necessary. Because they meant I could buy you this.' He opened his hand and there in his palm was a little blue box.

Kristen took it with shaking fingers and opened it, gasping as she saw a row of three diamonds winking up at her.

'Jimmy!'

'Kristen. Will you marry me? Will you agree to take me on, despite the ex-wife and the years of reluctance to get married? Despite the front room filled with wooden models, and the unsociable working hours during the tourist season?'

Kristen gave an excited little giggle. 'Of course I will!'

Jimmy bent forward and planted a fat kiss on her mouth before taking the ring out of the box.

'Do you remember which finger it goes on?' Kristen teased.

He grinned at her. 'Don't push it.'

'I think you might have to. It's a little tight!'

'Is it?'

Kristen laughed. 'Only joking!'

'Come here!' he said, giving her a hug that made her wonder if MGM should be sued over their happy endings after all.

CHAPTER 46

'It never really get dark in a city, does it?' Claudie said as she and Simon walked back to the hotel from the restaurant.

'There are so many lights,' Simon nodded, and then laughed. 'This is the City of Light, after all.'

'Would you ever live in a city?' Claudie asked, her boots clicking and echoing under the arches of the Place des Vosges.

'No. You?'

'No.'

'Whitby's urban enough for me,' he said.

'Me too.'

They walked in silence for a few moments.

'Thanks for dinner,' Claudie said, 'it was really lovely.'

'That's all right. It was the least I could do after last week.' They walked through the gates of the hotel and nodded to the girl on reception before heading to the lift.

'So what happened?' Claudie said quietly.

'What - with Felicity?'

'If you don't mind me asking.'

'No, I don't mind,' he said, and then gave a little laugh. 'We agreed that things would be better if we went our separate ways.'

Claudie nodded. 'And you're happy with that?'

Simon looked at her, his eyes twinkling mischievously. '*Ecstatic.*'

Claudie grinned back at him. 'And Kristen? Why did that never work out?'

Simon laughed again. 'God! I don't know. She's,' he paused, 'she's the closest thing I've got to a sister without actually having one.'

Claudie's eyebrows rose. 'That's so funny, because she thinks the same thing about you. Only that you're like a brother!'

'I know. It's so weird. But call it chemistry, or fate, or whatever, it just never worked out. But I couldn't be without her.'

'Me either,' Claudie said.

The lift door opened and they walked inside. Simon pressed for the first floor and they waited in silence.

'It's our last night,' Claudie said, and then wished she hadn't. What a thing to say! It was as if she were serving herself up on a golden platter.

'Yes,' Simon said, not seeming to notice her embarrassment. 'The time's gone so quickly. Still got all day tomorrow, though.'

Claudie nodded, and the lift door opened.

'Well,' he said as they reached their rooms. 'Eight o'clock again?'

'Why not make it quarter to?'

'Okay,' he said, watching as Claudie mirrored his smile. 'Quarter to.'

Simon lay wide-awake. He knew exactly why he couldn't get back to sleep, of course. It was because he was going to have to tell her.

He groaned and sat up in bed, turning to beat up his miserable pillow. It was Saturday night: the night things happened. The night for romance and fun and - declarations?

Surely the dress had been a signal? Surely Claudie wouldn't have chosen to wear quite such a red dress unless she was perfectly happy with the idea of him coming on to her? But, then again, she'd been expecting a weekend in Paris with Kristen - not him. She hadn't bought the dress to send out messages to him.

Still, she wanted to meet up quarter of an hour earlier for breakfast. That must be a good sign. Or should he not make anything out of that extra quarter of an hour? Maybe she just wanted an extra fifteen minutes of sightseeing.

He got out of bed and walked over to the window, peering down into the dark street beyond. Not completely dark, of course, as Claudie had pointed out, but the soft dark of a city at night.

It was nearly four o'clock in the morning. They were into their last day together and he felt as if an hourglass had been turned over and that time was slowly slipping away from him. He wondered whether she was asleep or wide awake like him, peering into the street wondering what to do.

A strange excitement rushed through his body as if telling him that this was meant to be; that his relationship with Kristen had never meant to work out: that it was but a prelude to this moment.

He scratched his chin and felt his bristles, rough as unglazed raku. And then, without stopping to reason with himself, he reached for the shirt he'd hung over the chair by the dressing table, putting it on and doing the buttons up. Then he pulled his trousers on over his boxer shorts and slid his feet into his socks and shoes. He did all this without a single thought running through his brain. His heart was pumping too loudly for any thoughts to be heard anyway.

He picked up the key to his room and stepped out into the corridor before knocking lightly on Claudie's door. If she was awake, she'd hear him. If she was asleep, he didn't want to wake her. Or did he? He knocked a second time and waited.

An eternity seemed to pass as he stood in the hallway. He looked up and down the corridor, anxious that somebody might appear at any moment. 'What do you think you're doing pestering that poor widow at such an indecent hour?' they'd say. Only it might be in French. 'Can't you leave the girl alone?'

Simon shook his head. No. He couldn't leave her alone. He had to see her.

He jumped as he heard the lock turn and watched the door open.

'Simon?' Claudie's snowy face peered round the door. 'Are you okay?' she looked up at him, puzzled by his presence.

'I - er - I,' he hesitated. He couldn't say it after all. The words, no matter how pressing, just wouldn't exit his mouth. 'I couldn't sleep.'

'Oh,' she said, hiding a yawn with a hand.

'And a quarter to eight is a long time away.'

Claudie gave the tiniest of smiles. 'I see,' she said, looking down at his shoes, making him wonder what it was exactly that she could see. 'Are you going out?'

He gazed down at his shoes too. 'I'm not sure. Why? Would you come with me?'

Her eyes widened very slightly. 'It's four in the morning.'

'That wasn't the question.'

'I know.'

They stared at one another as if trying to read each other's thoughts. At last Claudie spoke.

'I'd better put something warm on.'

Ten minutes later, they were out in the square again, the night air folding around them in a cold cloak. But it still wasn't dark. The streets were lit as if by a thousand stars.

There were still plenty of people around: on their way to, or on their way back from clubs or friends, but there was none of the gaudiness of the daytime. Colours had vanished and sounds and smells had morphed.

Simon and Claudie walked through the streets in companionable silence. Or was it embarrassed silence, Simon wondered? He tried to keep stealing sideways glances at Claudie, desperate to know what she was thinking.

'This isn't what you expected, is it?' he asked tentatively as they crossed a wide boulevard.

'What do you mean?'

'This isn't what you expected you'd be doing on your trip to Paris. Walking round the city at night - with me.'

'If there's one thing I've learnt over the last few months, it's that you should always expect the unexpected.'

Simon nodded solemnly. 'Claudie,' he said.

'Yes?'

'I'm really sorry about what happened to you. To Luke.'

They had reached the river in what seemed like no time, and Claudie looked down into its inky depths from the bridge, and then stared up at Notre Dame. As Simon joined her, he too looked up at the floodlit cathedral which loomed up into the night sky in dragonesque splendour.

'I hope I haven't overstepped -'

'No,' Claudie interrupted him, 'you haven't. And thank you for your sympathy. It isn't easy to give.' She continued to stare down into the river, her gaze seeming to dissolve in the steady flow of the water. 'That's something else I've learnt that over the past few months. People don't quite know what to say or do with me. You know that all these thoughts are skirmishing round their heads, but they say nothing.' She turned round and fixed her eyes on his. 'So thank you.'

'If you ever want to talk about it, I'll listen.'

She looked up at his face and knew that he was speaking the absolute truth. He *would* listen to her. And that was a great comfort to know, because there weren't many good listeners in the world.

After leaving the bridge, they followed the river. They didn't stop to worry where they were going; they just walked. Under and over bridges; through parks and squares; passed statues and tramps. The whole city was frozen in sleep. But always, they returned to the river.

'I think this river's following us,' Simon said at one point and

Claudie laughed.

And on they walked. And on they talked. Incessantly.

They talked about Whitby:

'Don't you think it strange that we never met before?'

'Not strange, exactly, but certainly a shame.'

They talked about food:

'I can't stand rice pudding.'

'Neither can I. It looks like sick.'

And, of course, they talked about films:

'Do you suppose this is where Gene Kelly danced?'

'Gene who?'

'Simon!'

'Only joking!'

And then they stopped talking and were just walking. Claudie thought it was probably to do with the lateness of the hour, as well as the amount of conversation that had poured from them. She'd been tongue-tied before, but this was the first time she'd been tongue-*tired*.

'It's late, isn't it,' she said, as they finally returned to the arches of the Place des Vosges.

'I was just thinking that it's too early,' Simon replied.

'Too early?'

They stopped just outside the iron gates of the hotel.

'Too early for me to say that I'm falling in love with you.'

As soon as the words were out of his mouth, there was a silence like they'd never heard before. It seemed to swallow up all the sound in the world, and seconds seemed to stretch themselves into aeons.

At last Simon spoke again. 'You probably won't remember any of this tomorrow.'

Claudie looked up at him and smiled. 'It is tomorrow,' she said.

CHAPTER 47

At Cabin Cottage in Whitby, two other people were wide-awake. But they were perfectly happy to stay put in bed, and had no intention whatsoever of venturing outdoors.

Snuggled under the duvet together, Jimmy was busy warming Kristen's frozen toes. It hadn't taken him long to get her to pack a bag and leave Claudie's cottage, and it had taken half that time again for them to find their way into the bedroom. There, they'd kissed, cuddled, made love, slept, kissed some more, made love again and were currently back to a period of prolonged cuddling. With a smattering of kisses thrown in for good measure.

It was good to be home, Kristen thought, as Jimmy lifted her hand into the air and stretched her fingers out so that he could admire the ring he'd chosen for her. Kristen gazed at it wistfully. Just wait till Angela saw it, she thought. And Claudie and Simon! They wouldn't be able to believe what had happened in their absence.

'I think,' Jimmy began a little hesitantly, 'a long engagement?'

'Yes,' Kristen agreed, not wishing him to back down now that she had a ring on her finger.

'Say two to three years.'

'TWO TO THREE YEARS!' the old Kristen kicked in as she turned round to face him. 'Do you want me to be grey?'

'It's a perfectly respectable time.'

Kristen set her mouth in a firm line. 'Two years - tops!' she said, withdrawing her hand from his.

'Two and a half,' Jimmy replied quickly.

'One year,' Kristen said, a half-smile on her face.

'One year?' Jimmy questioned.

'DONE!' Kristen quickly grabbed his hand and shook it.

CHAPTER 48

The lift ride to the first floor seemed to take an age. Simon and Claudie stood in silence, the space between his shoulder and her shoulder half of what it had been on their lift ride down a few hours before.

Claudie hunted desperately for something to say; something to put him at his ease, but the only thought spiralling around her brain was that Simon's face had flushed to the colour of a ripe strawberry. She'd never seen a man blush before, and it was peculiarly attractive.

'It's only an hour to breakfast,' Simon said as the lift door opened. 'Do you still want to meet at a quarter to eight?'

'Maybe we should make it quarter *past?*'

He nodded and smiled, and Claudie watched as he opened the door to his room and disappeared.

She bit her lip and found that she was frowning, which annoyed her. What on earth did she have to frown about? A man had just declared his love for her. Was that really a frowning matter?

She opened the door and stepped into her room. Her bedside lamp was still on and, as she walked in, she saw five little faces peering up at her from her dressing table. It looked as if the angels had been waiting up for her like anxious parents.

'Guess who hasn't had much sleep tonight?' Lily teased.

'Where *have* you been?' Mary asked. 'We got worried when we realized you'd gone out in the middle of the night.'

'I'm sorry. I didn't mean to worry you,' Claudie said, flopping down on the bed. And then she laughed. 'You look like a jury waiting to pass sentence.'

Jalisa stepped forward a little. 'It's funny you should say that.' She looked round and nodded to Mr Woo. 'Aren't you going to tell her?' she whispered.

Mr Woo shook his head. 'Jalisa - her job.'

'Yes,' Bert said, sticking up for Mr Woo for once, 'you're so good at these sort of things.'

Claudie rubbed her eyes and yawned loudly. 'Tell me what?'

Jalisa cleared her throat. 'Claudie –'

'Yes, Jalisa.'

'We've been having a little chat.'

'I can see that.'

'Yes. And we've all come to the conclusion that Simon is rather a nice young man.'

'Oh, you have, have you?' Claudie didn't want to get angry with them, but she didn't like the idea that they'd been discussing her and Simon behind her back.

'It's all part of our job, you see,' Bert chipped in. 'To help you on your way.'

'We make sure you okay,' Mr Woo said.

'When the time comes for what?'

Jalisa looked back at the others and then turned to Claudie. 'When we have to leave you.'

Claudie barely moved. Had she heard them right? 'Leave me?'

'We can't stay forever,' Jalisa said gently. 'You remember what we talked about? RTMO boxes and the like?'

'I know. It's just, I thought you'd be around a little longer than *this*.'

Mary stepped forward and linked arms with Jalisa. 'We're as surprised as you are, Claudie. But just look how far you've come since we arrived.'

'Paris isn't *that* far.'

'Claudie!' Jalisa chided. 'That's not what Mary meant.'

'I know,' Claudie sighed, suddenly visualising the angels in a meeting room in heaven, drawing up bar charts and measuring her grief.

'I think she's definitely ready now,' Jalisa might say. 'It's time we moved on and left her to face the world on her own.'

'This table shows how much she's improved since we arrived,' Bert might agree.

'It's the herbs,' Mr Woo would probably add.

Claudie shrugged, feeling helpless and hopeless. 'But this is so *soon!*' she said.

'We know,' Jalisa agreed. 'But you must feel positive about that.'

Claudie swallowed hard, as if she were having trouble digesting their words. 'But I can't see what's changed since you arrived. I mean, a little time has passed, but have I really changed that much?'

The angels gave her a beautiful group smile.

'You can't see what's under your own nose,' Lily tutted.

'What do you mean?'

'What exactly happened tonight?' Lily asked.

Claudie gave her a guarded look. How much did they know? Did they hover over her and follow her around all day and night? She wouldn't be a bit surprised. They did seem to have a lot of inside information.

'I really don't see how that changes things.'

'Don't you?' Lily asked, her voice rising in surprise. 'But it changes *everything!*'

'Bugger. Bugger. *Bugger!*' Simon grabbed a towel and patted his face dry, but the submersion in cold water hadn't reduced the redness of his face one iota.

He stared at himself in the mirror and shook his head at what he saw. He looked terrible. What must Claudie have thought of him?

Walking through to the bedroom, he sank down onto the bed and closed his eyes. He'd set his watch in case he fell asleep, but that wasn't very likely. Not with what he'd just told Claudie.

He groaned as he thought of their faces: his claret red and hers moonshine white. But at least he'd told her. The words were out. So let them do their work.

At quarter past eight on the dot, they found themselves in the lift again. Shoulder to shoulder this time, the space between them having vanished completely.

Under the arches of the breakfast room, they ate their last Parisian petit dejeuner with a few casual comments about what they should do and see during their remaining hours.

'We should go up the Eiffel Tower, I suppose,' Claudie said thoughtfully.

'And there's the boat cruise.'

'And the Mona Lisa?'

'Or Monet?'

'Or Rodin?'

'Or,' Simon said, struggling to cut his bread roll into two equal parts, 'we could just see where our feet take us again.'

Claudie met his gaze, trying very hard not to think of Whitby skies. 'Yes,' she said, 'that sounds perfect.'

The sun was blinkably bright as they left the hotel. Claudie had decided to wear her long black boots again, and had chosen her new lilac jumper, but was beginning to worry that she was going to overheat. She quickly glanced at Simon. He was wearing black trousers, black boots and a chocolate brown jumper which made his hair look even blonder than normal, and feather-soft as it blew around in the light May breeze.

They ended up by the Seine again, as if drawn by some internal navigational system, and Claudie watched as Simon browsed through the boxes of old black and white postcards for sale in the endless stalls along the riverbank.

'Do you think these are genuine?' he asked, handing Claudie a card with a postmark of 1902.

'Well, nobody writes like that any more. In fact, nobody writes much at all now.'

Simon pulled a face. 'How can you be sure that there isn't some out-of-work actor sitting in a garret somewhere writing stacks of these every day?'

Claudie frowned. 'You old sceptic!'

He shrugged, taking the postcard from her and putting it back in its box amongst the hundreds of others. 'They all look the same to me.'

Claudie rifled through the boxes, picking them up and examining them at random. They were beautiful. Fountains, streets, monuments, children at play. They were just so *Parisian*. She selected three views of the city and paid for them.

'What?' she said, seeing Simon's quizzical expression. 'It doesn't bother me if they're not genuine. I like them, and that's all that matters.'

Simon smiled at her. But it wasn't an ordinary smile. It was the sort of smile you can feel in your belly. The sort that warms your toes and softens your eyes. And she found herself returning it.

With its elaborate grey and gold decoration, bulbous lights and mythical dolphinesque creatures, the Pont Alexandre III was the most incredible bridge Claudie had ever seen. And she shouldn't have been surprised that the angels decided to make an appearance at the feet of a rather grand pair of cupids.

She gave them a big smile in greeting but, with Simon stood next to her, she didn't dare say anything. As much as she liked this man, she wasn't quite ready to confide in him about having angels.

'Has he kissed you yet, Claudes?' Lily shouted, causing Claudie to turn and glare at her. What a thing to say! And right in front of Simon too, even though he couldn't hear them.

'You can't come to Paris and not have a smooch,' Jalisa giggled.

'Leave her alone,' Mr Woo said.

'We will,' Jalisa said. 'Just give us a minute.'

Claudie turned round at Jalisa's enigmatic comment. She'd been feeling particularly nervous since Jalisa had started talking about expiry dates, and wanted to make sure that it wasn't going to affect her just yet, but she couldn't question her with Simon there. She'd have to wait, which made her all the more anxious.

A boat full of tourists passed under the bridge and Claudie saw several cameras pointing in her direction. Were they aware that they were photographing angels? And then she had an idea.

'Simon?'

'Yes?'

'Could you take some photos for me?'

'Sure. What of?'

'This bridge. It's so beautiful. And there's a great view of the Eiffel Tower.'

'You trust me with your camera?' he asked, taking it from her.

'Yes, of course!'

Okay,' he said, and she watched as he walked towards the centre of the bridge, leaving her alone with the angels.

'Jalisa,' she began, 'what exactly did you mean just then?'

'Oh, Claudie,' Jalisa said, her voice slow and weary after its earlier vibrancy. 'I think you know, don't you?'

'Know what?' Claudie could feel a stream of pure panic flooding her system, and she didn't like it.

'You don't need us any more.'

'But I *do!*' Her eyes widened in panic. What was happening? She was just beginning to trust them, to confide in them, and they were threatening to leave her? That couldn't be right.

Jalisa shook her head. 'You don't, Claudie.'

Claudie looked to the others for support. Mr Woo's head was

bowed, Bert had taken his hat off, and Lily and Mary were holding hands and looking as if they were about to cry.

'But I've only just got to know you.'

Jalisa's bright eyes looked up at her. 'It doesn't matter. You still don't need us.'

Claudie felt herself frowning again. They were teasing her, surely? They wouldn't be that mean really?

'But it's a *good* thing,' Jalisa said. 'It means you're ready to move on - to face the world.'

'I don't feel very ready.'

There were a few moments of silence. Apart from the sounds of Parisian drivers.

'We're going to miss you,' Bert said.

'Oh, don't!' Claudie all but cried.

'You've been so kind, so sweet,' Mary said.

'I miss you too,' Mr Woo whispered. 'Remember Mrs Woo in North London. She love to see you sometime.'

'Do you mean you're leaving me *right now? Here?*' Claudie gasped in horror. 'But I'll be so unhappy for the rest of the day. What on earth will Simon think?'

'Claudie,' Jalisa said slowly, 'I've always thought of happiness as a relay race.'

'Oh, don't go giving her that old speech!' Bert complained.

'Shut up!' Jalisa snapped. 'It's not old, it's something I was taught on my refresher course last year.'

'Good grief!' Bert said, shaking his head in disapproval.

'Yes,' Jalisa began again. 'Happiness is like a relay race. We all seek it in different things at different stages of our lives. For you, it was us for a while, but now-'

'Claudie!' Simon called from further along the bridge. She turned round to see him pointing her camera lens pointing at her. 'Smile!' he shouted.

And she did. The biggest, warmest smile she'd smiled in months.

She watched as he walked back towards her. 'Come on!' he said, holding his hand out to her. 'Time to move on, I think.'

Claudie turned round to say a final goodbye to the angels, but they'd vanished.

'Jalisa?' she mouthed.

'Bye, Claudie!' Jalisa's voice floated down from somewhere above her head. She looked up into the great blue sky, but there was nothing there but the Eiffel Tower.

'Take good care of yourself,' Bert's voice said.

'Don't forget Mrs Woo,' Mr Woo said.

Claudie looked from left to right, hoping for a last fleeting glimpse.

'Goodbye, Claudie!' Mary and Lily sang in unison.

'He's waiting for you!' Jalisa's voice whispered back.

Claudie looked back at Simon, his hand extended towards her, and a sudden feeling of peace flooded though her body. Should she? Could she?

She took a few tentative steps forward and took his hand in hers.

CHAPTER 49

The city of York was bathed in sunshine and had never looked more beautiful. Claudie had taken the whole day off work and had travelled in on an earlier train so that she could walk around the city at leisure.

She started with the tourist trail: the cathedral, the Treasurer's House, Clifford's Tower and The Shambles. And then she did the credit card trail, spending two week's wages on clothes from the boutiques that lined the backstreets.

Then, armed with three fat bags of goodies, Claudie made her way to fifteen Elizabeth Street for her three o'clock appointment.

It was with a heavy heart as well as heavy shopping bags that Claudie stepped into Dr Lynton's study. This, she thought, would be her last time here. She looked around the room and knew she was going to miss it: the books, the plants, the chairs, and even the terrible tea.

And Dr Lynton.

'Tea?' he asked as soon as she'd placed her carrier bags down.

'Please,' she said.

'Milk and one sugar, isn't it?'

Claudie's mouth fell open in surprise. 'Yes.'

'So, how was Paris?' Dr Lynton asked, passing her a perfect cup of tea, a smile hovering over his lips.

'Paris,' she sighed, 'was beautiful.'

'So you and Kristen had a good time?'

Claudie sat back in the chair and surveyed Dr Lynton. What should she tell him? The truth? *Why not?* Didn't he deserved the truth on her final visit?

'I didn't go with Kristen. I went with Simon,' she said, her voice clear and steady.

'Simon? Simon of the bookshop?'

Claudie nodded.

'With the eyes like a Whitby sky in winter?'

'The very one!' Claudie said, not bothering to hide her smile.

Dr Lynton leant forward in his chair and rubbed his chin thoughtfully. 'This is-'

'Quite some progress?' Claudie offered.

He nodded.

'I know.'

He nodded again.

Claudie sipped her tea. She was having fun.

There wasn't really any need for Dr Lynton to make any notes because Claudie didn't have anything alarming to tell him. Instead, they chatted away like old friends. Freud was completely forgotten, and there wasn't a single mention of books.

At the end of the hour, they stood up and smiled at each other.

'Well, it's been a pleasure, Claudie. And I wish you all the best for your future.'

'Thank you.' She held her hand out and he shook it firmly. 'Oh! I've got this.' She delved into her voluminous bag and retrieved his book. 'Thank you,' she said.

'You read page sixty-three?'

'Yes. I did.'

Dr Lynton nodded. 'Well,' he said at length. 'Goodbye, Claudie.'

Claudie picked up her shopping bags and walked down the hallway, waiting whilst he opened the door for her. As she stepped out into the bright afternoon, the sunlight reflected off his shiny brass plaque. And she remembered.

'Dr Lynton?'

'Yes?'

She bit her lip. Did she have the nerve to ask him? 'I was wondering - what does the "P" stand for?'

Dr Lynton smiled, almost as if he'd been expecting her to ask him. 'Paddy,' he said.

Claudie's first reaction was to laugh. Was he *sure* that was his name? Had he checked? It just seemed so undignified after she'd spent months believing it was Percival or Peregrine.

She looked up into the warm eyes that smiled down at her. No, she thought, Paddy became him. Paddy was perfect.

EPILOGUE

Whose idea had it been to go for a walk along the coast in November? November was definitely an indoor month in North Yorkshire. But Claudie and Simon weren't the only fools to think a stroll along the beach in winter was romantic. The trouble was, romance aside, the people they passed didn't look so much weather-beaten as weather-battered.

Claudie watched as the wind pushed and pulled at Simon's hair, as if it meant to rip it from his head. Her own hair was pushed under a headscarf, which wasn't exactly the height of fashion but, then again, the beach was definitely no cat-walk.

They hadn't spoken much since leaving the car. Claudie smiled at the thought of the little Fiat that was Simon's pride and joy. Not yet paid for, but an absolute godsend nevertheless.

They walked, gloved hand in gloved hand over the rock-hard sand, their bodies pushing furiously into the wind. It reminded Claudie of the day she and Luke had climbed Helvellyn in the Lake District, and how both the view and the weather had been breathtaking.

It was over a year since Luke had died. So many things had happened. So many new people in her life. Dr Lynton, Jalisa, Mary and Lily, Bert and Mr Woo. And Simon.

Claudie looked up at the great expanse of sky, her eyes widening to take in the white clouds like great daubs of whipped cream.

Simon Hart.

Meeting Simon had been a revelation. Like when you discover a piece of exquisite music and wonder if there was really a time in your life when you didn't know of its existence.

But did she love him more than Luke?

No.

She loved him *differently*. Just as page sixty-three had suggested.

'I think we should come back in the summer!' Simon laughed as they stood looking out to sea.

'Agreed!' Claudie shouted back above the wind.

Simon squeezed her right hand and then tucked it deep into one of his pockets. 'Let's go home.'

Walking back towards the car, Claudie took one last look at the beach and blew a kiss deep into the wind.

Luke would never leave her. He'd always be there. But Simon was there too now, and, for the first time in over a year, she felt as if she had a future.

ABOUT THE AUTHOR

Victoria Connelly was brought up in Norfolk and studied English literature at Worcester University before becoming a teacher. After getting married in a medieval castle in the Yorkshire Dales and living in London for eleven years, she moved to rural Suffolk where she lives with her artist husband and a family of rescue animals.

Her first novel, *Flights of Angels*, was published in Germany and made into a film. Victoria and her husband flew out to Berlin to see it being filmed and got to be extras in it. Several of her novels have been Kindle bestsellers.

If you'd like to contact Victoria or sign up for her newsletter about future releases, email via her website at www.victoriaconnelly.com.

She's also on Facebook and Twitter @VictoriaDarcy

ALSO BY VICTORIA CONNELLY

Austen Addicts Series
A Weekend with Mr Darcy
The Perfect Hero
published in the US as Dreaming of Mr Darcy
Mr Darcy Forever
Christmas with Mr Darcy
Happy Birthday, Mr Darcy
At Home with Mr Darcy

Other Fiction
Molly's Millions
The Runaway Actress
Wish You Were Here
A Summer to Remember
The Secret of You
Irresistible You
Three Graces
It's Magic (A compilation volume:
Flights of Angels, Irresistible You and Three Graces)
A Dog Called Hope
Christmas at the Cove

Short Story Collections
One Perfect Week and other stories
The Retreat and other stories
Postcard from Venice and other stories

Non-fiction
Escape to Mulberry Cottage
A Year at Mulberry Cottage

Children's Adventure
Secret Pyramid

CPSIA information can be obtained
at www.ICGtesting.com
Printed in the USA
LVHW04s1635260618
581952LV00004B/1027/P